MAFIA DARLING

The Kings of Italy - Part 2

MILA FINELLI

Copyright © 2022 by Mila Finelli

All rights reserved.

No part of this book may be reproduced in any form or by any electronic or mechanical means, including information storage and retrieval systems, without written permission from the author, except for the use of brief quotations in a book review.

This is a work of fiction. Any names or characters, businesses or places, events or incidents, are fictitious. Any resemblance to actual persons, living or dead, or actual events is purely coincidental.

Cover: Letitia Hasser, RBA Designs

Editing: Jennifer Prokop

Quando il diavolo ti accarezza, vuole l'anima.
When the devil caresses you, he wants your soul.
—Italian Proverb

CHAPTER ONE

Fausto

I often dreamed of blood.

Rivers of it, filling my mouth and choking me. Drowning me and everyone I cared about, with no hope of survival.

The dreams started back when I was a foot soldier, still being groomed under my father's watchful eye. In those days, the boss's son did not receive a pass on the more gruesome of tasks. No, they used those tasks to harden me, to turn me from a boy into a man.

A man capable of leading the world's most dangerous mafia. The 'Ndrangheta.

There had been no choice for me, no other life to consider. As the years went on, I followed instructions and never dared show a hint of weakness. Torture and killing became second nature to me, work I learned to love. It earned me respect from my 'ndrina brothers and fear from my enemies. Whispers followed me wherever I went, the tales of my cruelty spread far and wide.

This made my father proud.

He told me this often, especially after watching me at my worst. They called him in when I was too eager with my knife, the blood of our enemies staining every part of me red like the Devil. It was from this that the legend of *il Diavolo* was born. Gutting, dismembering, disemboweling . . . the pain I doled out was returned tenfold in my father's love.

It became a vicious cycle for me, more killing to earn more praise, until I hardly slept due to the nightmares. Even years later, I slept only three or four hours before I woke up in a cold sweat, a scream clawing at my throat. Then I would get up and exercise, running until I nearly dropped.

This was my life before she came along. I had more than most men could ever dream of, even if exhaustion stalked my every waking moment, so it was enough. I wouldn't ever trade my life for a clear conscience.

Then she arrived, with her fire and sass. And the bad dreams? They stopped when I was with her. For a few blissful weeks, I had a respite from the ghosts of my past, my first decent sleep in decades.

Then I sent her away.

The dreams have returned, but worse because they include her. My dolcezza, alone and scared, her body bleeding out in front of my eyes, and there is nothing I can do about it. My nightmares don't care that Francesca betrayed me, that she was not the person I believed her to be. No, my nightmares live to torture me and drive me insane night after night, pushing me to the limits of my endurance.

My son also featured in my dreams, and each time I find him dead. They always killed him before I can save him, leaving his lifeless body for me to find. My good boy, slaughtered like a pig.

So much blood. So much death.

Chi male comincia, peggio finisce.

A bad beginning makes a bad ending.

This is the life I have chosen. No matter what happens, there is no going back.

CHAPTER TWO

Giulio

Waiting at a stoplight, I took another hit from my weed vape and held in the smoke as long as I could. I exhaled, and the mellow sensation rolled through my bloodstream like a warm bath. Cazzo, that was nice.

I leaned against the headrest and closed my eyes. This feeling was much better than drinking alcohol, which only made me feel even more like my father. He'd taken to booze now that Frankie was gone. Fausto and I already had enough in common; no need to add a drinking problem to the list.

A car honked behind me. I opened my eyes and gave the driver the finger. *Stronzo*. I put my Ferrari in drive and sped off into the midday beach traffic. The music pumped from my stereo, a song I hadn't heard in ages. I tapped my hands against the steering wheel, changing gears swiftly, as I sang along. Dio, I felt good. Thirsty, but good.

I wish I could fuck Paolo right now.

The thought nearly ruined my buzz, so I shoved it aside. If I wanted to keep Paolo alive then I couldn't see him again. Except I didn't want to fuck anyone else. I still loved him.

My chest tightened and my heart thumped so hard, I swear it was louder than the bass in the song. I hadn't slept with anyone in three weeks, and it was torture. Even still, my dick remained limp at the strip club last night, much to the disappointment of the girl grinding on my lap. Life would be so much easier if I liked women.

Or if I could have Paolo.

My father believed it was so simple. The great Fausto Ravazzani gave his orders and expected us all to fall in line.

I told you, you can do what you like after you are settled and have children.

Except Paolo would never wait while I knocked my wife up enough times to fill out the family tree—and I didn't expect him to.

Cristo, was Paolo fucking someone else already?

The thought turned my blood to ice, even with the herb in my system. Had he forgotten me and moved on in the last three weeks? I bet he had. He seemed sad enough when I broke things off, but maybe those tears had been fake. Has he started posting on the hookup apps and meeting other men?

I had to find out.

I pulled into the drive of the beach house, and carried a box full of Zia's cornetti and sfogliatelle with me to the front door. Frankie still wasn't eating enough, but maybe I could coax her into a few bites. At least we were miserable together. Though I hated to see her sad, being with her every day has kept me sane after my breakup. That, and the weed.

I texted Sal, her guard, to let him know I was here then used my key in case she was asleep. I headed for the kitchen first. The rooms were empty and quiet, sounds from the beach faint in the background. An old cup of coffee sat on the kitchen island, Frankie's tablet resting there. Had she gone back to bed?

"Sal," I called quietly. Normally the big man sat at the back door, not quite inside but nearby in case of trouble. Except his chair stood empty. I checked my watch. Two o'clock. Sal should be here.

Were they on the beach? I scanned the sand stretching out along the edge of the water. Frankie hasn't felt up to long walks or swims in a while. There were lots of people on the beach but none of them were Frankie or Sal.

This was strange.

I dialed Sal's cell phone and retrieved my gun from the inside of my jacket. Keeping absolutely quiet, I went upstairs to see if she was in bed.

The master bed was rumpled but empty. She wasn't in the bathroom, either. *Ma che cazzo?*

Sweat broke out on the back of my neck, every part of me now on high alert. I quickly checked the rest of the upstairs then returned downstairs. I called Sal's replacement, Luca. He picked up on the second ring. "Where are you?" I barked.

"Just about to leave the house, why?"

"Did you hear from Sal today?"

"Yes, this morning. He wanted to know if we could swap shifts tomorrow."

"He's not here." I began opening closet doors and checking behind furniture. "Both Sal and Frankie are missing."

"That is impossible," he said, and I could hear him moving in the background. "I'm coming right now, but you should call Marco. They can review the security footage at the castello."

As I hung up on Luca, I returned to the kitchen to look in the pantry. As soon as I pulled open the door, my heart sank. Sal was there, unmoving. Minchia! Was he dead?

Worse, where the fuck was Frankie?

This was bad. This was very, very bad.

I had to call my father.

Fausto

I rubbed my eyes behind my glasses. The words on the screen were fuzzy, my body too tired to focus.

Sighing, I picked up my Campari and tonic. I'd taken to drinking early in the afternoons, a habit Marco disliked immensely but one I found necessary to dull the ache inside my chest. The past two nights I had fallen into bed in a drunken stupor and passed out for a few hours.

It was an improvement over weeks of sleepless nights.

Marco sat in the corner on his phone, pretending to ignore me while really watching me closely. He wasn't fooling me.

I read the numbers on my screen again, wanting to prove I was still on top of my empire. "Toni just made us over two million Euros by shorting a tech stock."

Marco grunted.

"Maybe we don't need D'Agostino for this computer idea."

He didn't respond.

I drummed my fingers on the desk and sipped my cocktail. When I drank, my thoughts frequently drifted back to *her*, even when I tried to prevent it.

She'd made a fool of me. I'd mooned over her like a lovesick teenager with his first taste of pussy. All the while she'd been keeping a secret from me, one that could destroy everything I'd built. I would never forgive her.

I narrowed my gaze on my cousin. "Why don't you take the rest of the day off?"

"I'm fine where I am."

He was babysitting me, like I was a toddler. I didn't like it. "Marco—" My phone lit up and Giulio's name appeared on the screen. I hadn't seen him since our argument.

Swiping to answer, I held the phone up to my ear. "Pronto."

"She's not here."

I heard the panic before I understood the words. Straightening in my chair, I immediately put it on the speaker so Marco could hear. "What do you mean? Where is she?"

"The house, it's empty. No Frankie, no guards."

Marco and I exchanged a look. What the fuck? Had she run? Or had something terrible happened instead?

My chest seized, my heart suddenly forgetting how to function, and I got to my feet. Marco began dialing on his phone, probably trying to reach the men I had stationed at the beach house, but I remained focused on my son. "Show me," I barked.

Giulio turned on the video and I saw he was in the kitchen, a gun in his other hand. "When I got here," he explained, "the back door was open. I found Sal out cold in the pantry."

He showed me Sal, pale and lifeless on the ground. "Is he dead?" I snapped.

"He's alive," my son said. "There's a syringe next to him on the floor."

"Where is she?" I shouted, yanking at the knot of my tie with one hand to loosen it. Had Francesca somehow drugged Sal and then escaped?

No matter what happens, I will leave here. Somehow, some way, I will get away from you.

"Search every inch of that house. I am on my way." I hung up and started across the room.

Marco held up a hand, talking rapidly on his phone. He grabbed my arm to stop me as I passed. "She left for a walk on the beach. Nothing out of the ordinary. Sal stayed behind at first, then went after her. Vic is watching the camera footage now."

I sprinted out the door and down the corridor. The security room was in the east section of the castello, and I ran there like a madman.

Vic was at the desk, a wall of screens in front of him. He was our best tech guy, a hacker, with skills that we put to use all over the globe. His gaze was locked on the screen with Sal in the chair at the beach house, his eyes tracking something on the beach. *Francesca.*

"She's been gone for about ten minutes," Vic said, moving the video forward. "Sal watches her and then gets up to follow."

"Why weren't you on the cameras today?" I snarled. "How the fuck did this happen?"

He swallowed but didn't meet my eye, his attention still on the screen. "I'm sorry, Don Ravazzani. I was working on a security update. I wasn't paying close attention to the cameras." On the monitor a dark shape crept into the kitchen—a man carrying Sal over his shoulder.

"Who is that?" I leaned in and watched as a man in a black mask tossed Sal into the pantry. A few seconds later another camera caught him leaving. Was this someone she'd hired to help her? Or was it one of my enemies? "Is she still on the beach? Can we get the CCTV footage?"

Vic shifted to a laptop and began typing. "It might take some time."

I pounded my fist on the desk. "There is no time. You're supposed to be this tech genius. So find those fucking cameras. I need to know what happened to her—"

"Rav." Marco held out his phone in front of my face. "You should take this."

"Not now."

"Rav," he implored, his expression as serious as I'd ever seen. "It's D'Agostino. He says he has something that belongs to you."

CHAPTER THREE

Francesca

These Italian motherfuckers, always kidnapping me.

The trunk opened suddenly and bright light flooded my eyes. Had we stopped? I'd been too deep in my head, too terrified, to even notice. My chest heaved as I desperately tried to suck air through my nostrils, which were clogged from crying and fear. Deep in the back of my mind I knew I'd hyperventilate if my panic didn't subside, but I couldn't control my body.

"*Calmati,*" I heard Enzo say as he leaned over, the phone in his hand pointed at me. Jesus. Now he was taking pictures of me? What, was there some mafia social media, where they bragged about their killings and kidnappings?

He moved to a different angle and snapped more photos. "I apologize, Francesca. This was necessary, but it's over."

In one quick motion, he ripped the heavy tape off my mouth. The burning pain seared my skin and caused my eyes to water. Fuck, that hurt. He flicked open a knife and I tensed. Was he going to stab me? Rape me? Cut my tongue out?

In a flick of the blade he cut through the zip tie around my wrists. I immediately cradled them to my chest, rubbing the deep indentations in the skin. Pins and needles started at my shoulders and worked their way down my arms as the blood flow returned. I winced, waiting for the pain to subside.

Enzo lifted me out because I was too weak to fight him, which I hated. It was like when Giulio found me in the dungeon. I was a shell of a terrorized woman. Mafia men were officially the worst.

Mariella and Enzo steadied me when my legs trembled and I almost toppled over. Shaky and sweaty, I licked my lips. "You fucking asshole."

He smirked, unrepentant over his evilness. "I know. *Dai, andiamo.* You may sit in the back seat."

"Where are you taking me?"

"To Naples. No one is going to hurt you, I promise."

"You held me at gunpoint and shoved me into a trunk. It's a little late for that, Enzo."

"I apologize, but I had to make it look convincing for the cameras." He led me to the back seat and produced a pair of handcuffs. "Get in."

"Why would I go anywhere with you two fucked-up psychos?"

He raised his shirt, showing me the pistol tucked into his waistband. "I prefer to do this nicely, but I am happy to put you back in the trunk, if you prefer. Either way, you are coming with me."

I wanted to fight. To run and escape. But we were on a deserted stretch of road, with nothing but flat ground all around us. I wouldn't get far.

And how could I risk my child? If he shot me, I would probably bleed out to death in the hot August sun.

You will find a way to escape, Frankie. Play along for now.

I slid into the back seat, and Enzo glared down at me. "I will handcuff you and put you back in the trunk if you try anything. Behave and you can sit back here with Mariella."

Mariella got in beside me as Enzo walked around to the driver's seat. "There is nothing to worry about," Mariella said. "Enzo won't hurt you. This is about getting what he wants from Ravazzani."

Great. *That* was certainly reassuring.

And just saying, if she thought we were still friendly, she could fuck right off.

Enzo got in and started the car. I leaned against the door and closed my eyes, exhausted. What time was it? I had no idea how long I had been in that trunk.

Mariella nudged me with a bottle of water. "Here. Drink this. I have a protein bar for you, too."

I wasn't too proud to refuse, not as a pregnant woman. "Thank you." Enzo was texting on his phone, so I asked her, "How much longer?"

"Four hours."

Oh, fantastic. This was going to be a miserable car trip. At least I wasn't in the trunk any longer.

Enzo started the car and drove off. "You've been staying at the beach a long time, Francesca. Trouble in paradise?"

Though I wanted to curse and scream at him, I said nothing. If he'd been watching the beach house, then he knew Fausto hadn't come to visit me, that I was staying there alone.

"Fausto has a temper," Enzo continued. "You must have pissed him off for him to send you to the beach."

"You can stop trying to pump me for information. He won't care that you've kidnapped me, if that's what you are wondering."

"Oh, I think he'll care very much." He smirked in the rear view mirror at me. "I'll soon have the proof."

Whatever that meant. "Listen, Enzo. You seem like a decent guy, as far as mafia bosses go, so I'm trying to save you a headache here. Even if Fausto wants me back, which he doesn't, I'm not interested. He and I are through, so your little kidnapping plan won't work. To be honest, you're actually doing me a favor by getting me out of there."

His smirk died.

"You cannot mean it," Mariella said. "The two of you were so affectionate on the boat."

I looked over at her and lifted a brow. "Well, guess what? He kicked me out—without parting gifts."

"I don't understand this. Parting gifts?"

"As in, I didn't get to keep my phone or anything else from him." Except a baby, apparently. Hooray. "So Fausto can drop dead as far as I'm concerned." I didn't actually want him dead; I just wanted him out of my life. For good.

Mariella gasped and Enzo frowned. They exchanged a glance in the rearview mirror. I could tell this development was not what they expected.

"I can't wait to see Naples, though," I said, changing the subject. "What do you guys do there for fun?"

They began speaking in rapid Italian, too fast for me to keep up and I was too tired to care. The excitement and adrenaline had taken it out of me. Growing a baby was exhausting. Leaning over, I rested my head on my arms and closed my eyes. Maybe they'd drop me off now that they knew a big payday wasn't possible.

If they did, I could walk to the nearest town and try to call my sisters. Try to arrange a plane ticket out of here, go someplace where I could make sense of my fucked-up life.

Something told me Enzo would not drop me off, though.

Which meant I was going to need to escape. Again.

I could do this. I could outsmart them. Outlast them. No doubt they thought I was weak and silly, the girl in the black bikini from the yacht. The *puttanella*.

They would underestimate me—as both my father and Fausto had —and I would make my way out of this stupid country. I would disappear to somewhere no one would find me, not even my family. A place with tons of open space and not a lot of people. I could grow vegetables and raise sheep. No, not sheep. They were too cute. Maybe chickens.

A phone rang over the car's audio system. "Pronto," Enzo said.

Deep, rapid Italian filled the car, and my muscles instantly went on alert. His voice was clipped and formal, but unmistakable.

Fausto.

I hadn't heard that sexy Italian rumble in weeks. My chest cracked, little fissures of misery opening up again, all the aches I'd tried to bury. I didn't want to miss him. I needed to keep hating him. I *should* keep hating him. He certainly didn't deserve my forgiveness, the dick.

"Go ahead," Enzo said in English. "You are on my car's speaker."

"Frankie," Fausto said calmly. "Are you well?"

Frankie. Not Francesca or dolcezza. Frankie, as if I was an acquaintance or old friend. Prickles of sadness coasted under my skin and buried in my chest like needles. If that was the way he wanted to play it, then fine. "Just great, il Diavolo. You?"

He didn't answer for a long second. "Enzo will take care of you. I will see that he sends you wherever you wish to go—with my blessing, of course."

A lump formed in my throat and I couldn't speak. He was washing his hands of me, for good this time. I shouldn't have been surprised. It was exactly as I had told Enzo. Fausto didn't want me back and he didn't care that I'd been kidnapped.

At least we were all on the same page.

I could hear him breathing normally, so unaffected, like this was only one of a handful of tasks he had to deal with today.

I never change my mind, not after someone betrays me. You are dead to me, Francesca Mancini.

God, why did that still hurt so badly?

I forced the words out. "Awesome. Tell Lamborghini I said bye. Oh —and rot in hell, eh?"

Fausto said something to Enzo in Italian, and the two conversed back and forth for a moment. Were they talking business? Jesus Christ, that was cold. Though I shouldn't have been surprised. That was all Fausto cared about anyway, his empire. His precious legacy.

Well, he would not get his murdering hands on my baby. No matter what, this child would be raised far away from Fausto, far away from the 'Ndrangheta.

Somehow I would get out of this goddamn country and they would never find me.

This ride was boring AF.

No one spoke after the call with Fausto ended. Enzo seemed lost in thought and Mariella played on her phone. I concentrated on not throwing up, which seemed like a real possibility with every minute that passed.

I had to get out of this car.

"Can we stop? I need to use the bathroom."

Enzo asked Mariella if she wanted to stop, and the other woman shrugged without glancing up from her phone. He found my eyes in the rear view mirror. "I will stop by the side of the road. There are bushes and trees."

"Fuck that. A real bathroom with a real toilet or I swear, I will ruin the leather upholstery in this car."

He glared at me, then made a call. Whoever was on the phone called him Don D'Agostino, so I assumed it was someone who worked for Enzo. Odd that he didn't travel with the level of security and paranoia that plagued . . . other mafia bosses. Was that confidence or stupidity?

When we finally stopped at a petrol station, two black SUVs were parked there. Four men got out of each car, a small army of thugs who looked more like military men, each wearing black cargo pants, black t-shirts and black combat boots. They formed a perimeter around the station, sharp eyes scanning the surroundings. Here was D'Agostino's army. Had I just thought him stupid a moment ago?

It was clear Enzo was anything but stupid, because he had two men follow me and Mariella to the ladies toilet. Any attempt to try to escape here was impossible. The men waited outside while Mariella and I went in. I closed the stall door and took deep breaths. The urge to vomit was strong, but I fought it, not wanting Mariella to know I was pregnant. When I finished and emerged to wash my hands, Mariella was touching up her makeup in the mirror.

Rooting around in her purse, she held up a stick of concealer. "For your eyes."

I examined myself in the mirror, horrified by what I saw. The misery of the last few weeks compounded by being kidnapped had not done wonders for my complexion. I looked tired, my skin sallow. Dark circles hung under my eyes, a perfect match for the anguish reflected there.

I will see that he sends you wherever you wish to go—with my blessing, of course.

"Do not look sad," Mariella said. "Many important men in Naples work for my Enzo. You will find another."

I nearly scoffed. No, thank you. I didn't want another mafia man. I wanted an accountant or an architect. A barista, maybe. Someone with a regular job that didn't involve killing people.

"I'll be fine," I said, waving away her concealer. "I'll go back to Toronto. Or to New York. I'm not staying here."

Mariella smoothed the edges of her lips. "I could never leave. There is nothing like a powerful man between your legs. Why would you want another?"

Self-preservation, maybe?

"Besides," she continued, "Fausto will soon lose everything. My Enzo is very clever with computers and he has eyes and ears everywhere."

What did that mean? Fausto had mentioned Enzo's computer fraud empire on the yacht, but this sounded more direct, like Enzo was targeting Fausto. How? Did this have to do with my ransom?

I couldn't worry about that at the moment. I had my own problems. As I watched Mariella fuss with her lipstick, an idea occurred.

"Can I borrow some lipstick?"

Eager to help me right the terrible wrong of my makeupless face, she handed over a tube. I accepted it then dropped it, and the tube rolled under the stall door. "Damn it," I said, hurrying into the stall after Mariella's lipstick. Once I had the tube in hand, I uncapped it and wrote furiously on the old metal.

Call police. Kidnapped by E. D'Agostino.

Then I slapped some lipstick on my lips and emerged. "How does it look?" I asked Mariella, who was applying more mascara.

"That is the wrong shade for you." She whipped out a pack of makeup remover wipes. "Here, use this and I'll give you another one."

Sure, right. Why not? Two mafia mistresses hanging out in a bathroom, trading makeup tips and dolling ourselves up for murderers.

Wake up, Frankie. You aren't a mafia mistress any longer.

True. And who cared what I looked like?

I used the remover wipe on my lips then threw it away. "No, thanks. I don't need lipstick."

"Suit yourself." She fluffed her perfect hair. "Come. Enzo does not like to wait."

I followed her out of the bathroom. "Do you have any food?"

"More protein bars are in the car."

The men followed us back to the car, where Enzo stood, frowning in our direction. He gave some orders to the men behind us, and the two soldiers turned around and returned to the ladies' toilet. Shit. Would they find what I'd written?

I tried not to panic as I settled into the back of the car. Enzo stood outside, not moving, and Mariella gave me a protein bar and another bottle of water before turning back to her phone. I ate it quickly, hoping to settle my stomach for the drive, and watched out the window.

The two soldiers reemerged, and one walked over to speak quietly to Enzo. When Enzo slid into the driver's seat, his dark gaze caught mine in the rearview mirror. "A message on the stall. Very clever, Frankie."

My stomach clenched and it had nothing to do with hormones.

Enzo continued. "You know, you and Ravazzani talk a good game, but I don't believe either of you."

Then he was a fool. "Just because Fausto and I are through doesn't mean I want to go anywhere with you. Let me go, Enzo."

"Not just yet." Starting the car, he drove out of the station. "I need you."

CHAPTER FOUR

Fausto

When most mafia soldati killed, they wore black. The color hid bloodstains better than any other.

I preferred to wear white. I wanted the next man to know what happened to the man before. I wanted to see the fear in his eyes when he realized what I was capable of.

Right now, my white shirt was soaked in blood. The metallic smell filled the dungeon and my nostrils, the floor sticky under my leather shoes. It had been so long since I let the darkness take over, and I welcomed the sensation. I needed to kill, to feel life draining out from under my blade, hear their cries as they begged for me to stop.

My heart pounded, my body alive after weeks of being numb. I had a purpose now and that was to get my dolcezza back. Anyone who stood in my way would regret it.

Two men lay crumpled on the stone floor at my feet, pools of red beneath them. They hadn't talked—but I was betting the third one would.

We captured three of D'Agostino's men yesterday, brought them back to Siderno, and tortured them for information on their boss's beach home. Francesca was being kept there, and I wanted to know everything I could about the inside. Rooms, security cameras, occupants—even down to the paint colors and carpet patterns.

I smiled as I sat down in front of D'Agostino's soldier. Though he couldn't move, he jerked against his bindings, trying to get away from me.

A waste of time. There was no escape for this man, and the terror in his eyes told me he knew it.

I set my knife on my thigh, the silver blade dripping red. "Do you think to leave here alive?"

The man, who looked only a few years older than my son, trembled and shook his head. "No, Don Ravazzani."

"Correct, but you have a choice. You may hold out on me and suffer, like your brothers"—I gestured to the floor—"or you may help me and die an honorable death. Quick, painless. I'll see your body returned to your family in Napoli."

He swallowed hard and a bead of sweat rolled down his temple.

"So," I continued when he didn't speak, "you will tell me what I need to know, no?"

"I swore an oath to Don D'Agostino."

"If you will not help me, that makes us enemies. Are you certain you wish to be my enemy?"

"No, but please. I have a child coming soon."

The words reminded me of my unborn child, the one Francesca was carrying while Enzo kidnapped her. Renewed fury had me lunging forward to hold my knife against his throat. "I don't give a fuck about you or your child. I will peel the skin from your bones until you tell me what I wish to know. See those IV bags?" I pointed to where Marco stood with the medical equipment. "That is to keep you alive until I get the information I need. You will not bleed out. You will watch as I pull your intestines from your belly and throw them onto the floor."

My prisoner shook his head, terrified but silent.

I began trying to get him to talk. At some point he passed out, and Marco had to rouse the soldier awake with smelling salts. Finally, I ordered Marco to strip off the young man's pants while I went to fetch a drill.

The second the metal bit touched his balls, the soldier began speaking. The words were slow and barely audible, but we eventually received the information on the house, exactly where they were keeping Francesca. The others inside, the number of soldiers on guard.

When we had what we needed, I took pity on him and told Giulio to take care of it, so my son put a bullet between the soldier's eyes. As I stood, Marco gave me a long look. "Are you all right?"

"Ask me that one more time and I will slice your tongue out of your mouth."

"Hard to have a consigliere who cannot speak, Rav."

"You could still write." I strode toward the stairs. "Get some men down here and clean up. I need to shower and then make a call."

"Papà, wait." Giulio now stood next to Marco, his gun at his side. "You need to sleep. It's been too long. Zia is considering putting sleeping tablets in your drinks. You cannot get Frankie back without a clear head."

I knew it, but I couldn't sleep. The nightmares were plaguing me, my regret like a tire around my neck. Every time I closed my eyes I saw her, pictured her face the day I had sent her away. The sadness, the anger. The disbelief that I would act so cruelly toward her.

I am the best thing that has ever happened to you. And it will be too late when you realize it.

Her words were all true. She had been the best thing in my life and I had thrown her away.

"I will," I lied as I stripped out of my clothes. Zia hated when I tracked blood in the house. "Do your jobs, both of you."

Dressed in briefs and dried blood, I made my way out of the dungeon and into the dark kitchen. As soon as I stepped inside the lights came on, startling me.

Zia stood there, scowling.

I was in no mood. "Do not start, old woman."

"Look at you. You look like a monster, which is why she left you. What kind of woman wants to bring a monster's baby into this world?"

She was not wrong. I was a monster, born from a long line of monsters. Molded and shaped to be a killer, a king. Feared and respected around the globe, with wealth greater than most countries. And I would not apologize for it.

Just to annoy her, I grabbed a glass and the open bottle of ciró on the counter. I filled the glass to the top. "Your husband was a monster. One of the 'ndrina's best killers. My father bragged that no one tortured better than Zio Dario."

"And how many babies did we have?"

I took a long drink of wine, trying to cool the bloodlust and rage inside me. "I assumed he had enough bastards that you didn't feel it necessary." Dario had six children by three different women, as I recall. The men were now all members of my 'ndrina, as were their young sons.

She made the sign of the cross and glanced heavenward, no doubt saying a prayer on my behalf. "You dare to disrespect me in this house? I should put a curse on you."

"I am already cursed. What's one more?" My first wife had been killed and the woman I loved had been kidnapped. Murder and heartache was all I'd ever known, outside of my short time with Francesca.

"Never have you spoken to me like this. In all the years I have known you, I said you were a good boy. Now I am ashamed of you, drinking wine when you should be out getting your unborn child back safely." She clapped her hands twice. "Give that man whatever he wishes and bring Francesca home."

As if it were that simple.

D'Agostino was dangling Francesca out like a piece of meat, hoping I would bite. The price he'd quoted me, half my drug operation on the west coast, was ridiculous. I would not bow to blackmail or intimidation. I was il Diavolo—I inspired the intimidation, not succumbed to it.

I chugged the rest of the wine and put the glass on the marble countertop. "I will have my vengeance and bring her home. D'Agostino will pay with his life first."

"Bah! You men worry so much about your pride that you cannot see what really matters."

Likely true, but this was all I'd ever known. "I am taking my pride and going to shower. You may chastise me more tomorrow."

I left her standing in the kitchen and trudged up the steps. All of a sudden, my body felt exhausted, my muscles heavy. Each step grew increasingly more difficult, like I was walking through quicksand. Ma che cazzo?

I put a hand on the wall as I stumbled down the corridor, just trying to remain upright. Something was wrong. I was covered in blood and sweat, but I hadn't been injured. I shouldn't feel like this.

Once I was in my room, my bed swung up to greet me. As I closed my eyes, it hit me what had happened.

Zia and her sleeping tablets. In the wine.

Minchia!

Francesca

Clean and modern, Enzo's beach home was the complete opposite of the castello. The property stretched out along the Gulf of Naples, each room boasting a magnificent view of the water and Vesuvius. Mariella lived here, while Enzo's wife and children were somewhere else, and he had the luxury of going back and forth, the cheating bastard.

Even though Enzo was hardly around, his guards were always present, as was Mariella, which meant I was never alone, and I was exhausted from it. Most of my time was spent wondering if this was the day I'd be tortured or raped in revenge against Fausto. Or worse, the day Enzo realized I was of no use to him and put a bullet in my brain.

I hardly slept. I ate to keep my stomach settled, but I worried that each bite of food was poisoned. Every noise made me jump, and my nerves felt stretched to the breaking point. How much more of this could I take? How much longer before they realized I was pregnant with Fausto's baby? What would happen then?

The possibilities were too terrifying to contemplate.

So despite Mariella's repeated attempts to forge a friendship with me, I kept to myself. I needed to think and figure out an escape. All I needed was an instant, any window of opportunity where I could sneak away. Or for Mariella to make a mistake, like leaving her phone lying around.

Something would eventually happen. They would underestimate this puttanella and then I would run.

I was slicing a peach in the kitchen when the front door opened. Enzo came in, trailed by three of his men. Unlike Fausto, Enzo never wore a suit, at least that I'd seen. He was always in tight designer shirts and jeans or trousers, like a Hollywood movie star on vacation. "Good afternoon, Frankie. I would like a word with you."

The peach turned to ash in my mouth and I watched him warily as I swallowed. "Sure."

Enzo sat on a stool at the kitchen bar and snagged a piece of peach off my plate. I didn't like how his eyes traveled my body as he chewed. He asked, "How do you like my beach house?"

"As prisons go, it's nice."

"Thank you. I would say you could thank Fausto for it, but he doesn't seem to be in the chatting mood lately."

Thank Fausto for kicking me out and allowing Enzo to kidnap me? Hell would freeze over first. "I told you he doesn't care about me."

Enzo didn't comment on this. "Has my Mariella been taking good care of you?"

"I suppose, but if you're taking requests I'd like a phone."

His lips twitched. "Strange we've not heard from Ravazzani, don't you think?"

Not strange to me. I knew him better than anyone, and Fausto never said what he didn't mean. He was through with me. I tried to sound braver than I felt. "You should let me go."

"Or perhaps I should send him a reminder."

I gripped the marble counter so hard my fingers turned white. Was this where he cut off one of my toes and delivered it to Fausto? I pushed the peach away, appetite forgotten. "That's a waste of your time."

"I don't agree." His gaze was shrewd. "I think he will mind very, very much."

I really liked having all five toes attached to my foot. "You heard what he said, right? He's given his blessing for you to send me anywhere I wish to go. Well, I wish to go to Toronto, please."

"Amore mio!" Mariella exclaimed, bounding into the room with a bright smile on her face.

He turned and opened his arms, and she came quickly, sliding between his thighs to press a deep kiss on his mouth. When they parted, he spoke in rapid Italian to her, too fast for me to translate, and she nodded before disappearing again. My stomach sank. Whatever he was planning must be truly terrible if he didn't want her to see it.

"Listen, Enzo. Signore D'Agostino. There's no reason to bother yourself with me. I'm sure you have better things to do. Let me go and we'll forget any of this ever happened."

He grinned at me. "You must have driven him crazy. I can see why he was staring at you like a starving wolf that day on the yacht."

That trip seemed like a lifetime ago. "I don't know what you're talking about, but it doesn't matter. Fausto and I are through."

Mariella returned, a long rope dangling from her fingertips. Oh, shit. I started to back up as Enzo stood. Except I was trapped by kitchen cabinetry and stainless steel appliances. I would need to sprint past them both and hope for the best.

It was now or never.

In a blink, I took off. I darted around the island and ran toward the sliding glass doors that led to the beach. No one tried to stop me, so I kept going. My feet slapped onto the wooden deck—and that's when I saw two guards emerge from either side of the house, their guns drawn and pointed at my head. I hesitated. Would they actually shoot me? I wasn't certain I could risk it.

That pause was all they needed to swarm around me. I tried to pull free, but they wouldn't budge, dragging me back inside.

Enzo didn't seem surprised. "Enjoy the fresh air?"

So many words burned my tongue. Most were creative versions of "fuck off," but I had to be careful with this man. "What are you going to do?"

"Come. Stand here, Frankie." He moved to the center of the room, the rope in his hand. Looking over his shoulder, he told his guards to bring me over. I knew there was nowhere for me to go, but I dropped back a step.

It did no good. The guards had a firm grip on me and they tugged me over to Enzo. "Hold her hands behind her back," Enzo ordered.

"No, please." I hated myself for begging, but I didn't want this. My heart pounded, my mind scared out of my wits. Why did he need rope? Was he going to rape me? Torture me? Oh, God. I couldn't breathe.

When the rope was around my wrists, pulled tight, Enzo continued winding the rope around my torso. His fingers brushed the underside of my breasts as he worked, and I tried not to react as revulsion ripped through me. Did he just cop a feel, the fucking perv?

The slight curve to his lips told me he had. God, how gross.

He's going to kill you. Stop worrying about whether he touched your boobs or not.

Right. There were far bigger problems at the moment.

When he had me trussed up to his liking, he pushed on my shoulder and forced me to my knees. That put my face at his crotch level, and fear clawed in my chest. Was he going to shove his dick in my mouth? I wobbled and certainly would've toppled over if not for Enzo's hand on my head to steady me. He ordered Mariella to get his phone, then held out his hand to one of the guards and a gun was placed in his palm.

Oh, Jesus. He finally realized I was of no use to him. "Enzo, no. Please, don't do this."

"Open your mouth, puttanella."

A tear slid down my cheek, my lungs incapable of pulling in air. I was going to die. I was going to die before meeting my baby, before seeing my sisters again. How was this fair? "Please, Enzo."

He pried open my jaw using his powerful fingers and shoved the barrel of the gun inside my mouth. The cold metal smoothed over my tongue and rattled against my teeth. It tasted like death.

I trembled, tears running silently down my cheeks. I couldn't believe this was happening. Fuck Fausto for kicking me out. I was definitely coming back as a ghost to haunt his ass for the rest of his life.

My mind went blank after that. I could only stare up at Enzo, the harsh edges of the gun tearing at the soft skin of my mouth. I don't think I was even breathing.

"So beautiful and so proud," Enzo murmured as he dragged a fingertip along my jaw, caressing me. "How could any man resist you?" Then he told Mariella to take photos with his phone.

I knelt in a grotesque display of cruelty, my body vibrating in terror as I waited for Enzo to pull the trigger. No doubt it would be soon, my gruesome death captured for his enjoyment. Would he share the photos with other members of the 'Ndrangheta? With Fausto? Was there a mafia Instagram where they posted these after the fact?

"Basta," he told his mistress, then slowly withdrew the gun from my mouth. He used his thumb to wipe the tears from my face while I tried not to hyperventilate. "You on your knees, so obedient. Did he like this, as well? I bet he did. This is why you are the perfect distraction."

Distraction? Something about his tone caused my skin to prickle. Danger cloaked the room, so thick I could smell it. Would he take me against my will now?

The moment was broken when Mariella threw her arm over his shoulder and handed his phone back. "Baby, her hands," she said in English.

I was quickly untied and left there, kneeling on the floor. What was happening? Relief flooded me as Enzo began texting on his phone, ignoring me, and the guards wandered away. Sagging, I caught my breath and tried not to think about how close I'd come to dying.

Mariella slipped a hand under my elbow and helped me to my feet. "He's very attracted to you," she said quietly. "If you want to join us, you are welcome. And, it might make Fausto jealous."

Inspiring jealousy in a man I hated seemed like a terrible reason to have a threesome. "Hard pass," I said. "But this is why you should help me. Please. I need to get out of Italy."

She gave one small shake of her head. "He will kill me if I help you escape."

"It's not safe for either of us here. Come with me. We can help each other."

Mariella's eyes were flat and resigned when they met mine. "There is no escape from these men."

CHAPTER FIVE

Fausto

I knew something was wrong as soon as Giulio, Marco and five of my men crowded into my office on the yacht. We had dropped anchor off the coast of Napoli, not far from Enzo's beach house.

"Papà," Giulio said in his most reasonable tone. "You should sit."

Marco grimaced, knowing me well enough to understand how this came across. No one told me to calm down or take a seat. I was the head of this 'ndrina, the capo, and I could never show weakness. "Tell me," I barked, remaining on my feet.

"A message has come in from D'Agostino," Marco said. "It's bad."

I appreciated his directness, but my gut cramped all the same. What had D'Agostino done to her? If he had hurt her, I would bomb the entire Gulf of Napoli, skull fuck his corpse, then go after his wife and children. "Show me."

Giulio handed me the phone and I froze. My glorious girl was on her knees, her face covered in tears while a Glock was shoved in her mouth. Enzo had her restrained, ropes crossing her body, under her breasts, and I could see the terror in her eyes.

A red mist coated my brain.

I couldn't think, the anger so swift and so violent that I threw the phone across the room, where it cracked open against the wall. With a roar, I flipped the desk over with both hands, papers flying and my laptop sliding to the floor. Out of the corner of my eye I saw Giulio ordering the soldiers out of the office, but I was too busy lifting a chair and hurling it across the room to care. I was a berserker, hell-bent on the destruction of everything in my path.

I tore the room apart. Broke furniture, cracked lamps. The framed pictures were thrown to the ground, where glass shattered. I cut my hand at one point but didn't stop. I couldn't rid my brain of that image, the woman I loved being mistreated. Tortured.

Because of me.

I caused this. I sent her away and left her a target for my enemies. And, for what? She had only honored my son's secret. I should have appreciated such loyalty to my own flesh and blood. Instead I cast her out. My love, the mother of my child.

Porca puttana! I shoved my hands in my hair and pulled hard on the strands, certain I was coming apart at the seams. I had to get her back. I had to get her back and rip the skin from Enzo's bones. Then I would somehow convince her to forgive me.

Please. God, please, do not take her from me.

I don't know if I could survive it. While Lucia's death had been a tragedy, it didn't destroy me. Instead, I had dedicated myself to killing those responsible and raising my son. Retribution for her death was enacted coldly, methodically, mostly because I knew it was expected of me.

But losing Francesca? It would break me.

The image of the gun in her mouth returned and I lunged for another chair, needing to throw it against the wall, but Giulio and Marco were suddenly behind me. They held me tight, even when I snarled and lunged like a wild dog.

"Papà, basta," my son said. "Let's work on getting her back."

It took a few minutes, but the haze slowly began to clear and I could think once again. "I'm fine."

Marco and Giulio released me and I straightened my cuffs with trembling hands. "We go tonight."

"Rav," Marco started. "We aren't ready. We are waiting on the Sicilians."

I made a deal with some of my Cosa Nostra associates in exchange for their help in killing Enzo and retrieving Francesca. "Tell them they have"—I checked my watch—"four hours to get here, otherwise the deal is off. And so is our truce."

"Fuck," Giulio muttered, rubbing his eyes with his fingers.

Marco frowned at me. "We cannot go to war over this. It's bad for business."

"I will start a thousand wars to get her back."

"Then think about Crimine," he said, reminding me of the annual gathering of La Provincia, the 'Ndrangheta leaders, coming up. It was held in the mountains and many of our important decisions and alliances were made there. "They'll expect you to answer for this."

"I will do whatever the fuck I want, cugino, and those old men can't stop me. Not when I bring in the most profits."

"Papà, she . . ." Giulio seemed to be struggling for words. "We are helping her escape D'Agostino, but then you must let her go."

I would do no such thing. My son, however, could believe whatever he wished. He'd soon learn how I planned to deal with Francesca. "Of course," I lied. "Now the two of you get out."

Marco glanced at Giulio. "Go tell them to be ready." Once we were alone, my cousin gave me a pitying look that set my teeth on edge. "Rav, you'd best prepare yourself for the worst. She is a liability and Enzo—"

"She is not a liability, she is the mother of my child. And Enzo will keep her alive, if only to use her to torture me." It was what I would do, after all.

"Do you think he knows she's pregnant?"

The sheer terror of that possibility caused my balls to nearly retreat up into my body. I had to believe Enzo didn't know, or else he would've used the information to his advantage. No doubt Francesca was smart enough to try to hide the pregnancy as best she could. "Doubtful, or else he would have mentioned it."

"Still, you need to remain practical and not let your temper get the best of you. That includes not growing angry if she wants to leave once we have her back."

She was my woman and I was never letting her leave. "You don't need to worry."

"My job is to worry, remember? And with everything going on, it seems to be more than a full-time job."

"You can take a vacation once we have Francesca back."

"And leave you to deal with Enzo by yourself? I don't think so. Not to mention we need to learn why no one was watching the beach house cameras when she was kidnapped."

Vic had been on duty that afternoon, but he wasn't a guard, per se. More like a computer hacker whiz. He'd been in my crew for almost seven years, and had worked in my home for the last three. "You don't believe Vic's story about a security update?"

"It could be a coincidence, but I don't like coincidences. And what of the others? Vic doesn't work alone."

I dug the heels of my palms into my eyes. "We'll deal with that when we return—including discovering how Enzo knew where to find Francesca."

"The beach house was no secret. You know how the men gossip."

I had replayed the video of the masked man dumping Sal's unconscious body a thousand times in my head. Something still bothered me about it. "Yes, but the man in the house . . . It was like he knew exactly where he was going."

"Maybe." Marco exhaled heavily. "We'll get Enzo to talk."

Yes, we definitely would. "Is everything in place?"

Marco folded his arms. "Other than the Sicilians, yes."

"Good. Call them now. Impress the importance of haste."

"I will. I hope you know what you're doing."

I knew exactly what I was doing. I would save Francesca from that bastard if I had to burn the entire world down to do it.

Francesca

Enzo stayed for dinner.

I tried to hide in my room, but I was ordered to the patio to eat with Enzo, Mariella, and six of his men. The outdoor space was softly lit and lined with beautiful, fragrant flowers. Gentle waves crashed onto the beach in a rhythmic soothing sound. The scenery would've been romantic under any other circumstances, but I couldn't enjoy it. I picked at my spaghetti alle vongole, aware that everyone was surreptitiously watching me. Was the food poisoned? Were they all waiting for me to eat it, then keel over at the table?

Mariella tried to keep the conversation going, but Enzo's men were uninterested in talking, remaining silent, and Enzo gave her one or two word answers. Finally, he looked at me. "Don't care for the pasta, Frankie?"

"I'm just waiting for the poison to kick in."

"Now, why would we poison you? You are much more valuable alive than dead." He pointed to my dish. "Take a bite."

"I'm allergic to shellfish." It was a lie. I loved clams.

"I have an adrenaline pen in the house. Go on. It's rude not to eat in our country."

I knew this to be true. Zia had given me a hard time about leaving food, even before I was pregnant. I swallowed and looked down. Was there poison in there? Probably not. If Enzo wanted to kill me, I'd be dead already. I twirled pasta on my fork, added a clam, then brought it to my mouth. Goddamn, that was good. Garlicky and rich, with the perfect seasoning and hint of the ocean. I wanted to hate this country, but its food won me over every time.

"If you start to feel sick," Enzo said with an arrogant lift of his brow, "please let me know."

Asshole. I ignored him and kept eating, suddenly starving. I guess being tied up and having a gun shoved in my mouth had really worked up an appetite.

"This is my nonna's recipe," Mariella said. "I make it for Enzo all the time."

"You mean when he's here and not at home." No idea why I'd said it, but these people were not my friends. We weren't at a dinner party where I was required to be polite. Fuck all of them.

Enzo chuckled and put his hand on Mariella's thigh. "It is no secret that I'm married. My wife is aware of Mariella. It's okay with her."

"How progressive of you."

"There is no such thing as monogamy in Italia, Frankie."

Super. Life lessons from my kidnapper. "I suppose Mariella is afforded the same privilege, then. What about your wife? Can she sleep around, too?"

His expression hardened, lips thinning into a cruel slash. I saw the capo in that moment, the one who killed and tortured for a living. "It is not the same for women."

"So much for being progressive."

Everyone's head swiveled back and forth, watching us. Mariella appeared horrified, but Enzo seemed amused. Mostly. "Did you speak to Ravazzani this way? Not holding your opinions back?"

"I have a brain and I prefer to use it. Anyone who doesn't like it can fuck off."

Mariella gasped, while Enzo's gaze darkened, sharpened into something hungry and fierce. "You have a mouth on you. Perhaps you need a lesson in respect."

Fear shot along my spine. Shit. Why had I spoken so openly? And why had I used curse words? Did he see this as a challenge? That was a dumb question. Of course he did. Now he had to put me in my place in front of his men. "I apologize. I shouldn't have spoken so rashly."

"Too late." He pushed back from the table. "Come. You are going to get on your knees and beg for forgiveness from every man here."

What the fuck?

Beg for the forgiveness of these murders? Was he for real? Everything inside me wanted to scream, *No, I won't do it*. I knelt in the past to Fausto during our sexy games . . . but those days were over. I bowed to no man, not any more.

Except how could I refuse? Not following Enzo's order was like a slap in the face. He would have to punish me—and who knew whether this house had a dungeon?

We stared at one another. Panic and dread filled my mouth, drying it out. Would he relent if I asked for his forgiveness right now? Damn it, why did I always make trouble like this? All I had to do was sit and eat quietly, and I hadn't been able to manage it.

The moment stretched with the entire group waiting to see what I would do. I gathered my pride and decided this would not kill me. I could endure a few minutes of humiliation to stay alive. Pushing back from the table, I started to rise—until a faint noise sounded and the soldier across from me fell back in his chair, a bullet hole in his forehead.

Oh, my God.

I watched as another soldier went down with a bullet, and then Mariella screamed. Chaos erupted, and I dove under the table. As the men scrambled, Enzo came after me, apparently unconcerned about Mariella, who was still screaming out there.

Another soldier dropped to the patio, dead. I covered my mouth, trying to hold down my pasta. What was happening? Some rival gang attack?

I knew it wasn't Fausto. He couldn't have been clearer on the phone in Enzo's car, especially after having ignored me for three weeks at the beach house. If there was a rescue team coming for me, it wasn't from Siderno.

My father?

That also seemed unlikely. Papà hated me more than Fausto did.

Enzo grabbed my arm. "Kick off those shoes. We need to run."

I obeyed, leaving my flip flops on the deck. If nothing else, I needed Enzo to keep me alive right now . . . though I would still be looking for a way to escape.

He began tugging me to my feet, but shots were still whizzing all around us. "Wait!" I shouted, not moving. "Is it safe to be running around right now?"

"There's a panic room in the master suite. I will take you there."

Oh, no way. No way in hell. That would send my claustrophobia into overdrive. And what if he locked me in? He could die and I would have no way to escape. "I can't go into a panic room."

"Dai, woman. I have no time for this." Carrying a gun in one hand, he jerked me up roughly with the other, not even caring when I stumbled. Instead, his hand pushed my head down and forced me into a half-crouch position, then he towed me inside.

The rooms were eerily empty. I supposed all of Enzo's soldiers were fighting the gunmen outside. Enzo cursed and shoved me toward the stairs. "Get moving."

"Let me just hide in a closet," I begged. "I won't move, I swear." I mean, I would run as soon as his back was turned, but Enzo didn't need to know that.

"No, I need to keep you safe. You're half of my plan to destroy Fausto."

"Fausto doesn't care about me!" Jesus, didn't he get it by now?

"Look around you. He cares very much. Now, get your ass upstairs."

As he tugged me up the steps, I looked around wildly for a way to avoid the nightmare of a panic room. Anything I could use to distract him or hit him with. There had to be a way out. No one was coming to save me—I had to save myself.

We arrived at the top of the stairs and I pretended to trip. When I slipped out of his grasp, I rolled to my back then used my legs to kick at the side of his right knee with all my might. The joint gave a sickening pop and he howled in agony, leaning over to grasp the iron railing for support.

I didn't wait. I shot to my feet and flew down the stairs as fast as I could, hurrying toward the front door. Enzo shouted at me to stop, but I kept going, praying his injured knee hindered him long enough for me to get outside.

There was no one guarding the front. Jerking open the door, I saw a Range Rover waiting in the drive and I sprinted toward it. Suddenly, I was lifted off my feet. "Let me go!" I tried to wrestle free, kicking and wriggling, as someone dragged me back toward the house. "Stop. Let me go, you asshole."

Whoever he was, he was too strong, and I found myself once more in the foyer of the beach house. Enzo waited inside, his furious eyes focused directly at me, the promise of retribution burning in the dark depths. "You fucking whore. I should snap your neck for that. Take her to the panic room," he told the guard. "I'll deal with her later."

The guard started marching me toward the stairs—then I heard a pop just before he fell forward, and I had to rip my arm out of his grasp to avoid collapsing to the floor. The back of the guard's head was now missing, blood pooling onto the tile, and I bit back a scream. I spun toward the door to see who was attacking—and found Fausto there.

Oh. My. God.

His white t-shirt and black pants were covered in blood, a huge knife strapped to his thigh. Flat, cold eyes swept over me for the briefest of seconds, almost dismissing me, before he took one step inside, his gun trained on Enzo. This was il Diavolo, the angel of death. A man who thrived on killing. A shiver went through me and I forgot how to breathe.

Fausto had come for me. How? Why?

While I was frozen there like an idiot, an arm wrapped around my throat and jerked me into a hard chest. Cool metal met my temple. I tried not to move, certain that I would die. Even if Fausto managed to shoot Enzo there was every chance that Enzo's gun would fire and pierce my skull.

Enzo's rasp sounded in my ear. "Did you like the photos I sent, Fausto?"

Fausto answered, his voice cool and detached. "Let her go. You've lost, Enzo."

CHAPTER SIX

Francesca

Enzo jerked me closer and started moving backward. "I've lost nothing. I still have your puttanella. I'll kill her."

Fausto prowled forward, his gun remaining trained on Enzo. "You die either way."

"Put down your gun or I'll shoot her. Right fucking now!" Enzo shook me, his arm coming around my throat, and I gasped.

Something flashed on Fausto's face at the sound, but he didn't take his gun off Enzo. "I don't think so. You are going to let her go."

"Wrong, I'm going to keep her. I think I will let her watch as I kill you."

"Marco!" Fausto shouted, his voice echoing in the large space.

Marco stepped into the doorway, but he wasn't alone. He had a woman and two small children with him. Their mouths were covered with duct tape, hands bound, eyes wide with fear. It looked as if they'd all been pulled out of their beds, with the kids still in pajamas. Marco's gun was aimed at the children.

Enzo went perfectly still behind me. His voice was low and angry as he slowly said, "You dare to kidnap my family?"

My stomach sank. Wives and children were supposed to be off limits. What had Fausto been thinking? Was he trying to get me killed?

"Drop your weapon and let her go," Fausto growled. "I won't ask you again. If you don't, you know what will happen. I won't hesitate, D'Agostino."

The cool metal left my temple and I saw Enzo lower the gun out of my peripheral vision. Then his arm loosened and he stepped back. I wasn't certain what to do, so I stood there, waiting. Was this it? Was I really free?

Giulio and two other soldiers hurried forward and quickly restrained Enzo. The D'Agostino children leaned into their mother, who tried to curl her body around them, protecting them. My heart went out to her. Soon I would be that mother, protecting her child at the expense of her own safety.

Fausto never took his eyes off Enzo. "Francesca, the car. Now."

He thought he could order me around? Had he lost his mind in the last month?

"Francesca," my baby daddy snapped when I didn't move.

I lifted my chin and stared him down. "I'm not leaving until I know what you are planning."

"That is not your concern. Go. Now."

"What are you going to do, Fausto?"

"Cazzo," he hissed. "Do as you are told. Get inside the car waiting out front."

"If you are planning on killing this man in front of his children, I will not allow it. Also, if you are planning on harming these children, I will not allow it."

His lips thinned as he stepped over to me, right into my personal space. Broad shoulders and a wide chest filled my vision.

Leaning close, he said quietly into my ear, "You think to tell me what to do, dolcezza? That is not how this works, if you recall."

My mouth dried out as the familiar tug between us roared to life, but I stood firm. He'd lost the right to call me dolcezza when he kicked me out. "This doesn't work at all, if you recall. We're done. So yes, I will tell you exactly what to do."

Shockingly, the edge of his mouth lifted slightly. "I am glad to see being kidnapped has not crushed your spirit."

"Maybe you Italians just suck at kidnapping."

He dragged the back of a knuckle across my cheek. "Dio, I have missed you."

I shoved his hand away. "Don't."

His eyes lost their warmth, and it seemed the temperature in the room dropped by forty degrees. Stepping back, he said, "We will discuss this later. Get in the fucking car."

I didn't move, except to cross my arms over my chest.

Enzo chuckled, which probably didn't help matters. Fausto stormed over to the other don and punched him in the face. Enzo's head snapped sideways, but Giulio and the other soldiers kept him on his feet.

"Fausto, his family," I hissed. No child should witness such brutality, even if their father deserved it. "Think about what you are doing for one goddamn minute."

Fausto's gaze cut to me and we stared at each other for several beats. I didn't flinch. Women and children were off limits, period. Just because Enzo broke that rule with me didn't mean Fausto should, too. He was a controlling asshole, but he respected tradition and rules. He knew Enzo's wife and children were innocent. If the roles were reversed, how would Fausto want his own wife and children treated?

Cursing, Fausto grabbed Enzo's hair and tilted his head back. Blood poured from Enzo's mouth but his eyes remained defiant. Moving in, Fausto spoke quietly, not loud enough for Enzo's family to hear, but I caught every word. "I am going to gut you like a fish and feed your entrails to the pigs on my estate."

Enzo spat on the ground at Fausto's feet.

Giulio shook his head, like he knew this would only make things worse. Fausto lifted his chin toward his son. "Get him on the boat."

Enzo was dragged out of the beach house by Giulio and the two soldiers. I went to the D'Agostino family and knelt in front of the children first. "I know you're scared," I whispered in my best Italian. "But your mamma is here to protect you. Always."

They didn't respond, just huddled closer to their mother, so I stood to face Enzo's wife. Reaching for the duct tape, I told her, "This will hurt. I'm sorry."

She nodded and I ripped the heavy tape off her mouth as quickly as possible. Surprisingly, she didn't make a sound, though I knew from experience it hurt like holy hell. "Grazie," she said. Somehow I knew she meant for not forcing her children to watch their father being brutally murdered.

I squeezed her bound hands. "Prego."

Fausto ordered Marco to take the D'Agostino family outside, which left me alone with him. He tucked his pistol into his waistband at the small of his back and crossed his arms over his chest. "You are angry with me."

I wanted to rail at him for asking such a stupid question, but honestly I was tired. "Actually, I'm over it. Just like I'm over *you*. Put me on a plane and send me back to Toronto. Now."

"Never. I will not let you go."

"Again, you mean. You will not let me go *again*. Because you did let me go, Fausto, and you can't decide you want your toy back just because someone else now has it. You gave your toy away, you selfish asshole."

The lines of his face sharpened, his cheekbones harsh slashes in the dim lighting. "You are the mother of my child and my mantenuta, therefore I can decide whatever the fuck I want when it comes to you. I know you are angry but you will forgive me in time."

He said this with such confidence, such arrogance, that I barked a laugh. "You are unbelievable. I'm not your mantenuta any more, and you lost all rights to this child when you kicked me out!"

"I apologize for my temper. I should not have reacted so harshly when we argued. If I could go back, I would handle things differently."

"That is what you said about the previous two times you sent me away. No more, Fausto. I'm done with you."

His right eye twitched. "I waged a war to rescue you, Francesca. I made a deal with the Cosa Nostra to help me extricate you from D'Agostino."

As flattering as he made it sound, I knew the real story. "Bullshit. You hated Enzo from that meeting on the yacht. He insulted you by refusing to allow you in on his computer fraud scheme." I hadn't picked up all the details, but my limited Italian had let me glean at least that much. Surprise flashed in his expression, so I gave him a smug smile. "I'm very good at eavesdropping. You should remember that."

Out of the depths of the house, a soldier appeared, a petrified Mariella at his side. "Don Ravazzani, what should we do with her?"

Mariella's gaze met mine and I could see her begging for help. Bitch, please. She had helped Enzo at every turn. "Leave her," I told Fausto. "Without his money she'll wither and die like an old prune."

Fausto turned to the soldier. "You heard my woman. Leave her."

My woman. I rolled my eyes. What a joke.

"Now," he said, giving me his full attention. "Let's return to the castello. The plane is waiting."

"Fuck off, Fausto. I'm not your woman and I'm not going anywhere with you."

Oh, he didn't like that one bit. His body seemed to swell, anger coming off him waves. "I cannot drug you this time because of the child, but I can tie you up, Francesca. I can force you to come with me."

"Why would you bother? I'll never sleep with you again and I'll try to escape at every turn. It's a waste of your time."

"Never is a long time, dolcezza. Would you care to bet on that?"

Based on the way my heart was pounding right now, absolutely not. "If you don't let me go, I will do everything I can to make your life a living hell."

He closed the distance between us and wrapped a large hand around my arm. "No need because I am already there. I have been since the moment I ordered you to leave."

While I was trying to make sense of that statement, he procured a pair of handcuffs from the pocket of his pants. Too late I realized what he was doing. In a flash he had a metal bracelet locked around my wrist, and he clapped the other around his own.

Great. Handcuffed to Fausto. Again.

Fausto

I watched her pretend to sleep next to me on the plane. Did she think I wouldn't notice the pulse racing at the base of her throat? Clearly she was awake, but I let her have this. She was pissed enough. It would take time to win her over once again.

But I would. What she and I had together was too strong, too wild to deny.

Had Enzo hurt her? I had no idea how she'd suffered at my enemy's hands, except for the photo of her on her knees, a goddamn gun in her mouth. D'Agostino would pay for that a thousand-fold before I was done with him. Was there anything else? I needed to find out what happened during her captivity—not only to exact retribution on Enzo, but to offer her support and comfort.

I examined her as best I could, but saw no bruises or cuts. No welts or broken bones. *Perhaps the damage is where I cannot see.* My blood ran cold at the thought. Had Enzo raped her? Or harmed my child in some way?

"Stop staring at me," she muttered. "It's creepy. And stop fidgeting. I'm trying to sleep."

"Cazzata. You cannot sleep any easier than I can." My adrenaline was still high from the attack, and worries over her clouded my brain. "Besides, the flight is only a little over an hour. By the time you fall asleep I will need to force you awake."

"God, I hate you."

I smothered a smile. If she hated me, she still felt something and I could work with that. Before then, there were practicalities to be dealt with, like the man who had dared to take her from me. "Did Enzo hurt you?"

"Worried that your toy is broken?"

"Francesca," I snapped. "This is serious. Did he touch you or hurt you? Or hurt our child in any way?"

"Other than brushing a hand over my boob, he didn't touch me. No, don't worry. He didn't hurt me nearly as badly as you did."

I winced, unable to help myself. I didn't like the idea of hurting her. I hadn't cared about a mantenuta's feelings before, but for some reason Francesca's *mattered* to me. It was strange.

When Lucia and I were married, I hadn't cared much for her feelings, either. She was there to oversee my home and care for my children, a part she had been raised to perform. There hadn't been any discord or arguments. She wouldn't have dared. My wife had bowed to my every whim, my every demand. The news about her death hadn't sent me into a tailspin.

So why had Francesca's kidnapping affected me so dramatically?

I didn't want to think about it. I had her back and that was what mattered. She would forgive me and everything would return to the way it was before, with fucking and laughter and our naughty games.

I cleared my throat. "Still, I will have the doctor examine you when we return home."

"Home," she sneered. "It's not my home."

"Lamborghini and Vincenzo have missed you. Zia, Giulio. Even Marco."

"Now I know you are lying. Marco hates me."

My cousin did not like Francesca, true. He thought she made me vulnerable. That she distracted me from 'ndrina business. Perhaps it was the case, which was why I needed our relationship to return to what it had been before as quickly as possible. "I missed you."

That got her to open her eyes, but there was no fire in them. No spark, just flat loathing. Even when I kidnapped her in Toronto there had been a flash in her gaze, a heat between us. "You missed a warm hole to shove your cock into."

I heard murmuring, which reminded me we weren't alone on the plane. A dozen or so soldiers were on board for protection. "Lower your voice," I told her.

"Why? I've done nothing to be ashamed of. I'm not the one who knocked up his mistress, then sent her away and put her under house arrest, alone. You didn't give a shit about what happened to me or our child."

"Is that what you think? I had guards and cameras on you every second. My son brought you food and gave you books to read. Ginger candies for nausea."

Her brows shot up. "You spied on me."

"My men sent me reports each day. I knew exactly what you were doing at every second."

"Except for when I was being kidnapped."

I ground my back teeth together. "Yes, that unfortunate oversight has been dealt with."

"Unfortunate oversight." She rolled her eyes. "You're an asshole."

"Careful," I leaned in to say. "I like when you show spirit, dolcezza."

She edged as far away from me as the handcuffs allowed and closed her eyes. "Noted. I won't do it again."

I decided not to push it. Not until the doctor examined her and declared that she and the baby were unharmed. Only then could I bring Francesca around. In the end, I would win this battle of wills.

She looked good. Even better than I remember. No baby bump yet, but her tits were bigger, her skin glowing. I wanted her so badly that my teeth ached with it.

I shifted in my seat and tried to concentrate on tonight. I needed to deal with Enzo. Marco and Giulio were on the yacht, bringing him to the castello dungeon, where I planned to keep him for a long time. No easy death awaited Enzo. He had dared to kidnap my woman and blackmail me. I had a feeling La Provincia would have something to say about this retribution against another clan, but I didn't care. The other 'ndrina bosses hadn't seen their woman on her knees, tied up with a gun shoved in her mouth. No, Enzo would remain my prisoner until I tired of torturing him.

When we finally touched down in Siderno, I led her to the waiting Range Rover and helped her up. She didn't speak, her movements sluggish. The car drove away from the landing strip and I pulled out my phone. After ordering the doctor to the castello, I called Marco.

"Where are you?" I asked, anxious to get started.

"We should arrive by early morning," my cousin said.

I tapped my fingers on my knee. I should have brought Enzo on the plane with me. It would have been faster. But I'd wanted to protect Francesca from him. "Keep me updated throughout the night. I'll be awake."

I hung up before he could chastise me about sleeping. I didn't want to hear it.

The castello's front door opened as soon as we pulled into the drive. Zia stood there, watching as the SUV rolled to a stop. I helped Francesca to the ground and took her hand like we weren't still cuffed together. We climbed the steps and Zia barely stepped back to allow us inside.

My aunt placed both hands on Francesca's face and began speaking rapidly in Italian. "Thank God that He has spared you a terrible fate. And the baby! You must rest, beautiful girl."

"Okay, I caught most of that, I think," Francesca said with a weary laugh. "Ciao, Zia."

Zia kissed both her cheeks. "Do not put Fausto through such agony again, please." Holding up Francesca's wrist, she snapped at me, "Unlock her, you pig."

I retrieved the key and removed the handcuffs. Zia took Francesca's hand and began leading her toward the kitchen. "The doctor is coming to check her," I called out to my aunt.

"He will have to wait. She is too thin and the baby needs food to stay healthy."

I followed. Though I needed to shower, I didn't trust Francesca not to bolt out the back door. She'd done it once before. I would need to put guards on her at all times. Until Marco returned and could organize security for her, I had to stay close.

When I entered the kitchen, Zia was placing a plate of chicken, roasted potatoes and asparagus in front of Francesca. There was a bottle of sparkling water on the counter. I reached for it and Zia smacked my hand. "That is not for you."

"*Dai*, old woman. I am the one who rescued her."

"And you are also the one who drove her away."

"I love when Zia yells at you," Francesca said. "Because you deserve it."

I dropped onto the stool next to Francesca and suppressed a groan. My back hurt and I think there were deep scrapes across my ribs. "May I also have a plate?" I asked Zia.

She ignored me. Instead she cut a slice of walnut cake and put it beside Francesca's dinner. Sighing, I rose and fixed a plate of food for myself. When I returned to my seat, I scowled at Zia. "You are forgetting who helped you when Zio Dario passed."

"Your father, as I recall. You were busy with your women and rising through the ranks."

Not true. My father planned to pawn Zia off on Marco's father until I intervened. I'd always liked her best growing up, constantly clinging to her as a small boy after my mother died. If not for me, Zia would be living in a tiny house fifteen miles away in the middle of nowhere.

Now ravenous, I started eating. After a few bites, I noticed that Francesca was picking at her food. Zia was at the stove, stirring soup, so I leaned over and asked quietly, "Do you not like it?"

"I feel sick to my stomach, but I don't want to hurt Zia's feelings."

"Eat what you can. I will make sure Zia understands."

She lifted a piece of chicken to her mouth, but quickly recoiled, her face turning white. I took the fork out of her hand and set it down. "So you don't feel up to eating chicken. Is it the taste?"

"The taste, the smell. The look of it. In fact, the only thing I want to eat right now is the cake."

Standing, I took our two dinner plates and moved them to the sink. Then I handed the cake platter to Francesca and stuck a fork in the top. Her brows knitted in confusion. "You're giving me the whole cake?"

Instead of answering, I lifted her off the stool and into my arms, cake and all. "Send the doctor to my room," I told Zia. "Francesca doesn't feel well."

CHAPTER SEVEN

Francesca

He was carrying me through the house. I tried not to think about how good it felt for Fausto to touch me, the warmth of his chest surrounding me after all this time. That was a slippery slope, and no way was I signing up to take that ride again.

My body's reaction to him annoyed me. "Put me down," I snapped. "You're still covered in blood and sweat."

"No."

I thought about smashing this cake in his face, but decided not to. While I would find it satisfying, it was a waste of great cake.

When we reached the top of the stairs, he turned left instead of right, walking toward his wing of the castello. "Where are you going? You went the wrong way."

"You are staying with me from now on."

The absolute nerve. "I want my own room, Fausto."

"You will stay in here with me."

God, no. Please, anything but that. Being close to him, smelling him. There would be no reprieve from my long-buried feelings. I grabbed the fork out of the top of the cake and held it up like a weapon. "My own room, or I swear to God I will poke your eye out."

The side of his mouth hitched as he shoved the door open with his shoulder. "There is my bloodthirsty dolcezza."

I slipped the fork back in the cake and went quiet. Damn it. I had to remember he got off on my spirit and sass. If I remained blank, an empty shell he couldn't play with or bait, he'd grow bored. He'd realize he didn't want to be a father at his age. Then he would let me go.

He carefully placed me on his bed, arranging me on the pillows. Then he picked up the house phone and began giving rapid orders about the doctor's imminent arrival, but I tuned him out. The smell of him permeated the room, so familiar and sexy. I'd almost forgotten it, the combination of oranges and spice and raw power. The man was a walking aphrodisiac—and I hated that he still affected me.

Miserable, I grabbed the fork and started on the cake. The moist, nutty flavor and creamy icing melted on my tongue. My God, that was good. I closed my eyes, wishing I could have Zia in my life without Fausto. Everyone needed a Zia who baked like this.

When my lids opened, I saw Fausto staring at me like I was his walnut cake. Hungry and desperate, a man on the edge of his control. I took another bite and let myself enjoy it, just to antagonize him. *Look at what you can't have,* I told him silently as I licked icing off the fork.

Suddenly, he gave a devious twist of his lips. Reaching for the hem of his shirt, he began to pull upward. The fork paused halfway to my mouth. Was he . . . ?

His t-shirt slid slowly up his body, higher and higher, revealing his flat stomach and the treasure trail I'd once licked. Then ribs and pecs, more clearly defined than I remembered, and his wide chest bisected with dark hair. Finally, his shoulders flexed and bunched as he tossed the shirt to the ground. That body . . . it wasn't fair. So manly, so hot. My stomach warmed and dipped, my lungs squeezing tight as I fought the urge to sigh.

I hadn't been horny in weeks and now it was like my body was wired, every cell electrified. All because he'd removed his damn shirt. I never should've told him how much I loved his chest all those weeks ago.

The skin along his side was scraped raw and it looked painful. At least, I hoped it was. Very, very painful. "Maybe the doctor should look at you first."

"I'm fine. He'll check you while I shower."

"You're leaving me alone with the doctor?"

"There's a guard outside the door. You won't be able to get away from me."

"We'll see."

His mouth curved into a frown but a knock sounded, interrupting our little standoff. Fausto called for them to enter and a handsome man stepped into the room, a backpack and a bike helmet in his hands. He and Fausto kissed cheeks as Italians liked to do. "Buona sera, Don Ravazzani."

Fausto pointed to me. "Ciao, David. Come, meet Francesca." He clapped the doctor on the shoulder and said to me, "Dr. Abruzzi will look you over. He has equipment to listen to the baby, too. Let him check you, all right?"

Fausto, asking for my permission? This was new. I nodded, hiding my surprise behind another bite of cake. He exchanged a few words with the doctor and disappeared into his bathroom.

"Signorina Mancini," the man said, setting his backpack on the bed. "I'm David. With your permission I'd like to do a quick examination. Nothing invasive."

This was the doctor? I had expected someone older with a stethoscope and black medical bag. "You speak English?"

"I do. Nine years in Michigan, first for my degree, then for my residency. I'm Fausto's second cousin."

So much for hoping the doctor would help me escape. I set down the cake and brushed crumbs off my fingers. "Nice to meet you. Let's get this over with."

David slipped on a pair of latex gloves then opened his backpack to find his instruments. He listened to my heartbeat, took my blood pressure, and asked me questions about how I'd been feeling. "Other than being nauseous, fine," I told him.

"That will pass in another few weeks. Are you taking prenatal vitamins?"

"Oddly enough, my kidnappers didn't grab them when they were shoving me inside a trunk."

He nodded once. "I'll send a prescription to the pharmacy. One of the men will retrieve it for you. Any bleeding or spotting?"

"No."

"You should be checked by an obstetrician, of course, but let's listen to the baby's heartbeat."

An obstetrician?

I nearly snorted. As if I'd been given the opportunity to visit a doctor during my "vacation" at the beach house.

He took a small box with what looked like a tiny microphone attached. We heard the rapid whoosh of the baby's heartbeat inside me and I relaxed into the pillows, relief rushing through me. With all the stress and uncertainty, I'd been worried about my little bambina.

Fausto appeared as the doctor was packing up. My baby daddy was naked except for the towel around his waist, his big body glistening from the heat of the shower. An ache pulsed in me and I shifted, willing it to go away. He and David exchanged words, then the doctor bid me goodbye and left.

I tried to ignore a mostly naked Fausto and concentrated on my cake. He went into his closet and I heard him getting dressed. When we were together I loved to watch him dress. His suits were cut to perfection, and seeing him go from the man who drove me wild in bed to the powerful don got me wet every time.

I could feel the dampness between my legs even now. What was wrong with me? A few hours ago I was in a gun battle. Shouldn't I be in shock? Afraid? Reliving the nightmare of being kidnapped and having Enzo's pistol shoved in my mouth?

For whatever reason, I wasn't. I was thinking about Fausto's big cock and the heat in his eyes when he stood by the bed and stared down at me. How he'd punched Enzo in the face and killed the guard who had been manhandling me.

You heard my woman.

Damn that possessive asshole—and damn me for liking it so much.

He kicked me out, broke my heart, and treated me like garbage. Again. The only reason he came after me was because someone else had dared to take what was his. That's all I was to him, a possession. His whore, breeding the next generation of killers and kidnappers. I would never forgive him for kicking me out and ignoring me, for leaving me alone and allowing me to be taken by his rival.

Sadly, my body was not on the same page.

I was broken. Fucked in the head. It had to be these pregnancy hormones—they'd restarted my sex drive tonight like a pair of jumper cables on a dead car battery.

But I wouldn't allow my feelings to show this time. I wouldn't give Fausto an opening back into my life. He'd never know how much he affected me or how my body still craved the mind-numbing pleasure he gave it. As far as he was concerned, I was now a frigid bitch.

Whatever I fantasized about in private was my own business.

When he emerged from the closet, he wore a white t-shirt that stretched across his powerful chest and hugged those delicious shoulders. His lower half was covered in a pair of old jeans. Was he going to the dungeon to deal with Enzo?

Sadly, the shiver that worked its way over my skin was not revulsion. Not at all.

I kept my eyes averted and forked up another bite of cake. He came over and covered my lower half with a soft blanket. Had he mistaken that shiver for a chill? I didn't correct him, too surprised at how careful he was being with me.

"Francesca," he said, his voice a deep patient rumble.

When I didn't respond, he put a finger under my chin and tilted my face. The fire in his eyes nearly scorched me. "How badly should I make him suffer, dolcezza?" he asked quietly. "Tell me. What retribution will make it easier for you to sleep at night?"

I swallowed. He was serious. Whatever I said would be carried out by this man without question, without mercy. Power surged through me, a feeling I'd been without for so long that it almost seemed strange. Enzo's fate rested in my hands. I thought of the trunk, the pistol in my mouth. How Enzo called me puttanella at every turn.

You, on your knees, so obedient. Did he like this, as well? I bet he did.

I hated Enzo for that.

But Fausto and I were not a team. This was not a partnership. There was no equality here, and I wouldn't pretend otherwise. "Since when are you taking my wishes into consideration?"

The smile fell from his face. "Do not worry. I will see that he suffers greatly for everything he has done to you."

Without another word, he walked out of the room, his heavy boots thudding on the carpet. When the door closed behind him, I put a hand to my chest, my heart racing. Would I ever be immune to him? This was unbearable, sitting here with tight nipples and a throbbing between my legs. Well, screw Fausto. I didn't need him to take care of this, not anymore. I didn't need any man ever again.

Without thinking, I slid my fingers under the blanket, into my shorts and panties to find my swollen clit. Oh, God. That felt so good. Better than I remembered.

Thank you, pregnancy hormones.

My other hand cupped a heavy breast as my fingers worked between my legs. Sparks shimmered in my veins, a weightlessness that carried my brain off to the place where only pleasure remained. I was drowning in lust, my sex drive back with a vengeance. It wouldn't take long to come, not with Fausto's words in my ears and his scent in my nose. It was like sensory overload.

The door suddenly flew open—and I jerked my hand out of my panties and off my chest. Shit!

Of course it was Fausto. He blinked at me, surprised, but only for a split second. Then he relaxed and gave a soft chuckle. Ugh. I filled my tone with all the venom I could muster. "What is it?"

"I forgot my mobile," he said and pointed to where his phone rested on the dresser.

I said nothing, my skin burning in humiliation and anger at myself. I should've waited a few more minutes before trying to ease this ache. Worse, I shouldn't be attracted to him.

Standing, I made my way to his bathroom, ready to shower and put this entire experience behind me.

As I locked the door, I heard him call out, "The shower head is removable and has both a high and low setting."

I gave the finger to the closed door.

Fausto

I descended the dungeon steps, a familiar calmness washing over me as I went below ground. Perhaps it was more like detachment rather than calm, but I relished it all the same. Down here, there was no need to hold back. Instead of fighting the demons of my past, I could let them rise up and take over.

Enzo D'Agostino was about to witness that transformation first hand.

I was almost ten years older than Enzo. He hadn't seen me at my worst, when they started calling me il Diavolo. He would learn, though, starting tonight.

Marco, Giulio, and several guards were leaning against the stone. Cigarette dangling from his mouth, Giulio watched me carefully, his face tired and gaunt. When had he started smoking? I didn't like it. Addictions made men weak.

I couldn't stop to mother him now, however. Besides, I'd already asked him to give up enough. Perhaps I should ignore the cigarettes. A tentative truce had been called between us while planning to retrieve Francesca, and I hated to see that broken.

Looking at Marco, I asked, "Any problems?"

"None. The men at the beach house were dealt with and the family returned home. They were scared out of their minds, but seemed all right."

"If we need them again, we know where to find them. Sicilians leave?"

"They could hardly wait. I offered to get them rooms tonight, but they declined. How is she? Forgive you yet?"

I thought of her, one hand down her panties, the other squeezing her tit. Dio, that sight. My dick twitched just picturing it. One thing for certain, Francesca's anger would not last much longer. Soon I would coax her back into riding my cock. "David says she's fine. Enzo give you any trouble?"

"He's been quiet. I don't think he's grasped the severity of the situation yet."

"Good. I like to be the bearer of bad news." I continued toward the last cell, the largest, where Enzo was strapped to a chair.

Grinning, I pulled over another chair and sat facing him. They hadn't gagged him yet. That would come later, when we tired of his screams. "Welcome to my home, D'Agostino. A shame you'll only ever see this one part."

"La Provincia won't let you get away with this. Whatever you think you are going to do to me, it's a bad idea."

I shook my head. "Your computer schemes don't bring in a fraction of what I do. I control the 'Ndrangheta's money, Enzo. And when you control the money, you control the people dependent on it. No one will dare say a word to me about this, because if they do I will burn it all down."

"The puttanella means that much to you?"

He wanted to make me angry, to hurry this along. It's what I would have done in his situation. A swift death was always preferable. But I intended to draw this out as long as possible. Months, if I was lucky.

"She is mine, which means she is off limits. You took her to blackmail me, to force my hand into giving you something you do not deserve. And you will suffer for it."

He sneered at me. "I bet you love her big tits. I certainly loved watching them jiggle as she and Mariella played on the beach. I even got to feel them when I tied her up with that rope—"

I didn't think, just lunged. My fist swung out and I popped him in the mouth. The chair rocked from the force of the impact, so I righted it with my foot. Both Enzo's lips were split open and blood coated the satisfied smile he gave me. "The great Fausto Ravazzani, pussy-whipped over a piece of Canadian trash."

Trying to get a handle on my temper, I exhaled and retook my seat. "I heard Mariella didn't make it." I pursed my lips and made the sign of the cross. "Such a tragedy."

He snarled and struggled then, trying to get at me. Yes, this was much better.

"*Figlio di puttana!* I asked your men to let her go, as well as my wife and children. What kind of man are you?"

"Your puttanella helped kidnap Francesca. Did you honestly think I would let her live after that?"

"I will kill you for this," he panted, his hair hanging down in his face. "Whatever it takes, I will kill you. I never hurt Frankie. I never intended to. She was treated respectfully while at my home."

"Except for your wandering hands," I remarked. "Giulio!"

"Yes, Papà?" My son was by my side in a blink.

"Bring me a cleaver and a small wooden table."

He walked to where the weapons were stored as I stared at Enzo. We said nothing, merely watched one another. I hadn't intended to start so brutally, but the idea of this man's hands on Francesca made me crazy.

Giulio arrived and handed me the items I'd asked for. "His right hand," I instructed. "Untie it."

Enzo jerked as Giulio freed his right hand, his jaw locked tight. Giulio tipped his chin to another soldier, who came forward to place the wooden table in front of Enzo. Then the two of them held Enzo's hand flat, fingers extended, on the wood.

I tested the cleaver blade while the boys worked. Sharp. When Enzo was in place, I stood and glared down at D'Agostino. "You restrained her and put her in a trunk. Then you tied her up and forced a gun in her mouth. You thought to use her against me, but it failed. You shouldn't have touched her."

CHAPTER EIGHT

Francesca

I woke slowly, my entire body sore. For a moment, I couldn't remember why. Then it all came rushing back.

Beach house. Attack. Fausto.

My lids flew open and I stared at the plaster ceiling. I was in the castello, but this was not my room. Fausto had brought me here last night and put a guard outside so I couldn't escape. Again. Jesus, being a captive really sucked. Would I ever have my freedom again?

I pushed up onto my elbows and did some deep breathing as the morning sickness washed over me. I'd stopped vomiting during my captivity at Enzo's house, so I hoped the worst of it was over. Now I just felt queasy all the time.

Two familiar suitcases waited inside the door. My things from Fausto's beach house. It was a relief to have my belongings, but it meant I was here for the foreseeable future. Well, just until I could convince Fausto to let me go.

I sat up and something on the nightstand caught the corner of my eye. It was a white box with a red bow. A gift? Excitement eclipsed the nausea for a brief second. I liked gifts, and he knew I was furious with him. Was this a peace offering?

Should I open it? I stared at it, thinking. I should throw it out. I didn't want anything from him. The only thing he could give me was my freedom—and we all knew that wasn't happening.

What was this? If lingerie was stuffed into that tiny box, he had a rude awakening coming. I wasn't wearing lingerie for him again, ever. Curiosity nagged at me as I stared at it. The box's size was more tailored to jewelry, like a bracelet or necklace. Whatever it was, I didn't want it.

But maybe I wanted to see it.

I reached for the box and slipped the bow off before I could change my mind. Then I pried open the lid and peeled back the white tissue paper. Was that . . .?

Holy fuck!

I dropped the box like it was on fire and watched a fingertip fall out and roll onto the carpet. *Oh my god, oh my god, oh my god.*

That was Enzo's finger. I knew it deep in my soul. Why in God's name had Fausto given me Enzo's *finger*?

Acid burned my throat and I bolted for the toilet. I barely made it to the bathroom in time before I vomited. My eyes watered with it, my body heaving in absolute horror.

What the hell was wrong with that man?

I sat there, wrung out and exhausted, disgusted with the entire male population, when I heard a knock on the outer door. "Frankie, you up?"

It was Giulio, the only man in this household I liked. Getting to my feet, I leaned out of the bathroom to call, "Come in."

Quickly, I rinsed my mouth out in the sink. I heard the door close and by the time I left the bathroom, Giulio was standing over the finger, frowning.

"What the fuck?" I asked, intentionally looking at Giulio and not the *human finger* on the floor.

"I tried to tell him it was a bad idea. He said you would appreciate it."

"Well, now you may return that and tell him I didn't. It made me puke my guts out. I hope he's happy."

"I'll get rid of it." Giulio bent to deal with the finger and I went to brush my teeth. I left the bathroom door open, so he came to find me when he finished. "It's gone," he said, dusting his hands back and forth. "Like it never happened."

"But it did happen," I said, putting Fausto's toothbrush back in the cup on the counter. Yes, I used his toothbrush to brush my teeth, and if he didn't like it he could fuck off. "He's absolutely crazy."

"I know, but he was worse after you were kidnapped."

This wasn't the first time in recent weeks that Giulio had mentioned his father's mental state being unhinged, but I couldn't allow myself to care.

I stepped forward and wrapped my arms around his waist. "I hate being back here, but I'm happy to see you."

"I am very happy to see you." He pressed a kiss to the top of my head as he hugged me back. "I was scared shitless for you. Did Enzo hurt you?"

"No, other than to insult me and shove a gun in my mouth."

"Fausto went berserk when he saw that photo."

"Good." Releasing him, I went to the bed and crawled back under the covers. "He shouldn't have sent me away."

Giulio sat on the mattress at the end of the bed. His hair was damp and he was dressed in a t-shirt and jeans. Not working today, then. He said, "I think he's paid for that mistake. Repeatedly."

"Except I paid for it, as well."

He shifted, getting more comfortable, and I rubbed my feet against his hip. I liked spending time with Giulio. We'd grown close during those weeks while I'd been at the beach house. Most days, he'd been the only thing keeping me sane. "I don't want to talk about Fausto. How's Paolo?"

Giulio's eyes turned bleak and sad, a look he only got when I brought up his former boyfriend. "Fucking every rent boy in town, from what I hear. He won't even look at me. He'll never forgive me and I don't blame him. I'll never forgive myself, either."

"I'm sorry, G. That absolutely sucks, but you had no choice."

"I know, but that doesn't make it any easier. At least there's no need to worry about marrying D'Agostino's sister now."

"Speaking of Enzo, is he . . . ?"

"Oh, he's very much alive. Fausto plans to draw it out as long as possible. We were down there most of the night."

"I don't want to know." Glancing over, I noticed that Fausto's side of the bed hadn't been slept in. What did that mean? If he was sleeping elsewhere, why make me stay here?

"How are you feeling?" Giulio asked. "I know yesterday was a lot to handle. The baby, he or she is okay?"

"Tired but fine. David came last night and said the baby sounds good, but I should see an obstetrician to be certain. I plan to call one as soon as their office opens."

"I'm happy to take you today, if you'd like."

"You mean I can leave this fancy prison?"

Giulio cocked his head and studied me. "I suppose this means my father didn't ask you whether you'd like to stay or not?"

Like, that was a choice? "Uh, no. He didn't."

Brow wrinkling, Giulio stroked his jaw. "I'll speak with him. Would you go home if you could?"

"Not to Toronto, but to New York or Boston, maybe. Anywhere but here. At least I'd be closer to my sisters there."

"I get it, but I would miss you, Frankie."

I rubbed my feet against him playfully. "I would miss you, too, but you know why I can't stay. He's hurt me too many times."

"What's a little love without hurt?" he said with a sad smile. "Italians have an expression, *'l'amore non è bello se non è litigarello.'* It means a little squabbling now and then does a relationship good. That you come out stronger for it."

"Squabbling?" I snort. "He locked me in a dungeon, left me on a yacht in the middle of a hurricane, and banished me to live under guard where I was kidnapped."

Giulio's mouth hitched. "At least you've seen him at his worst. Speaking of your sisters, you should call them. Both Gia and Emma keep texting me to ask about you. I've been playing dumb ever since D'Agostino kidnapped you, but I think they are starting to catch on."

"Thank you." I'd wondered what my sisters would do when they hadn't heard from me, whether they would talk to my father or not. I guess they reached out to Giulio instead, thank God. The last person I wanted involved in this mess was Papà. "Except I'll have to use your phone. God knows when Fausto will return mine."

"Your tablet is in one of those suitcases." He nodded to the bags by the door. "I packed all your things last night."

"Thank you, G. You're the best."

"I know."

I noticed his knuckles were torn and scraped, his hands swollen. "Is that from last night?" I tipped my chin toward his hands.

"Yeah." He flexed his long fingers. "Hurts like a bitch today."

"Do you like it? Hitting people and playing the mafia heavy?"

He cocked an eyebrow. "Should we be talking about this?"

"Why wouldn't we? Like, it's weird that we've never talked about it before, don't you think?"

"I do what needs to be done, like any good soldato."

"That's a bullshit answer. Be serious with me for one second."

He exhaled heavily. "I can't explain it, but there is this place inside me that feels unworthy, like I always need to prove myself to my father. He is the great Fausto Ravazzani and I'm supposed to follow in his footsteps. But how could I ever measure up to him?"

"He's not so great," I muttered dryly.

"Of course you'd say that. I'm his heir, though, and I want him to be proud of me." He fiddled with his watch, adjusting the thick metal band. "It's funny, I used to hate the violence, but the older I get the more I love it. I guess that makes me fucked up."

"Not fucked up. Your father is il Diavolo, after all. It's in your—"

I bit off the last word. Shit, I had half Fausto's DNA inside me, growing a baby. Would his genes guarantee a violent child?

"You don't need to worry about that if you leave," Giulio said, perfectly reading my thoughts. "I was raised in this life. The heir. I never had a chance. But your baby can grow up outside our world, somewhere nice with picket fences and no bullets."

That was only if Fausto let me go—and something told me he wouldn't.

Fausto

Mid-morning, I arrived in the kitchen to find my son and my woman laughing over caffè and cornetti. It was almost like the horror of the last month hadn't happened. I felt a smile tug at my mouth. Things would soon return to the way they'd been, including Francesca fucking me with abandon.

Their laughter died as I prepared another espresso. But I had other things on my mind. I was exhausted. Enzo hadn't broken yet, but he would. I had given him much suffering last night, enough to last for days.

Still, my mood was light. My dolcezza was back under my roof where she belonged.

"We should get going," she said quietly to Giulio. "I don't want to be late."

That got me to turn around. "Where do you think you are going this morning?"

Her right eye twitched but her voice remained flat. "To the obstetrician, Fausto."

"I will take you." My day was packed with calls and reports, but I would push them off to do this with her. For her to forgive me, we had to spend time together.

"You are going to take me to the doctor. *You?*"

"Me." I glanced at my son. "Tell Marco. I want six men with me, cars in front and behind."

"Sì, Papà." With a kiss to Francesca's cheek he disappeared from the kitchen to make arrangements for the trip. That left me alone with her, as Zia was outside in her garden already.

"You cannot seriously mean to go with me," she said. "You never leave the estate."

"Except for you, it seems. And what is the problem? I am the baby's father. I should go to these things." I hadn't accompanied Lucia to the doctor, so I had no idea what to expect. But these were things most men did when their women were pregnant, no? When Marco's wife had been carrying the boys, Marco had treasured the tiny black and white sonogram photos like they were gold bars, showing them to anyone in the vicinity.

She seemed to be struggling with a response, her mouth opening and closing several times. Finally, she said, "I'd prefer it if you didn't come."

I sipped my espresso and regarded her over the rim of the cup. If she was over me, as she claimed, why not let me tag along? We both knew she wasn't over me, though. I would never allow it. I was prepared to move heaven and earth to win this woman's forgiveness. "That is too bad," I said. "Besides, I want to hear for myself that everything is all right with our child."

"Suit yourself." She stood up and brought her dishes to the sink. "Though I just have to ask, what kind of lunatic gives a finger as a present to a pregnant woman?"

"Giulio already informed me it was a bad idea, but you deserve proof of his suffering, amore mio."

The porcelain clattered in the sink. "Shit," she murmured, righting the dishes.

Had it been the endearment that rattled her? If so, she should brace herself. There would be far more of those, as many as I could sneak in.

"Let's go," she said evenly as she strode past me.

Hmm. Her demeanor was unnaturally calm. I'd expected an argument or a biting comment, at the very least. I did love to argue with her. Back when we were together, our arguments usually led to fucking.

Was this new attitude a tactic to avoid arguing with me?

Ah, that made sense. I smiled as I followed her through the castello. I would love nothing more than a battle of wits with this woman, but she would lose. I hadn't risen to where I was in this world by being out maneuvered. Still, I relished the challenge.

She could act as calm and boring as she liked. It wouldn't work. Nothing about her could ever bore me. Didn't Francesca know that by now?

Once in the car, she studied the streets out the window, ignoring me. I didn't care. I had plenty of work calls to make during the ride.

One of those was to touch base with Toni, who oversaw the legitimate side of my business empire. During the call he talked about trades and our portfolio, and I listened with half an ear. From the corner of my eye I watched Francesca's foot bounce, her flat shoe dangling from the tips of her toes. It was unintentionally sexy and I wanted to pull her feet in my lap, slide my palms up her calves . . .

"Stop staring at me," she said without sparing me a glance. "It's creepy." She angled the other way, shielding her feet from me, and I tried not to laugh. Creepy? Then why were her nipples poking through her bra and shirt? She couldn't hide her body's reaction from me.

I finished my call as we arrived at the office building. She reached for the door handle but I grabbed her arm. "Wait here. Do not get out until you have guards surrounding you."

"Fausto, the only person I am in danger from is *you*." She flipped open the latch and left the car, and I was forced to let go of her. Damn it.

I hurried out my door and came around quickly. My men surrounded us and we all headed toward the door. "Cristo, Francesca! It's not safe for you to run around the streets of Siderno."

"I apologize." She slipped sunglasses on her face and covered her eyes from me. "Next time I'll wait."

Her voice was tight, as if the acquiescence nearly killed her. I had to credit her acting skills, though. If I didn't know her so well, I might have believed she meant it.

One person was already in the elevator when our entourage piled in. He took one look at the big soldati and bulges under our jackets and quickly excused himself, getting out before the elevator doors closed. Francesca sighed but said nothing.

The guards waited outside the main door to the doctor's office, while Marco and I escorted Francesca inside. The two women behind the reception desk perked up when they saw us, their eyes darting to me then back to my woman. I rested my hand on Francesca's lower back as we came forward, ignoring the stiffening of her small frame at my touch.

She removed her sunglasses. "Francesca Mancini to see Dr. Russo, please."

The receptionist swallowed and dared another glance at me. "Ciao, Miss Mancini." She clacked on her computer for a moment, and I looked around at the other couples in the waiting room. They were all staring at me, but quickly averted their eyes when I turned.

"Word will get around," Marco muttered to me. "This was a mistake." He'd been saying as much with his disapproving frown ever since we left the castello.

"It's what she expects," I said quietly. "And I won't handle this like I did before."

I wasn't certain whether I meant Lucia or how I had treated Francesca earlier. Perhaps I meant both. News of a Ravazzani baby would make Francesca more of a target, but I would go with her everywhere—along with an army of guards, of course.

An older woman in scrubs came over, one I recognized. It was the wife of one of my men who had retired two years ago. "Signore Ravazzani," she said, clasping her hands together. "Buona sera."

I kissed her cheeks. "Signora Mancuso. You are looking well."

"We hadn't realized . . . That is, Signorina Mancini . . ."

Had a different last name, therefore no one knew this baby was mine. I lifted a brow. "It is joyous news, no?"

"Of course, of course. Congratulations on your blessing. Come with me. I will see you settled in one of the exam rooms."

"Is it my turn already?" Francesca asked as I guided her after Signora Mancuso. "Normally I have to sit in the waiting room."

"A Ravazzani does not wait."

A sound of disgust escaped her mouth. "This is why I didn't want you to come."

"You should be thanking me. I have saved hours of your time."

I settled in a chair in the examination room, while Francesca sat on the big padded chair with stirrups. Signora Mancuso handed Francesca an empty plastic cup, the kind used for urine samples. "You know where the bathroom is?"

Francesca nodded and started to leave the room with the cup. I stood, ready to follow. "It's only around the corner, Fausto," she hissed. "Stay here."

"I go where you go." I didn't know these people. Therefore, I wasn't letting Francesca out of my sight while we were off the estate.

With a roll of her eyes, she went into the corridor and I trailed her. I hadn't been to a doctor's office in many years, but it seemed they hadn't changed much. Boring furniture, pastel walls. This one had photographs of babies everywhere, smiling mothers and fathers in hospital gowns. Hmm. For security, my son or daughter would need to be delivered at the castello, not a hospital. This was not the time for such a conversation with Francesca, however.

Soon we were back in the exam room. Signora Mancuso instructed Francesca to get in the gown and the doctor would be with us shortly. The door closed, leaving us alone, and Francesca stood there, unmoving, like she was waiting for me to do something.

I folded my hands on my lap. "I have already seen you undressed. That is how we found ourselves in this situation, if I recall."

"That was before," she snapped. "It's different now."

"Is it?"

Her arms flopped at her sides, as if I exasperated her. "At least turn around."

"You know how I feel about taking orders from you." I raked her body with a hot glance. "And I know you'd much rather follow my commands than give them."

"God, you are the worst."

With a huff, she turned and began undressing. She ignored me, but that didn't stop me from looking.

Cazzo, she was gorgeous. Her skin had turned a deep gold from the sun, and her long toned legs led to that round ass I loved to bite. Her waist hadn't filled out with the pregnancy yet, and I couldn't wait to see her all round and lush with my child. Dark blond hair spilled over her back and I longed to run my fingers through it, wrap it around my fist and pull as I rode her from behind.

Then she shimmied out of her panties, pushing the silk and lace down her hips, and let the scrap of fabric fall to the ground. She bent to pick them up.

Madonna santa, that sight.

I was nearly panting, my cock half-hard. My heart galloped in my chest like I had run a race, and I forgot all about the painful scrape on my side and my terrible night's sleep. I could only focus on her and this insatiable craving I had to touch her, to fuck her. To crawl inside her and never leave. She was a fever in my veins, an obsession, one I wasn't certain I'd ever overcome.

I had to have her soon or I would go insane.

After she slipped on the cotton gown, she strode over and handed me her clothes. "Here. For your lap." She tilted her chin toward the bulge in my trousers.

I spread my arms but made no move to take the garments. "Put them down," I ordered softly, unable to help myself.

Her breath hitched and she licked her lips. Her gaze darted to my crotch, where my dick pushed insistently against my zipper. For a second, I thought she was going to play along, that she would bend over and place the clothes on my groin, and perhaps brush her hand against my cock in the process. Instead, she looked away and let the bundle drop onto my lap, uncaring if it fell on the floor.

I was a tiny bit disappointed, but mostly pleased by her reaction. She was not immune to me.

Still, I couldn't help but wonder how different things would've been if I hadn't fucked up with her. We might've been here together for every appointment, teasing and laughing while waiting for the doctor. She would sit on my lap and kiss me, while I told her how much I looked forward to seeing our child but worried over my ability to keep them all safe.

I couldn't stand to lose anyone else.

Francesca hopped onto the examination table. "Don't say a word, Fausto. You're here as an observer only. I don't want you throwing your mafia boss weight around with my doctor."

More orders?

My dick twitched at her audacity. Though I longed to take her over my knees and spank her ass, I held up my palms. "You won't even know I'm here, dolcezza."

CHAPTER NINE

Fausto

"This must be the lovely Francesca," my cousin Toni exclaimed, walking forward. He kissed both of Francesca's cheeks "You are every bit as beautiful as I've heard."

"Thank you," she said, then looked to me for an explanation.

We had just arrived at one of the restaurants I owned in Siderno after the obstetrician appointment. I didn't like how thin she was, and the doctor had expressed concern over the amount of weight Francesca had lost. Though the baby was perfectly fine, the doctor had encouraged Francesca to eat more, whatever she could hold down. So I decided to bring her to lunch, also inviting Toni to discuss business. He'd been pestering me for an in-person meeting for months. Two birds, one stone.

"Meet Antonio, my cousin," I said. "He handles many of my businesses for me."

"Call me Toni," my cousin said. "Zio Toni, if you prefer."

I pulled a chair out for her and she sat. "You speak very good English," she said to Toni.

"I was raised in the Connecticut suburbs until I was twelve. Then my mother moved us back to Siderno and I became acquainted with my Italian cousins."

"Ah, I see."

"I was pleasantly surprised he agreed to meet in person today." Toni gestured to me, still speaking to Francesca. "Your influence, no doubt."

"Oh, I can hardly take credit," she said as the waiter passed out menus. "Fausto always does whatever the hell he wants."

I tried to hide my smile. "Francesca had an appointment at her obstetrician this morning. We came here directly after."

She bristled in her seat, no doubt furious that I had mentioned the pregnancy. But there was no use hiding it. Word of my presence at the doctor's office would spread all over Siderno by sundown. Besides, Toni was family. He deserved to hear it from me.

"Oh, this is wonderful news!" Toni exclaimed and leaned forward to slap my shoulder. "*Complementi*, cugino!"

Francesca rolled her eyes, then held up her hand to get the waiter's attention. When he arrived, she said, "I'll have the tiramisu and the frangipane tart."

"No." I proceeded to give the waiter a long list of things to bring to the table. She would eat actual food with vitamins and minerals first.

"You're impossible," she said when the waiter left.

Putting my hand on the back of her chair, I leaned over. "You may have whatever you wish for dessert, no? And I purposely did not order chicken."

Her lips parted, a flush deepening her cheeks and throat. "Fine."

Satisfied, I straightened. "Now we must discuss business," I said to her. "I hope you won't mind.'

"Yes, forgive us, Francesca," Toni added. "He's been too distracted lately, though now I understand why."

"Oh, he wasn't distracted by the baby. It was because he sent me away and then I was kidnapped." She gave me a bland stare that didn't fool me for a moment. "Right, paparino?"

Fury washed through me, even though I knew she was trying to get back at me for taking away her dessert and going to the doctor's appointment. My lips met the shell of her ear and I whispered, "I'm glad you are feeling better, piccola monella. I was worried you would need more time to recuperate. I see that's no longer the case."

Francesca didn't say anything, instead reaching for a slice of bread from the basket on the table. While she busied herself with eating, Toni and I caught up on the various matters I'd ignored the last month.

The meal dragged on, and I was surreptitiously watching Francesca enjoy her gnocchi when Toni nudged my arm.

"Are you listening?" Toni asked. "I know she's beautiful but surely I'm not that boring."

I frowned at him, though I was annoyed at myself. I should have paid better attention. "I heard you. There's a buyer for the media conglomerate and you want to sell. So, sell."

"No, Fausto," Francesca said, forking up another bite of gnocchi. "He wants to split the media conglomerate apart and form two companies. The less-profitable half would be sold."

Toni held out his hand toward her as if to say, *At least someone was paying attention.* I ignored him and concentrated on my woman. "Do you think it's a good idea?"

She lifted a shoulder. "I'd have to learn what each half of the company was responsible for."

"The profitable half," Toni explained, "would be data mining for advertisers through social media, dating apps, and online storefronts. The part I'd like to sell is the television and print side."

"Because ad revenue is down," I added to make sure she understood. "Everyone streams nowadays and gets their news on an app."

"True, but if the last few years have shown us anything it's that whoever controls the flow of information has the most power. People will believe anything."

Toni and I exchanged a look. This was true. "So, sell the data mining instead?" I asked.

"That would be a mistake," Toni said. "The revenue potential is incredible."

Francesca put down her fork and reached for her sparkling water. "You should split the companies but keep them both. Rename the data mining side, though, to something no one would associate with the media side. People don't like thinking their computers are spying on them. There was a big scandal a few years ago with one of the social media sites doing that."

"There was?" Toni asked. "I don't remember it."

"Yep. Everyone was deleting their accounts. That site was mostly for older people, though. Like Fausto's age."

Without thinking, I stroked my knuckles along the soft skin of her forearm. "Ancient, then."

Freezing, she stared at where I was touching her. Yet she didn't pull away, not at first. I took advantage, caressing her gently, not bothered that Toni was across the table. Finally, she shifted and moved out of my reach. Her hands ended up in her lap, her fingers knotted together.

"So we have a decision, then, yes?" Toni asked.

"Yes, and Francesca will choose a name for the new company."

She blinked at me. "I will?"

"You helped to make the decision, so it's only fair."

Her mouth stretched into a wide grin before she could stop herself. The sight of her pleasure hit me like a punch to the solar plexus, and I had to restrain myself from leaning over and kissing her. I wanted to taste her joy, drown in her happiness. I missed losing myself in her, the only woman who dared to antagonize and fight me at every turn.

The moment passed and she retreated, her mask firmly back in place for the rest of the meal. Toni and I moved onto the hedge fund he operated, as well as the real estate. I enjoyed the legitimate side of the Ravazzani empire, the strategizing over numbers and data. If I wasn't so suited to blood and violence, I could have been happy as an investment banker or CEO.

Toni cleared his throat and leaned in. "Rav, your former *friend* has made a request about the house."

I was distracted, watching Francesca lick tiramisu off a spoon. "Friend?"

"Katarzyna," he said reluctantly, referring to my previous mantenuta.

Francesca paused, spoon halfway to her mouth. "What about her?"

No way to hide it now. I waved my hand, indicating Toni should explain. My cousin shot me an apologetic look before saying, "She'd like to sell the house in Portofino."

I snorted. "Have we even finalized the paperwork? She doesn't even own it yet and she's trying to make a quick Euro."

"This is why she needs our—my—help. I wanted to check with you first."

"Is there a reason not to let her sell it?" Francesca asked, her attention on me.

I shrugged, annoyed that our day had been tainted by this unpleasant conversation. I didn't want Francesca reminded of the women in my past. "Other than her appalling sense of greed? No."

"You cannot blame her, Fausto," she said, her voice calm. "Both of you went into that arrangement with your eyes wide open. Do not penalize her for using it to her advantage now that she's on her own."

My soft-hearted *dolcezza*. This was the side of her I had missed the most, the one who looked out for her sisters. Who insisted on saving the baby lambs. The woman who stood up for my son, even when it had cost her everything.

Dio cane, I worshiped her.

Lifting her hand to my mouth, I pressed a kiss to the inside of her wrist. "Let Katarzyna sell the house," I told Toni, keeping my gaze on Francesca.

Her breath hitched and she licked her lips. I couldn't tell what she was thinking, but her hooded lids gave me a good idea. If Toni wasn't here, I would ask her if her panties were wet. Perhaps I'd even check for myself.

Without warning, she jerked away from me and pushed away from the table. "Excuse me. I must use the restroom."

Toni and I stood as Francesca hurried from the room. I had rattled her, which was very good. Glancing at Benito, who stood in the corner, I flicked my hand to indicate he should follow her. Because I owned the restaurant, I wasn't worried that someone would hurt her. They wouldn't dare.

But I was worried she might try to escape.

Francesca

I was weak.

I could feel my resolve crumbling like day-old bread. Those dark eyes of his, that sexy voice. It was like Fausto had a direct line to my hormones and he could pluck those strings at will, flooding my system with lust so strong I couldn't breathe.

Between my legs was a needy mess. My traitorous body had clearly forgotten all Fausto had done wrong, and no amount of reminders was keeping me immune to him.

I pushed into the ladies toilet and entered the empty stall. After I relieved myself, I came out to wash my hands and splash water on my face. I had to pull it together. I could not forgive him or start sleeping with him again. Both were terrible ideas.

God, but the look on his face when he saw our eleven-week old baby during the ultrasound. It was like he'd been the emotional one, his eyes turning glassy as he stared at the computer screen. I'd almost grabbed his hand, needing to share the joy and excitement for a moment, but somehow thought better of it.

You were very much my whore—and a good one at that.

Those words still hurt. He'd been so cruel, so cold. What was to say that wouldn't happen again when I did something he didn't like? I couldn't risk it, not when I had a child to think of. I could not be at Fausto Ravazzani's mercy ever again.

The door to the ladies room opened and an older woman walked in. I gave her a polite smile and finished drying my hands. As I went to go past her, she put a hand up. "Francesca Mancini?"

How did she know my name? "Who are you?"

She pulled a card out from her coat pocket. "I am Mia Rinaldo."

I glanced down at the card. Guardia di Finanza. Holy shit. Even I knew they were the police force in charge of smuggling and financial crimes. Basically everything Fausto did.

That they were approaching me, here in the ladies' room, couldn't be a good thing.

My anger at Fausto aside, I could never side with the police. That had been ingrained in me since birth. I thrust the card back at her and retreated a step. "No."

"You haven't even heard what I have to say."

I tried to move around her. "It doesn't matter," I hissed. "I don't want to hear it."

She blocked my exit. "You are in a very precarious situation, Miss Mancini. And I suspect you aren't as happy as Fausto Ravazzani's mistress as you let on. Especially after Enzo D'Agostino kidnapped you."

Jesus Christ. How did she know all this? Did she know I was pregnant, too? "Stop spying on me."

The agent laughed. "If you are in Ravazzani's orbit, you are being watched. Only a stupid woman would assume otherwise and one thing I suspect you are not, Miss Mancini, is stupid."

"You know nothing about me."

"I know you were raised in the life, albeit in Toronto. That makes you an asset to him, whereas the other women were just arm candy. He's paid more attention to you. Even went as far as to impregnate you."

I couldn't hide the shock from my face. Yes, they did know everything.

She moved in as I stood there, reeling, and slipped the card in my purse. "Is this what you want for your child? A lifetime of wondering when their father will be arrested? Blood and murder and drugs? Think, Miss Mancini. We can help you if you help us. We can work to keep you and your baby safe. We can put Fausto Ravazzani away where he can never get to you."

Did she honestly think that would work? I stood taller and pushed my shoulders back. "You know I'm smart, yet you try this line of bullshit on me. We both know there is no safety, even if I wanted to cooperate with you—which I don't. Fuck off, Agent Rinaldo."

I shoved on her shoulder to get her out of the way and slammed open the door. Benito was on his phone in the corridor, waiting for me while not paying a lick of attention. I rolled my eyes at his ineptitude.

A GDF agent had just tried to get me to turn on Fausto and Benito was probably searching for a date on Tinder.

I strode past him and went down the hall. When I entered our private dining room, Fausto glanced up and raked my body with a hot gaze, as if making sure I was all right. My entire body tingled and the enormity of what I'd done hit me in that moment.

I had chosen Fausto.

Oh my fucking god. I had chosen this man, the one who had hurt me and tossed me away. The one who'd said terrible things and forced his son to pretend to be straight. The chance to escape had presented itself through the Italian government a few moments ago and I had thrown it away.

What was wrong with me?

A sweat broke out on the nape of my neck as I sat. I ignored the quirk of Fausto's brow and finished my tiramisu, all the while contemplating my decision in the bathroom. Did I truly wish to get away from Fausto or was I kidding myself? What did I want?

Because if I really wanted to leave him, then—hatred of the police or not—I should have jumped at that opportunity.

Yet I hadn't. Why?

At my core, I was a mafia princess. I'd been raised in this world and I understood it. Even being sheltered from my father's day-to-day business, I knew how the organization worked and the men who ran it. Fausto had accused me many times of liking the danger, calling me bloodthirsty.

Do not ever try to tell me you weren't made for this life, that you weren't born to rule as a queen.

While I doubted that, I also would never stoop to working with the police. Doing so would get me killed faster than anything else. Fausto could never let that betrayal slide, regardless of the pregnancy, and his reach extended throughout the globe. There wasn't anywhere I could go that he couldn't find me, Guardia or not.

I put down my spoon, sick at the realization. There was no escape from this, unless he willingly let me go. And, considering he nearly cried at the sight of the baby this morning, it was safe to say he wouldn't, at least not until the baby was born. But I certainly wasn't leaving my child alone in Italy under Fausto's care, so I was stuck here.

There was also the problem of my libido. I was struggling—and failing—to resist him. What did that mean? Was I fooling myself in trying to keep my distance? More than anything, I needed him to suffer, to regret his treatment of me so that it never happened again.

Which meant I was already intending to forgive him.

Shit.

I rubbed my forehead, beyond exhausted by the mess of my life.

Fausto moved his chair and stood. "We'll finish later, Toni. I need to get Francesca back to the castello to rest."

I considered contradicting him, but I was tired. So I didn't protest when he led me out of the restaurant and helped me into the Range Rover. He settled beside me, his leg resting against mine. I didn't bother pushing him away. My head was too fuzzy. I just closed my eyes and let myself drift.

He placed something on my lap.

Looking down, I saw a to-go bag from the restaurant. "What's this?"

"I had them box up two orders of their tiramisu, since you seemed to like it. Don't tell Zia, though. She will think you don't like hers."

I loved Zia's tiramisu, so there was no chance of that, but his thoughtfulness touched me all the same. "You're impossible, you know that?"

The side of his mouth hitched, making him appear even more gorgeous. "Does this mean you are no longer mad at me, dolcezza?"

I sighed and decided not to answer. Instead I opened my purse, dug around, and held out Agent Rinaldo's card. "While I was in the washroom, I had a visit from the Guardia di Finanza."

CHAPTER TEN

Fausto

I stared at the card, not terribly surprised. It was a smart play by the Guardia, approaching Francesca. They had left my mistresses alone in the past, probably because none of them had lived with me and I never discussed business in front of them. Francesca was different. In every regard. "I see."

She dropped the card in my lap when I didn't take it. "I told her to fuck off."

Marco's eyes met mine in the rear view mirror. I knew what he was thinking. He didn't trust her, and he was wondering if this was a tactic, telling me about the Guardia to gain my confidence.

The familiar itch skittered across the nape of my neck, the one that whispered never to let anyone in. Never to give anyone power over me, over the business, especially a woman. These were words my father had repeated many, many times.

It wasn't easy, but I ignored them. I had been wrong to doubt

Francesca's loyalty before. There would be indisputable proof the next time I accused her of anything.

"Who did they send?" Marco asked from the driver's seat.

I picked up the card. "Rinaldo."

Marco snorted. "They must not be trying too hard."

"What does that mean?" Francesca asked, her gaze bouncing back and forth between Marco and me.

"We've never heard of her," I said. "Probably trying to make a name for herself."

"Do you know all of the Guardia agents by name?"

"Yes," Marco and I both said at the same time.

It was our job. Our livelihood. We had to know the enemy inside and out. I even had several GDF officials on my payroll. I would need to look into this Agent Rinaldo.

"Well, you didn't know this one," Francesca said, resting her head against the seat back and closing her eyes. "So, you're welcome."

I studied her face, the dark circles under her eyes. The sunken cheeks. She was exhausted. How had she slept last night in my bed? Despite my craving to be near her, I'd left her alone to rest and slept in a guest bedroom instead. Looking at her now, it was clear she needed more sleep. Hadn't her reports from the beach mentioned naps?

I pulled out my phone and checked my email. I answered when required, made some phone calls, and tried to catch up on the work I'd neglected for the last month. Toni was right, I had been distracted. Now I had Francesca back and things would slowly go back to normal.

The car turned a corner and Francesca's head dropped onto my shoulder. Asleep, she shifted to get more comfortable, and I remained as still as possible to avoid waking her. My poor dolcezza.

We pulled into the castello's drive and Marco turned the car off. He peeked over his shoulder. "I hope you know what you're doing. Because we're all fucked if you're wrong."

"I'm not wrong." I knew it in my bones. Rinaldo had presented Francesca with an opportunity and my woman had turned it down. If Francesca wanted to escape me, she would have accepted the Guardia's deal, turned me in, and disappeared.

Which meant she wanted to stay.

Hope expanded in my chest as I unbuckled her seat belt, then carefully maneuvered her onto my lap. Benito opened the door for me and I lifted Francesca out of the car. "You had better be in my office in five minutes," I quietly told my guard. "Where you will explain to me how a GDF agent was allowed to accost my woman in the bathroom."

Benito paled but gave me a nod. I went up the steps and into my home, the smell of basil and garlic in the air like the sweetest perfume. Zia must have started cooking dinner. I took Francesca up the staircase and into our wing.

She didn't rouse at all as I placed her on the mattress, not even when I removed her shoes. Then I found the soft blanket at the end of the bed. "Sleep, amore mio," I whispered before pressing a light kiss to the top of her head.

"This doesn't mean anything," she mumbled, her hands tucking under her cheek. "Just because I didn't help the GDF doesn't mean we are back together."

I didn't bother responding. We both knew she was wrong. This meant everything.

I went down the stairs and into my office, where Marco and Benito were waiting. "Ma che cazzo?" I snapped, pointing at Benito. "Explain yourself."

"I'm sorry, Don Ravazzani. She looked like a nice older woman. I never suspected she was a GDF agent."

Likely why Rinaldo had been chosen to approach Francesca. Still, this was sloppy. I didn't like sloppy, especially when it came to my woman.

I moved behind my desk but didn't sit. I wanted to loom over Benito and use my size to intimidate him. "You shouldn't have allowed anyone in there, old or not."

"I figured she was safe. It's your restaurant."

"Trust no one where Francesca is concerned. No one. And if it happens again, you'll be buried in the hole next to D'Agostino. Capisce?"

"Understood."

I flicked my hand toward the door. "Go, get out of my sight. Don't let me see you for a few days."

Benito nodded, then exchanged a glance with Marco before departing. "Rav," my cousin started. "He—"

"Don't make excuses for him." Benito was one of Marco's favorites. "He knows better."

"True, but none of us expected the GDF to be so bold."

"No one expected D'Agostino to kidnap Francesca, either. I'm tired of excuses. You know Rinaldo's arrival was no coincidence. The GDF obviously trailed us to the obstetrician, which means they are watching the castello more closely than we thought. How are you not aware of this?"

Marco's chest ballooned as he drew in a deep breath and let it out. "I'm stretched thin between the kidnapping, Enzo, and everything else I deal with on a daily basis. What more do you want from me?"

I slapped my hand on the desk. "I want answers! Put Giulio in charge of security, then, if you can't handle it. The extra responsibilities will be good for him and help keep his mind off his other problems."

"I'll speak to Giulio," Marco said. "I'll let him decide."

"No, you *tell* him what to do. My boy knows his place. And it's past time that he takes a larger role around here." Instead of waiting for Marco to argue, I grabbed the phone and punched a few buttons. "Get in my office now," I snarled, then hung up.

"Giulio is out on a job," Marco said.

"That was Vic." I dropped into my chair. "As long as I'm in this mood, I might as well get to the bottom of the security camera issue."

"I already talked to him. You heard his answers weeks ago. What's gotten into you?"

"You just said yourself that you're stretched thin. Maybe I can get more information out of Vic than you did. These men need to kept in line, cousin, and if you won't do it, then I will."

"Madonna," Marco murmured as he lowered himself into his favorite chair. "I hope you get laid soon."

So did I, but I didn't dare say it.

But this was a good reminder to calm down. I needed my wits about me at all times. I forced my hands to unclench and dragged in a few deep breaths. I had Francesca back, and she and the baby were safe. Enzo was in my dungeon, bleeding from my knife. I would have answers regarding security, then I could focus on everything else.

A second later we heard the knock. I called out and Vic entered, his hair disheveled like he'd been running his hands through it. I didn't stand or offer any greeting. Instead, I leaned back and folded my hands across my stomach. "Sit."

Vic slid into a chair and gripped the armrests. He rubbed his lips together, as if moistening them. "Don Ravazzani. How may I help you?"

"I want to hear for myself how my woman was kidnapped and no one noticed on the security cameras."

"I-I don't know. There was a security update. I was busy and not paying attention. Sal was on duty at the beach, and she usually stayed inside until Giulio's afternoon visit. I wasn't expecting anything to happen."

"But you are never alone in there. Where were the others?"

"We thought a camera went down. They went to investigate."

I resisted the urge to glance at Marco. This was too many coincidences for me. "And this was the precise moment that Francesca disappeared?"

"They were gone for about forty-five minutes, so somewhere in there, yes."

I scrutinized his expression. A man in my position learns quickly to tell when he's being lied to. Vic was nervous but I expected that. Was he lying? I wasn't sure.

With Francesca back under my roof, I wasn't going to take any chances. Everyone in my organization would now be under suspicion. "Finish up and go home for the day," I told him. "We'll discuss this later."

"Sì, Don Ravazzani." Vic got up and nodded at me and Marco.

When we were alone, Marco said, "I don't like it."

"Neither do I." I tapped my finger on the top of the desk. "Giulio is close with these young men. Have him do some digging. He can take them drinking, to the clubs. Someone will say something they shouldn't. No one can hide this big of a secret from me."

"And in the meantime? Are you going to let Benito and the others work in the castello?"

"Yes, except for Vic. Transfer him off site for now."

"No problem."

"Let's start some digging. If someone is working with Enzo or the GDF, there is going to be money changing hands somewhere. And I want Francesca watched carefully."

"All right." Marco didn't move, his mouth turned into a heavy frown.

My cousin clearly wished to say something. "Out with it."

"This could bring down everything we've built. Is she worth it, Rav? Is she worth losing the entire empire over?"

"She is worth ten empires—and don't fucking ask me again."

Rising, Marco pursed his lips and held up his hands. "Ask yourself what happens the next time the GDF approaches her, because there will be a next time. Are you so certain she wants this life for herself and her child?"

He left after that, and I could feel doubt creeping like poisonous vines in my veins. I pushed it away. Francesca had the chance to betray me with Agent Rinaldo and she didn't. While she might still wish to leave here, she wasn't a rat. She'd stab me right in the heart where I could watch her do it, before she'd ever stab me in the back.

No, she was still mine and soon she would admit it.

I found Francesca reclining on the patio, reading on her tablet, early one afternoon. When I sat on the end of the chaise, she slid her feet over, making sure not to touch me. A flush brightened her cheeks, color that had nothing to do with the Italian sun. "What do you want, Fausto?"

My eyes drank in her long sculpted legs and golden skin. For the last few days, I'd kept my distance, giving her time to readjust to life at the estate while I tried to find out if I had a traitor in our midst. I knew her trust would take time, but I was a patient man. She would require proof of my feelings, irrefutable evidence of my devotion to her, which I was perfectly willing to demonstrate for however long it took. I had no more pride when it came to this woman.

I leaned on the chaise, drawing closer to her. "I have a surprise for you."

"No, thank you."

"You will like this one, I promise."

"Let me guess? Your dick in my mouth? Hard pass."

Madonna, this woman. I craved her fire and spirit. Those qualities were some of the reasons she was such an extraordinary fuck. "No, but that offer is open anytime."

"I bet," she muttered, eyes locked on her tablet.

"Do you know what happens in September?"

"The leaves change color?"

"*La vendemmia*," I said. "The grape harvest."

Her gaze flicked to mine, and I could see the curiosity there. Before I sent her away she spent a lot of time in the winery and the vineyard. It was only natural she would be interested in seeing more. "What, machines go out and harvest the grapes, bring them back, and workers stomp on them?"

I shook my head. "Wrong and wrong. The grapes must be harvested by hand. It is the Italian way. And no feet in the wine anymore. That part is done by machines."

Her tablet fell in her lap as she cocked her head at me. "You mean people cut the grapes off the vines by hand?"

"Of course. You mean in all that time you spent peppering Vincenzo with questions, you never asked about the harvest?"

"How do you know I asked Vincenzo questions?"

Because I watched the security footage, hours of it, back when I was obsessed with having her. Not that I could admit as much now. "I was told you spent time in the winery, no? Regardless, I thought you might like to help."

"Help with the harvest?"

"Sì." I rose and held out my hand. "Come. Let me show you."

She ignored my hand but sat up and started to slip on her shoes. "Don't tell me the great Fausto Ravazzani is actually go into the vineyard and harvest grapes."

"I've done so almost every year."

Her mouth fell open, but she quickly shut it. When she was on her feet, we began strolling toward the vineyards. At a leisurely pace, it would take around twenty minutes. Did she plan to walk the entire way in silence?

Clasping my hands behind my back, I matched my stride to hers. There was no hurry and I didn't want to tire her out. Everyone should see an Italian grape harvest at least once in their lives, and I wanted this to be the first of many for her.

Normally workers were everywhere on the estate, buzzing about and chattering loudly. During la vendemmia, however, every able-bodied person was needed to help harvest the grapes. Workers from town and neighboring estates came over, as well. Nothing was more important than wine to Italians.

"How did I not know this is happening?" she asked. "The estate is like a ghost town."

"Today is the first day. Vincenzo declared the grapes ready only this morning."

"And he told you?"

"Nothing happens on the estate without my knowledge. Or, have you forgotten?"

"I haven't forgotten that you're a controlling asshole, no."

I chuckled. She was not wrong. "Yes, but at heart I am just a farmer, like my ancestors before me."

"Please. You get off on being a mafia boss. I saw you with Enzo, threatening to gut him like a fish and feed him to the pigs."

"I get off on many things," I said in a low rumble.

"Stop it. You're trying to get me back into bed and it isn't going to work."

"But I have you back in my bed. Every night when I pull you close to fall sleep, and every morning when I wake up and you're wrapped around me like a second skin." I leaned closer, my mouth hovering above her ear. "What I am trying to do is to get you to ride my dick again, because I miss it, amore. I miss *you*."

She swallowed, her throat working, but she edged aside. "You cannot throw me away and then decide you want me again. It doesn't work like that. You said terrible things to me. All because I stood up for your son!" She exhaled through her nose, a little huff of annoyance. "You broke my heart, Fausto. And I know you're sorry and you'd change it if you could, but you can't. You treated me like shit when I was pregnant with your child, for fuck's sake. Almost three weeks I stayed in that beach house, alone and miserable, sick to my stomach, and not a word from you."

She stopped and put her hands on her hips. "You didn't care whether I lived or died, as long as I was out of your sight."

This was enough. I had to set her straight.

I moved in and cupped her face in my hands. "Wrong. I couldn't sleep while you were gone. I couldn't eat, and I started drinking heavily. Ask Marco or Zia. I was miserable, a shell of a man. I poured over the daily reports about you, then lingered in doorways, hiding, while Giulio updated Zia on you." I stroked my thumbs along her jaw, the soft skin like velvet. My heart pounded so hard that I wondered if she could hear it. "Do you need me to tell you how I feel? Is that what you need to forgive me and believe I am worthy of your trust? Because ti amo, cuore mio."

Her eyes moved back and forth, as if searching my gaze for a lie. She would not find one.

I admitted, "I have never told a woman that before in my life, not even Lucia. I didn't want to lie and raise her hopes for that kind of marriage between us. But the way I feel about you, Francesca? It is a sickness, a cancer. Something that cannot be destroyed or removed. You are a part of me, from now until they put me in the ground."

"Until I make you mad again," she whispered. "Until you cannot control your temper and I am the one to suffer. Or our child."

"I would *never* hurt our child."

"Unless he or she turns out to be gay. Or trans. Or bi. What will you do then, Fausto?" She stepped back and my hands fell to my sides. "What if your next son doesn't want to join the mafia? What if your daughter wants to choose her own husband—or wife? Will you be so understanding, then?"

I clenched my jaw. "I do not wish to discuss the situation with Giulio. This is about you and me."

"No, this is about more than you and me now. It became more the minute you got me pregnant. I was perfectly happy as your temporary mantenuta, and you had to ruin everything by accusing me of being a gold-digging whore! Just because I was willing to keep Giulio's secret!"

I wanted to tell her she was never temporary, but why would she believe me? I had to prove it to her. My words were not enough, even if I meant them.

I gestured to the path. "Come. Vincenzo needs our help."

She didn't budge. "I changed my mind. I don't feel like hanging out with you this afternoon. I'm going back to the castello."

I put my hands together, shaking them. "Please, Francesca. You should see la vendemmia. It is magical. Let me show you. Or, let Vincenzo show you. I'll keep my distance, if that is what you prefer."

"Yes, I fucking prefer," she snapped and started off toward the vineyards.

I exhaled in relief and followed her. At least she was still coming to pick grapes with me. That was a small victory.

CHAPTER ELEVEN

Francesca

Vincenzo's tan wrinkled face brightened when he saw me. "Signorina! I wondered if you would join us." The vintner glanced over my shoulder and dipped his chin respectfully. "Signore Ravazzani. You honor us with your presence."

Fausto came forward, shook the vintner's hand, and spoke quietly. The people standing around us all laughed, grinning at him, and I tried not to look as annoyed as I felt. What, would they kiss his ring next?

A woman appeared at my side. She was slightly younger than Fausto, with a long braid of dark hair tucked under a sun hat. Her brown eyes were kind, her smile patient. "Is this your first time?"

I nodded. "I am a vendemmia virgin."

The woman chuckled. "That sounds like a t-shirt." Her expression turned serious. "I've wanted to meet you for a long time. I am Emilia, Vincenzo's daughter."

"Oh, hello! He told me all about you." Vincenzo often bragged about his daughter, the accountant who'd gone to university in London. "I'm Frankie."

"I know exactly who you are." Emilia shrugged then said *sotto voce*, "These old Italians are terrible gossips. Never trust them with your secrets."

"Noted." Of course they'd all been talking about me, the woman stupid enough to let Fausto Ravazzani knock her up.

"Hey, I didn't mean it like that," Emilia said, watching my face. "They think you are some kind of goddess, the woman who tamed the great Ravazzani."

Tamed, right. Shifting the attention away from me, I asked, "You work as an accountant in the city." She was also divorced, which Vincenzo mentioned through gritted teeth.

"I do. My father was hoping I would take over the winery, but I have a black thumb. Numbers are more my strength."

"I always hated math class."

She raised her hands. "Many people say the same, but numbers are useful, especially in our world." She tilted her head toward Fausto, and I wondered what that meant. I looked at Fausto and felt conflicted.

You are a part of me, from now until they put me in the ground.

I liked those words far more than I should, and I wanted to hear him say he loved me again and again. Something had changed in the last few days. He was softer with me, more open. At night, when I pretended to sleep, he pulled me close and whispered Italian endearments that made my heart melt. He rested his hand on my belly, stroking and soothing, like he was comforting our child in there.

It was a different side of him, one I craved—and that was dangerous. For all his talk and whispers, this was still the same man who said I was dead to him, who planned on taking our child away from me after the birth. A murderer and a drug kingpin. It was madness to feel any tenderness toward him whatsoever.

Yet I did, more and more each day.

"Here."

I looked up. Emilia held out a basket and pruning shears. Right, the grape harvest. Everyone else had started off into the vineyard, the sun coating the grapes in a burnished gold. Fausto, now wearing a baseball cap, was laughing with one of the workers, and that familiar tug of arousal in my gut grew stronger as I watched him. He was ridiculously handsome.

"Oh, you have it bad," Emilia said, nudging my arm.

"Hmm? What?"

"Come. I'm taking you to the other end. If you stare at him all day you'll never harvest any grapes."

When we found an empty row, Emilia showed me how to hold the cluster of grapes and snip the vine with the shears. Then the grapes had to be placed carefully in the basket. "There," she said. "It is important not to break or bruise them. Otherwise the fermentation starts."

"Like this?" I held and snipped a cluster, then gently put them in my basket.

"Very good. Now do it ten thousand more times." She chuckled and spread her hand out toward the rows of vines.

"This is hard work."

"Yes, which is why almost the entire village comes to help." She took the opposite side of our row and began snipping. "I took the rest of the week off from my job."

"This is a terrible way to spend your vacation."

"I don't mind. I don't see enough of my father anymore and it's nice to be outside." She placed more grapes in her basket. "I recently got divorced. I'm sure my father has mentioned it."

"Yes, he did tell me. I sense he doesn't approve."

"An understatement. Divorce is not common around here. Once you are married, they expect it to be for life, no matter how terrible he treats you."

Something in her voice caused my head to snap up. "Did he hurt you?"

"Not like that. He was a liar and a cheater."

"I'm sorry."

"Thank you. Most of the old guard—the new guard, too, I suppose —think you should stick it out. It's that Catholic mentality."

My sisters and I were raised Catholic, but we never really practiced. Once my mother died we stopped going to church altogether. "Were you married a long time?"

"Eight years. I was twenty-three when we married. At the time my father thought I was going to die an old maid." She sighed. "I should have waited. I was too young to marry, but I fell in love."

See? This was why you couldn't trust feelings. They steered you wrong every time.

"That's why I never want to marry," I said, bending to put another bunch in my basket. "It's not worth it."

"But you and . . ." She let her voice trail off. "I thought you and Signore Ravazzani were together. That you are pregnant with his child."

"We aren't together, not any more. And yes, I'm pregnant, but there is no wedding happening."

"Hmm."

I cocked my head at her, wiping the sweat from my brow. Didn't she believe me? "I know it sounds crazy, not to marry the father of my child. But I don't want to be tied to him for the rest of my life."

"But you are tied to him for life." Her olive skin paled in the bright sun. "I apologize. I should keep my mouth shut. None of this is my business."

"I don't mind. I have two sisters at home who are always sticking their nose in my business."

"You sound like you miss them."

"I do. Very much. I'd hoped to have them come visit but . . ."

"I'm certain Signore Ravazzani would bring them here, if you asked."

"I would bring who here?"

Spinning, I found Fausto coming toward me, his long legs eating up the dirt between us. I shielded my eyes from the sun and scowled at him. Had he been eavesdropping? "No one."

He went to Emilia and kissed her cheeks. "You are looking well," he told her. "Is he still going on about your divorce?"

"Of course. He's disappointed in the lack of grandchildren."

"Tell him that is what your brothers are for. Let's talk in my office before you leave today. I have some things I need you to check into for me."

Emilia nodded. "All right."

Did Emilia's accounting firm handle some of the mafia's money? Knowing it was none of my business, I returned to my grapes. Something suddenly dropped on my head, startling me. "Hey!"

Fausto had put his baseball hat on my head, which he was now adjusting. "Wear this. You need to protect your face from the sun."

I didn't know what to say. It was sweet of him, but I wasn't used to sweet Fausto yet. I probably never would be.

Bending, he kissed my cheek. "Have fun, amore. Try not to eat too many grapes, eh?"

Then he sauntered off, his ass total perfection in the worn jeans, while his broad shoulders stretched the fabric of his t-shirt. Would it be terrible if we slept together just once?

I nearly smacked myself. *Of course it would be terrible!* He had been a complete asshole to me.

Except my body didn't care. It seemed fully on board for treating Fausto's dick like an amusement park ride. Was this from the the pregnancy hormones, or would I still feel this way after the baby arrived?

When I turned, Emilia was watching me carefully. Grinning, she snapped her clippers at me like castanets. "What was that about not being together? Because that man is absolutely smitten over you."

I didn't have the heart to correct her. Fausto might seem smitten now, but what about the next time I did or said something he didn't like? "Have you known him a long time?"

"As long as I can remember. Which is why I must start shopping for a dress to wear to your wedding."

I plucked a grape off a vine and tossed it at her head.

Fausto

I opened the door to my office and found a stocky man waiting there with Marco. Everyone stood as I walked in.

"Fausto, my boy!" A contemporary of my father, Girolamo Condello was a don from another era and the head of Piedmont's biggest 'ndrina. Like me, he was a member of La Provincia, our ruling body.

"Ciao, Mommo." I kissed his cheeks. "What a pleasant surprise." I had a feeling what this meeting might concern, but I hoped I was wrong. Marco's worried expression told me he suspected, as well.

"You are looking well. It has been a long time since I have seen you out of a suit."

"Forgive me," I said with a self-deprecating shrug. "We began la vendemmia and I've just come in from the vineyard."

"Ah, I do envy you and your vineyards. I would never turn down a glass of Ravazzani ciró."

Marco poured wine while I sat. We both picked up our glasses and toasted. "*Salute.*"

I leaned back in my chair and asked the necessary questions about his wife and grandkids. Mommo had outlived two wives, and it seemed this last one might live long enough to inherit his fortune. Though who could say? The other two had disappeared suddenly.

He asked me about Giulio and business. I gave vague answers. Even with other capos I preferred to keep my information private. Besides, I wanted to move this along. I still needed to wash the vineyard off. Finally, I said, "I'm surprised to find you in Siderno. Are you on holiday?"

"I am here on business, unfortunately." He set his wine glass on my desk, then folded his hands across his middle. "Enzo D'Agostino has been missing for a few days, his beach house like something out of one of those horror films. I'm told no one survived save his mantenuta and two soldiers hiding in a secret room."

I resisted the urge to snarl at Marco. Sloppy work, leaving those two soldiers alive. No doubt they had opened their fucking mouths and spread tales of what happened far and wide.

Fury at my men aside, I tried to keep my tone light. "And you've come here to let me know?"

"I've come for information. I know you and your men were there. It's been rumored that you and D'Agostino had a disagreement of some sort."

That answered the question of whether D'Agostino's soldiers had talked. Cristo, what a mistake. I said, "I wouldn't expect you to bother yourself with a squabble between two capos."

"I'm here to reason with you." Mommo gave me a paternal smile, as if he was genuinely worried about me. "D'Agostino has powerful allies. This computer thing that he runs, with the scams and credit cards, it makes many people a lot of money. They are all wondering what will happen to this money if D'Agostino does not return."

I was in the process of assuming Enzo's operations, but I wouldn't tell anyone yet. Not until I wrestled control from Enzo's siblings, who were annoyingly stubborn about the entire thing. Fortunately, seeing their brother suffer on live video was going a long way to making that happen quickly. "And what of my allies? I also make a lot of money for people, including you." Mommo distributed my product through France and into Spain.

He held up his hands. "I am here as your ally. Your father and I were great friends in the day, and the Ravazzani name is one of the most revered. But we cannot attack each other, as the *Camorrista* do. We are heroic, valiant, not a bunch of animals who tear one another apart."

"I'm glad to hear we are not enemies," I said softly. "Otherwise I might wonder why you mistrust my judgment enough to come here and question it. If we were not allies, I might consider it an offense."

Sipping his wine, he stared at me. Then he set his glass on the desk, the big diamond on his finger flashing. I didn't remember him wearing such a gaudy piece when I last saw him. "Fausto, you wage war over a woman, a mantenuta," he scoffed, as though the idea was ludicrous. "Not even a wife. If you know where Enzo is, I beg you to release him before this gets out of hand."

I leaned forward, my hospitality gone. "Either you can set La Provincia straight now or I will do it myself during Crimine in a few weeks, I don't care. This matter is personal, not business. I will handle it as I see fit, without input from them or anyone else. What he took from me is irreplaceable, and I would expect any of you to do the same if such a move was made against your household."

"You have her back unharmed, as I understand. Do not let a woman make you weak."

Weak? Little wonder my teeth didn't crack from how hard I was clenching them. Standing, I signaled the end to this meeting. "Marco, won't you send a few bottles of ciró home with Mommo?"

My cousin inclined his head. "Of course."

To Mommo, I said, "I wish you a safe journey home."

He sighed and heaved out of the chair. "They will expect answers from you during Crimine, then. None of us acts alone."

Che palle. Did he think I was new, that I didn't know how this worked? And I didn't care who expected answers. In the end the other bosses expected money, which they saw plenty of from me.

We shook hands, then Marco saw Mommo to the door. I waited until they were safely out of sight before slipping from my office. Fury roiled inside me, the darkness in my soul burning and scratching to be satisfied. How dare anyone interfere? Enzo had crossed a line. He invaded my property, attacked my men, stole something precious, and tried to blackmail me.

If not for the kidnapping, I could've begged Francesca for her forgiveness at the beach. It wouldn't have been easy, but eventually we would have reconciled. The kidnapping had traumatized her and made her even angrier at me.

So, fuck Enzo. And fuck Mommo for daring to intercede.

Unlocking the dungeon, I slipped inside and rushed down the stone steps. The scent of damp and sweat greeted me, and I heard his labored breathing. I longed for my knife, a sharp blade to slide across skin, the bloom of warm red that followed.

To make sure he didn't die too soon, I knew he had to recover for a few days. But when he was well enough to suffer again, I would pick up where I left off.

For now, a short visit would have to suffice. I needed to see his pain.

You didn't care whether I lived or died, as long as I was out of your sight.

She was wrong. I cared. I cared a great deal.

Enzo was chained to the wall in one of the dungeon's cells. We allowed him enough slack on the chains to stand, not that he was capable of it at the moment. The swelling around his eyes made it difficult to see, but by the way he stiffened it was clear he knew who'd arrived.

I unlocked the cell and went in. Bending down, I grabbed his hair and slammed his head back against the stone, causing him to groan. I snarled, "They miss you, D'Agostino, coming to me and pleading for your life. But they should know me better. There is no mercy for you, no escape. You will die here, at my hand."

"Fuck . . . you," he wheezed.

To annoy him, I laughed. "You will not be so defiant after our next visit, I promise you." I let him go, and his head dropped forward. Standing, I relocked the cell, the old key scraping against the iron. "Get better, stronzo. I'm looking forward to hearing your screams."

CHAPTER TWELVE

Francesca

The castello was quiet when I came in from the vineyards, and my skin prickled in the air conditioning. It was time for a shower and a nap. Stretching out my arms to ease my aches, I climbed the stairs and turned toward my room. Rather, Fausto's room. How could I forget? At least his bed was comfortable. That was the only upside.

Closing the bedroom door behind me, I walked in and tossed Fausto's hat onto an armchair. I started to take off my clothes then paused. Was the shower running?

My hands froze, my mind stuck on that noise. Fausto was in there. And he was *showering*.

Oh God, I should leave. I shouldn't think about him naked and soapy, hands gliding over that body, his thick cock swinging between his legs. I used to love showering with him, getting on my knees in the hot spray and worshiping him with my mouth. He'd brace his hands on the tile and watch as he pumped his hips, dragging the heavy length of him in and out of my throat.

Desire, raw and undeniable, clawed in my gut and itched at my skin. I couldn't stop picturing him, couldn't stop *needing* him.

Then I heard a soft grunt. I knew that sound. I still heard it in my dreams.

Before I even realized it, I drifted toward the bathroom door.

What am I doing?

It was wrong, but I couldn't stop. I had to see. There was no harm in seeing, was there? I wouldn't touch him or let him touch me. But I could watch, couldn't I? He'd never know and I would only allow myself a quick peek.

I stepped inside, the tile cool on my feet. His back was to me, so he didn't notice my arrival. He had an arm propped on the tile, and water ran down his back in rivulets, smoothing over his ass and legs. A hand worked his legs as his hips flexed ever so slightly, muscles popping as he jerked himself off. I licked my lips at his magnificence, the sight of him like a cool drink after weeks of extreme thirst.

From now on, any time I needed to come, I would let myself imagine this right here. Before I could stop it, a soft sigh escaped my throat.

His head whipped around, blue eyes wide and surprised. I didn't move. Part of me had hoped he would catch me, drag me into the shower clothes and all, then have his wicked way with me. I was so tired of fighting this. I wanted him so badly.

Without breaking eye contact, he slowly turned and dropped his hand. Jesus Christ, his body was unfair. His flat stomach had more definition than before, his hips more pronounced. That cock, though. Fully hard, it stood out from his body, every bit as perfect as I remember—more than big enough to be a challenge. My pussy clenched, the stretch of his dick having imprinted there, and I had to grip the counter to keep from lunging at him.

He let me look for another few seconds, then wrapped his fist around the shaft once more and began stroking slowly from root to tip. "Do you want to know what I was thinking about?" he asked.

Yes.

"No," I breathed.

He cocked an eyebrow as if he knew I was lying. "I'm remembering the first time you let me fuck your ass. When we were in Roma." He sucked in a quick breath, his fist squeezing the head of his dick. "Madonna, that was fucking hot. Dirty and rough, my favorite thing in the whole world."

Mesmerized, I watched his hand glide over his dick.

"You took my cock so good, piccolina. You were so tight and warm. So sweet."

The words sent lust careening through me, like he'd injected a drug into my veins. My mouth was completely dry, while my pussy was the opposite. I was soaked and slippery there, a needy, throbbing mess.

"I loved to hear you beg," he continued, shifting to squeeze his balls. "Almost as much as I loved to see you come."

Fuck it. Why should *I* be the one to suffer? *He's* the one that did something wrong. My fingers found the button on my shorts. Flicked it open. His body went still, his entire attention focused on my hand. He seemed to be holding his breath, waiting to see what I would do.

"Maybe it's your turn to beg," I whispered.

"Please," he said instantly, his free hand falling against the glass barrier as if trying to reach for me. "Ti prego, dolcezza. I am so hungry for you."

I flicked the zipper down. "Again, paparino."

The nickname fell out of my mouth but I didn't think he heard me, thank God. Instead he leaned in and repeated, "Ti prego, baby."

I slowly pulled my shorts and panties to my knees.

Fausto's expression twisted, like he was in exquisite pain, and his hand picked up speed along his erection. His eyes were locked on my pussy, so I shifted to spread my legs as far as I could manage. The air felt cool on my overheated skin, and the shower filled the bathroom with a fine mist. I watched him pump, the muscles in his forearm bunching, working, and I slipped my fingers between my legs.

"Madre di Dio," he groaned, hips punching forward.

My clit was ripe, engorged, and the brush of my fingertips felt better than anything in recent memory. I swiped again, biting my lip to keep from moaning, my knees actually trembling.

"Show me," he said. "Pull apart your lips and show me how wet and swollen you are."

"Beg for it."

"Amore, please!"

More than happy to torture him, I parted my folds and let him see. Then I dipped a finger in my wetness and brought it to my lips, sucking the tip inside and cleaning the arousal off.

"Cazzo!" Fausto barked, his body tense as he rocked against the glass. "I want you in my mouth, little girl. I want to suck on your clit and tongue that pretty pussy."

Fuck, I wanted that, too.

I began working my clit, circling and rubbing, and pleasure streaked through me like lightning. I watched his hand pick up speed and thought about how good it would feel if he pinned me down and fucked me. His large body straining and thrusting, his cock delivering pleasure, driving me into the mattress. He knew exactly what I liked, what got me off, and he used that knowledge shamelessly. I loved it. I wanted to be his dirty slut, beg for him to let me come. I wanted to let him use me anyway he saw fit.

The words burned the tip of my tongue. I knew if I asked, he would rush from the shower like a man possessed. I would get fucked to within an inch of my life, the delicious soreness between my legs lasting for days . . .

Moaning, I picked up speed, wiping my fingers on my thigh when I became *too* slippery. Jesus, I was wet. I couldn't remember ever being this turned on before. But my clit craved the friction, and I moved faster, in time with Fausto's hand. I imagined he was fucking me, his body rubbing me on the downstroke.

This did not go unnoticed.

"There you go," he said, holding onto the top of the glass as he angled toward me, his hips rocking. "It would feel so good if I were fucking you right now, no? Your tight little cunt wrapped around my dick. I would fill you so good, piccolina. I dream about fucking you, about taking you hard and fast, until you are raw from it." He threw his head back. "Madonna, I have never jerked off this much in my entire life."

Panting, I grasped the counter. Tingles gathered and pulsed, little trails of light that multiplied until they became a wave of pleasure rushing toward me. I tried to hold it off, wanting to prolong this as long as I could. "You should get used to jerking off. It's the only satisfaction you'll ever have."

"We will see," he growled, his fist flying over his shaft. "Cazzo, Francesca."

The use of my name in his sexy rumble did it. The orgasm was right there at the edge of my mind, the strength of it stealing every bit of sense I possessed. I couldn't hold back the words of our game, the sexy secret only he knew. "Sono la tua puttanella," I gasped and came all over my fingers.

"Minchia!" he shouted. Thick spurts of come shot from his cock as his shoulders hunched, his muscles straining. We both trembled and shook, our eyes glazed as we watched one another, pleasure sparking between us like a live wire. I wanted to touch him, to taste him so badly that tears nearly sprang to my eyes. It was so unfair.

Reality crept back in as the orgasm subsided. The shower glass fogged with his exhales and my knees were weak. Holy shit, that had been unexpected. And hot. But wrong.

So wrong.

But it was so hot.

Damn it.

I jerked my panties and shorts up to my waist and ran from the bathroom.

I was halfway up the stairs later that night when the front door burst open. Glancing over my shoulder, I watched Marco march Giulio into the castello. My friend's face was slack, his limbs loose, as he tried to pull away from his uncle. "Let me go, Zio Marco."

"What's going on?" I called down.

No one paid me a bit of attention. Instead, Marco kept shoving Giulio in the direction of Fausto's office. I didn't like this. Was something wrong?

"I didn't do anything!" Giulio said with a laugh. "You're pissed for no reason."

"We'll see what your father says about it, eh?"

I was already trailing them. If Giulio was in trouble, I wanted to help. He was my friend—my only friend these days—and he hadn't abandoned me when I was exiled. I owed him for looking after me during those dark weeks.

So I didn't hesitate in following them directly to Fausto's office. Marco turned and frowned at me. "What are you doing?"

"Helping my friend."

"Frankie," Giulio said, smiling over his shoulder. "Thank God. Tell Zio Marco he's being dramatic and to let me go."

Ah, so this was the problem. Giulio's eyes were glazed and rimmed with red. He looked like my ex-boyfriend after he'd spent a few hours with his bong.

"Quiet," Marco snapped, then knocked on the door to Fausto's office. "Permesso!"

"Prego," my baby daddy shouted from within.

Marco opened the door and I slipped in before he could close it on me. Fausto sat at his desk, his suit coat off, the sleeves of his white shirt rolled up on his thick forearms. He removed the glasses he wore when he was working and stood. "What's this?"

A grinning Giulio pulled free of his uncle. "I didn't do anything wrong."

"I'll be the judge of that," Fausto snapped. Then his gaze traveled to me. "Francesca, you are not needed for this."

I lifted one eyebrow. "I'll be the judge of that."

Oh, il Diavolo did not like having his words used against him. He drew in a deep breath and his chest swelled, those bright eyes glittering as they narrowed on me. "This is a family matter. Go upstairs."

The words slashed like knives inside my chest, but I lifted my chin and stared him down. "Are you saying that I'm not family?" He told me he loved me earlier. Did he mean it? Because until I saw evidence of it, I wouldn't believe him. "Besides, I'm here for Giulio, who is like family to me."

He studied me, that keen mind turning over my words. "Sit," he finally said, pointing to the sofa. When I obeyed like a good mantenuta, he addressed Marco. "Explain."

"Papà—"

Fausto lifted a hand. "I will hear from your uncle first."

Marco said, "He missed an appointment tonight at the club. Gratteri called me, asked me to track Giulio down. I found him sitting outside Paolo's apartment. Turns out he's been doing that a lot lately." He walked over to Fausto's desk and set a small square cartridge on it. A vape. "I also found this in his pocket. It's a vaporizer for weed. There's also tons of weed in the car."

Fausto pinched the bridge of his nose with his thumb and two fingers. "Ma che cazzo?"

"I lost track of time!" Giulio folded his arms. "And this is not a big deal. Marco is overreacting."

Fausto didn't like that one bit. A muscle in his jaw twitched and he snarled, "This is a big fucking deal, Giulio."

"It's just weed, Papà—"

"Just weed? You're sitting outside Paolo's apartment, getting high, and neglecting your duties. Are you saying I should not be angry with you?"

Giulio chuckled, then worsened the situation by saying, "It's no different than alcohol—and I remember how much you drank every day when Frankie was at the beach house. So, come on, Papà. Spare me any lectures."

Oh, shit. All the air was sucked out of the room and Fausto's face flushed, the angles sharpening with his mounting fury. It was like watching a dragon readying itself to breathe fire.

But this was the weed talking. Giulio wasn't normally so disrespectful. I jumped to my feet and darted in front of him. I put my palms up toward Fausto, who was coming around his desk. "Wait a minute and calm down. He's not in his right head."

"Get out of my way, Francesca."

Giulio wrapped his arms around my shoulders and leaned onto my back, almost like he was snuggling against me. Fausto's mouth tightened. "Let her go before you hurt her."

"I would never hurt Frankie," Giulio said into my hair. "She's the best stepmother I could have asked for."

I closed my eyes briefly. Jesus. Baked Giulio was a blabbermouth.

"Listen," I said to Fausto, more than ready to put the stepmother comment behind us. "Let me grab some chips and I'll take him upstairs to watch a movie. Then you can yell at him all you want tomorrow."

Fausto's nostrils flared, his chest rising and falling with the force of his breaths. I didn't know if my suggestion would work, but I had to try something. The last time I saw him this mad was when he learned I knew Giulio was gay. I didn't want Giulio to suffer from one of Fausto's rash decisions.

"She's right, Rav," Marco said, shocking the hell out of me. I wasn't his favorite person, so I couldn't believe he was siding with me. "Let him sleep it off. We'll discuss it tomorrow."

"Fine," Fausto gritted out from between clenched teeth. "But he doesn't leave without my approval."

"Fuck, he's really mad, isn't he?" Giulio whispered with a chuckle.

"Get him out of my sight." Fausto spun and strode toward his chair. "Marco, see that his car is cleaned out and stored. He won't be driving it anytime soon."

I supposed that meant we were dismissed.

I took Giulio's hand and towed him from Fausto's office. "Let's go get some snacks and we'll watch that new Adam Driver movie again."

"He is so fucking hot." Giulio trailed after me like a sweet puppy. "He has huge hands, did you know?"

Yes, I knew. Giulio had talked a *lot* about Adam Driver's hands at the beach.

"Paolo also has huge hands," he said. "I miss him so much, Frankie."

"I know, sweetie."

"He's back on the dating apps. I don't understand it. How can he move on without me, like I never even mattered to him?"

I doubted it was easy for Paolo, but people coped with a breakup in different ways. "Come on. There's gelato in the fridge."

CHAPTER THIRTEEN

Fausto

A full glass of whiskey in hand, I stood in the dark at my office window and stared off into the night. With the lights out, the stars over the vineyard would be radiant, but I didn't even notice. Fury still burned bright in my chest, a ball of frustration that tightened with every breath I took.

Giulio was supposed to be my heir, the future of my empire. The men looked to him for leadership, an example of our strength and tradition. He needed to instill fear and respect. Instead, he was getting high and stalking his ex-boyfriend. Dio santo, if anyone should find out . . .

I rubbed my eyes. What did he want, to be the first openly gay leader of the 'Ndrangheta? This was a death sentence. He'd never make it to capo and everything I had sacrificed, everything I had done would be for naught. Did he care nothing for this family or his own life? For what I'd built?

There was only one solution to this problem, but my son would hate me forever. There was no turning back after I ordered it.

But order it I would.

That's why I was the don. I had to make the tough decisions and carry them out, even when I didn't want to.

I swallowed a mouthful of whiskey, the heat scalding my throat. Exhaling, I leaned against the window glass. I felt on the edge of my sanity these days. Perhaps a night of torturing Enzo D'Agostino would distract me from this ever-tangling knot of irritation inside me.

The door suddenly opened and light slashed into the room. Marco, no doubt. I didn't turn around. "I thought you went home."

The door closed and darkness returned. I heard light steps on the carpet, then the scent of olives and earth teased my nostrils. Awareness slid over my skin like a thousand tiny pinpricks. She always smelled like my estate.

This was not a good time, however. "I'm not in the mood for company, dolcezza."

"Too bad." She stood next to me and propped a shoulder against the window frame. "I want to know what you're going to do about Giulio."

"It is none of your concern."

"That means it's something bad."

She was learning. "Go to bed, Francesca. It has been a long day. I will come upstairs later."

"Don't send me to bed like a small child. I want to know what you are planning to do."

"What would you suggest?"

"Let him be with Paolo."

I snorted and finished the rest of the whiskey in my glass. "Impossible, for many reasons."

"What does that mean?" She grabbed my arm and forced me to look at her. "I know of one reason, because he's your son and heir. What other reason could there be?"

I just stared down at her. She would figure it out. Francesca was a smart woman.

"No. Fuck, no," she said, eyes wide as they searched my face. "You can't do that. You can't have Paolo killed."

"He will never focus until Paolo is gone. He's still watching him, for fuck's sake."

"Like you watched me when I was at the beach?"

I didn't care for the comparison. "It's hardly the same," I snapped.

"It's exactly the same." She gave a small shake of her head. "He's heartbroken. Fausto, I'm begging you. Don't do this. He'll never forgive you."

I looked out the window again, not answering. Of course she would think there was another way. But I knew this life better than she ever could, and there was no alternative. I would not justify it, either. My hand trembled as I shoved it into my trouser pocket. Violence lurked in the pit of my stomach, the darkness that resurfaced more and more lately, seemingly never satisfied. Even Marco had winced at some of the creative ways I'd hurt Enzo.

What happened when I could not shove the darkness away?

Francesca slipped between me and the window, her beautiful face looking up at me. Cristo, I wanted her so badly. But my feelings were too raw, too brutal. I needed to be alone.

I scowled down at her. "You should go."

"No, I won't leave you until . . ." Her palm came up to caress my jaw, her expression both understanding and resolved. "Do not purposely hurt your son like this. There are some things you can't fix once you break them."

She'd said this to me before. I hated the reminder of how I hurt her, how I ruined everything between us. "Like you?"

"This is a line you cannot cross. Giulio will find out and this will ruin any relationship you have with him. You're his father. I know you love him. Deep down, you don't want to hurt him."

"I care a great deal for you, amore. More than almost anything else." I brushed her hair off her face, loving the way the soft strands felt against my skin. "But don't ask this of me."

"I *am* asking—and I'll ask again and again until you listen to me. This is a mistake."

"I've already decided. I cannot change my mind."

"That's bullshit. You can change anything you like. You are the one with all the power over us, paparino."

The use of the word *us* was not lost on me, nor the nickname. I swallowed hard, stepped back, and went to pour another drink. "You should leave."

"No, I won't. I have to know what you're going to do. We're having a child together. I don't want to think you're capable of such cruelty when it comes to your own flesh and blood."

"You wouldn't understand," I snapped. "And unless you are finally ready to let me fuck you, you are wasting your breath."

"Is that what it would take to clear your head? Will fucking me calm you down enough to see reason?"

"No. It will only make me want to fuck you more."

"What if we make a deal?"

I paused, whiskey glass halfway to my mouth. Was she serious? "Are you trading your pussy for Paolo's life?"

"Would it work?"

I let my gaze travel the length of her body, my cock very much liking the idea. "I don't know."

"Then perhaps we should try it and see."

There was no hint of hesitation in her expression, but this wasn't enough. I didn't want her to ride my dick as part of a negotiation for some stronzo's life. I wanted her compliance and her full participation. I wanted her to *crave* what only I could give her, as I did with her.

We were both stubborn. Maybe she needed this as an excuse to fuck me again? She'd fingered herself earlier while watching me in the shower, her cunt so wet she had to wipe her fingers off to even continue masturbating. Desire was never a problem between us. So did she need a way to rationalize it?

Her breath quickened and I weakened, my resolve crumbling as my dick lengthened. If this was how I had to have her, then so be it. I was too desperate to refuse.

The words tumbled from my mouth. "Take off your clothes."

She reached for the hem of her t-shirt. The cloth fell to the ground, revealing red lace—and all the air left my lungs in a rush.

Madre di Dio. The red bodysuit.

"Look what I found in my drawer." She shimmied out of her yoga pants, displaying those long legs I loved to feel wrapped around my hips. Her waist was still small but the pregnancy made her tits even fuller. They spilled out from the top of the bodysuit cups. Kicking the pants aside, she said, "I guess you didn't get rid of all my lingerie after you sent me away."

I couldn't breathe, couldn't think. I was both grateful and angry, aware that she'd worn this to control me. And it was working. There was no resisting her, no refusal on my tongue. I wanted her too badly, the need in my balls too great. I loved her, and my body craved nothing more than to prove it to her.

I ran my tongue behind my teeth, contemplating, before growling, "Get on the sofa and spread your legs."

The slightest frown crossed her face. "If I do this, it doesn't mean I've forgiven you."

Though I had no one to blame but myself, I wanted to punch the wall. Five weeks ago she wouldn't have questioned an order like this, and I needed that acceptance again. Nothing less would do. She was *mine*.

Still, I knew what she needed to hear, even if I wasn't sure I believed it. I inclined my head. "Of course."

My agreement satisfied her. She started for the sofa, her ass high and tight, absolute perfection as she moved across the floor. I wanted to spank her, to mark her. To whip her just so I could lick her tears. I wanted every part of her, good and bad.

She settled on the cushions, faced me, and spread her legs. Her blond hair fell in waves around her shoulders, and the flush on her cheeks told me how much she liked being on display for me. "Open the snaps," I said.

Delicate fingers reached between her legs and the snaps flew open one by one, each soft pop a stroke to my poor neglected cock. I was so hard, the skin stretched tight over my shaft, and I couldn't wait to shove myself inside her, feel that warmth and heat again after so long.

When the fabric parted, there was her pussy on glorious display. She had recently shaved, leaving herself bare, and the glistening lips made my mouth water. My piccola monella, playing with fire.

I put the glass down carefully, then closed the distance to the sofa and dropped to my knees between her thighs. The scent of her arousal filled my nose and lungs, making my head swim. Fuck, yes. I had dreamed of this for so long—every time I closed my eyes for the last five weeks—that I almost couldn't believe it was real.

My chest heaved as I bent my head, my arms sliding under her thighs to pull her closer, but I paused just before my mouth reached her perfect skin. Breathing on her, but not offering any relief. "Beg me," I whispered. "Beg me to eat your pussy, dolcezza."

Francesca

I didn't have time to wonder whether this was a mistake or not.

I'd worn the red bodysuit as insurance, just in case I needed to break out the lace-covered girls and seduce him into not hurting Giulio or Paolo. In my head, I thought Fausto would take one look at me, agree to whatever demands I put forth, then ravish me in a frenzy.

I should've known better.

The soft exhales from his mouth teased my skin, and my clit pulsed with every beat of my heart. No way he hadn't noticed how wet I was at the moment. I needed his mouth on me. I craved the feel of his lips and tongue, the scrape of his teeth, the way he sucked and licked me like he was starving for me . . .

I hadn't missed the huge erection tenting his trousers, though. He wanted this every bit as much as I did.

Reaching down, I threaded my fingers through his silky hair, needing to touch him. God, this man. He turned me on like no one else in the entire world.

He snatched my wrist and pulled my hand away from him. "Place your hands behind your head," he ordered. "Give yourself over to me."

White-hot arousal shot through me, his dominance my drug, and I hurried to obey. The position put my body at an awkward angle, with my tits thrust up and out, barely encased by the bodysuit. Then he was back between my legs, his mouth hovering just where I needed him most.

"Ti prego," I whispered, unable to take one second more. "Please, Fausto."

That was all he needed to hear, apparently, because his mouth latched onto me like he was starving. Like my body was his sustenance and he'd been deprived for years. My back bowed, pleasure arcing through my limbs at his assault, his lips and tongue voracious as they sucked and licked, and I could only sit on the sofa and withstand it. I was forced to take the pleasure he gave me and return none of it, but his growls and sighs into my flesh told me he loved it every bit as much as I did.

Using the flat of his tongue, he massaged my clit, then drew it into his mouth to suck on it. Sweat broke out on my forehead and my thighs trembled. The tension was almost too much to take. Ribbons of lust were coiling inside my belly, but there was no relief, no gentleness coming from this man. It was almost like a punishment. Death by amazing head.

"You know what I want to hear," he said, nuzzling me with his nose. "Tell me."

What was he talking about? Everything throbbed. I was so fucking close. "Don't stop, please."

Two long, thick fingers worked inside my opening, filling and stretching me in the best kind of way. It pinched, the fit a tight one after so long, but I welcomed the burn as the digits tunneled inside me. "Holy shit," I breathed, and the glorious pressure of his fingers nearly made my eyes cross.

"Tell me who you belong to, Francesca."

I shook my head against the sofa. I couldn't. He asked too much. I wasn't ready to say it.

When the silence lapsed, he nipped at my swollen clit. I pressed my toes into the floor, the pain intense and bright behind my eyelids. "Fuck!" I shouted, and the ache quickly ebbed into a rush of endorphins. He gave the nub soft kisses, as if apologizing, and I panted, nearly sobbing, with the need to come.

He stood abruptly, the fabric of his pants soft against my legs. In a daze, I let him position me over the arm of the sofa, face down with my ass in the air. I heard his zipper and half a beat later his cock met my entrance. He shoved in without warning and the force of it moved the sofa across the wooden floor several inches. We both froze, and I struggled to breathe. He felt huge and perfect, the stretch painful but necessary, like he was a part of me. God, I had missed this.

He stroked my shoulder blades, my spine. Then he pushed the bodysuit up and over my head. I was completely naked while he was clothed. Was he aware of how much that turned me on? Knowing Fausto, yes.

His hand wrapped around the back of my neck, holding me down, and I went lax, more than ready for his dominance to take me to where nothing else mattered except having his cock inside me.

He began fucking me then, hard and rough thrusts of his hips, the best kind of punishment. I soared, the pleasure lifting me, replacing everything inside my head until my skin began tingling with an impending orgasm. Moaning, I floated, my pussy his to do with whatever he pleased. My climax hovered just out of reach, and I started shaking, my muscles trembling as I made nonsensical noises, and he finally reached around to pinch my clit.

White-hot sparks raced through me and I shouted, my walls clenching around his dick as I came. It went on and on, and my vision went dark for a second.

He withdrew and I immediately missed the feel of him. Coming around to the front, he sat down, that glorious dick on full display. Then he lifted me like I weighed nothing at all and settled me on his lap, facing him. He reached between us and lined himself up at my entrance, then put a hand on my hip, bringing me down to engulf him. When I had swallowed up his entire length, he stretched his arms along the back of the sofa and waited. A mafia king, content to be served.

Shit, he was sexy.

His gaze burned hot as it trailed over my body, my breasts, but he didn't touch me. He still hadn't removed his clothes, either, other than to free his cock. I wanted to rub up against him like a cat, nip and bite him, lick and suck him everywhere. I began rolling my hips, working his dick in and out of me, slow and sinuous, giving him a show.

The muscle in his jaw jumped, his chest rising and falling as I moved, grinding and gyrating, molding my tits with my hands. I presented him with a breast and he leaned forward to take the nipple into his mouth, sucking hard until I gasped. He released me and sat back again, watching me.

I started moving faster, and I soon felt another orgasm gathering at the base of my spine. I chased it, pulling him in deeper, and my lids drifted closed, my palms braced on his knees for leverage, as I rocked and rocked . . .

"Oh, God," I whispered. "Fuck."

I could hear his heavy breathing, feel the tremble of his thighs under me. Then the pleasure broke, my body convulsing as I came a second time. It was less intense than the first but went on longer, like a gentle wave. Fausto threw his head back and exhaled a few times, every muscle in his body growing taut just before I felt him expand inside of me. He groaned, his cock jerking as he clutched the sofa back, the tendons in his neck standing out in sharp relief.

Exhausted, I dropped onto his chest and tried to catch my breath, our bodies still connected. We stayed like that for a long minute, while he slowly stroked my spine with one hand. "That was fun," I said when he didn't speak.

He pressed a kiss to the top of my head. "I'm glad."

He was *glad?* The fuck?

Before I could ask him what that meant, he disentangled our bodies, tucked his glorious cock back into his suit pants, and pulled up his zipper. Naked, I watched as he rose and put himself back together, smoothing his shirtsleeves and fixing his cuff links. It was like watching a knight put on his armor, the protection he used against the rest of the world.

Did he want me to leave? Not that I wanted to hang around. I couldn't believe I'd fallen down this rabbit hole again. Though it was worth noting that two fantastic orgasms went a long way to dulling my disappointment over my lack of willpower.

Suddenly my yoga pants and t-shirt were in front of my face. "Thanks," I mumbled.

Slipping into my clothes, I realized we'd never come to a conclusion on the Paolo issue. "Will you let him live?"

Fausto strode behind his desk, sat down, and opened his laptop. "Is that what you'd prefer?"

"Yes," I said emphatically. "For God's sake, you can't have him killed. It would absolutely destroy Giulio. Send Paolo away, if you must, but do not hurt him."

"Then I will send him away."

He was acting weird. "Do you promise?"

"Te lo prometto."

Satisfied with his answer, I stood and stretched out my sore muscles. Who needed cardio with Fausto around? With his attention entirely on his laptop, he seemed to have forgotten about me. Wait, wasn't that what I wanted?

"See you around," I said on my way to the door.

"I don't know what time I will come to bed." He slipped on those reading glasses that increased his sexiness factor by a thousand degrees. "I have more work to do."

"Okay."

I stood at the door, confused. Then I felt the stickiness between my thighs and decided to go shower. So I slipped into the hallway and went upstairs. It was only when I stepped under the hot water that I realized something.

The entire time he'd been fucking me, he hadn't said a word. At all. Fausto was a talker and I loved his dirty mouth. But he'd been eerily quiet tonight.

He also hadn't kissed me on the lips.

Huh.

CHAPTER FOURTEEN

Francesca

A full bladder woke me in the middle of the night. After I used the toilet, I noticed that Fausto's side of the bed was perfectly neat. Was he still awake, or had he slept somewhere else?

I didn't care. I didn't need his warmth beside me to sleep. Or the tender way he wrapped around me in the mornings.

Besides, I was still annoyed at him. So what if he hadn't talked dirty or kissed me? Wait, that wasn't right. He had talked dirty at the start, right up until—

I sucked in a breath. That was it. He'd been his normal, controlling, filthy mouthed self right up until the moment he asked who I belonged to. When I didn't answer, that was when it all changed.

That *asshole*.

My chest burned as I stared at the bed. He had a lot of fucking nerve being upset with me—with me!—for not saying I belonged to him. What, did he think his magic cock just made all my anger and hurt disappear?

Filled with righteous fury, I grabbed my silk robe and stormed out of the bedroom. I checked the guest rooms in our wing, but they were all empty. Then I went down to his office, where I found the door open, the room unoccupied. Undeterred, I kept searching. I looked in the kitchen and the dining room. The sitting rooms. I checked the patio. No Fausto.

Hadn't he said there was a gym and an indoor pool?

The security rooms were on the east side of the castello, so I normally avoided that part. I went in that direction, opening a door I'd never been through before. A television show sounded from somewhere inside, so I followed the noise. A large room full of monitors sat on the right, with two of Fausto's men behind a desk, watching an Italian show on a laptop.

"Buona sera, signorina," one of the men said, rising. "Are you looking for Don Ravazzani?"

I pulled the robe tighter. "Yes. Do you know where he is?"

"The gym." He pointed in the direction I'd been going.

"Grazie."

I continued down the corridor until I found the gym. Sure enough, I saw Fausto through the tiny window in the door. He wore long shorts and no shirt, sweat rolling down his body as he ran on the treadmill.

I threw open the door. "You have some motherfucking nerve."

He didn't turn. "Why are you out of bed, Francesca?"

He wasn't even winded, which was mind-boggling, but I didn't have time to unpack that now. I moved directly into his line of sight. "You're pissed because I wouldn't say I belong to you."

His mouth tightened.

"Oh, my God! I don't believe it." I pointed at his face. "You do not get to be mad at me for anything until the end of time, you stronzo. What, did you think I would fall all over myself to declare my love for you the second you whipped your dick out? If so, you are completely fucking delusional."

He slapped the stop button on the treadmill and the belt began slowing. "Delusional? Is that what you call it when you undress for me? When you beg for my dick? You are the one who is delusional,

Francesca. We both know you belong to me. You will *always* belong to me."

"No, I don't. You lost your ownership rights the moment you kicked me and your unborn child out of the house! You said *I was dead to you*." Horrifyingly, my voice cracked on this last part. I took a deep breath. I would not cry in front of this man.

He put his palms together and bent his head, touching his fingertips to his lips. "I am sorry for ever saying that, for hurting you. But I took on the 'Ndrangheta brotherhood to get you back. Not to mention I risk going to war with every one of D'Agostino's allies to keep you, while the GDF is breathing down my neck. Everything I have is hanging in the balance, Francesca, but I don't care. I would fight to the death to keep you here."

I had no idea what he was talking about. "If you hadn't kicked me out, none of that would've even been necessary."

He threw up his hands, stepped off the treadmill, and began pacing. "I am aware, and I am drowning in fucking regret over it!"

Grabbing a small dumbbell, he hurled it against the mirror, which shattered in a million tiny pieces in an unholy crash. I covered my ears, ducking. One of the guards burst through the door, gun drawn, but Fausto held up his hand. They had a quick exchange and the guard left.

"What do you regret, Fausto? That you lost your little plaything? Or that I showed loyalty to your only son and heir, and you perceived that as some sort of slight against you?"

Fausto's chest heaved as he bowed his head. "I told you that I love you. I want every bit of you, like we had before. Yet you hold back. You want me to treat you like Katarzyna, then? Fine, I will treat you like Katarzyna."

"I don't fucking want you to treat me like Katarzyna. I want you to give me space so, I don't know, maybe I can wrap my head around what's happened to me over the last month. You are being incredibly selfish and butthurt for someone who's entirely in the wrong!"

"You come to me, begging me for a favor, wearing that red lingerie. And for what? You whore yourself out so easily? I don't want a whore. I want the woman who gives herself over to me, who surrenders to me so sweetly I could choke on it."

"If you call me a whore one more time, il Diavolo, I will stab you in your sleep. And fucking you on the sofa is surrendering. Did you need it in writing?"

"You let me have your body but that's all. Everything else is locked away and I am allowed to be pissed about it."

"Then be pissed at yourself. I'm giving you all I can right now, until I can trust you again. That is, *if* I can ever trust you again."

Growling, he put his fingers through his hair, tugging on the thick strands like he might rip them out of his head. "Tell me what I can say! *Mi dispiace, perdonami.* This is driving me crazy."

"There is nothing you can say. You claim to love me, yet you try to send me out of the room tonight, telling me it's a family matter that doesn't involve me. Am I your family, Fausto? Is our baby going to be your family? You need to fucking decide."

"You know that wasn't what I meant."

"Really? Do I? Because so far, you've broken every promise you ever made to me. So, forgive me if I don't believe a damn word that comes out of your mouth anymore."

He snarled, "I do not like being called a liar."

"I'm sure you don't, capo, but that doesn't change the fact that you are one."

Spinning on my heel, I stalked out of the gym and slammed the door behind me. Both of the security guards watched me pass, their mouths hanging open, eyes big and round. I kept going.

One thing I knew for certain, I was sleeping in my old room tonight. Fuck Fausto and his comfortable bed.

Fausto

The morning brought clarity to my problems with Francesca, much like the daylight that broke over my vineyards at dawn. As I drank my espresso and watched the workers arrive for la vendemmia, I thought about my family. For so long it had been Giulio, Zia, and me. Yes, there were cousins, but my son and my aunt were the two people who mattered most to me. I would gladly take a bullet for either of them at a moment's notice.

Now Francesca mattered to me, as well. Regardless of how it started, she and this child were part of my family. I'd waged a war to get her out of Enzo's clutches, and I would die before I let her go again.

It was past time to prove it to her.

But first things first. Picking up my phone, I texted my son that I expected him in my office in the next ten minutes. Marco arrived as I hit send. "Have a seat," I told him. "Emilia sent a text this morning and said she needs to talk as soon as possible." I'd asked her to quietly begin looking for money that might link one of my men to Enzo or the GDF.

"Is this about looking into everyone's accounts?"

"I fucking hope so. I want answers."

Marco settled into his favorite chair and crossed his legs. "I checked on our prisoner. Wounds are healing as they should. No sign of infection. He should be ready this afternoon for another session."

"Good. If Emilia can't find anything, perhaps we can get Enzo to talk."

Because Emilia didn't know our code system for phone conversations, I unlocked my desk drawer and took out a burner phone. Marco would dispose of it as soon as the call finished. Just as I started dialing, Giulio walked in. He looked healthy, freshly showered, not hungover in the least. Scowling at him, I pointed to a chair. "Sit and listen."

Emilia answered and told me to wait a moment. There was some scuffling, like she was walking somewhere, so I put her on speaker.

"Ciao," she whispered. "Can you hear me?"

"We can hear you. Are you free to talk?"

"Yes. I'm hiding in a storage closet."

"Have you found anything?"

Giulio's brow furrowed and he stared at the phone like it was a puzzle he was trying to solve. I felt like snarling that if he hadn't been stoned last night, he would know what was happening.

"Yes, but I don't yet know what it means."

My muscles tightened, a knot forming between my shoulder blades. "Tell me."

"Someone is stealing money from you."

I ground my molars together. This wasn't the first time someone had dared, but I didn't need another problem at the moment. "How much?"

"As far as I can tell, around thirty million Euros or so."

Marco hissed through his teeth and Giulio rocked back in his chair like he'd been struck. I tried not to react, other than curling my hand into a fist. It was a large amount of money, but it wouldn't come close to bankrupting me. What infuriated me was the principle. "Why am I just hearing about this now?" I snapped. "Where the fuck were your bosses on this, the head of the firm that I employ? This should have been caught."

"I don't know," she said. "I haven't told anyone. I can't imagine they are unaware of it, which means . . . ."

Which meant they were complicit.

Santo cazzo Madre di Cristo.

"Tell us what you know," I ordered.

"Small amounts are being siphoned off from the accounts in the Netherlands and deposited in various accounts in Haiti and Afghanistan."

Marco murmured, "Countries with relaxed laws on money laundering."

"Exactly," Emilia said. "I discovered this accidentally. I don't handle the Netherlands accounts for you, but I got a call from a friend at a bank in Denmark. He warned me that some of the transactions had been flagged for internal review. Then I started doing some digging."

"The GDF?" Marco asked, looking at me.

"They wouldn't steal it," I said. "They'd freeze the accounts."

"Agreed. This is someone very good with computers," Emilia said. "A hacker of some kind, one that knows exactly where to look to siphon off your money."

"Enzo," I gritted out. That motherfucker. I knew he was behind this. I could feel it in my bones.

Marco stroked his jaw, his leg bouncing in agitation. "That doesn't explain how he knew where to look. Which rocks to turn over. The accounts are complicated for a reason, Rav."

"Right," Emilia whispered. "This is someone who is very smart, with an inside knowledge of your accounts."

That was a very small list, one that didn't include either Benito or Vic. I wouldn't trust financial information to anyone outside of my small inner circle. Pretty much Toni and Marco were the only people who knew anything of use.

"I have to go," she said quickly, then the call was dropped. I tossed the burner onto the desk toward Marco and rubbed my face with my hands.

"Cristo," my son muttered.

"Exactly," Marco said. "This is some serious shit, Rav."

I did not have time for this. I wanted to talk with Francesca, make up with her, and spend the rest of the day fucking her into a stupor.

Instead I had to deal with Giulio, this missing money, Enzo, and a hundred other problems that came with my position. Exhaustion weighed down on me like a block of cement.

First things first.

I pointed at my son. "You are taking over security."

"Me?" Giulio glanced at Marco then back at me. "What about Zio Marco?"

"You'll work with him until you get up to speed, then relieve him."

"Why?"

I smothered the urge to sigh. I didn't like explaining myself, but he was my son. "Because it's time you took a larger role, more than just working with Gratteri. And it's too much for Marco to handle security alone with his duties as consigliere."

"I would like to see my family every now and again," Marco put in.

"But!" I pointed at my son. "No more excessive drinking, no more weed. No more sitting outside Paolo's house. From now on, you work with me and Marco on finding out how Enzo was able to get his hands on my woman as well as thirty million of my Euros."

"You suspect someone who works for us?"

"I suspect everyone," I said. "I want you to start with Benito, Vic, and some of the younger crew. Get close to them, see if you can get them to talk. In the meantime, we'll look at their families and expenditures. Anything that seems out of the ordinary."

"As well, we need to lean on Enzo," Marco said. "I suspect Mommo is involved somehow. Why else would he come and plead Enzo's case?"

Giulio's eyebrows climbed toward the ceiling. "Minchia! Anything else?"

"Yes, the GDF," I said dryly. "It's time you learn what being the don means. You'll sit in this chair one day."

His frown deepened. "I don't like to think about that."

"Not one of us escapes our destiny." I leaned forward and rested my forearms on the desk. He was going to like this news even less. "You should know that I've sent Paolo away."

His face lost all its color. "Did you . . . ?" He swallowed. "No, please. Please tell me you did not have him killed. I will do anything, just do not hurt him. I will not survive it."

"He is alive and unharmed, but he is no longer in Siderno." Paolo had boarded a flight for Belgium an hour ago. He would work for the 'ndrina there.

Giulio sucked in a sharp breath. "Where?"

"I'm not telling you." Giulio's eyes began to fill, his expression one of both profound relief and utter devastation. I added, "You have Francesca to thank for that. She begged me to send him away."

"You were going to have him killed."

I didn't answer. We both knew it was the truth. "I plan on inviting potential wives to dinner and you will consider one. But we'll wait until things calm down first."

"You're giving me time?"

"A little, yes. We have enough happening right now. This doesn't mean I have changed my mind about your need for marriage, however."

He sat forward and buried his face in his hands, saying nothing, and my stomach ached. I didn't like making Giulio miserable but what choice did I have? I wouldn't risk his life, his future, by letting him come out as openly gay.

"It won't be so terrible," I promised. "You'll forget about this boy and soon settle down with a nice girl who will give you babies."

Giulio's shoulders hunched. "Right. Not so terrible," he mumbled into his palms. "I can't wait. Is that all?"

"Yes. Go and see Zia, get an espresso."

He pushed out of the chair and moved slowly toward the door, his spine curved as if crushed under the weight of his unhappiness. It tore at my heart.

"Wait." I followed until we were face to face, except he stared at the wall. So I cupped his jaw and made him look at me. "I love you. You're a good son and you will make a great don one day." I kissed both his cheeks. "*Chi si volta, e chi si gira, sempre a casa va finire.*"

An old Italian proverb, it meant no matter where you go or where you turn, you will always end up at home.

"Especially true for me because there is no escape," he said before disappearing into the corridor.

When I didn't move, Marco said, "You have no choice, Rav, and the work will take his mind off the boy." Then Marco's mouth hitched, like when we were young and gave each other shit all the time. I knew what was coming. He said, "You let her talk you out of eliminating Paolo. That must have been some negotiation."

Yes, it had been. My eyes drifted to the couch. It felt amazing to fuck her again after so long, but she hadn't given me everything. I was a selfish man when it came to Francesca. I wanted her, body and soul.

And the only way to get it, apparently, was to give her everything in return.

CHAPTER FIFTEEN

Francesca

When I came downstairs for coffee, I was surprised to find Giulio already at the breakfast table. I assumed he'd still be asleep, considering last night.

"Buongiorno," I said, going to the espresso machine and finding my decaf supply. "How are you feeling?"

"Fine."

My espresso brewing, I turned to face him. "You were high as fuck last night."

"It wasn't a big deal. I smoked too much in the car." His gaze found mine and the sadness that lurked there gave me a moment's pause. What had happened?

He said quietly, "Thank you for convincing him to send Paolo away instead of . . ."

"Of course," I said immediately, my brows flying up in surprise. Fausto told Giulio about that? "I have your back, G. Always."

There wasn't anything else to say, no other kind words to ease his heart. So I focused on my espresso then took a seat next to him, waiting.

Finally, he rubbed his red-rimmed eyes. "I don't know if I can do this. I'm so tired of lying and pretending, of *hurting*. And it's only going to get worse. He's not even in the same city. He'll forget about me and I'm stuck here, marrying some woman I don't give a shit about."

The misery in his voice sounded more than theoretical. "Has Fausto chosen someone?"

"Not yet. He plans to bring the candidates here when things calm down."

How generous of Fausto. "I'll speak to him."

"I would say it's a waste of time, but you got him to change his mind about Paolo. You are the only one he listens to, apparently."

It hadn't been listening as much as letting him eat me out then fuck me. "I don't know about that, but he owes me after what's happened. I'll ask him to give you more time."

"Thank you, bella."

"It will get better, G. We'll figure something out. Drinking and getting high aren't going to help, though."

He slouched in his seat, not meeting my eye. "I know. Fausto wants me to take over security from Marco."

Wow. "That's huge. Are you going to do it?"

"You act as if I have a choice."

"You could tell him no."

He let out a dry, bitter chuckle. "That would go over well. I'm not you, Frankie."

"You have to be honest with him. You have to tell him what you want. Otherwise you'll grow resentful."

The edges of his mouth curled in a tiny smile as he sipped his espresso. "You are so wise, *matrigna*. No wonder Fausto knocked you up."

I rolled my eyes. "I think that had more to do with my boobs than my brain—and stop calling me that."

The sound of shoes clicking on tile grew louder, interrupting us, and Fausto soon strode into the kitchen. He wore a white dress shirt and navy trousers that hung loose on his trim waist, looking like a goddamn cover model for Hot Dad magazine. After a nod to Giulio and me, he went to the espresso machine. Normally, I loved to watch the graceful way he moved, but I averted my eyes and focused on the table. I was still pissed at him.

No one spoke as the machine whirred. I could still hear his angry voice ringing in my ears. *We both know you belong to me. You will* always *belong to me.* Wrong. He couldn't treat me like shit then think a few "dolcezzas" and "amores" would fix everything.

When he had his espresso, Fausto came over to the table. He bent and pressed a kiss to Giulio's head. "Have you eaten?"

Giulio shrugged, suddenly appearing like an angry youth. "Some."

Fausto's gaze flicked to me. "My office, Francesca. Now."

I blinked. Was he for real? Ordering me around after last night?

He stalked out, denying me the opportunity to tell him to go fuck himself. Then I remembered my promise to talk to Fausto about the potential brides for Giulio. Well, now was as good a time as any. He and I were already fighting. What was one more disagreement thrown onto the pile?

Grabbing a roll out of the basket, I stood. "I'll see you later, okay? We'll watch a movie this afternoon."

Giulio rose, as well. "I might be too busy. We'll see."

I kissed his cheeks, then carried my roll and coffee to Fausto's office. The door was open, so I slipped inside and closed it behind me. He was sitting behind his desk, glasses on, staring at his laptop. "Have a seat, Francesca."

I lowered myself into a chair, not speaking. Removing his glasses, he closed his laptop and picked up a piece of paper off the desk. "Read this."

I took it from his hand. "What is it?" A bunch of legalese was at the top, but the word "agreement" jumped out at me, as did our names. "Is this . . . ? Is this for you and me?"

"Yes. I was working on it before." He waved his hand. "I've had some alterations made since Napoli."

Since I was kidnapped, he meant. Still, this was what I had asked for—a legal agreement that offered security to me and my baby. I set down my roll and coffee to give the contract my full attention.

Thankfully, it was in English so I had no trouble following what Fausto was offering. It was a staggering amount of money to be set aside in a trust, plus stocks and even gold, but there were strings. I shook my head, frustration scalding the back of my neck. Was he looking for ways to piss me off? "So I collect only if I marry you? We aren't getting married, Fausto."

He slid a black ring box onto the desk.

My jaw fell open and my breath started coming sharp and fast, like my lungs were on fire. "What is that?"

"Open it."

"I don't want to open it." I was terrified of what was inside.

Reaching, he flipped the ring box open. Of course it was gorgeous. A huge emerald-cut diamond sat in a platinum band, smaller stones flanking the sides. Was I sweating? I felt like I was sweating.

"Do you like it?" he asked.

Was he serious? "It's . . . Wow, there are no words."

"Is that good or bad?"

"Good. It's stunning."

"Va bene. It belonged to my mother."

"So Lucia . . . ?"

He shook his head once. "She never wore this. She wanted a bigger stone."

Bigger than this? Wow, that was some Real Housewives-level shit. "I-I still can't accept it. I'm not ready to think about marriage."

"Unfortunately, you must. The Guardia will try to wear you down. They will threaten your sisters or our child. You will never be fully protected until you are my wife. It gives you security."

"And ties me to you for the rest of my life."

"True, but take solace in the fact that men in my position don't live very long."

"Jesus, Fausto." I rubbed my eyes and tried to ignore the way my stomach flopped at the idea of losing him. "That's grim."

"I'm a realist. Should something happen to me, say if I am sent to prison, then you would be protected and provided for. When I die, whether that's tomorrow or twenty years from now, you get a large portion with the rest going to Giulio. I'm giving you nearly everything, Francesca."

I didn't know what to say. I think my brain was in shock, stuck on what this would mean if I agreed. "This is quite the proposal."

His brows knitted and leaned back in his chair. "I decided on practical rather than romantic, after last night."

Fair enough. "You said you would never marry again. What changed your mind?"

"You."

"Because I asked for security in case things between us went up in flames?"

"That's not why I want to marry you. I need you in ways I can't begin to explain, and if this is what it takes to have you—all of you—then I will do it."

Everything was starting to make sense. "Ah, so instead of showing me you've changed and giving me time to trust you again, you are moving forward at warp speed and proposing marriage. Just so I will say I belong to you."

"You do belong to me. And if you agree to this"—he gestured to the paper in my hand—"then I belong to you, as well."

I stared at the wall and tried to think. This was all too much. Was he right about the Guardia? Would they try to use my sisters or my child against me? I knew without a doubt they would. Hell, Agent Rinaldo had already tried.

Is this what you want for your child? A lifetime of wondering when his or her father will be arrested? Blood and murder and drugs?

But marriage meant *forever*. It meant becoming Mrs. Fausto Ravazzani, staying in Siderno until one of us died.

No way.

Except realistically, what had I thought was going to happen? Fausto would never let his son or daughter go, and neither would I. Was I picturing some joint custody situation, where I lived in Siderno and our child spent every other weekend at the castello? That was ludicrous—and dangerous.

The safest place for our child was here, at the castello, protected by Fausto's men. Not to mention that I'd been kidnapped once already—

twice, if you counted Fausto in Toronto. I really couldn't handle a third time.

Fuck me. Was the best choice to say yes?

I stared at the paper in my hand, thinking it over. Yet the word would not come. I was still too mad and too hurt. He'd broken my heart, and I hadn't finished stitching the pieces back together.

Swallowing hard, I put the paper on the desk. "I need to think about this."

He dragged a hand over his mouth, probably to hold in a string of Italian curses. Finally, he said, "Okay."

"I'm sorry, but I can't decide on something this major in an instant. I need to think. I mean, I always pictured having my family at my wedding. My sisters . . ." I couldn't finish that thought without bursting into tears, so I just took a breath instead. "I appreciate this, I do, but I'm still trying to adjust to the idea of having a child, let alone the child of an Italian mafia king."

"King?" One dark eyebrow shot up arrogantly.

"This is not funny. I'm totally overwhelmed, Fausto."

"I am trying to help you, Francesca. Let me take care of you."

"If you want to help, give me some time." Head spinning, I stood up to go. I needed more coffee and food. This was too heavy of a conversation for an empty stomach.

"Wait," he said. I stopped but didn't look at him. Was he going to try to seduce me into giving an answer?

He pressed something into my free hand. "Here."

It was the ring box.

I tried to give it back. "Fausto—"

"Keep it." He curled my fingers around it and pressed a kiss to my forehead. "When you put it on I'll know your answer is yes."

God, this man. He understood me better than anyone. Saying the word, actually agreeing to something I knew was bad for me, would not come easily. I nodded and slipped the box into my pocket, where it sat heavily.

Just like my future.

―――

Over the next three days I dragged my tired ass to the vineyards to help with the harvest. It was nice to be outside, working in the dirt again. Emilia hadn't returned—she was doing something for Fausto at work—but I did convince Giulio to come with me once. He spent most of the time bitching about how the dirt and grapes would ruin his new custom sneakers.

I didn't mind the time alone. I had a very big decision hanging over my head, but the choice had basically been made the moment I decided to keep the baby.

Still, I couldn't put the ring on.

Fausto didn't push it. Nor did he try to have sex with me again. In fact, I was back in his bed, except he was never there. The only time I saw him was at dinner with Zia and Giulio. I hated to admit it, but I missed him. Yes, I'd asked for space but I hadn't expected him to really give it to me. Fausto liked getting his own way and he also liked to push my buttons. I wasn't used to this patient side of him.

You do belong to me. And if you agree to this then I belong to you, as well.

When I told Giulio about Fausto's proposal, I cried—and they weren't happy tears. Giulio's face had softened, his eyes understanding and kind. "I get this," he'd said, hugging me hard. "You've been through a lot. My father, he loves you. Marriage is inevitable, but sometimes the inevitable is a hard pill to swallow."

Exactly. God knew that Giulio understood my dilemma. If anyone could relate to having one's choices stripped away, it was him.

There were no answers, so I avoided the castello and stayed outside as much as possible. I clipped clusters of grapes, inhaled the salty Calabrian air, and pretended everything was okay.

The women around me began to whisper, tittering like schoolgirls, and I glanced up. Fausto was coming up the row, looking every inch the wealthy Italian businessman in a three-piece suit as he headed straight for me. My stomach fluttered. What did he want? Was he going to press me for an answer?

I'm not ready.

He nodded to the women, offering greetings and charming smiles, and thanking them for their hard work. I watched unabashedly, admiring the view. I figured I'd more than earned the right by putting up with his controlling ass.

When he reached me, he frowned. "Where is your hat?"

Really? I turned my attention back to the vines. "Hello, Fausto. Nice to see you, too."

Sighing, he took the small clippers from my hand. "Come with me."

"Is there a *please* in there somewhere?"

"Please," Fausto said, surprising me.

We gave my basket and shears to Vincenzo, then Fausto's hand wrapped around mine. The villagers stared as we passed, but the estate workers ignored us. I guess they were used to seeing Fausto drag me around.

When we reached the path to the castello, I yanked my hand out of his grip. That was enough touching for one day. My heart was already racing, his nearness conjuring wicked thoughts—like how much I wanted to pull him into the stables and peel that suit off his body.

"What's going on?" I asked. "Why did you come and get me?"

"I have a surprise for you."

My chest squeezed, excitement and nerves at war inside me. Instead of asking about the surprise, I blurted the question that had been on my mind. "Where have you been sleeping?"

He stopped abruptly and stared down at me, his brows raised. "You asked for time. I am giving you time."

"I didn't mean to kick you out of your room."

A familiar twist of his lips sent a bolt of heat through my veins. "I see," he said, shoving his hands into his trouser pockets. "You have been missing me."

"Only when I get cold."

"Liar."

I turned and started for the castello, my boots kicking up dust as I walked. He caught up easily. "Put on the ring and I'll come back to our bed."

Our bed. I shouldn't like the sound of that, but it made me feel all squishy inside. "We'll see. I'm still thinking about it," I lied.

He didn't say anything more. As we came up the small hill that led to the house, I noticed two figures sitting in chairs on the patio. They stood up as Fausto and I approached. Two girls, both in t-shirts and jean shorts. They were the same height and looked almost identical.

The air left my lungs and I stopped, frozen. No, it couldn't be. How . . . ?

Oh, my God.

"Oh, my God," I repeated, out loud this time. "Are those . . . ? You brought my *sisters* here?"

Fausto's hand swept down my back and settled on my hip. His mouth near my ear, he whispered, "Surprise, amore."

Tears flooded my eyes before I could stop them, emotion swamping me. My sisters were here. In Siderno. I couldn't believe it.

Without another word, I took off toward the patio. I sprinted, a huge smile on my face the whole time. Emma and Gia started forward, wearing matching grins, and we crashed together in an unholy mess of arms and tears. "Holy shit," I breathed. "I can't believe you're both here."

"Neither can we!" Emma said.

Gia added, "It was fucking wild, Frankie. One minute we're in class, and the next minute we're on a private plane to Italy."

I eased back to see their faces. "I can't believe Papà let you come."

"Your boyfriend has some serious pull," Gia said. "Whatever he said had everyone scrambling to do his bidding."

Not sure boyfriend was the right word, but I would have to ask Fausto about this later. Right now I needed to wrap my head around the fact that my sisters were here. I held onto their hands, unwilling to let them go in case they disappeared. "I'm so happy to see you both. You have no idea."

"Same," Gia said. "Plus I'm missing a calculus quiz and an English Lit paper."

"You'll have to make those up when you get back," Emma reminded her.

I heard footsteps on the gravel before I felt his presence at my back. He slipped a hand onto my hip and I suddenly craved the feel of his warm body next to mine. I shamelessly leaned into him, not caring if my sisters saw.

"Perhaps you'd care to show your sisters around the estate, dolcezza." He pressed a kiss to the crown of my head, his masculine scent filling my nose. "I will see you at dinner."

Releasing me, he strode toward the door that led inside, his broad shoulders stretching the fine fabric of his suit. My insides squeezed and I needed . . . I didn't know what I needed but I had all this emotion inside me, and my only thought was to stop him. When he opened the door and went inside, I held a finger up to my sisters. "One second. I'll be right back."

I darted through the door and into the cool house. Grabbing the tails of his suit coat, I pulled him to a stop. His brows lowered in confusion as he glanced over his shoulder at me, but I didn't speak. Instead, I pushed him toward the wall, uncaring of the guard that stood a few feet away.

Fausto's back hit the stone and he gave a soft grunt. I lunged for him, throwing myself at his chest and capturing his lips with mine, and he let me lead for a few seconds. Then he took over with a hand on my nape, holding me, while his tongue licked its way into my mouth. My toes curled inside my shoes. He devoured me, and if I'd ever doubted how much this man wanted me, this kiss obliterated it. The way his muscles trembled, the press of his fingertips into my skin . . . It was like he wanted to consume me.

And I'd never wanted so badly to be consumed.

Finally, he pulled back and pressed our foreheads together. "You like your surprise?" he said softly through heavy breaths.

"I do. Very much. Thank you, Fausto."

"I like to see you happy. " He eased me back then slapped my ass, hard. "Go, enjoy them. I will see you at dinner."

I gave him one last quick kiss and let him go, practically skipping as I went back outside. My sisters were sitting in the chairs and talking excitedly, finishing each other's sentences as they often did. I lowered myself in an empty chair, hoping I didn't appear like I'd been tongue-fucking Fausto a moment ago.

Gia smirked. "Your lips are swollen. You look like you've had a collagen treatment."

"You look beautiful," Emma said. "Being pregnant agrees with you."

"Only in the last week or so. Before that, I looked like shit. I do not recommend pregnancy, you guys."

"Noted," Gia said. "But the getting pregnant part must've been fun."

Yes, it had been. Too fun, in fact.

"You'll have a little baby soon," Emma said, her eyes growing soft. "Do you know what you're having yet?"

I shook my head. "No, and I don't want to know, either. There's too much at stake, and thinking about this baby's future is already doing my head in."

They both nodded. My sisters knew this world, knew what my child would endure, the kind of life ahead. Emma said, "Well, what names are you thinking about?"

"I haven't really thought about it. Choosing a name feels too . . . real."

Gia smirked, her voice dry. "Because the ultrasounds and vomiting didn't make it seem real?"

"Stop," Emma told her twin. "Let Frankie come to terms with it in her own time. I want to see the castello and the estate."

"Are you sure you aren't too tired from the trip?" I asked them.

"No way. I slept on the plane. I feel amazing," Gia said. "We should go clubbing tonight."

I knew Fausto would never allow that. "Slow down. How about we go harvest grapes instead?"

"Fun!" Emma said at the same time that Gia groaned.

Laughing, I stood up. "It is fun, actually. And you'll get to see the estate."

"Can we drink wine after?" Gia asked.

"Of course," I said. "Well, you two can drink wine. I'll keep you company."

"This is going to be the best trip!" Emma exclaimed as she rose.

"I know. I'm so glad you're here." I grabbed their hands and pulled them toward the path, happier than I'd ever been since arriving in this country.

CHAPTER SIXTEEN

Fausto

Francesca sparkled at dinner. Rarely had I seen her so animated, so happy, and I liked seeing her like this. As we ate, she entertained us all with tales of growing up, as well as her adventures so far in Italy—cleaned up, of course. Her sisters didn't know about the kidnapping, and I wondered if she would ever tell them what happened.

"The gelato in Rome was the best I've ever had," she was telling them.

"You certainly sampled enough of it," my son said with a grin, which caused Francesca to pick up a roll and fake throwing it at him.

Zia playfully reprimanded them both in Italian, which made everyone laugh.

I was quiet, observing. The dining room was lively and full, something I hadn't experienced in a long time. It was nice. If I had a big family like Marco's, every dinner would resemble chaos such as this.

My eyes flicked to Francesca, seated at my right. She would bear my child next spring, and I could hardly wait. I wanted as many children as she would agree to. An only child myself, I hadn't planned for Giulio to be alone, so I was thrilled at the prospect of more Ravazzani sons and daughters running around the castello. Hopefully I lived long enough—and stayed out of prison—to see it.

The Guardia had gone quiet after approaching Francesca. As we suspected, Rinaldo was no one, probably hoping to make a name for herself before retirement. This didn't mean the government wasn't working on a case against me, though. Except the case must not have been very strong if they were foolish enough to try to turn Francesca.

A bare foot slid over my shin and I tried to mask my surprise. My muscles clenched as I fought to stay still, not wanting to frighten her. If my dolcezza wanted to play, then I was more than ready.

Francesca leaned closer, her voice low. "Can I take my sisters to Rome? We could stay at your fuck pad."

"It could be your fuck pad, too, if you would put on the ring."

She bit her lip and slid her foot higher, teasing me with her toes. Sparks raced over my skin. "That doesn't answer my question," she said.

"Where is your foot going, piccolina?"

"Where would you like it to go?"

"My answer depends on if you are still angry with me or not."

She threw her head back and laughed, the sight causing my stomach to dip like a gull at the beach. Madonna, I loved her. I always wanted her this happy. I should have threatened her father weeks ago to get Emma and Gia on my plane. Instead, I had waited until yesterday. Lesson learned.

I shoved my leg closer to hers, desperate for more contact. Desperate for her to forgive me. While I understood the reasons for it, I hated that she didn't trust me. I would wear her down, though. It had already started, in fact. A few days ago she wouldn't have rubbed me with her toes and smiled at me. I had to be satisfied with whatever little progress I made each day.

Eventually I would have all of her.

"No trips to Rome," I told her. "Part of my agreement with your father was that the girls would stay here, nowhere else."

"Damn." She pushed a lock of her hair behind her ear. "How did you manage it? I can't believe he agreed."

I had plenty of material on Robert Mancini that he would much prefer to keep private. Not to mention I could cut off his income with a snap of my fingers. I think that threat scared him more than any public embarrassment over his drug and escort service habits. Tracing a fingertip over the fine bones in her wrist, I said, "I can be very persuasive. Or have you forgotten?"

Goosebumps traveled over her skin and I wanted to lick them, bite them. She whispered, "I prefer to call it bossy."

"A consequence of being the boss," I murmured, fascinated by the shape of her lips. I missed kissing her. The feel and taste of her mouth lingered all day after our kiss in the hall, the memory thickening my cock at the most inappropriate times today.

"They want to go clubbing tonight."

Fear and irritation tightened behind my shoulder blades. "Absolutely fucking not, Francesca."

"Calm down. I already told them no."

I relaxed slightly. I would need to watch these Mancini sisters, especially Gia. A troublemaker if I'd ever seen one. She had been eye-fucking every one of my guards under the age of thirty all day. I didn't want her upsetting Francesca.

"Papà," Giulio said. "Emma and Gia would like to see the nightlife in Siderno. I could take them."

"No." I wouldn't allow Francesca to go, and I didn't trust the sisters out at a club.

"Maybe tomorrow," Francesca told Giulio with a wink. "Let the girls have at least one good night's rest first."

I tensed, ready to argue, but then I felt her foot wrap around the back of my calf, and it stroked back and forth over my trousers. That simple contact mesmerized me, and I wondered if I could get her to move higher. My cock was so desperate for attention from her.

Her intention could not be more obvious, however.

"I know what you are doing," I said quietly. "It won't work."

"We'll see," she said with a teasing smile that caused my mouth to dry out.

Hmm. Perhaps she was right. I would agree to almost anything if she would get on her knees for me just one more time.

Soon.

If we were alone, I would pull her onto my lap and kiss her until she begged me to make her come.

"Too bad you didn't have your phone with you when you were vacationing in Naples," Gia said to Francesca. "I wanted to see pictures. Did you go to the catacombs or to Pompeii?"

An awkward silence descended. I didn't want to lie but Francesca obviously preferred to keep the kidnapping a secret from her sisters. The truth would only anger and frighten them. "We didn't get the chance," I said when no one spoke. "Allora. Next time."

Francesca gave the room a tight smile, one that did not reach her eyes. "Right. We hardly left the beach."

Marco entered and headed for me. He'd been waiting for Enzo to wake up. My cousin bent and said in my ear, "He says he's ready to sign it over to you."

Satisfaction rippled through me. This was what I'd been waiting for before killing him. Enzo's entire empire was about to be mine. "I'm coming."

Marco nodded to the table on his way out the door. I rose and placed my napkin beside my plate. Leaning over, I kissed Francesca's cheek. "I must go."

"But you haven't had dessert yet," she said, clutching my tie.

I held her jaw in my hand and caressed her soft skin for a brief moment. "You have it. I will see you tomorrow."

Straightening, I caught Giulio's eye and lifted my chin. He stood and excused himself to Zia and the sisters, then followed me from the room.

The two of us moved silently through the old house. "Why can't I take the girls to a club?" he asked. "You don't think I can keep them safe?"

He had pride like mine, so I had to tread lightly. "Of course I do, but I promised Mancini his daughters wouldn't leave the estate."

"Ah. Well, tell me next time. You made me look foolish in front of everyone."

The old instincts reared up, but I beat them down. He was right, as much as I didn't like explaining myself to anyone. "I'm sorry. I will try to keep you better informed."

My son drew to a halt and I did the same. He was studying me oddly. "What?" I asked.

"I can't believe I got an apology out of you. She is really having some effect on you, il Diavolo."

"Watch your mouth," I growled, then set off for the dungeon again. "I'm still your father."

He came up alongside me. "Has she answered you yet?"

"She told you I asked her to marry me?"

"Yes."

"What did she say?"

"You know I can't tell you. It wouldn't be right."

Irritation tightened in my gut. I didn't like that he was so willing to take her side over mine, as she'd done when she kept his secret from me. But I needed to come to terms with it. The two of them were close, part of my family, and I reminded myself to be grateful that they had each other. Loyalty to family was important, even if it didn't include me.

He continued, "If it helps ease your mind, I did call her la bella matrigna."

That drew a laugh out of me. "I bet she hated that."

"Give her time, Papà. She's put up with a lot over the last few months."

"I know. And I am. Even though it is fucking killing me."

"It'll be worth it in the end." He clapped my shoulder. "At least one of us will be happily married, no?"

"Giulio—"

He held up his hands as if to stop me. "Please do not tell me marriage won't be so bad again. I have been in love, and I have also seen you and Frankie. I know what true happiness looks like. What I will have is so far from that it's a joke."

He walked ahead of me as we passed through the dungeon door, and I pushed my son's suffering out of my mind for now. I had Enzo's to concentrate on instead.

Francesca

"Wait a minute," Gia said, shaking her head as if clearing it. "You were kidnapped at gunpoint, held for a week in Naples, before Fausto busted in like some action hero and saved you?"

"Yes," I said. "That is about right."

"The fuck, Frankie?" she snapped. "Why didn't you tell us?"

We were in my old room, which is where Emma was sleeping, with Gia just on the other side of the hall. I decided, after the comment about Naples during dinner, to tell them the truth about Enzo and the kidnapping. "I didn't want you to worry."

"Why did this other mafia don kidnap you?" Emma asked, always the practical, level-headed one.

"He was trying to blackmail Fausto. I'm not sure over what, but it sounded like a slice of the drug trade."

"Fausto deals drugs?"

This could not be a surprise to either of my sisters. "He imports them, other people deal them. Like our father."

"Are you shitting me?" Gia asked. "I thought Papà just ran casinos and bank heists."

"And drugs," I added. "He lost some product and owed Fausto a lot of money, which was why Papà traded me in the first place."

"Did this other mafia don hurt you?" Emma asked.

"He scared the shit out of me. Does that count?"

"I love that Fausto came and rescued you," my sweet sister said. "That must have been exciting."

More like terrifying. Men shot right before my eyes, Enzo holding a gun to my head. Sure. Good times.

"So they killed the other don, the one that kidnapped you," Gia said.

"Actually, no. He's in Fausto's dungeon as we speak."

Both of their jaws dropped open. "Fausto has a dungeon," Gia said. "Oh, my God. You have to take me down there!"

Emma shoved Gia's leg with her foot. "You know she doesn't like basements and cellars. Besides, you don't need to go down there and see a bunch of poor men being tortured."

"As far as I know, it's just Enzo down there—and don't feel bad for him. He locked me in a trunk and put a fucking gun in my mouth. He called me a slut. He's a terrible person."

"I can't help it," Emma said. "I don't like the thought of some helpless soul suffering down there while I'm up here drinking wine and eating tiramisu."

"Then don't think about it," Gia and I said at the same time.

Emma looked at me, a frown pulling the edges of her mouth. "Our father never brought his work home like this. How can you stand it?"

"Things are different in Italy," I told them. "We were sheltered from a lot of what went on in Toronto, even though we were raised in the life. But the men are more violent, more misogynistic here. So, keep your heads down. Don't cause trouble. Okay?"

"Okay," Emma said.

"I'll try," Gia said at the same time.

"I'm serious." I pointed at Gia. "Leave Fausto's men alone. Trust me, you do not want to get mixed up with one of them."

"You make them sound so awful." Emma gestured to my stomach. "But you're having a baby with one. They can't be all bad."

"God, you are such a bleeding heart," Gia told her twin. "You'd better hope your husband isn't in the life. He'll eat you alive."

Emma lifted a shoulder. "It's not my fault that I think everyone deserves compassion and understanding. Look at Frankie. She's forgiven Fausto after all he's done to her."

"Whoa," I said, holding up my hand. "I haven't forgiven Fausto."

Gia chuckled. "Sure, right. That's why you two were whispering and touching all through dinner, because you're still mad at him."

"Exactly, and I saw the way you looked at each other," Emma added. "He's in love with you."

"Maybe, but I can't trust him. How do I know he won't hurt me again?"

"You don't. You never will. Trust isn't something you can show or buy. It's in here." Emma pointed to her chest, then pointed to her head. "And here."

"He asked me to marry him," I murmured.

My sisters both squealed and clapped their hands. "Where is the ring?" Gia said, sitting up on her knees. "I need to see the rock."

I went to the jewelry box, which hadn't yet been moved to Fausto's room. I took out the ring box and pulled the platinum and diamond ring from the fabric. "It belonged to his mother," I said and handed it to Gia.

"Oh, Frankie," Emma said with a sigh, hand on her heart. "It's beautiful—and sentimental."

"The diamond could be bigger." Gia slipped the band on her finger. "It looks good on me, though."

"Give me that back," I said, taking my ring off Gia's finger. "The diamond is the perfect size. I'm not a Kardashian, for fuck's sake."

"Why aren't you wearing it?" Emma asked.

"Because." I flopped onto the bed. "I haven't decided my answer yet."

"You're having his child. You need to marry him," Emma said. "Even if just for the baby's sake."

"So romantic," I drawled.

"Do you love him?" Gia narrowed her keen gaze on me. "Like, really love him?"

Did I want to answer that? I stared at the ceiling and thought about it. How could I love a man who had hurt me so terribly? What was wrong with me that I still craved his touch and his dominance?

I couldn't begin to explain it. All I knew was that I did.

I nibbled on my lip. "Yes, I do."

"Then get your shit together and marry him," Gia said. "For yourself and your kid."

"Easy for you to say. Marriage means *forever*. I never expected to stay here forever."

"It means forever for him, too," Emma added.

Gia's phone dinged. She unlocked it and began texting someone. "I get it, but if you can't bring yourself to walk away, then let him put a ring on it and reap the benefits."

Hmm. Maybe they were right. I had a lot to gain from a marriage with Fausto. Money, status, protection . . . him. *You do belong to me. And if you agree to this then I belong to you, as well.* I wanted to belong to him so badly, I just didn't want to get hurt again.

Last night in the gym, Fausto's anguish and regret had been real. If Giulio and Zia were to be believed, Fausto suffered the entire time I'd been at the beach house, not to mention after I'd been kidnapped.

"You are the worst at making decisions," Gia said as she studied my face. "Life is too short, Frankie."

"You are terrible at making decisions," Emma added. "Which is why Gia and I always picked where to go out to eat in Toronto. You like when someone else decides."

Did I? Was that why I was drawn to Fausto's bossiness?

This time he was letting me decide, though. It must've been killing him. He wasn't a man used to waiting. Instead he made quick decisions and lived with the consequences.

Even when he got it wrong.

I stared at the ring. I wanted him and I loved him. He loved me, too. The contract would protect me and the baby, should anything go wrong. There was nothing to stop me from taking what I needed, even if we split. The money was mine.

I am giving you everything.

I think I was finally ready to accept it.

Looking at my hand, I slipped the ring onto my finger. I loved the way it looked. Even better was the way it felt—like ownership. Fausto's ownership.

Yes, I was fucked up. But he was, too.

"It looks good on you, Frankie," Emma said, nudging my thigh with her foot. "And I can tell you like it. Your face is beet red."

Was it? I pushed my hair out of my face. "I have to go. I'll see you both in the morning. Zia makes the most amazing pastries. You're going to love them." I kissed each of their cheeks. "Get some sleep."

"Wait, don't go yet," Gia said. "I want to talk more about this dungeon. Is it, like, a real dungeon with cells and chains? Or is it more like this?" She held up her phone and showed me a photo of a sex dungeon.

"Cute, Gia. And it's a real dungeon, with cells and rats and probably ghosts. I don't know why you're so interested in it."

"Frankie, you have to take me down there. I have to see it."

"We already covered this. No fucking way," I said.

"Why not?" Gia said, obviously irritated.

"There's no chance I'm going down there again."

"You don't have to go. Just take me there and tell me where to go."

"Gia," Emma said, "it's a dungeon. They kill people down there. It's not for fun."

"I *know*." The elder twin rolled her eyes. "Why do you think I want to see it? When else am I ever going to get another chance to see a real live dungeon? Please."

"Forget it," I said. "The man who is down there right now kidnapped me, kept me prisoner, and tried to hurt Fausto and his family. If he's still alive, he's in very bad shape."

"I'll be quick. One peek!" Gia begged.

Annoyed, I put my hands on my hips. Why was she being so difficult? "Don't make me regret the fact that you're here. It's been too long and I wasn't sure I'd ever even see you again."

Gia's expression instantly sobered. "I'm sorry. Of course you're right. I'm being a brat. Forget I even asked."

"Okay, good." At least I didn't have to argue anymore. "I'm going to find Fausto. If you need anything, see if you can find Giulio or Zia. I'll catch up with you both tomorrow."

"Have fun getting laid," Gia sing-songed as I walked out, and I shook my head. I'd forgotten what a pain in the ass she could be.

I went straight downstairs to the security room. Three guards were behind the desk, intently watching the screens. "Ciao," I said. "Can one of you tell Don Ravazzani that I need to see him upstairs. It's very important."

"Sì, Signorina Mancini." One of the guards picked up his cell and began texting.

"Grazie," I called and darted through the castello until I was in Fausto's wing. When I entered his bedroom, I immediately took off all my clothes and put on my silk robe. Then I wasn't sure what to do with myself. Nerves bubbled in my stomach, but there was no going back. The decision had been made.

I sat on the bed and waited. I was ready to face my fiancé.

CHAPTER SEVENTEEN

Fausto

Enzo was much stupider than I anticipated.

Despite what he told Marco, Enzo refused to sign over his business to me. It made no sense. He was weak, had suffered broken bones and internal bleeding. The air wheezed out of his lungs like a whistle. How he was still holding out through all he'd endured was a fucking miracle.

But I was tired of this. I had a woman to win over, and spending my nights in the dungeon with Enzo was not aiding me in that endeavor. I planned to get his cooperation tonight, no matter what.

He needed to die.

Marco had Enzo strung up in the cell, chains holding him to the ceiling. His toes barely reached the stone floor and his shoulder had dislocated hours ago. I pressed on the shoulder joint and Enzo shuddered, a whimper escaping his lips. "Are you going to sign?" I asked, pressing again. "Though I suppose you'll have to use your other hand to write."

He panted, his head hanging forward on his neck. No answer.

"Why are you doing this to yourself, Enzo? The pain will go away the instant you sign. That will be nice, for the pain to go away, no?"

There was no answer.

I sighed. "Should we squeeze your balls until they pop? It's excruciatingly painful I'm told and you won't live long after. Is that what you want?" I dug my fingers into his shoulder and he howled. "Sign the fucking papers, Enzo."

"Rav," Marco said, hanging up his phone. "You're needed upstairs."

I tensed. "What is it?"

"Francesca came to the guard room and asked for you. Said she needs to see you."

I didn't hesitate. She would not interrupt unless it was important. To Marco, I said, "Leave him hanging all night. Maybe that will make him more cooperative in the morning."

Marco nodded, and I headed up the stairs and out into the night. Why would Francesca need me? Was it something to do with the baby? My heart pounded as I entered the dark kitchen, fear propelling me forward. I assumed she was upstairs. Would I need to call David to come examine her? He didn't know anything about babies. If necessary, we would find her obstetrician, no matter the hour. Francesca and the baby were more important than anything else.

By the time I reached my bedroom, I was in a near panic.

Then I saw her.

Wearing her robe, she sat on our bed, her blond hair loose in waves around her face. I closed the door. "What's wrong? Are you ill?"

Her bottom lip disappeared between her teeth. "You have blood on your shirt."

I glanced down. My white dress shirt had a thick swipe of Enzo's blood across it, probably from where I leaned against him. I grimaced. "Perdonami," I said and began removing my cufflinks. I'd change into another shirt, so as to not offend her.

"No, leave it."

The breathless tone of her voice stilled my fingers. Her chest rose and fell swiftly, and the points of her nipples were evident against the thin silk covering her. Ah, I understood. The air in the room changed, and my skin crackled like I was in the midst of a thunderstorm. "You like seeing the evidence of my work?"

"I shouldn't," she whispered.

That didn't answer my question, but I let it go. "Why am I here, Francesca?"

Slowly, she lifted her left hand and I saw it. My mother's ring. Madonna, that sight.

Mine.

Satisfaction and possession twisted through me, a darkness that had me yearning to pin her down on the floor and fuck her until she screamed. My cock began filling, lengthening in pulses that matched my heartbeat.

I didn't bother to hide my thoughts as I slowly raked her from head to toe. "Do you know what this means?"

"Yes."

"Then say it."

She drew in a breath and let it out. "I belong to you."

The words sank into my muscles, tightening them in preparation of having her at my mercy. Her pussy was mine for the rest of our lives. "That's right. You do. And you will do whatever I say while we are in this bedroom, no?"

A slight hesitation and then she nodded.

That hesitation bothered me. Was she still angry? Or unsure about marrying me? I wanted to prove that she was ready to fully give herself to me. That she was ready to begin our games. "Stand up. Take off your robe."

With a graceful twist of her legs, she put her toes on the ground and pushed off the bed. Her fingers loosened the belt and the silk fell from her shoulders to pool at her feet. I had seen her naked in my office a few nights ago, but I was still dazed by her beauty. Madre di Dio, I would never tire of this woman. Creamy skin and ripe tits, long legs and a tight, hot cunt . . . There was no one who could ever compare.

I ran my tongue behind my teeth, the beast inside me howling to be let out. Instead, I tried to keep my tone cool and even. "You are gorgeous, amore. A vision. I've missed you so fucking much." She smiled, victorious, and took a step toward me. I held up my hand. "But I think you need a reminder of who owns you. Come here." I pointed to my feet.

When she tried to take another step, I said, "No, Francesca. Crawl to me."

Her smile faded, but her eyes remained dark with lust. Her hands fisted at her sides and I could see her rolling this command over in her mind. Five weeks ago she wouldn't have hesitated and I needed that acceptance again. Otherwise I would wait until I had it, until she was ready to submit to me. Nothing less would do.

Several seconds went by. Just when I thought she would refuse, just when I thought I would need to give her more time, she did what I'd been dreaming of for five long goddamned weeks.

She gave me everything.

Carefully, she dropped to her hands and knees, then began crawling toward me.

Her hair swung forward to frame her face but her eyes remained on me the entire time. Anticipation buzzed under my skin, my balls growing heavy, while I dug deep for patience and waited. The ring glinted on her finger as she moved, and I loved seeing the sign of my ownership on her. I would rip apart any man who dared to touch her, destroy anyone who caused her a moment's pain.

When she reached my feet, she sat back and looked up at me. Waited.

A smile curved my lips as I stroked the top of her head. "Ti amo, dolcezza. What a good girl you are." I reached for my belt, flicked it open, then unfastened my trousers. She didn't move, but her lips parted with the force of her breaths, and my freed erection bounced between us, the head aimed directly at her mouth. "You know what I want, no?"

She licked her lips and nodded, her attention never leaving my cock.

"Then begin," I told her, not moving to help.

Clasping her hands behind her back, she shuffled forward on her knees, edging closer, a little huff of frustration escaping her lips as she adjusted. Then the tip of her tongue emerged and dug into my slit, lapping at the drop of moisture there, and I hissed. Cristo, my greedy girl.

She licked the swollen head, her tongue flicking the underside, and a streak of pleasure raced down my legs. I locked my knees together to keep still as she pressed kisses down along the shaft reverently, like she had missed it. I hoped that was true because my cock definitely had missed her mouth—and her throat. It was time to reacquaint myself with both.

"Open," I growled. "Take me deep."

She twisted to get in better position, chasing my dick with her mouth. I liked to see her struggle to suck me without the use of her hands. With her hands behind her back, she angled her body, which thrust her tits out, their weight bobbing as she shifted. I didn't help her, either. I got off on degrading her, and Francesca got off on being degraded. It was why we worked so well together. I bet her pussy was dripping right now.

She finally got the head in her mouth and the tight heat made me grunt with satisfaction. "More," I barked.

Her jaw widened and she pressed forward, letting me slide along her tongue. When I hit the top of her throat, she paused. My fingers itched to take the back of her head and shove my way inside, but I let her do this. She knew what I wanted, and I needed to see how far she would go to give it to me.

She widened her thighs, changing the angle, and relaxed her throat muscles enough for me to slip in. "That's it," I crooned. "I will let you breathe in a moment. Eyes on me, baby."

Her wide, almost panicked gaze met mine and I saw the fear and determination. It made my dick pulse, and I gave a short thrust of my hips to tunnel deeper. We worked together for a few seconds until I was fully inside, exactly where I wanted to stay. "Relax," I instructed. "Don't pull off."

Tears gathered and spilled over her lashes, the most beautiful sight I'd ever seen. My cock filled her mouth and throat, her lips pressed to the patch of hair at the base. "Swallow, Francesca." Her throat muscles worked, squeezing me, and I gasped. "Va bene," I said, pulling back so she could take in air. After a few seconds, I lifted a brow in question, asking silently if she was ready, and she nodded once.

This time I didn't wait, unable to keep from grasping her head and ramming my cock in her throat. When I was as deep as I could go, I held there, loving the way she looked on her knees, suffering to make me happy. I could feel the orgasm building, my balls growing tight and heavy, the need to empty my seed in her mouth. She must have seen it on my face because she swallowed twice, then again, trying to force my come from my body, and the idea of it was so hot that I began roughly fucking her mouth. Every third or fourth stroke went in her throat, and I was like a man possessed. It was so much better than I remembered, her sweet tongue rubbing the underside while her lips pulled to give me suction. Like she couldn't wait to drink me down.

That wasn't what I wanted right now, though.

"I am going to shoot all over your face," I panted. "All over your tits."

She moaned in her throat as if she liked the idea, and the sound vibrated along my shaft. The thin threads of my self-control snapped and my balls sizzled with the impending orgasm. Pulling out of her mouth, I fisted my cock as thick jets erupted in pulses, and I coated her mouth and chin, then the creamy mounds of her breasts. She sat patiently, taking it, letting me paint her with my release, and I snarled in satisfaction, wishing I could drown her in my come.

When I finished it dripped off her chin and onto the floor, running down the mounds of her tits. "Cazzo," I said, slumping against the door. "I wish I could keep you like this. Just like this, my wicked girl. At my feet, covered in my come."

Grinning, she licked her lips, tasting the thick mess. "Yum."

With a snarl, I lifted her to her feet and slammed my mouth against hers. I couldn't wait to clean her up first. Instead, I smeared the fluid into her tits as I kissed her, the salty flavor on her lips only reminding me of how fucking hot she'd looked on the floor a moment ago. *Mine*. My lover, my toy. My entire life.

Holding her jaw in both hands, I broke off and pressed my forehead to hers. "You alone have the power to destroy me. I am nothing without you, absolutely nothing. And I will never, ever let you go."

Her hands wrapped around my wrists. "Good, because you've ruined me, il Diavolo. Absolutely ruined me, so there's no getting rid of me now. Which means you and I are going to rule the motherfucking world together."

Francesca

Fausto stepped back, and his eyes flashed with satisfaction as they raked my naked body, now coated in his come. He pushed his trousers off his hips, then toed out of his shoes. "Do you want to clean up before I fuck you, dirty girl?"

"No, paparino."

I didn't. I liked the sticky, sweaty mess of the two of us together, and I knew he got off on it, too.

"Dio, you are gorgeous," he rasped as he pinched one of my nipples. "I want to mark you and bite you, make sure everyone knows you are mine."

I held up the large ring on my finger. "More yours than this?"

His lip curled in a look so fierce, so dominating that my knees trembled. "I will always want to spank you, monella. Can you handle me rough tonight?" He began unbuttoning his shirt.

My thighs clenched as more heat flooded my veins. He'd spanked me before and I loved it. The slaps made my skin feel alive, incredibly sensitive. I was definitely down for it, especially if he fucked me afterward. "I love it when you're rough."

He slapped my butt once. "Get on the bed. Bend over, with your ass in the air."

I scrambled to obey.

I heard him chuckle behind me. "So eager. I love that most about you."

When I was in position at the edge of the bed, he came up behind me, now wearing only black boxer briefs. He growled and squeezed one of my butt cheeks. "I'm going to spank you, hard. Then I'm going to fuck you. Hard. Would you like that?"

I squirmed, barely able to contain my excitement as adrenaline spiked in my system. "Yes."

"Good. Allora, I will give you the choice. Would you like my hand or my belt across your ass?"

Oh, Jesus. I closed my eyes, a shiver running through me. Either? Both? "Should you be using a belt on a pregnant woman?"

"I asked your doctor that day at your appointment. She said it was fine as long as I didn't strike your belly."

I remembered him speaking Italian to Dr. Russo that day. He'd been asking about *spankings*? My God, how mortifying.

Still, the idea intrigued me. The belt had come up that first time we'd fucked, and I remembered the way he'd caressed the leather in his long fingers. Could I take it? "Belt."

"Perfetto. Put your feet flat on the floor."

I shifted into position and he walked to his discarded trousers and picked them up. With a flourish, he pulled the leather from the belt loops, and the swooshing sound caused an echoing throb between my legs. Why was that so hot?

He returned, standing slightly to the side. "I think *dieci*. You will count." Smoothing a hand along the small of my back, he asked, "Ready?"

I nodded—and pain exploded across my bare ass. "Holy shit!" I tried to move away, kicking my legs. The skin stung, like I'd been attacked by bees back there.

The pain eased and the area turned warm, tingly. Hyper sensitive. I sucked in a breath.

"Count, or you will receive more than ten."

I wasn't certain I could endure even ten. "One," I said, quickly.

"In Italiano," he snapped, fire cracking across my skin with another strike. "Now, Francesca."

"*Due*," I gritted out, my fingers digging into the soft duvet.

Three, four, and five happened in rapid succession, every slap in a different place along my ass and upper thighs. I shouted each number, my brain struggling to keep up. My lungs labored to drag in enough air, and I wasn't certain about this. At all.

Then he paused and brushed gentle fingertips over the skin . . . and I sighed. The pain sparkled bright, my ass all sensation, and the light touch echoed in my clit. Fuck, that was nice. Painful, but nice.

"Va bene," he crooned, arousal evident in his voice. "You are halfway, amore. So close to your reward."

"Please," I said on a long whine. I needed him to fuck me, right now. "Ti prego."

"Oh, how I love to hear you beg. My dick is already hard for you again."

My pussy contracted around the emptiness, and I could feel the wetness drip onto my inner thighs. "Ti prego," I repeated. A blunt finger shoved inside me, stretching me, and my back bowed. God, yes. "More."

He pumped lazily a few times, not nearly enough to give me what I needed. I tried to push back, urging him on, but he pulled away. "Soon. Very soon."

The next crack of the belt across my skin stole my breath. It hurt worse than the first five combined. "Fuck! Shit! *Sei!*"

"That dirty mouth. Again, Francesca."

Another strike, this time across the tops of my thighs. I panted, sweat breaking out all over my body. I couldn't do this. "*Sette,*" I whimpered.

"Three more," he said. "I will make them fast."

"Wait, please—"

The belt rained down three times in quick succession and I howled. Then the leather hit the floor and Fausto's mouth was between my legs, eating at me like a man possessed. He tongued my slit, shoved the tip into my entrance, then flicked my clit. His hands held onto my ass, separating my cheeks, and that slight bit of pressure on my sore skin felt delicious, the flesh throbbing and alive. Like he'd brought it to life.

It went on and on, his mouth torturing me in the very best way. He licked everywhere, even the ring of muscle between my cheeks. When my legs began shaking he circled my clit with the flat of his tongue, and the orgasm slammed into me, fiercer than I expected, and I shouted as my body convulsed. *Holy fuck.* It went on and on, his tongue dragging out the sensations until I sagged onto the bed. My brain floated, every muscle gone liquid.

He stood and then I felt the tip of him, hard and blunt, at my entrance. His cock shoved inside, the wetness easing his way, though it was still a stretch. It took him a few thrusts to get all the way inside, and I sighed at the fullness, the sweet invasion of his body into mine. "Oh, God," I gasped. "You feel so good."

Draping over me, he kissed my spine and began speaking a string of Italian my blissed-out brain couldn't comprehend. But I did understand, "*Mi fai impazzire*," something he'd told me before.

"You make me crazy, too," I said dreamily, reaching behind to grab his ass.

Straightening, he took my arms and folded them behind my back. His grip was punishing as he held onto me, but I didn't notice. I felt light and airy, my body pliant and filled with sensation. He began fucking me then, punches of his hips that rattled my teeth as he jerked me onto his cock again and again. Then his thumb slid between my ass cheeks and began toying with my hole. I couldn't even complain because everything he was doing felt so fucking good.

"I think I must reacquaint myself with all your holes," he said as the digit dove inside. "Would you like that? Your paparino's cock in your ass again?"

My tongue was thick and awkward, desire making me stupid. I could only nod, craving everything filthy he would give me. There was no reason to pretend I didn't want it when we both knew I did.

This man was going to be my husband. Holy shit.

He hissed through his teeth when my body clamped down on him. "*Cazzo.* Yes, squeeze my dick again."

I did it once more and he groaned. "You are trying to make me come, no? Because it is working."

When I did it a third time he smacked my butt cheek and pulled out. Limp, I couldn't do more than roll my head to watch him reach into the drawer beside the bed and retrieve a bottle of lube. He popped the cap and poured a generous amount in his hand before jacking himself, coating his cock and making it slippery. I watched the muscles of his forearm shift as he worked, and whoa, that was hot. I made a mental note to request a video of him masturbating soon.

Moving behind me, he drizzled liquid down my crack and massaged it into my hole. "I want you to ride me. I want to see your face when I claim your ass again."

Fausto got into position on the bed, flat on his back, then lifted me over him until I straddled his hips. Bringing me toward his face, he kissed me hard, his tongue invading my mouth and letting me taste his desperation. The tips of his fingers probed the tight ring of muscle, smoothing, massaging, opening me. Eager, I rolled my hips, dragging my mound over his shaft.

"So needy," he murmured against my mouth when I whimpered. "Don't worry, little girl. I am going to fill you up."

His fingers slipped inside, but there was only pressure. It was as if the pain receptors in my body were on vacation at the moment, and the pleasure center of my brain was firmly in charge. He pumped his hand slowly, widening me, while his mouth remained demanding. I took it gladly, letting him use me. I would always be his puttanella, even with a ring on my finger.

He broke off and grabbed my hips. "Up, piccolina. Take me inside."

I braced one hand on his stomach, then reached with the other to take his thick cock, lining him up at my back entrance. His warm skin was slick and hard, and I began pushing down, hissing when the head slipped in. He threw his head back, his expression nearly feral in its intensity, and I loved watching this powerful man come undone by my body. By our connection. I dropped down a little more, gave myself time to adjust, then continued, working steadily, with Fausto's big chest heaving the entire time. His fingertips sank into my skin, pressing on my hip bones and I knew I would have bruises there tomorrow.

The thought sent a punch of arousal through my middle and I lowered my hips all the way down, meeting his pelvis. God, it felt so good, my sore ass rubbing against his rough skin. The width of him split me open and I panted, loving the way he overwhelmed me. Loving him, period. "Baby," I whispered, hoping he understood.

He knew. Of course he did. No one could read me better than Fausto.

He cupped my breasts with both hands, pinching my nipples. "Tell me, gorgeous girl. Ride me and tell me. Don't hold anything back from me."

I began moving then, churning my hips slowly, dragging his shaft in and out of my ass, all the while watching his face. His eyes burned hot as they raked over my body, possession stamped on his features, and I let the words fall out. "Ti amo, bello."

His reaction was instant. Snatching me in his big hands, he leaned up and brought me to him for a blistering kiss. Then he braced his feet on the mattress and began pounding into me, his body thrusting upward in short jabs that bounced my tits up and down. His hands kept my hips steady, our bodies straining and working together. Whatever spot he was hitting deep inside me sent sparks down my legs, along my spine, sending me higher and higher.

When I started trembling, he said, "Your clit, dolcezza. Play with it and make yourself come. Right now."

I didn't question him. My hand flew between my legs and I rubbed my swollen flesh, desperate for release. The rush was instant, a wave of color and light that exploded behind my eyes. My muscles contracted around him, clamping down, and I heard Fausto grunt as his movements became uncoordinated. Then he held me still, his back arching, as his cock pulsed in my ass, hot jets filling me. God, he was sexy as fuck.

And he was mine.

"Madre di Dio," he panted. "I hadn't expected you to say that." He pulled me down to lay on top of him and wrapped his arms around me, his cock still buried in my backside. He kissed the top of my head. "I do not deserve you, amore."

I stared at the glittering ring on my left hand, the heavy jewelry that belonged to his mother. The words were true, I did love him. I'd been falling for him since the day he told me I could keep Lamborghini. Possibly even before. I liked the darkness inside him, the barely leashed violence. He was the most powerful man in Europe, richer than a king, and he fucked me like he couldn't ever get enough.

I tilted my head to meet his eyes. "I love you, but if you break my heart again, I will carve yours out of your chest and feed it to your pigs."

The look on his face told me he liked my words. "There is my bloodthirsty queen." He gently lifted me off his softening erection and rolled me onto my back. His hand cradled my face. "You are everything to me. I tried to survive without you but could not do it. No matter what happens, I will always love you. I want you right here with me until I take my last breath."

My heart thumped hard as my chest expanded with emotion. "I never thought when you drugged me and dragged me all the way to Italy that I would marry you."

"I can be very persuasive when there is something I want." He pressed a quick kiss to my lips. "Speaking of, I want to get married as quickly as possible."

I rolled my eyes and pushed him off me. Give this man an inch . . . "Slow your roll, Ravazzani." I got to my feet and started toward the shower. "I know we're having a shotgun wedding and all, but give me a minute to breathe."

He came up behind me and smacked my ass. "That is for your sassy mouth, monella. Get in the shower and I will see if I can convince you."

CHAPTER EIGHTEEN

Francesca

Fausto was still in the shower and I was starving.

Being pregnant and fucking that man had really taken it out of me tonight. I slid on my robe and left our bedroom. There had to be leftover pasta somewhere in the fridge.

As I started down the stairs, I heard arguing from the other wing. It sounded like Gia and Emma. God, these two fighting was the last thing I needed right now. I hurried toward Emma's bedroom and threw open the door.

They both started and spun toward me. The silence didn't last, though, and they both began talking at once. Lifting my hand, I cut them off and hissed, "Will you keep it down?"

Emma blurted, "Frankie—"

"Keep quiet," Gia ordered her sister.

I inhaled and let it out slowly. "What is going on with you two?"

"I have to talk to you," Emma said, her expression troubled.

"About what? What's wrong?"

"It's nothing," Gia said.

"We saw what was down there," Emma said.

Gia cursed, but I was still confused. "Down where?" What the hell were they talking about?

Gia shot Emma a look that could have withered the entire vineyard. "It's no big deal, Frankie. We just had a quick look in the dungeon."

My jaw fell open, my post-orgasm high evaporating. "What the fuck? I said you couldn't go down there. How did you manage it?"

Emma folded her arms across her chest and glared at Gia, doing their twin mind-meld thing where they spoke silently to each other.

"We knew you didn't want to go down there, and we didn't want to push you." Gia sat on the bed and shrugged. "So we just figured we'd ask Giulio to take us instead."

"And he agreed?"

"Gia told Giulio that you said it was okay," Emma said flatly.

"What the fuck? I can't believe you would lie to him like that."

"I'm sorry. Don't be mad."

"Too late. I'm beyond mad. I'm furious. They kill and torture people down there, Gia!"

"I know. We saw the blood."

Oh, my God. No wonder why Emma looked upset. "Are you okay?" I asked her, studying her face carefully.

Instead of answering, she said, "I need to talk to you. Alone."

"Gia, go away," I said. "I'll deal with you in a minute."

"Okay." Gia closed in to kiss my cheek. "Sorry, Frankie, I couldn't resist. There aren't any dungeons in Toronto, that's for sure. At least none that I know of."

I wasn't swayed. Gia was definitely of the "act first, apologize later" variety, but she knew better. "That still doesn't make it right."

We waited for Gia to leave, then Emma put her hands on my shoulders. "You have to do something."

"About what?"

"That man down there."

I blinked at her. "Excuse me?"

She stepped away and began pacing. "He's . . . really bad off,

Frankie. I can't believe he's still alive. There's blood everywhere. Sharp instruments and chains. Medical equipment. It's like the movie *Saw*, but in real life."

Was she kidding me right now? Was I seriously supposed to pity Enzo? "Emma, that is a bad man. I told you what he did to me. I have absolutely no sympathy for him whatsoever."

"Come on. Don't be like that. You aren't one of these mafia types. You know what's happening down there is wrong."

Did I? I hadn't lost a wink of sleep over Enzo's fate since arriving back at the castello. I was more than content to let Fausto handle it as he saw fit. "Enzo's a murderer, too, babe. Who knows what might have happened if Fausto didn't rescue me? Enzo probably would have killed me."

"You don't know that."

"Oh, sure. He would've just let me walk out the door in Naples. Think, Emma. If this man goes free, I'm at risk. Fausto is at risk. Giulio, Zia, everything and everyone here is at risk."

Emma crossed her arms and hunched her shoulders. "Can't they, like, negotiate a peace treaty or something?"

I wasn't sure Enzo deserved peace of any kind.

I gentled my voice. "Remember how I said things were different here? This isn't the United Nations. These men are brutal killers. It's very old school."

She squeezed her eyes shut. "I know. I just . . . I can't stay here knowing that man is going to be killed at any moment."

"Then why did you go down there? You knew what you were going to see."

"Because I had to know. I'm telling you, I can't celebrate your engagement and have a nice vacation here when a man is murdered right under my nose."

I rubbed my forehead, the beginnings of a headache settling in my temples. "Emma, you're being a pain in the ass."

Her eyes went glassy and tears pooled. Oh, crap. I made her cry.

"I'm sorry," she choked out as I dragged her into a hug. "Just send me home."

"I'm not sending you home. You just got here."

"But I can't stay, Frankie. I can't stay if they are going to kill him while I'm here."

"What if . . . ?" I swallowed hard. "What if I could get them to hold off on dealing with Enzo until after you leave?" Fausto would need to agree, but I could convince him. Hopefully.

"Oh, please, Frankie. Please, talk to Fausto."

"I'll talk to him, okay? But I can't make any promises."

"Okay." She hugged me back. "I'm sorry. I wish I was like you and Gia but—"

But she wasn't.

"Don't apologize," I said.

"Thanks, Frankie." She drew back and wiped her face. "Love you."

"I love you, too. Let's forget about this for right now and go downstairs for something to eat."

When we left, a figure shifted from his position against the wall.

Fausto.

Damn it.

I plastered a smile on my face. "Hey, baby. What are you up to?"

He pushed off the wall and stalked forward. "I could ask you the same thing, but I've already been alerted by the men in the security room."

Those blabbermouths. I touched my sister's arm. "Go back to your room, Em. I'll see you later."

"Okay. Good night."

Emma went back inside, but I didn't look away from Fausto. I couldn't decide if he was angry, annoyed, or merely bothered by the dungeon excursion. So I played dumb.

Wrapping my arms around his neck, I licked his earlobe. "Want to come to the kitchen with me? I'll feed you."

"Why did my son take your sisters into my dungeon?"

Sighing, I let him go. We were doing this now, I guess. "I need to talk to you."

Oh, the suspicion that coasted across his handsome face. "Is that so, amore? What about?"

"Can we go to our room first?"

"And why would we need to do that? Are you going to give me bad news?"

"No, of course not. But I don't think this is a conversation you want to have in public."

He leaned in to grab my hip, tugged me close, and put his mouth near my ear. "Get going right now, monella, before I spank your ass here in the hallway."

Fausto

As I trailed my soon-to-be wife to our wing, I didn't know what I was feeling. Angry, yes. But mostly I was very confused.

Lucia never would've dared allow her family into my dungeon. She wouldn't have asked or even entertained the idea. Our world has clear boundaries and my first wife understood them perfectly.

Francesca didn't seem to care or even be aware of those boundaries. Not only had she allowed her sisters to traipse into the dungeon, but she somehow also convinced my son to give a tour.

Ma che cazzo?

I would have words with Giulio tomorrow, but in the meantime I had to deal with Francesca. Just because we were getting married, this did not mean she had control of my men and my estate. I was the boss, not her, and she needed to concern herself with our children and home—not mafia business.

She would respect our boundaries.

I closed the bedroom door and watched as she sat on the bed. I leaned against the wall and crossed my arms. "Explain."

She nibbled her lip and twisted her hands in her lap. "I can't tell if you're mad or not."

I wasn't certain, either. "Francesca."

"My sisters wanted to see the dungeon. Giulio agreed to take them down. It's not a big deal."

The words confirmed what I thought, and I felt my chest heat in frustration. "It is a big deal, amore. A very big deal. This is not an amusement park or playground. This is a dangerous place with dangerous men. Bad things happen here. You understand, no?"

Her brows lowered. "Of course I understand. I'm not a child, Fausto. They asked and, frankly, I said no."

"And how did that work out?"

I could see the guilt in her expression. It was a look I'd seen many times. She made a face. "They didn't listen to me, apparently."

I gestured with my hands. "See?"

"I guess I should've expected it," she said with a tiny chuckle. "They are my sisters, after all. But they won't ask to go down again."

"And what happens when they ask for something else they shouldn't?"

"What do you mean?" She tucked one long leg under her opposite knee, distracting me for a second with all her golden skin.

I focused on her face once more. "I need you to understand how this is going to work, dolcezza. You will be my wife, not the boss. You don't order my men around and you don't interfere in my business. Everything goes through me, whether it's the estate, the 'ndrina, or my family."

Her jaw fell open. "Are you kidding?"

"Not even a little bit."

"I have no desire to interfere with your business, but you're talking about *our* family. You really think I'm going to be that kind of wife, the one that shops and lunches and doesn't ask questions? Don't you know me *at all?*"

"Don't you know *me* at all?" I countered. "Because if you do, then you must know I will not be managed, Francesca. I will not have my balls cut off by my wife."

"I don't want to cut off your balls. I happen to like them very much."

I lifted a brow at her. "That's good because they are staying exactly where they are, which means you answer to me. That is how this works."

"That is not how this works, Fausto. This marriage will be a partnership. We will be equals. I respect you and you respect me. The end."

I took a deep breath, struggling to remain cool and level-headed. "We are not equals. I make the decisions and accept the danger. If someone must die or go to jail, it will be me. This is to protect you and our children."

"That is not protection; that is bullshit Italian misogyny. What happened to, 'I am giving you nearly everything, Francesca,' and 'I can't live without you, Francesca'?"

I ignored her terrible imitation of my accent, which sounded like an American pizza commercial. "You are not getting involved in my business. It is too dangerous. You will ignore whatever happens and allow me to handle things as I see fit."

"Ugh!" She grabbed a square pillow off the bed and threw it at me. I didn't move as it bounced off me. She said, "I am not going to be a good little housewife, waiting for you at the end of every day with a cocktail and dinner on the table. If that is what you picture our marriage being like, you might as well take your ring back."

"I wasn't thinking that before," I said with a sly smile, "but I am now. Will you do it naked?" I let my gaze travel the length of her. "Yes, I like that very much."

"Stop it, you sex fiend. Do you want to marry me?"

"You know the answer to that question."

"Then I have a request to make—and your answer will prove if you're ready to treat me as an equal or not. Because I am telling you that this marriage will not survive if you think of me like an underling. I expect a partnership, Fausto. If you're unwilling to give me one, then I don't want to marry you."

My muscles tightened. After all this time, after all I'd shared, she was still testing me? I snarled, "I don't like ultimatums or threats."

"I don't want to threaten you any more than I want to be ordered around. But we have to straighten this out before we get married—*if* we get married. Are you ready to hear my request?" I gave her a single nod, too furious to elaborate, and she said, "I want you to promise me that Enzo won't be killed while my sisters are here."

I didn't move. I didn't even blink. It was like ice filled my veins, a calm washing over me. "You think to dictate Enzo's future to me?"

"I am not dictating. I am asking. And it's only temporary."

"But if I do not agree, you won't marry me."

"This is what it means to be married. Compromise, even when you don't like it. Giving in to your partner sometimes. If you are incapable of it, why on earth would I ever marry you?"

"I will not compromise when it comes to D'Agostino."

"I'm not asking you to set him free. I'm just asking that, if you're planning to kill him, to wait until my sisters go back to Toronto. Emma is traumatized at the idea of murder happening during her visit."

My lip curled into a sneer. "I don't care if she is traumatized. No one tells me how to deal with my enemies."

"Again, I'm asking. But think very carefully before you answer, Fausto."

Outrage and venom poured into my blood like a river, a torrent of resentment at the position she was putting me in. Enzo was near death and the instant I had what I needed from him, I wanted him dead. I didn't want to give him extra time on this earth because Emma Mancini might get her feelings hurt. "I could force you to marry me," I snarled.

"No, you can't. I will never say the vows, not if I don't believe you respect me."

I stalked over to the bed. If she wanted to negotiate before our wedding, fine. I had a few things I'd like to ask for. "Stand up."

She heard the steel in my voice and didn't hesitate. Licking her lips, she slid off the bed and stood. Unafraid, she met my eyes and I knew I would give her this one thing.

I grabbed her hips and pulled her into my chest, my forehead resting on hers. She wrapped her arms around my neck, holding on while her breasts pressed against me. We stayed there a moment, breathing in one another, and the simple embrace soothed me, a balm on my stained soul. "I love you and I cannot live without you. If I must agree to this, then I will. For you. But don't push me too far. We will be *partners*, no?"

"Grazie, baby." She pressed a kiss to my jaw. "I am going to make you the very best wife. You won't ever regret it."

"And if I am compromising for you, then you will compromise in return for me." I could feel her body stiffen in my hold, so I grabbed her tighter. "Wait until you hear what I am asking."

"Fine."

I held her face in my hands gently, like it was a precious gift. "You will give me at least three more children in addition to this one." I tilted my chin toward her belly.

Her eyes went wide. "Kids? This is what you want in exchange?"

Then her eyes went unfocused, like she was thinking about it. Thinking about me shooting deep inside her, filling her up with my come to get her pregnant. When she bit her lip and swayed toward me a little, I knew I was right.

Madre di Dio, my woman was hot.

"Okay," she whispered.

A flash of possessiveness whipped through me. Cazzo, I couldn't wait to make more babies with her.

When she leaned back, I said, "Wait. I have one more compromise."

"What?"

"You will marry me as quickly as possible. Tomorrow. I will allow your sisters to stay for the ceremony, but they must return to Toronto immediately after."

She gasped, ripping out of my hold and moving away from me. "Fausto, no! They just got here. I'm not ready to let them go."

"That is my final offer, Francesca. Every man in my command will question why I have not yet killed Enzo. It makes me look weak, capisce?"

"What if—?"

"No. I will not delay the inevitable any more than necessary. Every day he remains alive is a threat to me, to you. To everything I have built. You may see your sisters another time."

Tears welled up in her eyes, but I didn't give in, even when those tears spilled over her lashes and tracked down her cheeks. She wiped her face. "I'll miss them."

I moved in and hugged her, smoothing my hands down her spine. "I know, dolcezza. I'll make it up to you."

The next morning, I went down into the dungeon alone. I wanted my enemy to see me in my wedding suit, see my happiness, and realize he would never have the same. He would never see his family again, never stand in the Italian sun. He would die soon at my hand, and I couldn't fucking wait.

I considered this a wedding present to myself.

He cracked one swollen eye as I came in with a chair and sat down. Smoothing my tie, I took my time, letting him wonder why I was there. Marco, thanks to his training as a medic in the army, could keep a man barely alive, just enough to suffer, and Enzo was hovering on that line. He was thin and weak, a shell of that smug, smiling asshole who came onto my yacht and leered at my woman's ass.

It was a beautiful sight.

"Buongiorno, D'Agostino." I gave him my blandest smile. "Come stai?"

He said nothing, merely watched me, his breath rattling in his chest.

"Today is a good day. Would you like to know why?" When he didn't answer, I jammed the toe of my dress shoe into his dislocated knee. He whimpered and I smiled wider. "Today is my wedding day. I will marry Francesca in a few hours out in the sunshine, surrounded by my family and friends. Then I will spend the rest of the night fucking her. You remember what that was like, no? Fucking your wife?"

His breathing picked up, but otherwise he didn't react.

"Did you know she's pregnant, my woman?"

That got a reaction from him. He blinked several times.

I folded my hands in my lap. "The entire time you had her in that trunk, when you shoved the gun in her mouth, she was carrying my child. A Ravazzani son or daughter." I let that sink in. We both knew the importance of legacy and children. "Too bad you didn't know," I said with fake sympathy.

"Her sisters are here. Perhaps you met them last night? Francesca has asked me to keep you alive while her family is visiting. Remarkable, no? Even though you kidnapped her and scared her, my woman is kind enough to ask me to spare your miserable life for another few hours. So with every breath you take today you should thank her."

I rose and moved the chair out of his cell, then returned and bent by his head. "But don't worry, stronzo. When I've sent her sisters back to Toronto, I'll come down and finish what I've started." I lowered my voice. "And I promise you this: you will sign everything over to me before I kill you."

Straightening, I turned and walked out of his cell. Over my shoulder, I called out, "Enjoy your last hours on Earth, D'Agostino."

CHAPTER NINETEEN

Fausto

I married her in the vineyards.
As she bound herself to me for eternity, the rows of plants, my family's legacy, stretched out to honor us. Francesca was barefoot, wearing the Celestina cream gown I'd chosen for her back when we thought she would marry my son. It was tight in the chest, thanks to her pregnancy, but still fit otherwise. A simple bouquet of white roses and lilies rested in her hands, while a delicate crown made from lilies of the valley and grape leaves sat atop her head, blonde hair long and loose down her back.

She'd never looked more beautiful.

We repeated our vows in front of the small group gathered to witness the ceremony. My family and her sisters were here, along with Emilia and Vincenzo. Tommaso was invited, and he brought Lamborghini.

Days ago, when I gave her my mother's ring, I started the marriage paperwork with the government. So though today seemed like a surprise to my bride, I'd been planning it for a while. After the ceremony we would be wed in the eyes of man and God, until one of us left this earth.

The mayor of Siderno, Antonio Volpe, presided over our service. It was the least he could do, as I'd handed him the election three years ago. "*Vi dichiaro marito e moglie!*" the mayor announced at the end of the ceremony.

I exhaled in relief and turned to my bride, happiness sending my heart flying. I put one hand on her hip and another at her nape, then bent to kiss her. The cheers barely registered as I took my wife's mouth, uncaring of who saw how much I wanted her. Her lips were soft and pliant, and she gave me command of the kiss, even when it turned hungry.

"Dai, andiamo!" Giulio finally called. "Break the glass, Papà, and let's go eat."

I eased off my wife's mouth, pressing a few additional small kisses just to prolong this moment. I hadn't felt a fraction of this joy, this intense satisfaction in my bride at my first wedding. I never wanted to forget this.

By the time I straightened, Francesca was clinging to me, her lips swollen and wet. Madre di Dio, she was beautiful. Marco handed me the red wine glass and left the small wooden dais, along with everyone else. "What are we doing?" she asked.

"Haven't you been to an Italian wedding before?"

"No. Are we drinking wine together?"

I often forgot how young she was, how sheltered she'd been. I pushed a strand of hair behind her ears. "No, mia bella moglie. We break it. The number of shards represents the number of years we will be happily married."

"Oh." Her cheeks grew an adorable shade of pink. "Fun. I'm ready."

We both held the delicate wine glass. "Uno, due, tre," I said, then we dropped the glass.

It bounced but didn't break. The stem broke off, but otherwise the glass remained intact, rolling sideways until it came to a stop. Francesca gasped, while Zia quickly made *mano cornuto,* the sign of the horns, toward the glass to ward off any evil spirits.

"Fausto!" Horror laced Francesca's voice. "It's supposed to break."

I put my arm around her waist and spoke quietly in her ear. "It means nothing, a stupid tradition from the past."

"No, no." She clutched my tie. "This is bad. Like very, very, very bad." Wild eyes stared at the glass as if it was some harbinger of doom, while it was just nonsense.

I had to reassure her. "Francesca, the glass broke into hundreds of pieces at my first wedding, but Lucia and I were never happily married, nor did our marriage last long. Do not put faith into silly wives' tales."

Her fist tightened around my tie, crushing the silk, as she tugged me closer. "You had a healthy son together and you've lived this long. The 'ndrina is prosperous. To spit on your good luck is wrong."

"You are spending too much time with Zia," I muttered.

She shoved my stomach. "I am serious. Let's do it again. We'll really throw it this time."

The guests were waiting, talking amongst themselves, eager for this to be over, but I knew my bride would not let this go. I didn't want Francesca thinking about this all during the wedding dinner or—more importantly—the wedding night.

Walking over to the glass, I lifted my foot, brought it down, and smashed the bowl beneath my leather shoe. Shards of glass went everywhere, tiny pieces that glittered in the late afternoon sun.

"There." I announced to the crowd, "Let's go eat."

Francesca didn't move, her mouth open. "I can't believe you did that. That's worse, Fausto!"

Shaking my head, I scooped her up in my arms so she didn't cut her bare feet on the glass. Once on the ground I was reluctant to let her go. I kept walking and she nestled her face into my throat. "We're married," she breathed, as if she'd just realized it.

"We are married, Francesca Ravazzani."

"Oh, shit," she whispered. "Why is that so hot?"

I chuckled. If she liked that, she was going to love what I had planned for later.

I carried her toward the winery. When she realized where we were going, she lifted her head. "Wait, we aren't eating in the castello?"

"No." I continued over the threshold and set her on her feet, then kissed her mouth. "I wish there had been time to give you a big wedding and party. It's what you deserve. But I hope you like what I arranged for tonight instead."

"I don't need a big wedding and a fancy party. Just you."

My chest expanded, the words falling easily from my mouth. "Ti amo, cuore mio."

She leaned up on her toes and pressed her lips to mine. "Ti amo, paparino."

I smiled, feeling lighter than I had in years. "Come. Your paparino wants to feed you." I took her hand and led her into the tasting room, which had been transformed for the wedding dinner.

Sheer fabric and tiny lights criss-crossed the ceiling, while candles burned all around the room, their soft glow bouncing off the wine casks and exposed brick walls. Tables had been pushed together to form a hollow square, chairs on the outside, with candles and flower arrangements every few place settings. Boxwood trees and more flower arrangements dotted the edges, giving the tasting room a romantic, intimate feel. I hoped she liked it. Giulio and Vincenzo had worked hard on this together today, knowing how much my wife loved the grapes and the process of making wine.

"Oh, my God. Fausto," she said with a sigh as she took it all in. "It's beautiful. I can't believe it. How . . . ?"

"Giulio and Vincenzo oversaw this. For you."

"It's perfect."

Everyone filed in and began taking their seats. Francesca and I sat at the head of the table together, where a basket of wrapped *bomboniere* waited. She leaned over. "What is this?"

"Those are wedding favors. You give them out to the guests."

"What's inside each little box?"

"*Confetti.* Five sugared almonds."

"Is this another luck thing?"

"Sì, they symbolize health, wealth, happiness, fertility, and longevity for the newlyweds."

She gestured to her belly. "I think you have the fertility one covered, baby daddy."

I leaned in and kissed her. "We still have three more of those to come."

She rolled her eyes, though I was not fooled. I could see the way her eyes sparkled at the idea.

Ready to get this dinner over with, I stood up to welcome our guests. I very much wished to get my wife alone.

Francesca

I was a married woman.

Even though I was wearing a wedding dress, it seemed surreal. Married. To Fausto Ravazzani.

Holy shit.

I was a mafia wife, a role I'd sworn to avoid. As I snuck a glance at my handsome husband, I couldn't regret it. I would spend the rest of my life at his side, in his bed, hearing that sexy growl and playing our dirty games together. Yes, please.

As I passed out the favors to the small number of dinner guests, they all kept shoving money at me. I knew it was an Italian custom, but I wasn't prepared for this much. The mayor gave me ten thousand Euros, for fuck's sake. Giulio said more money and gifts would arrive in the coming weeks, once news of Fausto's marriage spread around the globe.

I guess that's what happened when one married a badass international criminal.

When I finished with the favors I walked back to my chair, which was now occupied by Marco. Instead of being deterred, I slipped onto my husband's lap and draped my arms around his neck. He smelled so good and felt even better. Fausto stroked my thigh and held me close, while he and Marco spoke quietly to one another. I was in no hurry to move.

I'd spent the entire day and most of the evening with my sisters.

Though I was happy to have them here, their visit was bittersweet and way too short. Emma and Gia were sad, as well, but they had to get back to their lives in Toronto.

I would miss them, there was no doubt about that. I thought back to when I wanted nothing more than to leave Italy and return home, but I didn't feel that way anymore. I was Team Ravazzani now. My loyalties were with Fausto and his 'ndrina. His family and our children. Someday, I'd see my sisters again. We would find a way to reconnect.

"He's weak but still holding out on us. We should track the money," Marco was saying. "That thirty million went somewhere."

Were they talking about Enzo?

"His men will be too smart to spend it now," Fausto said. "Besides, when he signs everything over to me, it will no longer matter."

Wait, they were discussing Enzo. Holy shit, did this mean he stole thirty million dollars from Fausto?

What was it Mariella had said? *Besides, Fausto will soon lose everything. My Enzo is very clever with computers and he has eyes and ears everywhere.*

Why hadn't I remembered that before?

I straightened, angling so I could see both of their faces, though I kept my voice low. "When I was with Mariella, she told me you would soon lose everything and that her man has eyes and ears everywhere."

My husband's fingers tightened on my body as he exchanged a dark glance with Marco. "Anything else you can remember?" he asked. "Any mention of who might be helping him?"

I searched my memories. So much of that time had been spent in a panic, with a dash of morning sickness to boot. Staying alive and keeping my shit together had taken most of my energy.

This is why you are the perfect distraction.

Yes, it made sense. I hadn't understood Enzo's words at the time, but he'd obviously taken me to distract Fausto. When I repeated the words to my husband, he scowled.

"A misdirection," Marco said, rubbing his eyes. "Cristo."

"That *brutto figlio di puttana bastardo*," Fausto swore, then returned his attention to his cousin. "Tomorrow morning, I want you and Giulio in my office first thing. We need to strategize."

"Can I come, too?" I nuzzled into his throat. "Seeing as how I was so helpful tonight?"

"No. I want you sleeping and resting."

"But—"

"That's enough." He patted my hip. "Go and say goodbye to your sisters. They depart now for the airport."

My heart sank as he helped me to my feet. "Okay."

I started to leave, but his warm fingers wrapped around my wrist, stopping me. He brought my wrist to his mouth and kissed the inside of it, sending goosebumps up my arm. "After you finish, I get you all to myself."

"Okay," I repeated, but breathier this time. I don't know how he managed to turn me on with the simplest touch.

He let me go and I went toward the twins, who stood near the wine barrels, drinking. True to form, Gia flirted with every seemingly unattached male tonight, while Emma watched from arm's length.

"Is it time?" Emma asked quietly when she saw me approach.

I nodded. "I'm going to miss you both so much."

Surprisingly, Gia hugged me first. She wasn't usually the demonstrative one. "Bye, sis. I'm going to miss you, too."

"Stay out of trouble, Gigi, and keep up with your birth control shots," I said with a laugh, even though tears had started leaking from my eyes. "I love you."

"I love you, too. I hope this isn't the last time we see you."

My chest felt hollow and more tears slipped free from my lids. "Of course it won't be. We'll figure it out."

Finally, I let her go and turned to my other sister. "Sweet Emma," I said and wrapped my arms around her. She held on tight, already crying, as well. "I love you. And you should definitely stay out of trouble, too."

"I will," she whispered.

I pulled back and held onto their hands. "Remember what I said about Papà and college. He might say you can go for four years but he could be lying. So, make the most of that first semester away at school."

Benito came over to hover behind us, his face conveying his unhappiness in being tasked with this errand.

My sisters and I fell into a big group hug with more tears and whispers of keeping in touch. I made them promise to text me the minute they landed in Toronto. Then Benito cleared his throat and we were forced to let go. A sob tore at my throat as they turned away.

Watching Emma and Gia walk out of the winery was one of the worst moments of my life. It felt like a part of me was going with them, like maybe the old Frankie, the version of me who'd hoped for a normal life filled with college, drinking and random boys. None of that would happen now. I was about to start a new chapter as a wife and mother. A mafia queen.

Arms wrapped around my waist and I felt Fausto's strong presence behind me, easing some of the rawness in my heart. He kissed the crown of my head. I sighed and leaned into him, wiping away tears. I'm sure I looked like a mess.

"They will be fine," he said softly. "*Te lo prometto.*"

Turning, I slid my arms around his neck and held on. My makeup was probably running and ruining his shirt, but that was too bad. I was allowed to cry right now.

When I quieted he tilted my chin up. His eyes were gentle and adoring, the kind of look he saved just for me. "Are you ready for your surprise, *mia bella moglie?*"

My toes curled inside the shoes I'd put on for the dinner reception, and I accepted the handkerchief he handed me. Real cotton, because my man was fancy. "I can't wait." I wiped my face and tried to clean up as best I could.

"*Va bene.* Come." He turned to the guests and spoke in Italian too quickly for me to translate. Whatever he said made everyone laugh and break out into applause. "*Auguri!*" everyone shouted, offering their best wishes, as he led me to the door.

"What did you say?"

"I said the time has come for me to claim my bride, and the only blood on the sheets would be my own if I did not satisfy you properly."

"Jesus, Fausto."

He chuckled and kissed my hand. "Tell me I am wrong."

"If you don't satisfy me, I will just take care of myself."

He hummed deep in his chest. "I still watch the video of you trying on lingerie in the dressing room from Rome. It gets me so hard."

We stepped out into the darkness. I expected him to turn right but he went left, as if we were going to the vineyards. "Wait, shouldn't we head toward the castello?"

"This is a surprise, amore. That means you do not ask questions."

"You're a pain in the ass, you know that?"

"You will like this. Trust me."

The night was perfect. Not too brisk and a clear sky for a bright three-quarter moon. There wasn't a sound anywhere around us except for our feet on the gravel path. It felt like we were completely alone out here, the only two people in the entire world.

"We're going into the vineyards?"

He didn't answer, just led me down the rows of vines. The look on his face was predatory, dark . . . the same man who'd watched me deep throat him in the stables and ride him in a red bodysuit. It was the face of a man obsessed, who would have me at all costs. And I had given up everything for him, had followed him down the path of darkness where he made the rules and no one dared question him.

But I knew the power I held, the way he'd suffered without me. He would bend at my request, as he had with Paolo and Enzo. The thought of this great man willing to change his mind for me, his wife, made me hot and reckless, like I wanted to do anything he asked, no matter how depraved. It made me giddy and light, a supplicant ready to worship at his feet.

It made me want to play.

I kicked off my flats and took off running.

I didn't need to look back to see if he was chasing me—I knew he was there, right behind me. I could feel his breath, his *lust* as I lifted my heavy skirts and flew across the bare ground. The cool dirt cushioned my toes and the wind caused my hair to stream behind me like a banner. I was free and outside, with the one person I loved beyond reason. The hunger for him was like these grape leaves—steady and strong and lasting.

He caught me, his big hands finding my waist and pulling me to a stop, and he caged me against his chest with his arms. I gave a pitiful struggle, which caused his muscles to strain as he held me tighter. "Where do you think you are going, piccola monella?"

Oh, shit. I heard it in his voice. That rough domination, the kind he got when he wanted to conquer me.

And I desperately wanted to be conquered.

"You don't have to do this, signore," I panted. "I'll be good for you, I promise."

His body jerked slightly, then he spun me around. His glittering gaze searched my face, as if to check what was happening, so I added in a plea, "Please, just let me go."

I heard his quick intake of breath, watched his nostrils flare. His fingers dug into my ribs, the strength he normally kept in check flaring to life. Mmmm, yes. I wanted to feel that strength, to drown in it tonight. To wake up tomorrow with his fingerprints and bite marks all over me.

We'd played these games before, though not quite this particular one, but still he knew his part. He knew what I wanted from him, because no one had more insight into my mind than Fausto.

His hand wrapped around the front of my throat, not cutting off air but squeezing my flesh enough to send my pulse racing. "You belong to me now, little girl, and I will never let you go."

"No, please—"

I lost the ability to speak when he bent and tossed me over his shoulder. He marched through the vines, ignoring my half-hearted struggles and protests until he found the row he wanted. The plants surrounded us, parallel lines of brown and green, and it was a world away from soldiers and guns. A simpler place where men claimed their women in the dirt and open sky.

He set me on my feet but didn't release me. Instead his hand came under my jaw to hold me still. "You are going to be very good for me, capisce? You will do exactly what I say, won't you?"

I rolled my lips, more turned on than I could stand. "But I've never done this before. I'm afraid you're going to hurt me."

His grip gentled and his accent became more pronounced, his voice dark with desire. "I will not hurt you, sweet girl. I will get you ready, stretch your tight pussy wide to take my cock." His palm swept over my breast, and my nipple pebbled at his touch. "You will try for me. You want to make me happy, no?"

God, yes. My knees were like jelly as I nodded. "Sì, Signore Ravazzani. I will try."

CHAPTER TWENTY

Francesca

Fausto swallowed audibly, then said, "Turn around."

I presented him with my back, and he wasted no time before taking the two panels of the dress and pulling hard. Buttons flew to the ground as the expensive silk parted like gauze. He pushed the fabric off my shoulders, down over my hips, and let it fall to my feet. I stood bare in the moonlight.

He hissed through his teeth. "Naked beneath your gown. Sei la mia puttanella, no?"

Even a thong left panty lines, so I'd gone commando all night. "No, I'm a good girl," I said, covering my breasts with one hand and my mound with the other.

He pushed his hips against my ass and let me feel the erection through his trousers. "You might be a good girl now, but you will soon be a dirty, filthy girl for me." He knocked my hands out of the way and walked around to my front. "No, don't hide yourself. Let me see you."

I slowly let my hands fall and his eyes raked over me, inspecting me. He dragged a fingertip over the peak of my breast and I arched toward him, unable to help myself. The corners of his mouth curled upward. "See? You are eager for it. A dirty girl who wants to get fucked."

My mouth was dry with wanting, but I said, "No, I'm not dirty. I saved myself."

His fingers trailed along my stomach, over my mostly bare mound, and into my slit. He hummed in his throat. "Allora . . . just as I thought. Dripping for me. Get on the blanket, piccolina. Let's fill that needy pussy with its first cock."

Jesus, okay. He was going to make me come with his words alone. When Fausto decided to play with me, he drove the game to better places, heights I never could imagine.

My body on fire, I stepped on the blanket and laid down. He was still fully dressed, his tailored black suit absolute perfection, and I ran my eyes over him greedily. I had been admiring him all night, his white shirt showing off the olive skin of his throat, the black tie hanging down his powerful chest and flat stomach. And he was *mine*.

While staring at my pussy, he shucked his suit coat and unbuckled his belt. The outline of his cock was evident in his trousers, proof of how much he liked what we were doing. I pulled my legs together, shielding myself.

He growled. "Widen them. Let me see what belongs to me." I tentatively spread my thighs, but not enough for his liking. "More. Show me where you need me."

When I was fully open, he unfastened his trousers and lowered the zipper. Then he reached inside his briefs and took out his dick, now harder than I'd ever seen it. The size of it was fucking impressive and my intake of breath was one hundred percent real.

"No, it's too big," I whined. "You're going to rip me in half."

He gave himself a rough stroke. "You can take me. You're going to take all of me and love every second of it."

Dropping to his knees, he settled between my thighs, spreading me wider to make room for him. I kept my hands at my side, a sacrifice for his pleasure. "That's it," he praised, sliding his palms over my skin toward my hips. "Relax, my sweet girl, and let your paparino take care of you."

Then he switched to Italian and said things not covered in any translator app, while strumming his thumb over my clit. It was obscene how wet I was now, my body aching everywhere as the tension built inside me. "Please," I breathed, forgetting what we were doing.

His face was taut and flushed, eyes wild, as he reached to line himself up at my entrance. His trousers and briefs rested around his hips, his shirt and tie still on, and I had never wanted him more. I tensed, clenching my pussy to give resistance as he worked the head inside. "Relax," he crooned. "Let me in. It's going to feel so good."

"Okay, signore. I'll try." I gave a little huff of air and squirmed as he slid in a bit more. "Is it in yet?"

"No, baby. Just a little bit more. I'm going to need to thrust soon, though. You're so tight."

"Will I really be yours after it's done?"

His hips jerked, sending him deeper, and we both gasped. "Sì, you will be mine. *Sempre.*"

Forever.

"It feels strange," I said, putting a good amount of wonder in my voice. "Way down deep inside me."

"That is my cock, saying hello to your pussy. We are going to make each other very happy in a moment."

Inch by inch he stretched me, the invasion so slow, just as if I were still innocent. He was being careful with me and it played into the fantasy, making me hot. I was naked on the ground, and everything around us—including me—belonged to him, and I could think of no better place to spend our wedding night than out in the dirt of his ancestors.

"Yes," he said, "that is nice, you squeezing me so tight. Do you like the way I feel inside you?"

"I don't know yet. I feel so full."

He watched where our bodies were becoming joined. "Look at your beautiful pussy, so wet and ready, sucking me in. Take all of me, like a good girl. I'm going to make this so perfect for you, dolcezza."

He kept going and the pinch I experienced when he bottomed out was not faked. Fausto was a lot to take. I loved it, though. My man was not easy, but I wouldn't have it any other way.

"Ow." I tried to shove him off me. "It hurts."

"No, just relax." He leaned down and kissed me, though I tried to resist. Undeterred, he held my jaw and kept at it until I began kissing him back, my body softening beneath him. "Oh, my sweet girl," he murmured. "Va bene, no?"

I nodded and put my hands on his shoulders. "It's a little better."

"I am going to move now. Let me fuck you and show you how good it will feel." He flexed his hips, withdrawing slightly before returning, the thick length dragging over my sensitive walls.

"Oh," I said, making my eyes round. "I liked that. Will you do it again?"

"Madre di Dio!" he hissed, his eyelids slamming shut as if he were in pain. "Fuck, Francesca."

I loved driving him wild like this. Could I make him lose his self control and ride me like an animal in the dirt? "Please, Signore Ravazzani. Don't stop. I'll be good. Let me feel it just once more."

That did it.

With a growl, he began pounding into me, thrusting with his powerful body, planting himself inside me like he was trying to imprint on my soul. His clothes were rough against my skin and I held him close, my legs wrapped around his hips. The game was lost in the frenzy, and it became the two of us working, straining in the darkness, with grunts and sighs carried away on the salty breeze. I tasted his skin, his lips, writhing beneath him as he pinned me down and called me filthy and dirty, his little slut—all the names I pretended to hate but secretly loved.

And when he whispered that he was going to fill me up with his seed and get me pregnant with his child, I came so hard I nearly blacked out. My back arched as I trembled, my walls convulsing around his cock, and then he was coming too, thick pulses that sent warm jets into my body. He threw his head back and shouted, his body sealed tight to mine like he never wanted to leave. Like he didn't want to waste a single drop, like all his come needed to stay inside my pussy.

Finally, he pulled out and pushed onto his knees. Chest heaving, he pinched the bridge of his nose between his thumb and forefinger. "I am too fucking old for this. You are going to kill me."

I laughed and ran my bare foot up his thigh, onto his chest. "You love me."

His expression softened as he captured my leg and held me close. "I do. Ti amo, mia bella moglie."

"Same, paparino. Did you like your wedding night?"

He yanked up his briefs and trousers and stretched out beside me. His hand came to rest on my abdomen. "I did, very much. I guess it will never be boring with you, at least."

I leaned up to press a quick kiss to his mouth. "I will always be your dirty mantenuta."

"You liked it when I said I was going to fill you up and give you a baby."

Fuck yes, I had. "You liked it when I acted like your little virgin wife, seeing a cock for the first time."

He cupped my breast and squeezed gently. "I never believed this would turn me on so much, especially as I have fucked a virgin wife before and it was nothing like this."

"What was it like that first time with Lucia?"

He frowned. "I don't like discussing her. It feels disrespectful."

"Why? You aren't going to trash her, are you?"

He made a face that showed exactly what he thought of my youthful slang. "I don't like speaking ill of the dead."

"Afraid you'll go to hell, il Diavolo?" That earned me a sharp pinch to my nipple. "Fuck, Fausto!"

"That is for your smart mouth, monella."

The pain spread throughout my body, followed by a rush of endorphins that made my clit pound. "I like that," I murmured.

"I can tell." He did it again. "I will buy you nipple clamps. Do you know what they are?"

"Everyone knows what nipple clamps are," I told him dryly. "You know I have access to the internet, right?"

He pinched me harder this time and I yelped. Heat radiated behind the pain when he let go. "Stop turning me on," I told him, slapping at his hand. "I want to hear about your first wedding night."

"Why?"

"Because I want to know about your life before me. I'm curious about Lucia."

"Nothing good can come of digging into the past, amore."

I tilted my head to stare at him. "Will you just tell me and stop being so dramatic?"

He sighed heavily and caressed my stomach. His platinum wedding ring winked in the moonlight, a sight that made my heart sigh with happiness. He said, "The ceremony was held at the castello, followed by a nine-course dinner. I could feel her getting more nervous with each course that passed. The crowd also grew rowdier, with chants of *'bacio'* louder and louder as the night went on. I hadn't slept with a virgin before, so I had no idea what to expect, but I assumed she had been prepared by her mother or her sisters."

"Or Google," I added.

"*Esattamente*. When we got upstairs, it was clear she was ignorant of what was to come. I knew I had to treat her carefully, as a wife and not a mantenuta. There is a very clear distinction here between the two."

"Except for me."

His grin was wicked. "Except for you. Allora, I tried to be patient with Lucia, but she wanted it over with as quickly as possible. As if she was determined not to enjoy it, capisce? And we needed the blood on the sheets."

This didn't sound like it was going in a positive direction. "So?"

He leaned in and pressed a kiss to my stomach, his breath warm and moist on my skin. "I was not as careful as I should have been with her. She endured it and then it was over. My father was pleased by the blood, though."

He hardly ever talked of his parents. I had hundreds of questions burning my tongue, but I held them. Something told me I could only prod him so far tonight, and I'd already opened up the wound on his first wife.

His tongue swirled in my belly button. "You are so beautiful. It makes my heart ache just to look at you."

My chest swelled, and I ran my fingers through his soft hair. "Are you hoping for a boy or a girl?"

He dropped more kisses where our baby was growing. "It does not matter to me. I have an heir already, so whatever we have is a gift. But I would be lying if I said I wasn't looking forward to a daughter."

"The powerful mafia king, sitting at tea parties and letting her paint your nails?"

"It would be an honor. I always wanted many children."

"That's because you get to do the easy part."

He chuckled and repositioned his body between my legs, his mouth moving toward my mound. "Let me repay you, then."

CHAPTER TWENTY-ONE

Fausto

Early the next morning I was back at my desk, reviewing a city contract we were bidding on. Mayor Volpe assured me the job would go to my construction company, even if my bid was twice the others. That was the way of things here. No one got ahead by playing fair.

The Mancini twins landed in Toronto during the night. Mancini asked about the wedding, but I didn't feel like talking. I wanted as little to do with Francesca's family as possible. That part of her life was over. She belonged to me, no one else. Her future was with me and my family, this estate. She would remain at my side until I died.

My wife.

I would never tire of saying the words.

After screwing in the vineyards last night, I brought her inside to clean up and then fucked her again, this time in a bed. My back screamed in protest this morning because of it, but I didn't regret it. I'd take her as often as she'd let me.

Giulio entered with two cups of espresso. I was impressed. He was up early, clear-eyed, and well-dressed. It gave me hope. "Buongiorno," he said and sat one cup near my papers.

"Ciao." I thanked him for the espresso. "Have you—?"

My phone rang and I checked the display. Marco was due any moment, but it wasn't my cousin. This was a number from Piedmont, one I didn't recognize . . . but I suspected. Not many people had my direct number, except for the other 'ndrina leaders and governmental officials I worked with closely.

Exhaling, I slid to answer then put it on speaker for Giulio's benefit. "Pronto."

"Ciao, Fausto!"

It was as I thought. I would know his voice anywhere. "Ciao, Mommo. Come stai?"

"Va bene, va bene. That package you need to return? Have you given it more thought?"

I wasn't fooled by his code. By package he meant Enzo—and I wasn't returning that stronzo except in pieces. Plus, Mommo had already tried this. Why was he pushing the matter again?

"I decided to keep it. It's fragile and won't last much longer."

There was a long silence on the other end. Finally, Mommo said, "That is disappointing to hear. Your father would want you to do the right thing, especially on the heels of the joyous wedding last night."

Cazzata. My father would have relished torturing Enzo to death right away, no matter which members of La Provincia complained about it.

But what worried me was how Mommo had learned of my wedding so quickly. My come was practically still drying on my wife. How the fuck had word spread so quickly?

"I am surprised you heard."

"You know these men." He chuckled, a deep smoker's rasp that spoke of a lifelong habit. "They gossip worse than old women."

Marco walked in and he frowned when he saw my expression. I turned my attention back to the call. "Yes, they do. Still, I would feel better if I knew where your information has come from."

"It's not every day that one of our most powerful leaders gets married, Fausto. Everyone is talking about it. Jealousy, no doubt, over your beautiful wife."

I squeezed my fingers, making a fist over and over. "And yet I haven't heard you offer up your congratulations."

The resulting pause told me everything I needed to know. "Congratulations, my boy. *Evviva gli sposi!*" The traditional well wishes sounded forced.

"Thank you," I said coolly. "Was there anything else?"

"No, but they will demand answers regarding that package in a few weeks when I see you. This will not go unnoticed."

He was talking about Crimine, the yearly meeting for the highest 'Ndrangheta leaders. "I am more than happy to explain myself, but this is a private matter. They will understand."

"I hope for your sake that you are right. I must go. Ciao, Fausto."

We rang off and I tossed my phone onto the desk with an angry clatter. I dragged a hand through my hair. "I don't like this," I said to Giulio and Marco.

My cousin rubbed a hand over his mouth. "How did he hear of your wedding so quickly?"

"That is a good question." I leaned back and exhaled toward the ceiling. Madonna, it wasn't even nine o'clock and this day had already turned to shit. "Where are we with our investigations into the men?"

"Emilia thinks Benito is clean. I spoke with her yesterday," Marco said. "There's nothing in his finances that suggests any money coming in or out, not more than the usual. At least that she could find."

"I'm close with Benito," Giulio agreed. "I would know if he was working with one of our enemies."

Maybe. I wasn't willing to risk my family's safety on *maybe*, though. "Where are we with the others?"

"Emilia's working on it. I gave her more names to investigate. She did say Vic's stuff is heavily locked down. She's coming up against dead ends everywhere."

"That is suspicious."

"Maybe, but maybe not," Giulio said. "He's a tech guy. He's not some clueless soldier who'd keep his money under the mattress."

The pit of my stomach churned as I considered this. I wanted answers. Normally, I was a patient man, but every day this traitor remained in the shadows was a risk to everything I loved. "Still, I don't like it. We're keeping him off the estate?"

"Certo," Marco said. "He's working on beefing up the security at one of the warehouses. I've got a few guys watching him."

"Should we try to sweat him? Bring him to the dungeon and see what we can find out?"

Marco shook his head. "It's too risky until we have more information. If it's not Vic, it will tip off the real traitor and we may never learn who it is."

"That's true. The men will notice," Giulio added. "The second Vic disappears, word will spread."

I turned the problem over in my mind, examined it from all sides. "What if we take this woman, this GDF agent? Rinaldo? We sweat her instead?"

Marco and Giulio exchanged a look. "She's a woman, Papà," Giulio said. "We can't . . ."

He let it hang there, but I was already leaning forward. "I don't fucking care if she's a woman. She approaches Francesca? She should die for that alone."

"It would look very bad," Marco said carefully. "And it would bring a ton of shit down on our heads. The GDF and the press would go crazy."

I knew this, but part of me didn't care. "What if we take a trip to Piedmont?"

Marco pursed his lips, which he did often while thinking. "Take one of Mommo's guys? I like it."

"Won't he suspect us?" Giulio asked.

"Not at first," I said. "He treats me like I'm an idiot, like he's a mentor in my father's absence."

"I like this," Marco said. "I'll organize a trip tomorrow, after we see who in Mommo's crew would most likely have answers."

"Good." I looked at Giulio. "Sit with Francesca today. Have her write down everything she can remember from her time with Enzo, even if she thinks it's insignificant. She mentioned some things last night during the reception, and maybe she can remember more."

"I will, after her doctor's appointment."

Francesca had a doctor's appointment today? "Why wasn't I told she was going out?" I frowned at my cousin. "Did you know?"

"Yes. We've arranged security."

"I want her doctor coming here," I snapped. "No more trips off the estate."

My son winced and held up his palms. "She won't like that."

"Too fucking bad. She should—" I bit off the words, too angry with everyone. "Forget it. I'll tell her as soon as she's awake."

Francesca

I finally rolled out of bed and carried my exhausted ass downstairs for coffee. Granted, decaf because of the baby, but I wasn't complaining. To relax and sip a hot beverage sounded heavenly right now. Fausto had really taken it out of me last night.

Our wedding night, though? Absolute perfection.

As long as I live I'd never forget the way he looked at me, the way he devoured me in the vineyards. Then he brought me inside and melted my heart by fucking me slow and sweet, hardly breaking eye contact the entire time. God. Just thinking about it gave me shivers.

Giulio suddenly appeared beside me at the espresso machine. "You're finally awake."

I gave him serious side-eye. "I'm usually up before you, so I don't know what the hell you're talking about." My cup finished, so I took it off the machine and brought it to my mouth, blowing on the liquid to cool it down. "Speaking of, why are you up so early?"

"I was meeting with Fausto and Marco."

"Your new security role?"

"Yes."

He didn't say anything else as he started to make another cup of espresso, so I nudged his shoulder with mine. "Well?"

"Well, what?"

"What did you talk about? What's going on?"

He frowned as he worked the buttons. "You know I can't tell you."

"Why not?"

"Because it's business."

I put my hand on my chest. "But I'm family now. Team Ravazzani. I'm allowed to know business."

The noise that escaped his mouth said he didn't agree. "If my father approves, then I'll tell you whatever you wish to know."

Irritation prickled along my skin. I didn't like being kept in the dark. Weren't Giulio and I supposed to be friends?

Leaning in, I said, "If you don't tell me, then I'll tell you all about my amazing wedding night with of tons of rough sex and orgasms—"

"Dai, matrigna! Basta!"

I laughed at the genuine horror in his expression. "Every time you shut me out then I'll talk about all the orgasms your father is giving me."

"Gross, Frankie. Knock it off."

"Knock what off?" Fausto asked as he appeared in the kitchen doorway

My husband strode in, looking sexy as fuck in a three-piece gray suit that hugged his body. But it wasn't the bespoke clothing or expensive leather shoes that held my eye. Or even the classy silver watch peeking out from under the cuff of his dress shirt. It was the platinum band on his left ring finger that captured my attention. He was really mine.

"Oh, bella," Giulio chuckled under his breath before he sipped his espresso. "You have it so bad."

Not quite done torturing Giulio, I focused on Fausto, who was putting his cup and saucer into the porcelain sink. "I was just telling your son about all the amazing sex we had last night."

Giulio choked on his espresso, then immediately started for the hallway. "*Bacha ma culo, matrigna!*"

I rolled my lips between my teeth to keep from laughing. "Same to you, *figliastro*!" Yes, I had researched the word for stepson for this very reason.

Fausto shook his head, like Giulio and I were two obnoxious kids trying his patience. "I need to speak with you," he said to me, leaning against the counter and crossing his arms.

I didn't like the sound of that. "Oh?"

"You have a doctor's appointment this afternoon?"

"Yes. At two o'clock."

"You need to arrange it so the doctor visits you here."

He didn't elaborate or explain, which made me bristle a tiny bit. "Why?"

"Because I said so, Francesca. It's safer this way."

"But—"

"There's no 'but.' Your safety and our child's safety is my responsibility. The doctor may come here."

"Fausto," I snapped. "That's fine for future appointments, but I can't cancel at the last minute. I've already confirmed that I'll be there."

"Then call and tell them you won't." I started to argue, and he held up his hand. "I'm trying very hard not to raise my voice or lose my patience, but it's safer for you in the castello."

"And I agreed to have future appointments here. But we don't have any of the equipment yet. How are they supposed to do a check-up? Also, who knows when she'll be able to squeeze me in?"

"Have you forgotten your last name? She'll squeeze you in, do not worry."

This was ridiculous. "Giulio can take me today if you're busy."

"It has nothing to do with whether I am busy or not. I don't want you off the estate. Not now, maybe not ever!"

His voice rose steadily to a roar but I held my ground. "Have you lost your mind? I can't be a prisoner here."

"You will, if I ask it of you."

The conversation had taken a drastic turn, one I definitely didn't like. "Are we compromising? Because it doesn't feel like it right now."

He stared intently at my face, the bright blue depths swirling with emotion. I knew he was coming from a place of love, that he was worried about me and our bambino, but I didn't like starting off this marriage as a dictatorship. He needed to learn to work with me, to respect my feelings. To confide in and trust me. I asked, "Is there something you aren't telling me?"

"No."

"Then I'm keeping my appointment. I'll talk to her about moving them here for the future and ask for a list of equipment to buy, but I want to make sure everything is okay with the baby."

He straightened off the counter, his body instantly taut. "Have you been feeling any pain? Any discomfort?"

"You mean after you fucked the shit out of me last night?"

"I'm serious, monella."

"No pain, no twinges. But I *am* sore everywhere. We haven't exactly been, like, gentle."

He grimaced, almost as if he felt guilty. "Fine, I'll take you. We'll put your mind at ease about the baby."

Warmth spread through me. He was learning.

I drifted over to where he stood and wrapped my arms around his neck, pressing close. He dropped his hands onto my hips. "Baby," I whispered, nuzzling into his scratchy jaw. He hadn't shaved this morning and I loved the feel of his scruff on my skin. "Did we just have our first fight as a married couple?"

He put his face in my hair and inhaled as his hands swept up my back. "I like when you are sweet with me. My little kitten."

"Then I promise to be very sweet to you later, after my doctor's appointment."

He grunted. "I worry that something will happen to you. That something will happen to the baby."

"You can keep us safe, paparino. There's no one more capable than you and your men."

He dipped his head and kissed behind my ear, then moved along my throat, his lips soft and adoring. "You are going drive me crazy for the rest of my life, aren't you?"

"That is the plan, amore."

CHAPTER TWENTY-TWO

Enzo

I had no idea how long I had been imprisoned in the Ravazzani dungeon. Days? Weeks? Time had no meaning anymore as I drifted in and out of consciousness.

My entire body screamed in pain. I was fairly certain my left lung was punctured, which could happen when one's ribs were broken like mine. I couldn't hold my head up without getting dizzy. My right shoulder was dislocated, as was my left knee. Every breath was agony.

But I never broke.

Somehow I had endured Fausto's cruelty. I thought of my wife and children, my family. I thought of the beach in Napoli, my home there that I loved so much. I thought of my favorite places, my favorite meals—anything that allowed me to escape this nightmare, if only in my own mind.

I just had to keep my mouth shut and survive.

Fausto still didn't have what he wanted—access to my empire. I would die before signing it over to anyone. It had taken me years to establish the computer fraud scheme, and the other bosses ridiculed me along the way. Then, when I started making piles of Euros, they all wanted to reap the benefits. Fuck them.

And fuck Fausto. He'd maintained a stranglehold on the European drug market for years, never sharing with the rest of us. And if anyone else tried smuggling, he reacted with swift retribution, like a bully in primary school.

So I'd been smarter. Creative and more progressive. I alone brought the 'Ndrangheta into the twenty-first century. Drugs may be better understood by the old school, but I earned hundreds of billions every year with fraud. Fausto Ravazzani would never get his hands on it, either.

A key turned in the metal lock at the top of the stairs and I froze.

That sound haunted me. It signaled hours and hours of terrible suffering, and I wasn't certain how much more I could endure.

Besides, he'd promised to kill me the next time he visited.

When I've sent her sisters back to Toronto, I'll come down and finish what I've started.

My heart began racing as I tried to suck in air. At any second the heavy door would swing open and I would hear the scrape of their shoes on the stone steps. Their laughter and glee as they anticipated hurting me over and over.

Nothing.

There was only silence. I didn't understand. Where was Fausto? His consigliere, Marco, or his son, Giulio?

I was sweating. My breath wheezed as I tried to force enough air into my damaged lungs. Had I imagined the sound? Or was this just another way to torture me, to build my fear until I was nearly catatonic.

Cazzo. I didn't know anymore.

The room swam, even though my eyes were closed, the darkness swallowing me up. And I welcomed it.

Fausto

As we drove to the doctor's appointment, Francesca's face was nearly pressed to the car window, her wide eyes, taking in the city. It was like she'd never seen shops and restaurants before.

Because she hasn't seen much of Siderno before.

Guilt settled at the top of my spine, regret weighing heavily on me this afternoon. If I were a normal man, I would have taken her out to dinner, shows. Nightclubs and parties. Everything a girl her age deserved.

But I wasn't a normal man and our life would always be lived in the shadows. She and our children would need to stick to the estate, as I did. It was too dangerous otherwise, and Francesca would eventually come to respect my orders without question. My first wife had died at the hands of my enemies. I'd never survive it if I lost Francesca, too.

I wondered whether I'd been too lenient in giving in to this appointment today. Her concern over the baby convinced me, though. I had been rough with her recently, so it would be good to reassure us both.

Extra precautions had been taken for the outing, including tripling the number of soldiers accompanying us. The car had been swept for bugs and tracking devices as usual, and the route had been secured. While Enzo no longer posed a threat, I still had other enemies. I wasn't taking any chances with Francesca and our child.

Marco's phone rang, interrupting the silence. He answered and spoke quietly in cryptic sentences, as we always did with our business when using phones. When he finished, he turned toward me. "It's nothing. I'll tell you later."

Because Francesca was in the car. "Anything serious?"

"No. I had to shuffle people around today while you're gone and the men were confused. Also, I worked out who is going to Piedmont."

"Good. Are you keeping Giulio apprised?" My son was in the car behind us, riding with more of my men.

"I'll text him now."

"Is this about Enzo?"

At Francesca's question, Marco winced and slowly faced forward, like he was removing himself from this conversation. I angled toward my wife. "You know I can't discuss these things with you."

"But you were just discussing it in front of me."

"A good wife would pretend she didn't hear anything," I teased, knowing it would make her mad, while I ran my fingers along her arm.

She lowered her voice and leaned in. "You don't want a good wife. You'd be bored with her in an afternoon."

She was probably right. I shifted to kiss her, my chest swelling with the magnitude of what I felt for this woman. I loved her so fucking much.

I didn't care that the men in the front knew I was kissing my wife, not when Francesca's lips were this eager, her mouth this hot. Her tits were pressed against my arm, her leg moving restlessly along mine, like she was trying to get closer. I slid my hand up her bare thigh, eager to hear her little whimpers.

Then her stomach growled. Loudly.

I pulled back to see her face turn bright red. She bit her lip. "Sorry. I didn't get a chance to eat lunch."

"Why not?"

"Don't scowl at me," she snapped. "Nothing sounded good at the time. It's not a big deal."

"This is a very big deal. My son or daughter needs you to stay healthy, wife."

"I've got it covered. I don't need you all up in my business."

Her flippant attitude did nothing to reassure me. "Your business is my business. Or have you forgotten?"

There was a gelato store a few doors down from the office building where her doctor's office resided. I glanced at my wife and came to a quick decision. "Pull over, Nesto."

Enzo

A noise roused me. But there was no one in the dungeon. Now I was sure I was hearing things.

My brain tried to focus, but it was like slogging through quicksand. I was numb and weak, and every second I was conscious felt like an hour.

There. I heard it again. It was the door.

Cristo! No, no, no.

I shivered, the dread filling my veins like ice water. I tried to remember what little words of prayer I could still recall. *Please, help me.*

There were more of them this time. I counted at least eight men coming down the stairs. They were moving slower than usual. But why hurry, I supposed? I wasn't going anywhere.

I heard whispers but couldn't make them out. That was odd. Usually Fausto was shouting at me, taunting me the second he entered the dungeon.

They came closer, but I didn't bother looking. I didn't need to see the smug satisfaction when he saw me, naked and crumpled, on the dungeon floor. I prayed he killed me quickly, but I knew he wouldn't.

Please.

"Don D'Agostino."

No one had called me by that name in quite a long time. I opened my good eye and squinted, trying to make out a face.

I knew that face.

It was one of my own men.

"Don D'Agostino," he breathed, his gaze sweeping down my mangled body. "Thank God you are alive."

The overwhelming relief caused tears to form, so I closed my eye and relaxed into the dirt floor. Dio santo! They had come for me. Fucking finally.

Ravazzani hadn't known that I had people close to him, people who would work to get me out, and I prayed each morning it would be the day. I'd all but run out of hope. I was certain after Fausto's last visit that my time was up.

But I held out long enough. I would soon be free.

Voices carried on around me. "He can't walk. We'll need to carry him."

"But I think his shoulder is dislocated."

"We can't fix it now. We don't have time."

There was rustling and I felt my body shifting as they got into position. I made a pitiful whine when they lifted me, sounding more like a wounded animal than a man. The pain was excruciating.

I must have passed out going up the stairs because the next thing I knew we were out in the fresh air. Gunfire popped in the distance and I cracked my eyelid to see where we were.

They were carrying me around the side of Fausto's castello. Bodies dotted the ground, the dirt dark and wet beneath them. My men surrounded me, at least ten of them, some holding me and the rest offering protection. The jostling and shifting nearly caused me to vomit, not that I had anything in my stomach.

One of my men fired his gun, the sound both familiar and strange after so long in isolation. I could barely breathe as more shots were fired, the hope and terror lodging in my throat. To be stopped now, when I was so close to freedom, would be worse than never having a chance at all. They would need to put a bullet between my eyes right here because I would not return to that dungeon under any circumstances.

They started yelling, but I was too weak and nauseous to understand what was being said.

Instead, I began to pray.

Fausto

Nesto cast a worried look at Marco before glancing at me in the rear view mirror. "But, Don Ravazzani . . ."

"Here," I repeated in a sharp tone, the one my men knew was an order. I appreciated his caution, but we were well guarded and the obstetrician was just a few doors down. There was no reason I couldn't treat my woman to gelato right now.

Nesto slowed the car, guiding us to the curb, then came to a stop. Francesca peered over my shoulder. "What's going on? Why are we stopping here?"

I threw open the door and got out. The car behind us had also pulled over, and my men were hurrying onto the sidewalk to offer protection. Marco was there beside me, his keen gaze taking in the street, his body tense and ready. I could hear his phone buzz, but he ignored it.

"Anything?" I asked him.

"No, but let's make this quick."

I held out my hand to Francesca and her fingers met mine. "Dai, andiamo." I helped her out of the big car. "I want to feed you. Let's get you some gelato."

"You're buying me gelato. Right now?" She gave me that secret teasing smile of hers, the one that said she knew how much I loved her. I would do anything for that smile.

"There is never a bad time for gelato, no?" I threw my arm around her waist and tugged her close as we strolled inside. "I know how much you love it. And I know you're hungry."

The shop was empty, so she took her time deciding, asking for samples of three or four different flavors. By the time she settled on the mint chocolate chip, she was smiling and laughing. Marco and Nesto waited outside like a protective wall, so I opened the door for her. She waited for me on the walk, then held up her spoon. "Here, try this."

"Are you sure?" I grinned at her. "I was told never to take food away from a pregnant woman."

She rolled her eyes but chuckled. "Oh, the misogyny. You are hopeless, husband."

Her happiness sank into my bones, a balm for all the violence and cruelty I dealt with on a daily basis. It was like the dark clouds that loomed over my soul parted just for her, enough to let in her sassy mouth and resilient spirit.

I snatched her hand and bent down for the gelato.

Enzo

I was too dizzy, so I had to keep my eyes closed. The shouts and gunfire grew louder, more intense as we went. One of the men carrying me stumbled, and horrendous pain went all throughout my body. I felt my stomach revolt, but I was somehow able to keep from retching.

If they dropped me, I'm not certain I would survive it.

"Almost there, Don D'Agostino," one of my men said.

I could hear the rumble of a car engine, the most beautiful sound I'd ever heard save for the first cries of my children when they were born.

"Open the door!"

More shots nearby and then they laid me down on a cool leather seat. Someone threw a blanket over me.

"Dai, andiamo!"

A car door slammed. Dio, was I really going to get out of this place? It seemed too good to be true. I tried to listen to what was going on, catching pieces here and there.

"Wait!"

"What is it?"

"The shots have been reported and the carabinieri are on the way. They'll approach from the north, so you must head south to avoid them."

"Grazie. We couldn't have done this without your help."

"Just make sure he knows when he wakes up. I want a promise that my family will be safe."

Ah, so this was Fausto's man, the one who had helped me bring down the Ravazzani empire. While he'd been useful to me over the last year, I had to wonder why he didn't tip me off about the attack on my beach house. Had he wanted Fausto to capture me?

"Of course, of course," my soldier said. "Now, let us leave."

More doors slammed, and then the tires squealed as the car drove off. They held me to keep me from tumbling about, but with every bump and twist I fought to remain conscious.

"Should we take him to the nearest hospital?"

"No. To the docks, as we discussed."

"But—"

"We just need to get him on the ship. The doctor can attend to him there."

"I think he needs more than a doctor."

"No . . . hospital," I wheezed.

It was hardly more than a breath, but they heard me. We had to get as far away from Siderno as possible—and quickly.

If I was right, then all hell was about to break loose.

Fausto

When I licked gelato off my lips, Francesca gave me a sly grin. "You want some now, don't you? I can see it in your eyes."

"And what is it you think I want, amore?" I asked, leaning close.

"Stop. You're not getting that until we get home." She glanced back at the gelato shop. "I'm kind of regretting not getting the chocolate, though."

"Cioccolato," I corrected.

Her eyes glazed over, like she did when I talked dirty Italian to her in bed. "God, I love the way you say that."

I kissed her forehead. "Go back to the car with Marco. I'll go get you some for later."

"You will?" She fed me another spoonful of mint chocolate chip gelato. "You are the best husband I've ever had."

I playfully slapped her ass right there on the walk. "The only husband you'll ever have."

Spinning toward the store, I suddenly felt a hard punch to my side, but saw no one close enough to hit me. Cazzo, that hurt. The impact threw me back a step, then I dropped to one knee. I couldn't control my body, the pain was so great.

Then I knew what had happened. What was happening. I supposed it had been inevitable.

My brain couldn't function but my mouth still worked. "Francesca,"

I wheezed, wanting them to get her to safety. She was what mattered in this moment, not me. She was the only thing that mattered.

I watched her mouth open in a scream but nothing came out. My men rushed around me, their footsteps silent, as I collapsed on the hard ground and blue sky filled my vision. I heard nothing, the pain in my lower half roaring in my mind, my ears ringing. I saw Marco, who seemed to be shouting at me . . . and then I slipped away.

CHAPTER TWENTY-THREE

Francesca

I was screaming.
They were dragging me away from him and I couldn't stop screaming. I clawed and dove, struggled as hard as I could to get back to him, my entire world laying there on the ground, his blood seeping out onto the cement.

No, this isn't happening. They can't take him from me.

"Fausto!" I cried. And cried and cried, his name a refrain on my lips, my only thought to be with him. "No, please! I have to be there!"

They didn't listen. Three soldiers packed me into the Range Rover and shouted at me to stay low. I was hysterical, crying and shaking. Marco was with Fausto, pressing on his side, and my husband—oh, God. His eyes were closed and he was as pale as death. *No, please. Don't take him from me.*

Marco began giving orders and they lifted Fausto up quickly, carrying him to my car. I moved over, making as much room as possible. Nesto jumped behind the wheel, Giulio in the passenger seat, as the men put Fausto into the back seat with me. I grabbed under his shoulders and pulled with all my might to help get him into the car, settling his head on my lap, and Marco climbed into the back, too.

"*Vai, vai!*" Marco punched the back of the driver's seat as if to hurry Nesto.

The car sped off, but I couldn't pay attention to anything but my man's face. Tears streamed down my cheeks, and I could barely breathe through my sobs. He could not die. Not here, not now.

I stroked my husband's forehead and held him. He was so still, his chest barely moving. His olive skin was dull, like someone had unplugged the light inside him. "Paparino," I whispered. "You can't leave me."

"Francesca," Marco barked. "I need your help."

I sucked in a deep breath. "Tell me what to do."

"I need you to keep pressure on his wound while I work."

I gently laid Fausto's head on the seat and joined Marco in the footwell. I reached for Fausto's middle and put my hands on the bloody towels covering the wound. There was so much blood. Fausto's blood. It seeped through the fabric and onto my hands. My arms shook as I pressed, hoping I could stem the flow of red.

"Just keep firm, even pressure on him, Frankie. I won't know what we're dealing with until I see the wound." Marco said as he pulled a case from under the front seat.

Fausto groaned and I started to ease off. "Ignore him," Marco snapped. "It's better that he lives. Keep doing what you're doing."

Oh, Jesus. I didn't move, just kept pressing down on the bloody towels. *Don't die, don't die, don't die.* It was a mantra in my head, a prayer of desperation in my darkest hour.

Now wearing surgical gloves, Marco flicked open a knife. "Here, let me in there."

When I backed away, Marco shoved aside the bloody cloth then quickly cut through Fausto's vest and shirt, exposing the wound. Blood ran in rivers out of my husband's body, and I covered my mouth, trying not to howl in terror.

Marco wasn't phased, his expression calm. He doused Fausto with water from the kit and pushed a plastic tube filled with white stuff into

Fausto's wound. Then he pushed on a plunger and forced whatever was in the tube into Fausto.

I could see the white stuff instantly expand, the blood slowing.

"What was all that?"

"Saline to clean the area and special sponges. They expand to pack the wound and stop the bleeding."

"How do you know about this stuff?"

He went back to the case. "I was a medic in the army."

I felt a burst of hope. Thank God Marco was here. "Now what?"

He took out a large plastic pack, ripped it open, and placed a bandage over Fausto's abdomen. It had a large pad and what looked like a strange plastic handle attached. "We need to wrap his middle with this. I'm going to lift him a bit. Hold this pad and push the other end of the bandage under him."

Marco slid his arms under Fausto and lifted, and I quickly did what he described.

"Now bring the bandage up, twist it once and slide it through the plastic cleat."

Looking closely, I realized that what I thought was a handle had a small gap and I was able to pass the bandage through it.

"Now, go the other way now. Pull firmly, not too hard, in the opposite direction. Kind of like you're cinching up a belt."

I understood and pulled toward me and pushed the bandage under from the front.

"Good, keep going. This is a compression bandage. It will maintain pressure. Wrap it around as many times as you can."

When I finished, Marco rested Fausto back on the seat and took the end of the bandage from my bloody hands. He tucked two small hooks under the wrapped edges of the bandage. "That will hold it in place. You did well, Frankie. Now the hospital must do the rest. How long?" he shouted up front.

"Five minutes," Nesto said.

Oh, God. Was that close enough? Did Fausto have that long? Tears streaming once again, I grabbed my husband's hand, squeezing hard, trying to give him strength through my fingers.

Nesto drove wildly, cutting through traffic, while Giulio talked on the phone, barking Italian at someone. When he hung up, he said, "The hospital is ready for him."

That made me cry harder. People *died* in hospitals. My mother died in a hospital.

"Get David there, too," Marco snapped. "He'll assess the surgical staff and whether we need to fly anyone in from Rome."

To work on Fausto. Oh, God.

"Frankie, be strong." Marco's voice was quiet and reassuring. "He needs your fire right now. Your spirit, not your tears."

I nodded. Marco was right. I couldn't fall apart. I was married to the most dangerous man in Europe, so I had to be prepared for the blood and violence that came with it. It was just . . . .

"I cannot lose him," I whispered. My God, we hadn't even been married for twenty-four hours.

"You won't. He's tough. This is the fifth time someone has attempted to kill him. He'll survive."

I stared at the red coating my hands, the blood all around us. It stained the front of my dress, the leather seats. There was so much of it. Why had I insisted on coming today? This was why he was so secretive, why he stayed close to the castello. But he relented because I'd asked. Had stopped to buy me gelato because I hadn't eaten lunch. How could I have been so selfish as to demand this trip?

My chest splintered, so full of anguish and guilt that I could barely breathe. I'd never recover if something happened to him. I wanted to fuck in the vineyards and see him hold our babies, drink wine and take showers together. I needed a lifetime of memories with him.

I needed more time.

Please don't take him from me.

We arrived at the hospital a few minutes later, tires screeching as Nesto turned into the drive. A team of nurses and doctors awaited, an empty gurney at the ready. Terror clawed into my throat. I wasn't ready to let him go. If those people took him away, I might never see him again. *Just like Mamma.*

I swallowed hard. *Be strong. They will fix him. He will not die.* I repeated the words over and over as they took my husband from the car, put him on the gurney and wheeled him inside the building. My feet were rooted to the ground, my eyes focused on the doors, now closed. An arm slid around my shoulders.

"Let's go inside." It was Giulio. He had to be hurting, too.

I flung myself into his arms, wrapping around him. "Tell me it's going to be okay."

He hugged me, his heat and strength surrounding me. A long moment passed before he answered, his voice raw. "I can't. You and I, we've never lied to one another."

Oh, God. I clung to him, more tears leaking from my eyes. I hadn't known I could cry this much.

"This is my fault," I sobbed into his shirt. "He tried to talk me out of it but I wouldn't listen. I can't . . ."

I can't live with myself if something happens to him.

"We were very careful." Giulio squeezed me hard. "This shouldn't have happened."

Marco eased up alongside us. "You two need to get inside. I have to go. I need to find the shooter."

Nesto came over, his phone pressed to his ear. "Enzo's escaped," he told Marco. "His men attacked the castello."

I gasped as Guilio shouted, "*Figlio di cane!*"

Marco dragged a hand down his face, his eyes solemn. "A distraction. Of course."

I wasn't sure what that meant, but I knew it was bad.

"I'll keep you informed of his condition," Giulio promised Marco.

Marco put a hand on Giulio's shoulder. "You're in charge. Until he recovers everyone answers to you. Be ready, Giulio."

Giulio nodded. "Grazie, Zio."

"He's proud of you. He knows you can handle it, okay? And make sure she eats and drinks. For the baby."

"I will."

Marco took Nesto and drove off, and Giulio led me into the hospital. We were waved in, immediately sent to a private waiting room. I thought there would be paperwork to fill out, but no one asked us any questions. I supposed they all knew my husband. Presenting an identification card really wasn't necessary.

I sat next to Giulio and stared at the blood on my dress. Was this the last part of him I would have? Dried blood on some expensive fabric? I didn't want to wash my hands. I didn't want to change. I needed to keep him close, even if it was just his blood.

Zia soon arrived, looking a decade older than she had this morning, and she asked Giulio questions in rapid Italian but I was too out of it to follow. All I could do was clutch the bottle of water in my blood-stained hands and stare at the wall.

What was I going to do if he died? Our child would never meet its father. I would never hear Fausto call me "dolcezza" or "piccolina monella" again. No more naughty games. I would live the rest of my life without his formidable presence, an empty hole no one else could ever fill. I wouldn't survive it.

So much blood. His skin had been so pale.

I started trembling, my teeth chattering. Suddenly, Giulio was there, throwing his suit jacket around my shoulders. He knelt in front of me, his hands stroking up and down my arms. "You're in shock," he said. "Take a deep breath."

I shook my head. I couldn't. Air wouldn't help fix him.

"Frankie, breathe, bella. Think of your baby. Fausto's baby. He would hate it if something happened to either of you."

I dragged in a deep breath and Giulio encouraged me. "That's it. Keep breathing. He's going to be okay."

"You said you wouldn't lie to me."

"That was before I thought you'd faint on me. Keep going. In and out. I'll see if I can find a blanket."

Then he was gone. I blinked back tears and tried to focus on my breathing as Zia sat next to me. She didn't speak and soon Giulio came back with a hospital blanket, which he wrapped around my shoulders.

Zia motioned to Giulio and started speaking rapidly, which Giulio translated for me. "Enough, Francesca. You must be strong. You are a Ravazzani now, his queen. You cannot sit and snivel and faint like a weak little woman. Everyone will look to you, his wife, regarding his condition. If you project strength and power, everyone will be reassured—" Giulio stopped abruptly and said, "Zia, basta."

He gestured to my hands and my dress, apparently defending me, but Zia remained firm. She told him to shut up and keep translating.

With a sigh, Giulio kept going. "You are his wife, the one who bears the future of the family inside you. He will expect you to shoulder this, whatever happens, with grace and courage. Like a Ravazzani."

I sat straighter, knowing she was right. This was not the time to fall apart. I had to be strong. For Fausto. For our child.

"Excellent," Zia said, slowly this time. "You show them, Francesca. Show them the Ravazzanis cannot be defeated."

CHAPTER TWENTY-FOUR

Francesca

After six hours, Fausto came out of surgery in stable but serious condition, and was taken to the ICU. The doctors explained the bullet went in through his back and out his side, and Marco had likely saved Fausto's life by packing the wound with the sponges in the car. During the operation, they repaired one of Fausto's kidneys and a torn portion of his small intestines, and removed his gallbladder. They were optimistic about his recovery, but the risk of infection was high.

He hadn't woken up yet, and they were keeping him on a ventilator for now. But he was alive. Pale, but alive.

We arranged for a large private room, one with a small bed for me. Guards were posted outside the room and throughout the hospital itself. Anyone coming into Fausto's room had to wear special identification, including doctors and nurses. Considering Enzo had escaped, we weren't taking any chances.

Zia began praying over Fausto's prone form, while Giulio and I talked quietly off to the side. "I will have someone bring you clothes," he said. "Anything else you want from home?"

"I'll text you a list. Has there been any word from Marco?"

"Yes. It was a professional. They found his location, up on a rooftop across the street from your doctor's office. Probably hired by Enzo's men as a diversion from the attack on the castello."

I rubbed my eyes, trying to take it all in. "And Enzo?"

"We don't know. I can't imagine he'll stay in Siderno. It's too dangerous and he's too weak. My guess is he's being taken back to Naples." He hugged me. "We have to focus on Fausto right now. Thankfully, it looks like you won't be a widow quite yet, matrigna."

"I feel as though today has taken several years off my life." I leaned into his solid warmth. "Thank God he let you come with us. I'm so glad you were here."

"Same, bella. I'll take Zia home and we'll return in the morning." He kissed my cheeks. "Try and get some sleep."

"I will. You too, G. Stay safe. We have a long road ahead of us."

Nesto poked his head in, takeout containers in his arms. "Signora Ravazzani, I brought food."

I let go of Giulio and held out my hands. "Bless you, Nesto. I hope there is pasta in there." With Fausto now out of surgery, I felt like my stomach could finally handle food.

"Just as you requested. And plenty of tiramisu." He gave me the containers and kissed my cheeks. "Take care of Don Ravazzani for us."

"I will. Grazie, Nesto. Seriously, this is amazing."

"Prego, signora. We are all thinking of you and praying for the don's recovery."

"Please, call me Frankie."

Giulio made a hissing noise through his teeth, then barked orders at Nesto. When the younger man left, Giulio frowned. "They must respect you. Do not get close to them. Let them address you properly as the don's wife."

"Aren't you being a little harsh?"

"You and I must hold everything together until Fausto recovers. No one can suspect we might be weak. This world, it preys on weakness.

Marco will help, but we are the Ravazzanis responsible for the future. It falls to us to carry on when my father cannot, capisce?"

This version of Giulio was worlds away from the one who'd splashed me in the water and helped me buy lingerie. He was deadly serious, his shoulders stiff with the weight of all that rested upon them. I gave him a grim smile. "I understand. This isn't going to be easy for you, is it?"

"No, but it is what's expected."

"I'll help you."

"Good, because those spreadsheets and stock reports are like Japanese to me. I've never been good with numbers."

Math wasn't my best subject in school, but I wasn't terrible at it, either. And I remembered my lunch with Zio Toni. Talking over the business stuff had been interesting. "I think I can handle the legitimate side with Toni." Probably.

"And I'll handle the other side."

"I can help with the 'ndrina business, too."

Giulio immediately shook his head. "Fausto would kill me. You stay clean and out of prison."

"G—"

"No, Frankie."

I gave him my sweetest smile. "We'll discuss this later."

"You're going to be a pain in my ass, aren't you?"

I sobered, realizing this wasn't the time for teasing. He had enough to worry about that I didn't need to add to it. "No, we're a team. I only want to help. I'll see you tomorrow?"

"Certo," he said and kissed my cheek.

Then Giulio wrapped an arm around Zia and pulled her away from Fausto. "*Domani, domani,*" he kept telling her. She wasn't happy, but she finally kissed my cheeks and left. Then I was alone with my husband.

The beeps and whirs echoed in the empty room as I went to his side. Only his chest moved as air was forced in and out of his lungs, his face serene. I placed a kiss on his forehead, letting my lips linger on his warm skin to reassure myself he was still here. Still alive. I never wanted to relive a day like today ever again.

"Paparino," I whispered. "I don't know what I would do without you."

I took a shower, finally changing out of the bloody clothes and into a pair of scrubs they gave me. Then I ate dinner and sat with Fausto some more. I considered the tiny bed awaiting me, but I was wound too tightly. Every time I closed my eyes I saw Fausto on the ground, bleeding out. Or in the car, his blood seeping all over my hands.

Sleep would not come anytime soon.

I went to the door and found the soldier stationed there. "Stay with him, Carlo. I'm going down to the cafeteria for coffee."

"I will get you coffee, signora."

"No, that's all right. I need to walk around a bit."

Carlo motioned to the young man stationed at the end of the hall. "Leo will go with you."

"I'll be fine. That's not necessary."

"Signora, Marco and Giulio will gut me like a fish if you go alone."

I took pity on him. Carlo was just trying to do his job. "Fine. I'm sorry."

I smiled at Leo and let him follow me to the cafeteria. When we arrived he waited near the entrance, his eyes roving as he checked the area. There weren't many people there at this hour, just a few women milling about and some nurses laughing together at a table. I went to the cappuccino machine and began making three cups, one each for me, Leo and Carlo.

A woman with a baseball cap on her head came to stand next to me. I switched out the cup and started another one. "I'll just be another second."

"No problem, Signora Ravazzani."

She knew me? Surprised, I glanced over and came face-to-face with Agent Rinaldo.

My muscles tightened. "What the hell are you doing here?"

"I thought with what happened today you might be ready to chat. It's not too late for us to help you."

"You have to be joking. I married him."

"The marriage can be annulled." Her gaze searched my face from under the bill of her hat. "You don't realize how close you were to getting shot, do you? Two inches to the right and that bullet would have torn through you and your baby."

I hadn't thought of that, but now I couldn't think of anything else—and it made me very angry. What right did this woman have to come to the hospital where my husband almost *died* and say these things to me? She was trying to scare me, to get me to betray Fausto.

I considered alerting Leo, but I really couldn't handle any more bloodshed today. So I hurried with my task, ready to get away from the agent as quickly as possible.

She continued, oblivious to my mounting fury. "Is this a risk you want to take with your child?"

"Don't presume to know what is best for my child—and I'm not leaving my husband, ever. You are wasting your time."

"You are making a mistake, Frankie."

I sneered as I stepped closer and lowered my voice. "That is Signora Ravazzani to you. Stay the fuck away from me and my family, Agent Rinaldo."

I grabbed my cups and hurried toward the register. Flustered, I reached for my wallet . . . and realized I didn't have one. "Perdonami," I told the cashier and looked up for Leo. "I forgot my money."

She waved me off. "That is not necessary, Signora Ravazzani."

How did she know . . . ?

Oh. I supposed everyone in the hospital knew who I was.

"No, please. We can pay." I didn't like the idea of getting things for free because of my husband's last name.

My last name now, too.

Leo arrived and held out a few Euros. "I'll pay you back upstairs," I told him as we walked away.

"That is not necessary, signora. It is an honor."

"Well, this is for you," I said, lifting one of the three cappuccinos.

"Grazie," he said as we walked back to the elevator.

The antiseptic smell clung in my nostrils, a perfume of loss and pain, a cocktail of human suffering that lingered inside these walls. I could still remember visiting my mother, holding her thin hand and crying. The twins hadn't visited as often, so I'm not sure what their memories were of Mamma's last weeks, but seeing her waste away had been fucking awful.

The elevator doors opened and we stepped in. I had to forget those memories and forget about Agent Rinaldo. Only my husband mattered right now.

———

Time moved slowly the next few days.

They took Fausto off the ventilator two days after his surgery. Not long after, his eyes fluttered open. There he was, alive and still with me. I pressed my forehead to his cheek. "Ti amo, baby."

There wasn't much more to say than that, because he drifted back into unconsciousness. The knot in my chest eased a tiny fraction. Our problems were far from over, but it was good to see his gorgeous blue eyes staring at me once again.

We decided I would spend nights at the hospital, while Zia would sit with Fausto during the day. This would allow me to go home and clean up, as well as see to the estate and business matters during Fausto's recovery. The doctors were keeping him heavily sedated for the time being and they didn't anticipate him leaving the hospital for at least a month.

Marco and Giulio took over Fausto's office, the two of them sequestered in there for hours at a time. I knew they were trying to find the shooter and Enzo, as well as going over other mafia business. Every time I asked about what was going on, they evaded the questions, clearly trying to shield me. Except there was no reason to shield me any longer. I made my choice when I married Fausto, then again when I cursed out Agent Rinaldo in the hospital cafeteria.

Still, Giulio was steadfast in his refusal to involve me.

Zio Toni took me under his wing. He came over and met with me in my new office, which had been an old library that no one used anymore. We walked through all the legitimate businesses—the number of which absolutely made my head spin—and he shared the financial documents with me. I spent one whole day just trying to wrap my brain around Fausto's laptop, including the bizarre naming system he used to keep the Guardia off his ass.

If nothing else, this experience taught me that my man was clever. And rich.

I knew he was rich, but this was on another level. He owned companies throughout the world with hundreds of thousands of employees, and this didn't include the illegitimate businesses. Those made money hand over fist. Put it all together and I couldn't even fathom his net worth.

I enjoyed the work. It gave me something to do, something to distract me from worrying about everything else going on. The first thing I did was tackle his email in-box, which was something of a catastrophe. Fausto wasn't big on responding, clearly, which left tens of thousands of unopened emails. The number of notifications made the back of my neck itch.

"You can see he's old school. He prefers to talk rather than write," Zio Toni said with a chuckle when I pointed this out.

"But how does he know there isn't something important in here?"

"He waits until I call him to tell him something important is in there."

I rubbed my forehead and stared at the overflowing in-box. "Isn't that incredibly inefficient?"

"Yes," Toni said without hesitation. "But I can't get him to change, no matter how many times I bring it up."

"He needs, like, an executive assistant to manage his shit."

"I agree, but he's too paranoid to ever hire anyone to do it."

This I believed—and Fausto's paranoia was hardly unwarranted. Enzo had stolen thirty million Euros from him recently. Did Toni know? I didn't ask. It wasn't my news to share, if Fausto hadn't confided in Toni. Besides, someone had helped Enzo steal that money. Until we knew who, I was keeping that information to myself.

Guilt settled in my stomach like a stone. Would Fausto's cousin really betray him?

Jesus, I didn't know. I hadn't thought anyone would dare an assassination attempt in broad daylight on the street, either. Showed what I knew.

"Well, I'll go through his email for now," I told Toni. "Then, while I sit with him at the hospital, I can go through the larger issues and type out his responses."

"Va bene, signora. That would be a big help. In the meantime, you can sit in on the meetings, take notes, and relay the information to him as you see fit."

I could do that.

While I hated the reasons behind my involvement in Fausto's business, I was excited to help. I didn't want to be a clueless mafia wife, whose only purpose was to raise babies and look good on my husband's arm. That would drive me slowly insane. I needed to do more and this was the perfect way to contribute.

Toni set me up with a separate email and calendar just for me. The next day I began joining conference calls and introducing myself, taking notes and learning who was who. Most everyone conducted business in English, and Toni hired translators for those who didn't.

I was in the midst of a call with a chemical company in Germany when Giulio walked in. He looked *terrible*. Like he hadn't slept or showered since before Fausto's shooting more than a week ago. I frowned at him and made sure I was muted on the conference call. "Hey, G. Everything okay?"

"You know the answer to that." He dropped heavily into a chair. "What are you doing?"

"Listening to a chemical company in Germany whine about the construction delays in their expansion."

"That's an excuse on the part of the construction company to drag it out and earn more money. The construction company is either one of ours or belongs to another 'ndrina, someone my father is doing a favor for. Ask them." He nodded toward the laptop, where I had my video and sound off.

I unmuted and interrupted. "Excuse me, but what is the name of the construction company?"

"Bosporus Construction Limited, Frau Ravazzani," someone answered.

Giulio gave a nod, then motioned for me to cut the sound. "That's the North Rhine-Westphalia 'ndrina," he said. "Papà's undoubtedly given Bosporus the job in trade for something else. I'll make a call today, see if we can't resolve it. That'll be one less headache for you."

"But one more thing on your plate." I reached over and rubbed his shoulder, which was tight. "Should I be worried about you?"

"No, because it wouldn't change anything. And I don't want you under any additional stress."

That didn't reassure me in the least. I stood and began giving him a shoulder rub. "What about your stress?"

His head dropped forward and he groaned. "Mamma mia, that feels good."

"I'm serious. Are you sleeping?"

"I'm okay. You have enough happening right now. Don't worry about me, too."

That was not a great answer. "Talk to me, then. How is it going? Can I help?"

"No, no one can." He exhaled long and loud. "I keep thinking, this is my future. This is what it will be like when he steps down. Which he could do tomorrow, if he wanted. He has you and a new baby on the way. After almost dying, he might decide to hand it over to me."

I didn't think Fausto would do this. He was too much of a control freak to let it go, at least for now, but I could see a scenario where he slowly turned more over to Giulio in the next few years. "Is it so awful?"

"I probably shouldn't tell you."

"But I want to know."

"They know he's hurt and they're coming for us. For me. We've had three of our supply houses hit in the last two days, and it will only get worse. So I have to make a show of strength to prove that we aren't weak. That I'm strong. It's such bullshit. Like proving my manhood or something."

"Gross."

"Exactly." He rolled his neck as I continued to rub. "I've tortured and threatened so many men in the last thirty-six hours that I'm sick to my stomach. I'd much rather sit in here and take conference calls and make stock trades. Use my brain instead of killing people."

"You have to tell your father."

"Sure, right. He'd love to hear it, no?"

"You've already proven yourself, G. You've worked for the 'ndrina for years. Marco has boys who could take over. So does Toni. This doesn't need to fall on your shoulders."

"You know Fausto better than anyone. Do you honestly think he'll let a nephew take over?"

I grimaced. No, my man would not be receptive to this idea *at all*. "Probably not, but we can work on convincing him together."

"I won't put that on you. No, I need to stop complaining like a little bitch. I'm better off just accepting it." He gave a rusty laugh. "Maybe I just need to get laid."

"There's always the hookup apps."

"When the fuck would I have time? I'm guarded every second." He scrubbed his face with both hands. "Another glimpse of my future as boss. Celibate, except for sleeping with a wife I don't love."

I lowered my voice. "You need someone on the estate. A man you can see here."

"Someone I sneak off with, hoping not to get caught. Someone who can never tell anyone and risks death with every encounter. Sure, what man wouldn't sign up for such an honor? It's too depressing. Sometimes I wish—"

When he didn't continue, I asked, "You wish, what?"

"Nothing. Forget it. Just pointless daydreams." He drew in a deep breath and let it out slowly. "I'm fine."

He didn't look or sound fine. "I love you, G. I'll find a way to help you. Let's just get through this and get him home, okay?"

He reached to rub my shoulder as I had done with his. "Love you, too, matrigna. Now, the reason I came in here was to ask about Enzo. Marco wants me to sit with you and see if you can recall anything else from your captivity. Anything that might help us learn who the traitor is."

"Traitor? You mean the person who helped Enzo steal thirty million Euros?"

"That, and everything else. How was Enzo's crew able to get onto the estate, get into the dungeon, and carry him off? And at the exact time Fausto was shot, no less."

"A misdirection, Marco called it."

"Yes. And someone helped to facilitate your kidnapping. The cameras cut out at very inconvenient times."

"Then it's whoever was on the cameras."

"It's not that clear. Vic was on the cameras when you were kidnapped, but he wasn't anywhere near the estate when Enzo was released."

"I see."

"Let's focus. Anything else you overheard or saw with Enzo?"

I repeated what I'd told Fausto and Marco, which was all I knew. "Enzo wasn't around much. He was mostly with his wife."

"That's what I thought, but I had to ask." He pushed away from the table and stood. "Your conference call is over, by the way."

Damn, I hadn't noticed. I logged off from the conferencing software as Giulio walked to the door. "Can we have dinner together?" I shouted to his back.

"Can't. No time. I'll see you later, bella."

I watched him slip through the door, not liking this one bit. I knew it wasn't forever, just until Fausto returned, but something needed to give.

CHAPTER TWENTY-FIVE

Fausto

I almost died. Again.
 This time was different, however. The other attempts on my life had been sloppy, easily avoided. Except for the car bomb, I saw them coming.
 The sniper caught me by surprise. I hadn't expected a coordinated attack to facilitate Enzo's escape. I suppose I should have—he knew it was me or him, that one of us would end up dead—but I'd been shot on the street like a foot soldier. In front of my wife.
 What had I been thinking?
 I'd been careless, which was unforgivable. She was carrying my child. Nothing mattered more than the two of them, along with Giulio. I should've held firm and had Francesca cancel the appointment. Instead I let her manipulate me to get her way.
 I would not make that mistake again.
 Consciousness once more tugged at me and forced me awake. My brain swam toward the sounds until my eyelids fluttered. I hoped to

find the beautiful face of my wife, who stayed here at night with me, but instead Marco was there. It was the first time he'd visited, at least while I was awake, since the shooting more than a week ago.

"Cugino," he said. "They say you won't be able to eat solid food for months."

"*Vaffanculo*," I whispered, my mouth dry.

He chuckled and helped me sip some water. "How do you feel?"

I gave him a pointed stare, not bothering to answer such a stupid question.

The doctors said Marco probably saved my life by packing my wound and stopping the bleeding in the car. I remembered nothing after dropping onto the sidewalk, but my cousin had acted quickly, apparently. I'd never be able to repay him for that. "Thank you."

"You would have done the same, if the roles were reversed. And you're welcome." He lightly touched my shoulder. "I'm not ready to lose you, you stubborn bastard."

"Have you learned who took the shot at me?"

"A professional, hired by whoever is working with Enzo. I saw the rooftop. It was a clean, patient job. They were there for a couple of hours, at least. They knew you were going to be there."

Fucking Enzo. Killing him was my top priority once I was released from the hospital. And that shooter had better watch his back because I would slice him into tiny pieces the instant I learned his identity.

"Francesca?" I asked.

"A rock. She's safe, working on the legitimate side with Toni. He says she's very capable."

"How is Giulio?"

Marco nodded, knowing exactly what I was asking. "He's fine. Got a good head on his shoulders and he's making all the right moves."

This pleased me.

"Everything is in good hands, Rav. You don't need to worry. Just get better."

"No one can know." I was so tired, I couldn't finish the thought. But I knew Marco would understand.

"Of course, of course," Marco said. "We've covered up most of the reports and bribed the staff to keep quiet. No one knows the full extent of your injuries. I convinced La Provincia to push Crimine back a week, but if you don't feel up to going I can go in your place."

We both knew this was a terrible idea. I needed to be at the meeting with all the other 'ndrina leaders, or I'd be seen as weak. Luckily I had a bit more time to recover before I had to make the trip, and the conference was in Calabria, not far from Siderno.

I raised my brows. "I want to come home."

"They think by the end of the week, if necessary, but it doubles the risk of infection. No one is advising it, Rav."

"I don't care." I would be safer, as well as hidden from prying eyes, inside the castello.

Marco held out his palms. "Your wife won't like it."

"She'll be fine." I would make her understand. Every day I lingered here made me and the entire empire vulnerable. If I had to build a sterile hospital room in the castello, so be it. I had to get out of here.

"Any problems?" I asked him.

"None I'll bother you with. I told you, stay focused on getting better."

"Tell me."

He shook his head, the bastardo. "Some people making plays, speculating that you're too weak to stop them. Giulio and I are handling it. They all know he speaks for you."

Cazzo. I'd wanted more time to groom my son, to guide him in what it meant to rule. To throw him in like this seemed almost cruel. "Bring him to me."

Marco said, "I will. Maybe tonight, if you're awake."

"Wake me if I'm not." I tried to speak the words urgently.

"Your wife will gut me if I do that. She's been hovering over you at night like a mama bear."

My dolcezza. The best thing that has ever happened to me. I loved her beyond reason. Which was why she needed to stay at the castello from now on. Coming here was too dangerous. "No more."

"You mean no more visits?" When I nodded, Marco grimaced. "She won't like it."

"No more visits."

"I'll try, but I'm not certain she'll listen to me. Between her and

Zia, the two of them never leave you except when the other is here. Zia hasn't let anyone come visit you. I had to threaten her just to get her to leave for a few hours."

Picturing Marco squaring off with Zia would have made me laugh, if I didn't hurt so damn badly. Francesca needed to obey orders. I was her husband and I made the rules. No more bending when it came to her safety. "What about Enzo?"

"Not a trace. If I had to guess, he's recovering up in the mountains surrounding Napoli. What do you want to do? Hire a hitter?"

"Yes." Francesca wasn't safe as long as Enzo continued to breathe. I could feel my energy waning, the darkness calling me again. "Sicilians," I got out. They had several snipers we could hire, competent men they used to take out politicians and Guardia officials.

"Good idea. You'll owe them another favor, though."

"Worth it." I closed my eyes, unable to fight any more.

When I fell back under, my dreams were of blood and death.

Francesca

The conversation with Giulio bothered me all afternoon.

When my business calls ended, I decided to go to the hospital early. I needed to talk to Fausto about his son. I didn't like the way Giulio looked. Perhaps one of Marco's sons could help out, just until Fausto was back on his feet.

Nesto agreed to drive me, and he took two more soldiers along in precaution. Since the shooting, security at the castello had been beefed up considerably, all the men armed to the teeth. I wasn't complaining. I still had trouble sleeping when I pictured Fausto on the ground, nearly bleeding to death.

In the back of the armored SUV, I closed my eyes and wondered how I could help Giulio. I knew he had Marco, but Marco was old school. Was there something I could do, something they hadn't considered? I tapped my phone against my thigh, thinking. What about some cyber-stalking? While Fausto's guys wouldn't be stupid enough to have social media accounts, their relatives might. I used to follow David's sister's Instagram account back in Toronto because she posted way more personal information about their family than he did. It was how I learned he went to a party in Richmond Hill instead of staying home to study, like he'd told me.

So, maybe one of the men had a distant connection to Enzo we didn't know about.

Giulio said Vic was on the cameras during my kidnapping but not when Enzo escaped. If he was any good at security and computers, though, he'd probably figured out how to access everything remotely.

I unlocked my phone. "What is Vic's last name?" I asked the young men in the car.

"Benedetti, why?" Carlo answered.

"No reason," I murmured. I began searching for bread crumbs, family members who might be on social media. I quickly found an aunt on Facebook without a private account. Perfect.

She was older and posted a lot of family photos. She also liked to share religious memes, but I ignored those. I even caught Vic in some, when he was a scrawny teen. I wouldn't have recognized him if not for her caption naming everyone in the photo. I kept going back, waiting for the page to reload with more photos.

My eyes swept the posts, not sure what I was looking for except some connection to Enzo. A hint that Vic knew someone from the D'Agostino crew. A photo with a large group went by and a face caught my attention.

Holy shit. Wait, it couldn't be. I stared closer. Enlarged it to be sure.

Yes, I was right. It was her.

Agent Rinaldo was in the background.

My mind reeled with the news. What the fuck? This was no coincidence. Vic was related to a GDF agent? How was that possible? Was Rilando even an agent? She'd handed me a card, but anyone could print those online.

"Turn around!" I slapped the headrest of Nesto's seat. "Go back to the castello. Right now!"

Nesto didn't question it. Immediately, he turned around in the middle of the street, causing the SUV's tires to squeal against the pavement. I hardly noticed. I began texting Giulio that I needed to see him and Marco right away.

The drive seemed to take forever and the men in the car were quiet. More than likely they didn't know what to think about my erratic behavior. I didn't care. I wasn't about to explain myself to them, not with news like this.

Once inside the castello I didn't bother knocking on the office door. I turned the knob, went in, and closed the door behind me. Giulio looked up from behind the desk, Marco standing at his side. I blurted, "Agent Rinaldo is related to Vic."

Marco went stiff and Giulio narrowed his eyes at me. "How do you know that?" my friend asked. "We've looked into his family and his background and found nothing out of the ordinary."

I found the screenshot of the post I'd saved on my phone. "This came from his Aunt Rosemary. I found her on Facebook and started scrolling back through old photos." I pointed to the woman's face. "This is her right there. That's the woman calling herself Agent Rinaldo."

"This is from seven years ago," Giulio said, passing the phone to Marco. "Minchia! How did we miss this?"

"Because we weren't looking on Facebook," Marco murmured. "This explains why we hadn't heard of her. She's not a real GDF agent."

"Why would Vic's relative pose as a GDF agent and approach me? It makes no sense. If he's working with Enzo to embezzle money, why bother with me?"

"Chaos," Marco answered. "You are Fausto's weakness. If Enzo can get you thinking about leaving or turning over information, that's all he needs."

Giulio nodded. "Who knows? If you agreed to go with Rinaldo, you might've been kidnapped again."

Jesus. This was making my head spin. Was Enzo really so devious?

"So now what? You're going to go and find Vic, right?"

"I know exactly where he is." Marco took out his phone and began texting. "I'll have the boys get him and bring him here. That way he won't suspect anything."

"Then the dungeon?" I asked, my gaze bouncing between the two men.

Giulio cast me an odd look. "Why do you sound excited by that?"

"I'm not excited." I heard the lie in my voice. Damn, I *was* excited —but not at the idea of Vic enduring whatever hell awaited him in one of those cells. No, I liked that I'd played a part in discovering his treachery. I was good at this mafia shit.

"Okay, they are bringing him," Marco said. "He thinks we need his help with a problem in the security room."

I dusted my hands and took a bow. "Well, my work here is done. Good luck, boys. I think I'll head over to the hospital now."

"Wait, Frankie." Marco gestured to the chairs in front of the desk. "Let's sit down. I have something to tell you."

Giulio's face went completely blank, and I knew I wasn't going to like what I was about to hear. "I don't need to sit. Tell me now."

"He said you can't come to the hospital any longer. It's too dangerous."

My jaw fell open. That fucking husband of mine! Anger flared to life in my chest like a match had been struck. "He can't keep me from visiting him."

"No, but I can." Giulio sighed heavily, looking serious and resigned, very much like a young mob boss. "I don't want to, Frankie, but I will. Until Enzo is dealt with, we all need to remain cautious. And our enemies are crawling out from under the floorboards now that Fausto is injured. I can't worry about everything else and you, too."

The nape of my neck turned hot and a familiar defiance burned in my chest. No way was I staying inside the castello for months while Fausto recovered alone in the hospital. These two had to know me better than that.

"Do not get that look on your face," Giulio warned. "I'm serious, Frankie."

I wasn't going to argue. If I did, they would only watch me more carefully. "Then I want a way to talk to him. Set up a video feed in that hospital room."

"I can do that," Marco said.

"What about Zia? She won't like being kept from him, either."

Marco shifted on his feet, evading my gaze. Giulio rolled his lips together tightly, his shoulders growing tight like he was bracing for impact.

"Oh, I see." I gave a brittle laugh. "Zia's allowed to go but I'm not. Sure, that makes sense."

"You're pregnant," Giulio snapped. "And his wife, which makes you a target. You can't seriously think Zia is in the kind of danger you are."

I resisted the urge to yell at him. This was not Giulio's doing. I knew exactly who was responsible. Fausto was making decisions again without consulting me, that controlling asshole.

And if he thought I would obey blindly like a weak little wife, then he obviously didn't know me very well.

"I have more work to do anyway to prepare for tomorrow," I told them as I walked toward the door. "Let me know if you need any more help with Vic."

"Frankie, promise me," Giulio said to my back.

I crossed my fingers in front of me, where he couldn't see. "I promise. See you later, G."

CHAPTER TWENTY-SIX

Francesca

A nurse was in Fausto's room, reading his vitals, when I walked in. His heart machine started beeping wildly when he saw me.

"Ma che cazzo?" Fausto rasped.

"Hello, husband." I walked over to the bed, ignoring the dark glare he sent my way. "How does he seem today, Angela?"

"Much better, signora. No sign of infection and he is gaining his energy back."

"Oh, good." I smiled at him and leaned in to kiss his cheek, which was now coated with whiskers. "Ciao, baby."

Fausto was absurdly attractive when he was clean-shaven, but that was nothing compared to how hot he looked with a beard. There were even some gray hairs in his scruff, which gave him a daddy vibe I definitely dug. I would beg him to keep some facial hair when he felt up to playing with me again.

"You are not supposed to be here," he said when the nurse walked out.

"And yet, here I am."

"I should call Marco and have him lock you up in the dungeon."

"But you won't because they are busy with other things that are more important than me."

"Nothing is more important than you."

"Aw, that's sweet." I pressed my lips to his. Even though he didn't have much energy for kissing, I still liked the warmth of his mouth, the feel of his breath on me. The reminder that he was still here.

"Who brought you?"

"I'm not telling you." I knew better than to rat out my accomplice. I dragged an armchair closer to the bed. "Maybe I drove myself."

"If you did, then I will spank your ass, moglie."

"You'd have to catch me first, *marito*."

"I won't always be in this hospital bed. Then I will make you pay."

"Boy, you are feeling better," I grumbled. "I almost miss the groggy-and-too-tired-to-boss-me-around Fausto."

"You like when I boss you around."

I kissed his temple and whispered, "True." Then I dropped into the armchair. "How do you feel?"

"Like I've been shot. You look tired."

"I'm fine. Just working long hours."

"Are you eating and sleeping enough for a pregnant woman?"

I chewed on my bottom lip. "I think so? I mean, I don't know. My last doctor's appointment didn't happen for obvious reasons, and I've been too distracted with everything to reschedule it."

Fausto grabbed the controller on the bed and pressed the call button for the nurse.

"What are you doing?" I asked. "Do you need something? I can get it for you."

Angela came in right away. "Yes, signore?"

Fausto didn't give me a chance to speak. "Send up the best obstetrician on call. It's an emergency."

Oh, he was too much. I gave Angela an apologetic look. "No, it's not. Just whenever the doctor is free. Grazie, Angela."

Whatever the nurse saw in Fausto's expression had her nodding. "I'll send the doctor in immediately."

"You're a pain in the ass," I told him when we were alone. "They will all be very glad to see you go when you leave in a few weeks."

"Days, you mean."

"What? You're coming home in a few days? Is that safe?" I looked at the machines and thought about his injuries. He'd almost died ten days ago, for fuck's sake. No way was he ready to leave this place.

"Do not worry. Marco is having a bedroom in our wing converted to a hospital room. It'll be safer for me there."

I supposed that was true. And it made my banishment from the hospital a non-issue. "He's hiring a team of nurses, I hope."

"Of course. I wouldn't expect you to play nurse, dolcezza. Though I would very much like to see you in the outfit."

Dirty man. God, I loved him. "I'll buy one for when you're feeling better." Then I remembered we had things to discuss. I quietly told him about the sleuthing I'd done on Facebook and what I learned about Vic and Agent Rinaldo.

His eyes were soft and proud when I finished. "You are very clever. Good work."

"Thank you. It felt really nice, I'm not going to lie."

"Toni says you are very good with the businesses. That you have an easy way with the employees and a head for the work."

I grinned and batted my lashes at him, preening. "I like it. I mean, some of the conference calls are boring, but for the most part I'm enjoying it."

The side of his mouth curled. "It's good that you took it on, so Giulio could focus on other things."

I licked my lips. "Yeah, about that. We need to talk."

"Oh?"

"Yes, it's about Giulio." Fausto's face went blank, like a window had been shut, and I winced. "Look, I know you don't want to hear it, but he's miserable. Not only that, he looks terrible. He doesn't want to do it, baby."

"He will come to terms with it. Don't worry."

"You're wrong. He's seeing a glimpse of his future right now and he doesn't like it. He's deeply unhappy."

"I did not take to it right away, but I came to settle in and accept it. The same will happen for my son."

He wasn't hearing me. He was stuck in his primogeniture mafia fantasy world. I pressed my hands together like I was praying. "Fausto, please listen to what I'm telling you. Giulio is not you. He's a completely different person, and I'm worried about what this is doing to him. He's in a dark place."

"What does this mean, dark place?"

He practically sneered, so I gentled my voice. "His mental health. I'm worried."

"You young people and your *mental health*. Your generation needs to toughen up."

The number of offensive things in those two sentences made my throat ache. "Listen, boomer, this is not about toughening up. This is about your son being miserable enough to do something drastic."

He grew very, very still, his blue gaze watching my face very carefully. "Such as?"

"I don't know, but I'm concerned. You are asking him to sign up for a life of celibacy and loneliness. Of misery and death. Don't you want him to be happy?"

"Money and power make men happy, dolcezza."

Oh, he was annoying. I gave him a pointed stare. "Really, husband? Is that what makes you happy? When we were separated, was all that money and power keeping you warm at night?"

A muscle in his jaw jumped. "What would you have me do? Give it all to one of Marco's boys?"

"Yes," I said emphatically. "Toni also has sons. There are other Ravazzanis to take over besides Giulio."

"It should be my son," he hissed. "The leader has always come through my family."

He was starting to get agitated, the beeps on the monitors growing louder, so I patted his shoulder and gave him one last piece of advice. "Perhaps it's time for change, then. Because you have to let Giulio choose."

"I will handle my son," he said harshly.

I knew he was irritable and feeling powerless, but I would not allow him to take it out on me. "In case you've forgotten, this marriage is a partnership, Fausto. There isn't your life and my life. There is only *our* life. Capisce? And the lives of our children, who we will parent *together*."

Closing his eyes, he let out a tired breath. "This is why Marco should have locked you up."

I bent and pressed a kiss to his hand. "It would never work, bello."

He remained silent and kept his eyes closed. I could tell he didn't have the energy to argue, and I hated to push him while he was still recovering, but I was truly worried about Giulio. This problem couldn't be ignored, and it would take time for Fausto to wrap his mind around the idea of offering Giulio the choice.

A knock sounded on the door and Fausto's guard appeared. "A doctor for the signora," he said.

"They may come in," I answered, rising.

An older man walked into the room. He immediately bowed his head toward my husband. "Signore Ravazzani. An honor."

Fausto explained that I had missed a doctor's appointment, so he'd like me and the baby checked out.

The doctor smiled and nodded at me. "Sì, sì. Signora Ravazzani, come."

"No," Fausto said. "You will do it here. She does not leave my sight."

"But signore—"

"Here," my husband insisted. "Bring the machines or whatever."

I opened my mouth to argue this was too much, but Fausto's expression said I'd better not. He was deadly serious that I remained in this room. I smothered my irritation. I'd already upset him enough about Giulio. No need to add to it.

The doctor nodded and backed out of the room. I smirked at my husband. "Do you have a secret pelvic exam kink I should know about?"

Frowning, he closed his eyes. "That attitude. You get bratty when you think I cannot discipline you."

True. "Then get better, amore, and you can spank me again."

"Believe me, I will."

Minutes later, an orderly brought in a padded table and set it up, then a nurse brought in an ultrasound machine. He instructed me to change into a gown and wait for the doctor. The obstetrician returned and washed his hands, while asking me simple questions about my last exam and general health. He gloved up and dabbed at his forehead with a paper towel, casting nervous glances at my husband, who was watching everything very intently.

The doctor listened to the baby's heartbeat first, and the reassuring *whoosh, whoosh, whoosh* made me smile. Then came time for the internal exam and his hand was shaking as he inserted the wand into my vagina. I tried to make jokes and talk, anything to keep the mood light, but nothing really helped.

On the small screen there was the tiny bean, shifting and moving inside me. The doctor began taking measurements and pictures, and praised Fausto for creating such a beautiful baby. I rolled my eyes toward the ceiling.

"The bambino, he looks good," the doctor said when he finished. "Your son will be strong."

My mouth fell open. Did he just . . .? Without asking first?

Fausto, on the other hand, grinned. "A son?"

The doctor's head swiveled between me and Fausto. "Sì. I assumed . . . You were told, no? You are having a boy."

Fausto

I didn't sleep much that night.

Lost in thought, I watched Francesca on the bed in the corner, the even rise and fall of her chest as she slept. A *son*. I hadn't lied when I said I preferred a daughter. Sons brought too much heartache, too much worry. I had done everything to mold Giulio into the man to lead my family, yet I'd failed. He didn't want it.

You have to let Giulio choose.

Two weeks ago, before I was shot, I wouldn't have cared about his feelings. He was the Ravazzani heir with a duty to me, to the family, and his wishes didn't matter.

But I could no longer say this was still the case.

As I bled out on the sidewalk, I thought of those I was leaving behind, including Giulio. My good boy, who'd only argued with me once, and it had been over his lover, Paolo. He would do whatever I asked, even at the expense of his own happiness. But did I want that life for him?

I'd hated my own father, who hadn't once shown any regard for my thoughts or feelings. We weren't close and his death had come as a relief. Did I wish for my own son to feel the same at my passing? When Giulio was born, I vowed to have a different relationship with my son, but life came along and I fell into predictable patterns.

You have to let Giulio choose.

My heart twisted, more pain flooding my body. I didn't want to do it. Probably because I knew what my son would choose—and it would not be me. I would lose him. And I wasn't certain I could bear it.

The door opened and I assumed another nurse was coming to check on me. Except it was Marco, and he looked as exhausted as I felt.

When he saw I was awake, he came in and pulled a chair over to the bed. "Giulio told her not to come," he said. "She's a force of nature, your wife."

My eyes drifted toward my sweet girl once more. Such trouble, my dolcezza. "I know."

"Did she tell you about Vic?"

"Some. Why don't you tell me the rest?"

Quietly, he outlined the confession he and Giulio had obtained an hour ago from Vic. "Enzo threatened Vic's mother and sisters to gain his cooperation in stealing the money. So Vic hacked into your laptop and put keystroke software on it, just long enough to get access to the bank accounts. Enzo wanted to steal more, but Vic grew nervous after the kidnapping."

I also changed my passwords routinely, so this would've made it harder. "What about Rinaldo?"

"After Frankie's return, Enzo made it clear she was still a target, and Vic claims he worried something terrible would happen to her. He sent in his aunt to pose as a GDF agent. The hope had been to make the GDF threat credible enough that Frankie would lie low, be on her guard, and stay inside the castello."

I let out a derisive sound. "Does the *coglione* think this will win favor with me?"

"No, he isn't that stupid. What do you want me to do with him?" Marco asked.

My chest burned but it had nothing to do with my injury. I wanted to make Vic suffer for allowing Francesca to be taken. For turning against me and helping my enemy. An example had to be set. "Let him sit until I get home. I want to see to it personally."

"Before you do that, maybe we can use him to draw out Enzo's location?"

"Good, yes. Do that sooner rather than later, before Enzo grows suspicious over Vic's absence."

"I will."

"How is Giulio?" I asked.

"Tired but he's holding up."

"Francesca said he's miserable."

Marco shifted in his chair and smoothed his trousers, something he did whenever he was trying to buy time before offering up an answer. "It's tough. He's not like you, Rav. I don't know what to say."

I swallowed past the lump in my throat. "We're having a son."

"Complimenti, cugino!" He nudged my shoulder. "*Auguri e figli maschi!*"

The popular wish for many sons twisted in my chest. With sons came disappointment. "I hoped for a daughter," I said with a heavy sigh.

"Don't worry about Giulio. He's still young. You know men his age.

They are full of come and rebellion. After marriage he will calm down."

I didn't think so. I hadn't been like this at his age. I had taken on more and more responsibilities, eager to prove myself. Listened to my father's advice and the advice of my elders. I never questioned orders, never let my father or my crew down. But I'd failed in instilling this same drive in my son.

I shoved all that aside to worry about later. "How are the plans to bring me home?"

"The room should be finished tomorrow or the day after. The equipment is being rushed and we've hired three nurses, all vetted. David is moving in until further notice."

Good. I liked having a doctor in the family. "I want you to come back in the morning and take Francesca home. And keep her there, Marco."

"I will, I will."

"Check on Giulio tonight before you go home, will you? Make sure he's eating and sleeping."

"Of course. Do you need anything before I go? Something to eat— oh, wait." He tapped his temple as if he'd just remembered. "I forgot. You cannot have food."

Bastard. He hadn't forgotten. "Zia is still trying to sneak in her veal ragù. It's torture."

Marco chuckled softly. "Should I grab anything for your wife when I go by the castello tonight? Something she might need in the morning?"

This was new. Marco wasn't usually so considerate toward Francesca. "No. She chose to slip out the door so she will live with the consequences."

He stood and leaned to kiss my head. "Try and get some sleep, eh? It'll help you heal faster."

"I know this isn't easy on you, cugino. Thank you—and tell Maria thank you, as well."

"My wife and I would do anything for you, Rav. You know that. But you're welcome."

My cousin left, closing the door softly, and I looked over at my wife. "You can stop pretending to be asleep."

She rolled over and stretched her long limbs. The low hospital lighting casted her in a soft glow and she was like a beautiful golden angel. My heart turned over, the love I felt for her nearly spilling out of my body.

"I didn't want to interrupt," she said.

"Come here."

Instead of obeying, she put her hands under her cheek and looked at me. "Where?"

"Come, lay down next to me."

"Fausto, there isn't enough room in that bed. I'll hurt you."

"No, you won't. I need to hold you right now. Ti prego. Come squeeze in next to me, bellissima."

Her gaze softened and I knew I had her. She unfolded from the small bed and padded over to me. She wore just a t-shirt and panties, and she'd removed her bra, so her breasts swung beneath the thin fabric of her t-shirt. Cristo, I wish I felt better. My dick hadn't even twitched since I had been shot, but mentally I still craved fucking her, touching her.

Brow furrowed, she went to my uninjured side and lowered the rail. "How is this going to work?"

I lifted my good arm and tried to make space for her. "Get in."

It took her a while and I had to hide a wince or two, but she made it work. She stretched out on her side and cuddled ever so gently to me. It was the first time I'd held her since the shooting and my body relaxed, settling into the uncomfortable mattress. "I have missed this," I murmured, closing my lids.

"Me too." Her lips found my throat. "Don't ever scare me like that again, okay?"

"Ti amo, Francesca. No matter what happens in the future, know that I love you with everything I am. When I was dying on that street, my last thought was of you."

"Oh, baby." She pressed closer. "I don't want to think about that ever again."

"Nor do I."

"I should never have asked you to delay killing him. If I hadn't—"

"It does no good to dwell in the past. I don't blame you or Emma. I had plenty of time to kill him before your sisters came, but I enjoyed toying with him."

We were both silent for a few minutes, the sound of the machines in the room our only companion. She finally said, "I can't believe we're having a boy."

"Are you disappointed?"

"I'm . . . nervous. I want for him to be able to make his own choices when the time comes."

I thought of my first son, at home and miserable. "No one has a choice in this life."

"That's not true. Furthermore, it *shouldn't* be true. Would you have chosen anything different if your father had allowed it?"

"No. I loved the life. Never once did I want to do anything else."

"But that's you."

I forced myself to give voice to my greatest fear. "He won't choose me."

She was quiet, her breath gusting over my throat and making me shiver. Finally, she said, "No, but he will choose himself. And isn't that more important?"

"You will never see him again," I snapped. "*I* will never see him again. He will need to disappear to stay safe. Change his name, his looks. All because he refuses—"

"Stop right there. He's not refusing anything. He's done everything you've asked of him, even at the expense of his own sanity. He wants to make you proud, but think about what you're doing for a second. What kind of life are forcing him into, secrecy and lies? Celibacy and loneliness? It's beyond cruel."

"It's the only way to keep him safe."

"Except for letting him go and giving him a chance to find true happiness outside the mafia. You have to accept it and let him decide."

The plaster ceiling wavered as my eyes filled. She made it sound so easy, to give my son a choice and watch him walk out of my life. That wasn't how things were done here. We were all about family and legacy, and even Italians not in the mafia stuck close to home. I raised him myself after Lucia died, every moment of his young life forged into my brain. It was like asking me to cut off my arm and never notice its absence.

"Baby, I know this is hard," she said quietly. "But as parents our job is to put our kids first. Always. I know you love him, which means you have to give him a choice. If you don't, it will kill him."

I was too exhausted to think about it any longer. I closed my eyes and let myself drift to sleep.

CHAPTER TWENTY-SEVEN

Fausto

I was too weak for the dungeon steps, so I instructed Marco to bring Vic up to my new hospital room upstairs. In the middle of the night, they dragged him in and threw him on a plastic tarp spread out on the ground by my bed. He moaned and curled into himself, his broken and bloody body trembling from the pain.

Va bene. This pleased me.

"Can you hear me, *pezzo di merda?*"

When Vic didn't answer, Giulio kicked him in the ribs. Vic dry heaved a few times, and after he quieted, I snapped, "Answer me."

"Yes . . . Don . . . Ravazzani."

"Know this, Vic Benedetti. I will make an example out of you. They will whisper about the horrors of your death for years to come. You will suffer, coglione. You will suffer for spitting in the face of my trust and for what happened to my wife. The wife and sisters you were trying to protect from D'Agostino? They receive nothing from me after your death, not even my protection."

"No, please," he wheezed. "Please."

"He put a gun in my wife's mouth. A gun. In my wife's mouth!" I was shouting by the end, and pain tore through me. I think I popped open a stitch. Gasping, I relaxed and tried to keep breathing.

"Perdonami, perdonami," he repeated, his one good eye focused on me.

"There is no forgiveness," I rasped. "No mercy for you. But I won't make the same mistake with you that I made with Enzo. You won't be kept alive to prolong the torture. You will die tonight. And pieces of you will be delivered all over Calabria, all the way up to Napoli. I will sprinkle you all throughout Italia like snowflakes so everyone knows of your disgrace."

He closed his eyes and began praying.

I sneered, "There is no redemption for you—or your family. Which body part should I deliver to them first?"

He started sobbing and I gestured to Marco. My cousin put a gun in my hand and everyone stepped back from the tarp. I didn't aim for his head, which would've been too quick a death. With two shots, I put bullets through Vic's kneecaps. It was painful but not life-threatening. He howled but I ignored it. When I handed the gun back to Marco, I said, "Cut him up. Leave him alive for the worst of it."

The men rolled the tarp around Vic and lifted him up. Giulio started to walk out with Marco, so I said, "Giulio, stay."

His brows drew together and he glanced at Marco. "I'll come down when I'm done here."

Marco told Giulio to take his time, and then I was finally alone with my son. The past few hours had been busy ones, with getting settled into my new room and letting Zia and Francesca fuss over me. This was the first chance I'd had to speak with my son. "Come. Sit down."

Francesca hadn't been lying. Giulio did look terrible, like he hadn't slept in days. He'd been such a carefree and happy child. I wondered where that boy had gone. Was he still inside there, buried under layers of responsibility and expectation?

What kind of life are you forcing him into? Secrecy and lies, celibacy and loneliness?

He started to pull over the armchair, but I waved him to the bed. "Sit here. Where I can see you better."

"I don't want to hurt you."

"I'm fine. This is my good side."

He lowered himself gently onto the bed and folded his hands. "What is it?"

"First, Marco told me of your intelligence and leadership in my absence. I'm very proud of you."

Giulio's mouth hitched and his back straightened ever so slightly. "Thank you, Papà. I did my best for you, for the 'ndrina."

"I know, and I'm very pleased. I always assumed I had more time to ease you into the role, to guide you. I know it couldn't have been easy to be thrown in like that."

"It's given me a whole new appreciation for what you do. I will definitely pay better attention from now on."

"This is the second thing I wished to speak with you about." I paused and tried to organize my thoughts. "When you were born I paraded you in front of all the men. 'Look at your next leader,' I told them. We had a big party with everyone there."

He watched me carefully, saying nothing.

"When your mother was killed I raised you myself. I can still remember the way you used to follow me around, playing with your trucks and cars in my office while I worked, asking me questions. I have loved you with every part of my heart. You are my sweet boy, the only good thing in my miserable life until Francesca came along."

I stopped to clear my throat, afraid I was going to start crying too soon.

When I recovered, I said, "I wanted so many things for you. A wife, children. To carry on the legacy built by my grandfather and father, the legacy I've expanded upon. To be feared and respected throughout Europe as Don Ravazzani. But those were things I wanted. Things I demanded without giving you a choice."

The beeps of the machines filled the silence when I couldn't force out the words. Once I did, there was no going back.

As parents our job is to put our kids first. Always.

"My wife," I started, "she is very wise. She sees things I do not, and she's convinced me that I must let you choose. That your happiness depends on it."

Giulio blinked a few times. "Choose? Choose, what?"

"Whether to take over as don one day."

He stared at me, still as a statue. I wasn't certain he was even breathing. "Is this a joke?" he asked.

"Absolutely not. I'm letting you decide your future. I would prefer that you decide quickly, though. Word can't get out that there's any question, any hesitation."

"You are letting me leave? I can walk away from it?"

"Yes. That is what I am saying."

"I can't believe it." He covered his mouth with a hand, then repeated, "I can't believe it."

I could see a light return to his eyes as he began to contemplate a future outside of the mafia. I didn't wish to influence his decision but he had to understand the risks. "Giulio, before you decide, you must understand something." I put my hand on his knee. "If you leave, you cannot come back. This isn't like moving to another city or going off to university. You will no longer be a Ravazzani. You must change your name, your appearance. You can't—"

My voice cracked and I couldn't say it.

You can't be my son any longer.

My lungs burned like the fires of hell were inside them. If he chose to leave, how was I going to bear it?

"Papà," he whispered. "I don't know what to say."

"Talk to me. What are you thinking?"

He scrubbed his face with both hands. "I know Frankie is having a boy. You'll have another son. And maybe he won't be such a disappointment."

My voice grew stronger. "You have never disappointed me, figlio mio, not a single day in your life. Whatever your decision, I will respect it. I will still love you and I will *always* be proud of you. But there's no straddling these two worlds. You are either in or you're out, and if you stay that means living a lie. To do otherwise puts you in grave danger."

"And if I leave, I can be whoever I want. Go wherever I want. Date whoever I want."

"Sì, that's true."

"Why can't I come visit secretly? Or we could meet up somewhere."

That he was asking this meant he'd already made his decision. I smiled sadly at him. "I will not put you at risk. Perhaps attitudes will change in the mafia in the coming years. Who can say? But I can't make any promises. For your safety, you must go far away and live as someone else."

He made a noise in his throat. "I wouldn't even know where to go."

"I hear Belgium is nice."

He sucked in a harsh breath. "Papà . . . ."

"Don't ask me more."

He stared at the floor, his expression troubled. "I don't know if I can actually say it. I'm scared you're going to change your mind."

"No matter the name you use, know in your heart, you are a Ravazzani. You come from a long line of powerful men who were born to rule. Don't live your life in fear. Whatever you decide, be strong." A tear slipped free but I didn't brush it away. I needed to feel the pain now, to steel myself. I had to be strong for what was to come. "And I won't change my mind. I want you to be happy."

Moisture pooled in his eyes and fat tears trailed down his cheeks. He leaned in and kissed my cheek. "Grazie, Papà. Grazie."

I held onto his head and pressed my lips to his forehead. I didn't like it, but Francesca had been right. How could I deny him happiness? "Ti amo, figlio mio, per sempre." More tears fell, my cheeks wet, as I breathed him in. He used to smell like lemons, back when Zia would sneak him lemon candies. I'd forgotten that until now, but it was a nice memory. "Per sempre," I repeated.

Leaning on my cane, I threw open my office door and hobbled inside. Marco and my wife were there, with Francesca sitting in my desk chair, and the two of them looked up from a laptop. Alarm bloomed on her face. "Fausto! What are you doing out of bed?"

I didn't answer, my full concentration required to keep me from falling on my face like a small child. My side hurt like a son of a bitch and sweat already rolled down my back.

Marco reached me first, grabbing my arm to steady me. "You should go back upstairs."

"I'm fine. Just help me to my chair."

It had been just over two weeks since the shooting and I was impatient to be better. I needed work to distract me.

"Rav, you should be in bed. David said—"

"No." I put enough strength in that one word to prevent anyone from arguing with me.

Marco exchanged a look with my wife, which caused irritation to swipe across my skin. My cousin no doubt believed she could control me, as she'd convinced me to change my mind about other things. But I'm the boss, and I made the decisions for the 'ndrina. No one else.

Besides, there was work to be done and all of it was my responsibility. The weight of an empire rested on my shoulders, and I could no longer shirk it.

He got me into my leather chair and a sharp pain ripped through my side, so fierce it took my breath away. Closing my eyes, I sucked in a deep breath and let it out slowly. I could sense my wife's disapproval without even looking at her. It hung heavily in the room, but I ignored it. "Tell me what is going on."

Francesca sat in a chair across from my desk, while Marco took his usual seat in the corner. Her gaze swept over my face. Whatever she saw there caused her to ask, "Are you all right?"

I hadn't seen her since my conversation with Giulio last night. We decided he would break the news to her, and I knew he was still asleep. I'd instructed Marco to leave the boy alone today. There was no reason to burden him further with affairs that weren't his concern any longer. So I was fairly certain Francesca didn't know yet.

Instead of answering her question, I said, "Fill me in."

She began reading out her notes on the most pressing issues, and I closed my eyes, listening. She and Toni had done an excellent job. Toni was right—she did have a head for this sort of work. I made comments when necessary, but I was happy to turn the bulk of this tedium over to her. Reading emails and sitting in on conference calls wasn't a good use of my time.

When she finished I smiled at her. "Va bene, Francesca. You've done well in my absence. But then I expected nothing less from you."

She bit her lip, color staining her cheeks at my compliment. "Thank you, baby."

"Would you like to continue this? Working with Toni on the Ravazzani businesses?"

"Yes," she said instantly, a grin nearly splitting her face. "Definitely yes. I can be, like, your personal assistant."

"No, you can be, like, my Chief Operating Officer." I was the President of the conglomerate and Toni was the Vice-President. We didn't have a COO, but I would create the position for her, if she wanted it.

"Oh, my God. Yes. Thank you. That would be amazing."

"It will be a lot of hard work, amore. Toni will be your boss. I'm not sure this will leave you much time to spend outside or laze about with Lamborghini."

"It won't leave me much time for nooners with my demanding husband, either," she said, lifting a bratty brow in my direction, and Marco snickered.

"We'll see about that," I promised darkly.

Smiling, she rose and closed her laptop. "Let me know when you're done talking about everything else and I'll come back."

I made a very quick decision. "Stay."

She glanced at Marco then back at me. "But I thought you needed to discuss the other businesses?"

"You may stay. There is only *our* life, remember?"

I'd been thinking a lot about these words, about merging our lives completely. She was my wife, clever and brave, and she'd already seen me at my worst. There was no reason to hide from her any longer. We would be stronger together.

"Really? I can stay?"

"Do I need to repeat myself?" I lifted a brow at her, giving her the stern expression I knew she loved.

"No," she drawled and lowered herself back into the chair. "I'd like to stay."

Marco began reporting. "Some guns came in two days ago and Carlo took them all to the safe house. We have buyers lined up coming from Serbia next week."

"The rebels?"

"Yes. We'll charge them double what we paid."

"Good. What else?"

Marco kept at it, his memory sharp, even for details. The shipments in, the purchases out, the status of our construction projects . . . he gave me all of it. I sorted and stored the information in my mind. "Good. Anyone get ideas while I was in the hospital?"

"A few of the suppliers mouthed off and some of our supply houses were raided. It was taken care of. Things should calm down now that you're back."

It was to be expected, but I didn't like it. "You'll give me the names of those suppliers. I'll deal with them personally. What about Vic?"

Marco cleared his throat and cast a nervous glance toward Francesca. This was new, discussing murder and disposal in front of her. I waved my hand, telling him to hurry up. "She can take it."

"We did as you ordered," he said. "Small pieces were delivered to the appropriate people first thing this morning."

"Enzo?"

"We sent the head to the last known address we could find for D'Agostino."

My lips curled. I would've loved to see Enzo's face when he opened that box. Even if he wasn't home, Enzo would hear of it. News of the delivery would travel fast amongst the 'Ndrangheta, serving as a warning to others who considered betraying me. "Let's call him and see if he picks up."

"Right now?"

I nodded. "I want him to know that I've recovered, that he hasn't beaten me."

Marco pulled out his phone and began scrolling. "If you're intent on calling him, then you should try to determine where he's staying, who he's with. Any information we can get to help us take him out. Do not lose your temper."

"Yes, baby," Francesca said. "Please, do not lose your temper."

I wanted to lash out at them both, but deep down I knew they were right. I stared at my wife's beautiful face, letting the tranquility she instilled in me settle into my bones. Then I pointed at the phone. When it started ringing, Marco put it on speaker and set it on the desk.

"Pronto," a voice said, weaker than usual but stronger than it should have been.

"Enzo, come stai? How are you feeling?"

"Never better, Fausto. But enough about me. I hear you've been unwell."

"I'm fine. Stronger than a bull. It's too bad you couldn't stay longer."

"Yes, well. Thank you for your generous hospitality. I will have to see how I can repay you."

"There's no need for that," I said. "It was truly my pleasure."

"Perhaps you can come visit me next time. Your wife seemed to like the beach house."

I closed my eyes and dragged in a deep breath through my nostrils. My wife's delicate fingers touched my hand, telling me to remain calm, so I said, "Last I heard your beach house was destroyed."

"Everything can be rebuilt, not to worry. Congratulations on your marriage, by the way."

"Grazie. No need to send a gift. You already left one behind." The tip of his finger. "Speaking of gifts, did you receive the one I sent you? It should have arrived this morning."

"No, I haven't seen it yet."

"A special token, just for you. I hope you enjoy it."

There was a long pause. "I'm sure I will. I'll be sure to send you something in return."

I leaned forward and hardened my voice. "If I were you, I would focus on my business and family instead."

"Then it is fortunate you are not me, no?"

This stronzo never learned, apparently. "How is your wife and children? Your young sister? They must have been happy to see you upon your return."

Enzo didn't say anything, likely not wishing to divulge whether he'd seen them or not. In the background, I heard church bells. Not particularly revealing, not in Italia, but it could mean he was in a city, not out in the country.

Marco gave me a sign to finish up, so I said, "I must go, Enzo, but I hope you take care."

"Yes, you take care, as well, Fausto. Please give your beautiful wife a kiss for me, eh?"

I ground my molars together so hard I thought they might crack. "Please do the same with Mariella. Oh, wait. She left, didn't she? A shame. I know how attached you were to your mantenuta."

I hung up the phone, unwilling to let that bastardo have the last word.

The silence stretched. Marco shook his head. "We should have killed him when we had the chance, Rav."

"I fucking know, Marco." I didn't look at my wife. I knew she already felt guilty about this.

"He won't rest until you're dead. Our only option is to get to him first."

I scrubbed a hand across my forehead. "Who do we use, the sniper from Rome?"

"You mean Lesso?"

Alessandro Ricci. The best shot in Europe and always available for the right price. I nodded. "See if you can track him down. Whatever he wants but I need proof. Also, let's find Mariella."

"Why?" Marco asked.

"Based on what she told Francesca, I think Mariella knows a lot about Enzo's operations. More than a regular mantenuta. We should find her, discover exactly what she knows, and how we can use it."

"She's with some designer in Milan," my wife said. "She loves to post pictures of herself on Instagram."

"Excellent. Call one of our friends up there. Have her questioned."

"Have them get her drunk on white wine," Francesca said dryly. "It's her favorite."

"One more thing," I said to Marco. "We need to discuss Crimine."

"What's Crimine?" Francesca asked.

"A meeting with all the leaders. It's where decisions are made and problems are solved. It's sort of like . . ."

"A mafia boss conference?"

A smile tugged at my lips. The first hint of one I'd felt since my meeting with Giulio last night. "Yes, that's close enough." I turned to Marco. "You will come with me."

Marco nodded once. "What about Giulio?"

"No, he's not coming."

If Marco suspected anything, he didn't let it show. Instead, he asked, "Think D'Agostino will attend?"

"Not unless he wants to die."

"But he might kill you if you go," Francesca interrupted to point out. "You can't seriously be considering going."

"I have to be there. It's a sign of strength."

"Let Marco go and be your sign of strength."

"It doesn't work that way, amore. We have to appear strong—*I* have to appear strong."

"No." She lifted a brow, much in the way I did when she was arguing with me. "I forbid it."

That was a line too far. Even Marco realized it, because he stood and headed for the door. "I'll give you two a moment."

"We leave in three days," I told him. "Make whatever arrangements are necessary."

He nodded and disappeared into the castello. My wife didn't wait for the door to even close before she started. Fire snapped and crackled in her gaze as it narrowed on me. "Do you have a death wish?"

"Of course not," I said calmly. "But this is business."

"This is not *business*," she spat. "This is your pride. This is you not wanting anyone to think you are weak. Which is ridiculous! No one in their right mind would ever doubt you or your ability to lead, Fausto."

And yet Enzo had dared to steal from me, to kidnap my wife. To blackmail one of my men. To try to have me killed. I would not allow another to get ideas.

Anyone who worked against me would pay.

"I will be going, Francesca. So make your peace with it."

"Why are you doing this to me?" Her eyes grew glassy and she put a hand to her chest, dragging in a breath. "I just watched you nearly *die*. You were bleeding everywhere." She closed her eyes. "Do not make me go through that again. I can't take it, baby. I really can't."

"Come here." I motioned with my hand.

"No. Do not try to seduce me into changing my mind."

"I can hardly seduce you. I'm weaker than a kitten. Come *here*, piccolina."

Scowling, she walked over and stood by my chair. I patted the desk. "Up."

She slid her ass onto the wood and her shoulders slumped. "You said this was *our* life. That means I get to protect you just as much as you protect me."

"Within reason, wife. I have responsibilities you won't always understand, but you have to trust me. There are reasons why Crimine is important, especially this year. I cannot miss it."

"Then let me come with you."

"Absolutely not." I set my hand on her thigh, caressing her through her jeans. "You are the most important thing in the world to me. I can't lose you. I can't bear to lose—" My throat closed and I couldn't finish it.

I can't bear to lose anyone else.

I would soon watch my oldest son walk out the door forever. If something happened to Francesca, I would never recover.

"Oh, paparino," she whispered, her expression full of understanding. "Can't you see I feel the same about you?"

"You have to trust me. I was raised in this life. I know how to stay safe."

"Says the man who was just nearly killed by an assassin."

"Francesca," I said tiredly. "I am going. Now, stop arguing and come lie down with me upstairs. I want to kiss you."

"I thought you said you were weak as a kitten."

"I am, which is why you are going to do all the work." I really was exhausted. Coming downstairs and sitting here had taken all my strength.

"The doctor said no sex, Fausto. Not until you are healed."

My mouth curved. I liked this very much. "You discussed sex with my doctor?"

Her cheeks turned pink, as if she'd been in the sun for hours. "You discussed sex with *my* doctor. I don't see the difference."

"Is your pussy needy? Does it need to be filled, monella?"

She squirmed a little on the desk and I had my answer. Still, she shook her head. "You are not fucking me."

I doubted I could get an erection, my body was in so much pain, but that didn't mean I couldn't help get her off. "No, I'm not, but I have toys upstairs that can serve as a substitute. And, you're going to let me watch."

"Dirty old man," she said, but I could see the way her eyes darkened at the idea.

"Help me up the stairs and I'll show you how dirty I can get."

CHAPTER TWENTY-EIGHT

Francesca

I couldn't stop crying.
Five of us were gathered in the foyer, surrounded by three suitcases. Fausto was on his feet, propped up by a cane, with Zia and Marco nearby. Giulio and I stood off to the side, close to the luggage, and his arms were wrapped around me as I sobbed on his probably very expensive shirt. There was nothing left to be said. I had pushed for this outcome, hoped it would come to pass, but it *hurt*.

Giulio was the most composed out of all of us, which was understandable. It had been his decision to leave, after all. Fausto gave him a choice and Giulio had grabbed the opportunity eagerly. Now he would start a new chapter in his life as a whole different person. When he walked out this door, he was no longer the Ravazzani heir. Not a Ravazzani at all, in fact.

And I would never see him again.

I hated it, but I understood the reasons why he couldn't live happily here. And really, this was best for Giulio, which was all that mattered. When he gave me the news I heard the excitement in his voice over his future, his chance to live proudly and openly as a gay man. Deep in my heart, I knew he would be okay.

Still, I couldn't let go of him.

"Bella," he whispered in my hair, "you will be fine without me. My father will take very good care of you."

I couldn't speak, I was crying too hard. He'd been my first friend, my rock here in a strange place. I would miss him so fucking much. This felt unfair, a punishment none of us deserved.

"Dolcezza," my husband said gently. "The plane is waiting."

Nodding, I stretched to press a kiss to Giulio's cheek. "Be happy, G. Be safe."

Giulio's mouth lifted slightly as he kissed my forehead. "However you made this happen, I will always be grateful for it, matrigna. Ti voglio bene, bella."

"Ti voglio bene," I choked out.

Marco, of all people, put an arm around my shoulder to comfort and guide me away, his free hand holding out a pack of tissues. I took them gratefully and tried to clean myself up as Zia walked over to Giulio. She pressed a bag of food in his hands, telling him to eat and to make his bed everyday. She asked him to write her a card every Christmas to let her know he was all right. He hugged her hard, saying he would, then released her.

Fausto went over to his son and the group of us edged away to give them privacy. My husband clasped the back of Giulio's head and pressed their foreheads together. Then Fausto whispered softly in Italian, too quiet and too fast for me to understand, and Giulio nodded in response. It went on for some time, until Giulio's face crumpled, his composure faltering at whatever Fausto was saying.

Fausto kissed both of Giulio's cheeks then stepped back. Giulio wiped his face and nodded at him, their eyes locked in some silent understanding. My husband had been uncharacteristically quiet in the hours leading up to Giulio's departure, and I'd given him space to process his emotions. This was not easy for him. How could it be? His son was walking out the door to start a new life somewhere else, never to return.

Marco let me go and took two of Giulio's suitcases. Zia cried softly at my side, using a fancy lace handkerchief to wipe her eyes, as Giulio followed Marco out the door. When the heavy wood closed with a snap, Fausto didn't move. He just stared at the empty spot where his son had been. Zia began reciting prayers and hurried toward the kitchen. *"Padre Nostro, che sei nei cieli..."*

Pain swamped my entire body. It felt like someone had carved out my chest with a spoon. I couldn't catch my breath, my lungs struggling for air as I continued to cry. Then Fausto's shoulders dropped, like he couldn't bear the weight of them any longer, and my heart broke a little more.

I couldn't stand it. I closed the distance between us and wrapped my arms around him, careful of his injury, and pressed my cheek to his shoulder blades. His big body trembled and he put his free hand on top of mine. We stood there for a long time. "Ti amo," I said into the thin cotton t-shirt he wore.

He nodded, but didn't speak, and that tore me apart. My man felt deep, and this was undoubtedly the worst day of his life.

"I need to go lie down," he said after another minute.

"I'll help you." I shifted to his side, but he held up a hand.

"No, please. I need to be alone for a bit."

His expression was ragged. Destroyed. Bleakness like I'd never seen haunted his beautiful eyes. "Okay," I said, swallowing past the lump in my throat. "Ring if you need anything."

Leaning in, he pressed his lips to my temple, pausing there for a long second. Then he pulled away and began making his way up the stairs, his movements stiff and heavy. I waited until he was at the top, then I went outside into the bright sunshine, to breathe fresh air. To remind myself that life was worth living, no matter where we were.

Fausto

San Luca
Sanctuary of Our Lady of Polsi

The drive up the mountain was slow and bumpy. I winced with every twist and turn, but didn't complain. The church and monastery were situated in the Aspromonte mountains in Calabria, nestled in the bottom of a gorge. I was grateful for the road, rough as it was. A few decades ago, the place was accessible only by foot.

Tradition dictated the 'Ndrangheta leaders meet here, and I had never missed Crimine. I wasn't about to start now, even though I felt terrible.

I could endure it. I had a lot to accomplish today.

"How are you doing back there?" Marco looked over his shoulder from the passenger seat.

"Fine," I gritted out.

"Stitches feel okay?"

They burned like the fires of hell, but I didn't want him to baby me. "Yes. Stop worrying. You are worse than Zia."

"Zia's not half as bad as your wife. I already have fifteen text messages from her."

I picked up my phone and texted Francesca:

I am fine.
We are almost there.
Stop texting Marco.

Her response was almost immediate:

Then answer my texts and I won't have to!
If you get hurt I'll never forgive you

Then she sent a string of emojis that made me crack a smile. It mostly included eggplants and water droplets, but I knew what she meant. I sent her back a heart.

*Paparino! You sent me an emoji!
I feel so proud*

I rolled my eyes, though my smile widened. My piccola monella, always pushing and teasing me.

When the car pulled up to the front entrance, I gripped my cane and got out as quickly as I could manage. It was imperative that I appear mostly recovered, not as an invalid. Mommo was there, talking to one of the monks out front, and he came right over when he saw me.

"Fausto, ciao!" He kissed my cheeks. "You are looking well. Much better than I'd heard."

"A scratch," I said with a shrug. "I hardly even notice it any more."

He slapped my shoulder and I grinned through the pain. "Va bene, va bene. We need you strong, my boy. Your father, he was strong, too. I remember how he took two bullets in the thigh and kept chasing a rival dealer through the streets." Mommo chuckled as he led me inside, and I left Marco and Benito to deal with the car.

"Is everyone here?" I asked, removing my sunglasses and tucking them in my jacket pocket. The guards patted us both down for weapons, as these meetings were supposed to be friendly. No guns, no knives.

"Sì, sì. We were just waiting on you, even though you live closer than the rest of us, eh?" He shook my shoulder roughly, jostling me.

"That's because I'm busier than all you lazy fucks," I teased back, though I felt lightheaded from the pain.

"Come in. We were having a drink, but now we can get started."

"Excellent."

In truth, I could not wait to sit down again. But instead, I made the rounds in the big hall where the round table was set up. I shook hands, kissed cheeks, slapped backs, and acted as if I hadn't almost been assassinated three weeks ago. Someone handed me a Campari and soda, and I saw it was Marco. I sent him a grateful look and drank half the cocktail in one swallow.

Inside the room were the members of La Provincia, the board of control. The one person missing was Enzo D'Agostino. It was smart of him not to show up, because I would have strangled him on the spot.

Finally all the leaders sat, with our men standing behind us. I was sandwiched between the dons from Reggio Calabria and Platì, both men I knew well.

Pasquale Borghese was the *capo crimine*, also the diplomat and mediator of the group, so he called the meeting to order. "Signori, let us begin, as we are all anxious to return home. Some more than others."

"Yes, the ones with girlfriends!" someone shouted, causing everyone to laugh.

Borghese held up his hand. "We must start with the most recent conflict among us, which has escalated and turned ugly. Too ugly, in my opinion, and I know many at this table feel the same. Ravazzani, would you care to explain?"

I pushed back my chair and rose slowly. "You all know me. You know I do not attack unless provoked. It started small, with a group of pirates stealing my shipment, hired by D'Agostino. Then D'Agostino kidnapped my wife, put a gun in her mouth."

"Was she your wife at the time?" Mommo asked, though everyone already knew the answer.

"No, but she is the daughter of Roberto Mancini, one of our leaders in Toronto, and she was pregnant with my child at the time." I dragged in a breath and went on. "D'Agostino also blackmailed one of my men into embezzling thirty million Euros from me." Eyebrows went up all around the table. "And he hired an assassin to shoot me on the street."

I let all that sink in. Every man at this table would exact retribution in my shoes. They knew what I was feeling.

"So I ask: Would any of you let D'Agostino live after all he had done?"

No one had the balls to say yes. If they did, I would call them a liar.

"Dai, Fausto," Borghese said, puffing on a cigar. "You kidnapped and tortured D'Agostino. For *days*."

I held up my hands. "I don't deny it, but I will say I was justified.

Francesca is the love of my life. If your wife was kidnapped, you would do the same."

"He thought he was taking your mantenuta, a whore." Mommo shrugged like this was acceptable. "We all know the Mancini girl was impure when she came to Siderno."

My temper flared and I beat it back through ruthless willpower. This was not the time.

"Basta," Borghese told Mommo. "That is his wife you are talking about. The mother of his child."

Mommo apologized and I continued, looking at every face around the room. "I would prefer to handle the situation with D'Agostino myself. I am requesting that no one here interferes."

Borghese puffed on his cigar and leaned back in his chair. "Does anyone object to Don Ravazzani's request?"

Another older don said, "What happens if it turns into a conflict like the '80s? We all barely survived."

"That is a good point," another don said. "We cannot afford to draw the attention of the Guardia or lose our soldiers."

"I promise to keep the violence limited to Napoli. You have my word, on my oath, it will not bleed out into any of your territories."

That seemed to satisfy the room. Borghese nodded. "We are in agreement, then. Ravazzani and D'Agostino will settle this amongst themselves. Let's move on."

"Wait," I said, remaining on my feet, using my cane for balance. "I have two more related items of business."

"Related to D'Agostino?"

"Yes." Borghese gestured for me to proceed and I nodded my thanks. "It occurred to me," I said, "as these things unfolded that D'Agostino could not be working alone. Enzo, he is ambitious but he is not smart, capisce? There had to be someone older, perhaps wiser, giving him advice. Convincing him I would make the perfect target. After all, I control the most here at this table. And in the end this was really about money, not my wife."

Every eye tracked me as I began limping around the table. "So I began to think. Why would someone help D'Agostino? Who needed more money? Maybe someone was in debt from too much gambling or had an ex-wife demanding too much alimony? Or maybe a wife that constantly overspent her allowance."

When I was directly behind Mommo, I said, "One thing my father taught me was never trust the friend who comes to you wearing a smile during a crisis. Because he is plotting your murder behind your back."

Mommo froze, cigar half-way to his mouth—and that was when I pounced.

With a whoosh, I pulled my cane apart to reveal a thin blade, which I shoved directly against Mommo's throat. Chairs scraped and a scuffle behind me signaled that Marco was holding back Mommo's man. Ignoring everyone else, I kept the sweaty fuck in my grasp, the steel at his windpipe. "It was you, Mommo, my father's friend, who turned against the Ravazzanis to help that miserable piece of shit."

"I would never betray you," Mommo choked out.

"Cazzata. You did—and the man in my crew, the one D'Agostino was blackmailing, confirmed it."

Mommo tried to look at Borghese. "Let us settle this amongst ourselves. Let Ravazzani and I speak privately."

"No," I snapped, then leaned to whisper in Mommo's ear. "Remember when you advised me not to let a woman make me weak?"

"Fausto—"

"But you let your wife make you weak, Mommo. She spends more than you make, doesn't she? It's never enough and you don't have the balls to tell her no. So you decided to join with D'Agostino to steal from me, kidnapping my woman to distract me. Allora, does that sound like something a *strong* man would do?"

"You are a fool," Mommo hissed. "Fucking that whore in your father's house."

"That is the difference between us, you miserable pig. My woman doesn't make me weak. She makes me stronger, so strong I am willing to slit your throat right here in front of all these men."

I jerked my arm and sliced through his throat, making certain to cut both carotid arteries. Dark red spurted out all over my hands and the table, a fountain of death, but no one moved as Mommo slumped forward. No one came to try and save him. They knew better.

Blood pooled onto the floor as I put my cane back together. Mommo's gasps grew fainter as I returned to my seat. By the time I sat down, Mommo was dead.

Borghese's eyes were big and round. "Ravazzani, you can't—"

"Mommo and D'Agostino were working together, which means Mommo knew of the attempt on my life. That makes us enemies. And let me say this now, any other man who betrays me will be dealt with in a similar manner."

The room was silent, except for the dripping of blood onto the old stone. Clearing my throat, I said, "I have one more matter for discussion, then I must return to Siderno."

"You are not staying for the rest?" Borghese asked.

"No. However, I have something to tell all of you." I forced myself to relax. "My son, Giulio, is gay."

Disbelief stared back at me from every angle. Some of the expressions quickly turned to pity, because they knew what my revelation meant.

I continued, "He has chosen to leave, to live a life outside of our world. Though I continue to love him very much, he is no longer my heir, and has nothing to do with my family or our business. I ask that you all let him go freely, safely, to build a life he can be proud of."

The men shifted uncomfortably. "Sì, sì," one mumbled, while another said, "Certo." Round and round it went, with every man agreeing to let my son live free of the 'Ndrangheta.

Borghese came to his feet and addressed the room. "I think we can all agree that times are changing. No one at this table should cast a stone unless they can be certain their house is not made of glass, eh? And besides, the business is what really matters."

"The money is what really matters," someone said, and chuckles erupted around the room.

I stood and pulled on my cuffs to straighten them. "I vow here, in front of all of you, that any gay members of your families are irrelevant to me. As Borghese said, what matters is business."

Without waiting another second, I strode out of the meeting room, Marco right behind me. The monks had a collection box near the front door, so I took out my wallet and removed all the cash I had, like seven or eight thousand Euros. I shoved it all in the collection box, then walked out and got in my car.

It was time to go home.

CHAPTER TWENTY-NINE

Francesca

I worried the entire time he was away.
When Fausto was set to return, I paced in the entryway while Nesto leaned against the wall, watching me. He hadn't left my side during my husband's absence, except when I used the bathroom. I knew this was to keep me safe, but I would much rather have Fausto's gaze on me.

After scolding me for scuffing the entryway tile, Zia dragged me to the kitchen for chicken in lemon sauce and a side of roasted eggplant. She had a tartufo for dessert, which reminded me of Giulio and our dinner way back when I was first in Siderno. I started tearing up.

Zia shook her head at me. "He is better off. He's a good boy but he never liked this life, not like he should in order to lead. Your son will take over when it's time."

This was a conversation for another day. No way was I deciding my child's fate like that. I didn't care what Fausto said—our children would make their own decisions.

"It's the hormones," I told her. "I cry all the time." Lately, it was true. Losing my close friend and Fausto's shooting had turned me into a weepy mess.

"Basta," Zia said. "You must remain strong. You are La Donna."

"La Donna?"

"Sì, Donna Ravazzani," she said. "You are Don Ravazzani's wife."

I looked at Nesto for confirmation. He nodded once. "It is what we call you, especially after Don Ravazzani was injured."

La Donna. Holy shit.

I hadn't expected that.

"These last few weeks, you have stepped into your role," Zia said with a nod. "You make us all very proud."

I bit my lip to hide my smile. They were proud of me? No one had ever said that to me before, other than Fausto. "I will do my best. I never thought this was how my life would turn out."

Zia shook a wooden spoon at me. "He needs you. Never forget it."

And God, I needed him.

The front door opened and closed. I started to get up, but Zia hissed at me. "You stay. Let him come and find you. These men, they are hunters, capisce?"

I couldn't help but laugh. Was this really her advice?

I waited, trying to appear calm as the ticking of the cane grew louder. Then my man appeared, his face weary but gorgeous. I started to grin—until I saw the blood on his suit.

Jumping up, I blurted, "What the fuck happened to you?"

He held up his free hand. "I am fine, amore." Then nodded at Nesto, who quickly disappeared into the hallway.

Zia went over and Fausto bent to kiss her cheek. "The blood is dry," he said. "I didn't track any into the house, I promise."

She patted his face. "Good boy. Now go, be nice to your wife. She's been very worried."

Zia left the kitchen and Fausto came over, his gaze soft as it raked me from head to toe. "Mia bella moglie," he murmured, pressing his mouth to mine. "I like this t-shirt."

I looked down. The shock of seeing him covered in blood made me forget what I had on. Oh. It was my new "Baby Mama" t-shirt. It was a little big, but I would soon grow into it.

I very carefully wrapped my arms around his shoulders. "I am your baby mama, paparino."

His good hand slid to my ass, which he squeezed. "Best decision of my life was knocking you up, dolcezza."

I eased back to stare at him. Something about the way he said it . . .

"Did you get me pregnant on purpose?"

The edge of his sexy mouth lifted. "I'll never tell."

"I swear to God, Fausto. If I find out you were using me to breed more Ravazzani babies—"

"You'll what?" His brow arched. "Come right here on the spot? You know the idea of it gets you hot."

Fuck, he was right. "You're annoying."

He just laughed. "Because I know you so well? You'd better get used to it. Now, help me upstairs. I want to wash the blood off and lie down with you."

"Does this mean I get to help you in the shower again?" This was quickly becoming my new favorite pastime.

"Of course. This is a wife's job, no?"

"I thought my job was to suck your dick?"

"Soon, baby. Very soon. Dai, andiamo. Help me get cleaned up."

As we went up the stairs, I asked, "Are you going to tell me whose blood this is?"

"No."

"Did you kill someone at your mafia conference?"

"Yes."

I would like to say it didn't turn me on . . . but that would've been a lie. "Was it Enzo?"

"No." He was breathing hard by the time he took the last step. "Cazzo, I am exhausted."

When we entered our bedroom, he pointed to the bed. "What's this?"

Two t-shirts were waiting on the mattress. "A gift for you."

"For me?"

"Yes, so close your eyes."

He shook his head but humored me. I held up the first shirt. "Okay, you can look." When his lids opened, I said, "This one is for you."

It was a white t-shirt with black letters that said, *I'M THE BOSS.*

"Damn right I am," Fausto said.

"But wait." I lifted the tiny onesie. "This is for our son."

The block letters read, *LOL, OK.*

His lips twitched like he wanted to laugh. "You think this is very clever, don't you?"

"Yes, because it is. Admit it, they're perfect."

Giving me the soft smile he reserved just for me, Fausto limped over and kissed me on the mouth. "I love them. I love you."

"So, are you going to tell me what happened today?"

"No."

"Why not?"

Slowly, he began removing his jacket. "Because there is a code of silence, an unspoken rule that we don't discuss what happens there."

"But it's me. We're supposed to tell each other everything. And I'm La Donna."

He threw me a surprised glance as he tossed his jacket onto the bed. "Who told you this?"

"Zia. Wasn't I supposed to know?"

The frown he wore was deep. "It makes you a target."

He grunted, struggling with his shirt, and I began to help. "I'm already a target. Our life, remember."

"My job is to protect you and our children. Promise me you'll not take any unnecessary risks, especially while Enzo is still breathing."

"I won't—as long as you do the same."

Putting a hand on my jaw, he tilted my face toward his. The look he gave me was full of adoration and reverence, and I wanted to melt into a puddle on the floor. He whispered, "My piccola monella, don't you know that everything I do is for you? I will cheat and steal and kill for you. I will burn down the entire world to keep you safe."

"I don't need any of that. I just need you here, growing old with me."

"And that's exactly what you'll get, even when you tire of me."

"Never." I pressed up on my toes and kissed him quickly. "I'll never get tired of you."

"Liar."

I removed his shirt and smoothed my hands over his strong, warm shoulders. "What are you going to do about Enzo?"

"Kill him."

"When?"

"He's been hard to find, but I'm working on it."

He unbuckled his belt and unzipped his trousers, and my eyes glazed over with memories and longing. Chuckling, Fausto shook his head, knowing exactly what I was thinking.

"I'm sorry," I said. "I can't help it. You've conditioned me. Your pants come off and I lose my train of thought."

"You are going to be the death of me, dolcezza."

I took his hand and led him to the bathroom. "But you'll love every second of it."

CHAPTER THIRTY

Fausto

Four and a half years later

The door knob rattled, followed by a thump. More rattling.

As Marco started to stand from his chair, I put my hand up. "Wait," I mouthed and hid my smile.

A few seconds later my office door opened and the beautiful face of my two-year-old daughter, Noemi, appeared. She strode in like she was in charge. "Papà! Zio Marco! Mamma says it is time to come."

I pushed back from the desk and patted to my lap. "*Polpetta!* I've been waiting for you. Come, give me hugs and kisses."

"Ah, me first!" Marco scooped up my daughter before she could get to the desk and spun her around. She squealed with delight, her short blonde curls flying.

When he set her on her feet, she grinned and wobbled. "I'm dizzy."

I gave her a second to get her bearings. "Now may I have my hugs and kisses?"

She ran right over and jumped on me, squirming onto my lap. Noemi was aggressive and energetic, just like her brother. And her mother, now that I thought about it.

Noemi stood on my thighs as her little arms wrapped around my neck. My heart turned over as she pressed her lips to my cheek. "There," she announced. "Is that enough?"

"For now," I told her. Then I held her hands and let her lean back, one of our favorite games.

"Are you working?" she asked.

"Yes, of course."

"Mamma said it's time to come."

"All right, but only if you lead the way."

Holding her hands, I stood and let her dangle before swinging her side to side. She begged me to do it again, but I set her down instead. "Later. Right now you have to help Marco and I find everyone."

"Follow me!" She ran out of the room, expecting us to keep up with her.

"You are in for years of heartache with that one, cugino," Marco said, chuckling as we walked into the corridor together. "She is going to give you gray hair."

"I already have gray hair." A tiny bit on my temples, something my wife liked very much.

"More gray hair, then."

We headed toward the stables, Noemi charging along the path in front of us in the afternoon sun. Every now and again, she turned around to ensure we were following as she galloped along. Beside the paddock, a long table had been set up, colorful decorations along the fence and chair backs. A group of people stood by the table, but my eyes landed on my wife first.

Every time I saw her, it was like a punch to the gut. Dio santo, she was gorgeous, her blonde hair wild in the breeze, a long flowing dress on. I bet she smelled like my land and the March sunshine.

Terra e sole.

"Papà! Hurry," Noemi called. "Cake!"

A little boy climbed the wooden fence, jumped off the top, and landed into a pile of hay. I sighed. "Raffaele!" I boomed when he emerged and began to scale the fence again. "Get down."

He didn't like hearing this one bit. "But Mamma said I could."

"I did not," Francesca told our son. "And you don't get any presents if you lie on your birthday."

I went over and kissed my wife first. "You look good enough to eat, monella."

"Later. Right now, I need you to get your son under control so we can start."

"Good, because I have a surprise for you after."

Raffaele was a strong-willed child. Francesca often said I was the only one who could deal with him, especially when the boy was angry. All I did was talk softly but sternly, holding his eyes. It calmed him down every time.

By the time I reached the fence, my son was picking up dirt clods and throwing them as far as he could. He loved being outside every bit as much as my wife did. "Are you ready for cake?"

"What about presents?"

"The presents come after the cake."

"But he's not here yet."

"He's coming, don't worry. But we should start."

"No," Raffaele said, throwing more dirt. "I want to wait."

Dio, save me from four-year-olds. "Raffaele, get out of the dirt and come here. Now."

He brushed his hands off and ran over, his little brow furrowed in unhappiness as he stared at me. I knelt so that I was at his level. "You have to listen to me. I'm your father."

"Mamma says she's the boss."

Oh, she did? I tucked that information away for later.

"That's true, so you must listen to both of us. He will understand if we start without—"

"There he is!" Raffaele scrambled through the fence and tore past the table, sprinting as fast as his little legs would carry him toward the path.

I rose and shoved my hands in my trouser pockets, trying to hide my pleasure. Part of me longed to run to see him, too.

Giulio grabbed Raffaele and tossed him in the air. "It's the birthday *signorino*!"

I pressed my lips together, the tightness in my chest nearly unbearable. My first-born son hadn't been here in seven months, but each time he returned almost had me in tears. I knew where he lived and what he was doing, because of course I did, but we never discussed it. He was happy, which was all that mattered. He visited the castello once or twice a year, and that had to be enough for me. His life was elsewhere now.

Francesca had been the one to convince me a short visit every now and again wouldn't hurt. She said the other mafia men were too terrified of me to ever hurt Giulio. That was probably true, but I still worried. I didn't want my choices to ever hurt my children.

Noemi dragged Francesca toward Giulio. My daughter didn't know her half-brother as well as Raffaele did, so she could be a little shy around him. Giulio put Raffaele down and held out his arms for Noemi. She looked up at her mother, unsure. Francesca lifted Noemi and they hugged Giulio together.

Giulio was surrounded after that, first by Zia and then Marco. Benito and Nesto came over and shook Giulio's hand, slapping my son on the back. Finally, he caught my eye and excused himself. I hadn't moved, merely stood by the fence and watched all the people I treasured most in this world.

Raffaele tried to follow his older brother, but Francesca grabbed the boy and took him to see his cake. I was grateful, as I always liked a moment alone with Giulio. My son looked good. Strong, fit. The haunted expression he'd worn in those last few months here had disappeared completely.

"Ciao, Papà," he said quietly.

"Figlio mio. You are looking well." I kissed his cheeks and hugged him.

When I released him, he gestured to my temples. "More gray hair. Is it from Raffaele or Noemi?"

"Both, most likely." I cupped his face in my hands. "Everything is well? You have enough money?"

"Papà," he sighed and rolled his eyes. "Stop worrying. I told you, I'm fine."

"It is my job to worry."

"You and Zia and Francesca. I keep telling all of you to stop."

"We love you."

"I know. Come on. Raffaele's going to throw a tantrum if we don't have cake soon."

"We'll catch up later? I kept that bottle of cognac you sent."

"I brought a different bottle you might like, as well as some gifts for Francesca and the kids."

Putting my arm around his shoulder, I led him to the table. There was cake and singing, and then Raffaele opened his presents. Paper was everywhere by the time he was done.

"Wait!" Giulio said. "There's one present missing."

"There is?" Raffaele clapped his hands. "What is it?"

Giulio put his fingers in his mouth and gave a sharp whistle. One of the grooms emerged from the barn, leading a pony out toward the table.

"Oh, shit," Marco murmured at my side.

"Tell me you didn't, G," my wife said, shooting Giulio an angry look. "Giulio! We said no big gifts this time."

"He's my brother. I'm allowed to spoil him." Giulio went and took the reins from the groom. "Raffaele, come see your pony."

With an excited whoop, Raffaele darted off his chair and hurried toward his half-brother. The joy on my youngest son's face was infectious and I found myself grinning.

"Fausto," my wife growled. "This is serious. He cannot do this every time he visits. It's too much."

"Can I have a pony, too, Papà?" Noemi's eyes were wide and hopeful, a father's weakness.

"Yes," I told her, ignoring my wife's gasp. "When you turn four."

Francesca turned away in her seat, her jaw clenched. She wanted our kids to grow up humbly, not as spoiled mafia princes and princesses. I respected her wishes. Usually. But I would not deny my daughter equal treatment.

I had to put my wife in a better mood. "Dolcezza, come with me."

"No. I need to clean up and get the kids back to the house—"

"Zia and Giulio will see Raffaele and Noemi inside. You're mine for the rest of the night." I'd already arranged everything. All I needed was her.

I plucked a half-full bottle of wine off the table and two glasses, then went to her. I held out my hand. "It's time for your surprise."

"Is Papà taking you someplace special?" Noemi asked Francesca. "Can I come?"

"No, this is just for Papà and Mamma," I said. "Kiss us goodnight and we'll see you in the morning."

Noemi did as I asked, then we said goodnight to Raffaele. The sun had begun its descent and soon the kids would go to bed. They would barely miss us, if at all.

"Wait." Giulio held out a piece of paper. "That's a present for you, Papà."

"For me?" I put down the wine and glasses, then accepted the paper. It was an address in Pozzuoli, outside Napoli.

I instantly knew, but I still had to ask. My gaze flew to him. "Is this . . .?"

"Sì. A friend of a friend found that for me."

Sensing the direction of the conversation, Marco was suddenly at my side. I handed my cousin the slip of paper. "Four and half years and my son is the one to find him."

"Dai, I can't believe it." Marco clapped Giulio's shoulder. "Grazie."

The repercussions of this, of what it could mean for Giulio, dimmed my happiness. "Does this put you in any danger? I don't want anyone connecting you to me."

Giulio shook his head. "The friend, he's like me. He knows who I am but he'll keep it quiet. Don't worry."

I did not find this reassuring. I growled, "Giulio—"

"Papà, it's fine. He has more to lose than I do, trust me. I'm safe."

"I want to hear more about this later." I pointed at him. "I won't have you risking yourself to help me."

"Okay, that's enough business talk for now." Francesca snatched up the bottle and glasses, then grabbed my arm. "You two can settle this tomorrow, when we're not in front of the children."

I took Francesca's hand and started toward the vineyards. After a moment, she rested her head on my shoulder as we walked, cuddling close. "You aren't really going to buy her a pony, are you?"

"In two more years, yes."

"Paparino. . . ."

"I don't want to talk about the kids tonight. I want to spend time with my wife."

"Are we going to the winery?"

"No."

"It's too cold for the vineyards."

"I'll keep you warm."

"Seriously? We're going to the vineyards?" When I smirked at her, she shook her head. "You're up to something."

"Always, mia bella moglie. You should know that by now."

By the time we reached our vineyards, the sun had set. We walked hand in hand to the middle, and Francesca stopped when we reached the row where I'd asked Vincenzo to place a pile of blankets.

"We have a perfectly good bed upstairs," she said.

"Yes, but I like to fuck you in the dirt."

"That is because you like me dirty and filthy."

"That's true. You know what else I like?"

She loosened my tie and tugged it off, then slipped the silk into my coat pocket. "My ass? My pussy? My tits?"

"Sì, I like all of those things. And I also like when you are round with my child."

Her hands paused in the process of unbuttoning my shirt. The moonlight played off her gorgeous face as she stared up at me. "So that's what this is about."

"We conceived Noemi out here. I want to get you pregnant with another baby."

She bit her lip, her breath coming faster. "You're going to come inside me?"

I'd been pulling out for months. It was no hardship, as I loved seeing her drenched in my come. But the idea of shooting inside her was hot, too.

I lowered my voice and shifted closer, crowding her with my body. "Are you going to drain me dry like a good little girl?"

"Oh, God." She swayed a little then put a hand on my chest to steady herself. "Yes, I want that so badly."

"Then get naked and get on the blanket. I'll fill you up, pump you full of my come."

Turning serious, she put her hand on my face. "Games aside, are you sure? We could stop at two."

Her second pregnancy had been easier than the first, but I still had to ask, "Do you want more?"

"As long as you hire another nanny so I can finish my MBA, I'll have as many babies as you want, paparino."

I smacked her ass. "You promised me four. We're only halfway there."

She whipped her dress over her head, and the beauty of her mostly naked body sent lust rolling through me. "Then you better get to work."

THE END

Thank you so much for reading MAFIA DARLING!
I hope you enjoyed it!

The Kings of Italy series continues soon . . . with Enzo and Gia in MAFIA MADMAN. For a sneak peek, keep going!

Want to get updates about the next Kings of Italy book? Sign up for Mila's newsletter at milafinelli.com.

Help other readers discover books!
If you read **MAFIA DARLING**, I'd be so grateful if you'd leave an honest review on Amazon. Please and thank you!

A peek at
MAFIA MADMAN
The Kings of Italy, Part 3

"The best weapon against an enemy is another enemy." —*Friedrich Nietzsche*

Enzo

Four Years Ago

The memories haunted me.

Though I had been rescued from Fausto Ravazzani's dungeon three weeks ago, there were moments when it felt as if I was still there, a broken shell of a man, weak and delirious on the stone floor. Now I couldn't close my eyes without remembering. Sleep became impossible, the dreams too agonizing to bear.

My body would recover. Each day that I remained on this yacht, healing, I grew stronger, the bruises fading. My mind was another story.

I was no stranger to bloodshed. Raised in a violent world by a violent man, I was taught to hide the cruelty under a smile and a designer suit. I had balanced this easily, never losing my grip on reality while committing even the most heinous of acts.

What happened in Ravazzani's dungeon changed that.

I was no longer the same. My brothers asked me to explain what happened and provide them with details, but I couldn't voice the words. The horrors were too fresh, my humiliation too great. I couldn't stand to be touched. They had to restrain me the first time the nurse changed my bandages because I kept thrashing to escape.

The gentle rocking of the yacht lulled me toward oblivion, but I fought it. I didn't want to relive the horrors of the dungeon in my dreams. When I heard my brothers whispering in the next room I spoke as loudly as I could manage. "*Che cosa?*"

Vito and Massimo appeared at my bedside. "Did we wake you?" Vito said. Closest in age to me, he was my second-in-command and consigliere. "You should sleep."

Impossible. I'd rather learn why they were gossiping like a pair of *nonne.* "*Dimmi.*"

My youngest brother, Massimo, cleared his throat. "I was telling Vito that Fausto Ravazzani has been released from the hospital."

Che cazzo? This soon?

"Surprising, no?" Vito said. "All reports said he was near death."

Getting out of the public hospital was a wise move. Far safer for Ravazzani inside the castello, protected by his soldiers. This was what made him such a difficult target to eliminate.

I had nearly succeeded, though.

Hiding for me was more difficult. Right now I was on a yacht in the middle of the Mediterranean with my brothers. My wife and children, as well as my younger sister, had been secreted out of Italy, far away from me and anything connected with the D'Agostino family, in case Ravazzani's men found me.

Licking my dry lips, I forced out, "When?"

"Yesterday."

This meant I didn't have much time. He would be looking for me, using every resource available to seek retribution. I had to be smarter.

"Water," I said, and Massimo helped me take a long drink. My hand was still bandaged from where Fausto cut off the end of my index finger, and my shoulders throbbed from being strung up by my hands for days. When I finished I pushed a button to elevate the bed. My brothers built an impressive state-of-the-art hospital room on the yacht, complete with three nurses and two doctors. Thank God, because I've never been closer to death.

And for what? Because I dared to grab more power? Because I dreamt of a better empire for my children?

I would not feel guilty for wanting those things. Yes, I had listened to the wrong advice, but my desires had not changed. I was alive and recovering, safe in the middle of the ocean, and soon I will make him suffer.

One thought kept me sane. *An eye for an eye is not enough.*

"Open your phone," I told Massimo. "Find background noise. A city, preferably in Italia."

Vito rubbed his jaw. "You think he'll call you."

I knew it deep in my bones. "Fausto likes to taunt his enemies. He will also try to learn where I am. Tell the captain to cut the engine."

My prediction proved correct an hour later.

As a nurse fed me soup, my phone rang with a blocked number. I looked at Vito and nodded. The nurse was ushered from the room and Massimo began playing background sounds. Vito hit accept and held the phone to my face.

"Pronto," I said as strongly as I could manage.

"Enzo, *come stai?*" Fausto's voice was tight and too loud, a performance if I'd ever heard one. "How are you feeling?"

My stomach burned with fury and frustration. I gripped the sheet in my fist, but kept my tone even. "Never better, Fausto. But enough about me. I hear you've been unwell."

"I'm fine. Stronger than a bull. It's too bad you couldn't stay longer."

Pezzo di merda. I hated his smug arrogance. "Yes, well. Thank you for your generous hospitality. I will have to see how I can repay you."

"There's no need for that," he said. "It was truly my pleasure."

No doubt this was true. Il Diavolo's thirst for blood was legendary in the 'Ndrangheta. But I wouldn't let him get the better of me ever again. "Perhaps you may visit me next time. Your wife seemed to enjoy the beach house."

There was a pause and I knew I'd hit my mark. My lips curled with satisfaction.

He finally said, "Last I heard your beach house was destroyed."

I made a noise like this was nothing. "Everything can be rebuilt, not to worry. Congratulations on your marriage, by the way." He wasn't the only one who remained well informed.

"Grazie. No need to send a gift. You already left one behind."

I stared at my bandaged hand, anger clogging my throat. *Madre di Dio*, he was a *coglione*. He'd maimed me. I would never forgive that.

Before I could respond, Ravazzani said, "Speaking of gifts, did you receive the one I sent you? It should have arrived this morning."

I looked at Vito, who shook his head and began typing on his phone. "No," I said. "I haven't seen it yet."

"A special token, just for you. I hope you enjoy it."

What had Ravazzani delivered? I couldn't begin to guess, but I was certain I wouldn't like it. "I'm sure I will. I'll be sure to send you something in return."

"If I were you, I would focus on my business and family instead." His voice was low and hard, a clear threat.

Except I didn't take threats from this man. I didn't take threats from anyone.

I smiled. "Then it is fortunate you are not me, no?"

"How are your wife and children?" Ravazzani asked. "Your younger sister? They must have been happy to see you upon your return."

More taunts. I wanted to wrap my hands around his neck and squeeze until his eyes bulged from his head. Until blood vessels popped and his skin turned purple. He'd taken my wife and children from their beds, held them at gunpoint. It was inexcusable in our world, where wives and children have always been off-limits.

Ravazzani must've tired himself out, because he said, "I must go, Enzo, but I hope you take care."

"Yes, you take care, as well, Fausto. Please give your beautiful wife a kiss for me, eh?"

I could hear his heavy angry exhales, and I relished knowing I'd rattled him. As if we were friends, he said, "Please do the same with Mariella. Oh, wait. She left, didn't she? A shame. I know how attached you were to your *mantenuta*."

Had he mentioned Mariella instead of my wife to fuck with my head?

The line went dead and I snatched the water glass by the side of the bed with my good hand and threw it across the room. Pain ripped through my shoulder as the glass shattered against the oak paneling. I shouted, *"Brutto figlio di puttana bastardo!"*

"Calm yourself," Vito snapped. "You'll tear open your stitches."

"Angela, the kids—they are safe, no?" I asked.

"Sì, certo. Do not worry," Vito said, already texting on his phone. "Ravazzani will not find them in England."

I prayed not. Though our marriage had been arranged, I cared for Angela. She was a good wife and a great mother to my son and daughter. Seeing the three of them held at gunpoint had been the worst moment of my life. After I was captured, Vito sent my family to a friend in England to keep them out of Ravazzani's reach.

"The package," I said. "What was it?"

My brother checked his phone. "They found the box. It was down by the road, dumped by a passing car."

"What was inside?" Massimo prodded.

"Remember Ravazzani's computer expert, the one that we blackmailed to help us kill Ravazzani? Vic, I think." Vito's gaze met mine. "It was his head."

Cristo. "The rest of him?"

"No idea."

I felt no remorse. Vic had been a means to an end, the right tool for the job in the moment. That tool had failed, so it was of no use to me now.

Massimo looked between me and Vito, his expression eager. "What now? Do we send a message back or do we go kill him?" Massimo cracked his knuckles one by one, an annoying habit left over from childhood.

"We are not strong enough," Vito said. "Enzo needs to recover, and we need to undo the damage from the kidnapping."

My brother was not wrong. Being Ravazzani's prisoner had weakened my position in the 'Ndrangheta. Many of our allies had deserted us, and our enemies were using the opportunity to encroach on our businesses. Thankfully the computer fraud enterprise, worth billions of Euros, hadn't been affected. We were still making money hand over fist, which meant I could rebuild everything else.

Ravazzani had tortured me to get that fraud business, doing unspeakable things to force me to sign it over. I never broke, though. He was not the first to hurt me, to make me bleed. My late father, the former Don D'Agostino, head of the Napoli 'ndrina, taught me pain. Taught me to endure agony.

"Do not flinch or I will hurt you more," my father said. *"You must be strong, Lorenzo. Stronger than everyone else."*

But this had been different. Ravazzani had maimed and humiliated me. Treated me worse than a dog. Left me chained and naked for days, and now I lost my family and my freedom because of him. It twisted my mind and fueled my rage.

I had changed. The civilized man from before no longer existed. Now I was inhuman, a creature filled with hate and revenge, and Ravazzani would pay.

Looking at my brothers, I said, "He'll be searching for me on land, so we stay on the water. We stay safe and we stay smart. Stronger together."

"Stronger together," my brothers repeated the D'Agostino family motto.

"Purchase a new boat," I told Vito. "Make sure no one knows it's mine. We'll sail west and hide out on the French Riviera."

My brothers left me alone and I closed my eyes, exhausted. Fuck Fausto Ravazzani. This had always been my game to play, not his, and I needed time more than anything else.

In the end, I would destroy everything he cared about until nothing remained.

———

Start reading MAFIA MADMAN today!

ABOUT THE AUTHOR

Though she is a *USA Today* bestselling author in another genre, Mila finally decided to write the filthy mafia kings she's been dreaming about for years. She's addicted to coffee, travel and Roy Kent.

Visit her website at milafinelli.com.

Want to get updates about the next Kings of Italy book? Sign up for Mila's newsletter at milafinelli.com.

facebook.com/milafinelliauthor

instagram.com/mila_finelli_author

bookbub.com/authors/mila-finelli

ALSO BY MILA FINELLI

MAFIA MISTRESS

Part One of the Kings of Italy Duet

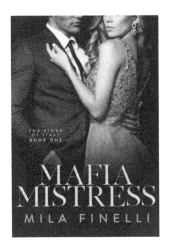

FAUSTO

I am the darkness, the man whose illicit empire stretches around the globe. Not many have the courage for what needs to be done to maintain power... but I do.

And I always get what I want.

Including my son's fiancée.

She's mine now, and I'll use Francesca any way I see fit. She's the perfect match to my twisted desires, and I'll keep her close, ready and waiting at my disposal.

Even if she fights me at every turn.

FRANCESCA

I was stolen away and held prisoner in Italy, a bride for a mafia king's only heir.

Except I'm no innocent, and it's the king himself—the man called il Diavolo—who appeals to me in sinful ways I never dreamed. Fausto's wickedness draws me in, his power like a drug. And when the devil decides he wants me, I'm helpless to resist him—even if it means giving myself to him, body and soul.

He may think he can control me, but this king is about to find out who's really the boss.

****

Start at the beginning with Mafia Mistress, Part 1 of the Kings of Italy duet!

Available on Amazon in eBook and print.

Made in the USA
Coppell, TX
08 November 2022